I0771280

BOOK THIRTEEN IN THE RAIDING FORCES SERIES

THE TIP OF THE SWORD

PHIL WARD

A RAIDING FORCES SERIES NOVEL

Distributed by Military Publishers, LLC
Published by Military Publishers, LLC
Austin, Texas
www.philwardauthor.com

ISBN 13-978-1732766921
ISBN 10-1732766924

Cover design by Stewart A. Williams

For ordering information or special discounts for bulk purchases, contact

MILITARY PUBLISHERS LLC
3616 FAR WEST BLVD., SUITE 117, BOX 215 AUSTIN, TX 78731

DEDICATION

To the First Responders and Medical personnel on the
front line of the war against the Great Pandemic of 2020.

Color by Adalyn

RANDAL'S RULES FOR RAIDING

RULE 1:   The first rule is there ain't no rules.

RULE 2:   Keep it short and simple.

RULE 3:   It never hurts to cheat.

RULE 4:   Right man, right job.

RULE 5:   Plan missions backward (know how to get home).

RULE 6:   It's good to have a Plan B.

RULE 7:   Expect the unexpected.

RANKS, DECORATIONS AND **NICKNAMES**

RANK PROTOCOL:

The first time a person is named in a chapter or after a chapter break their full rank and name is given. Addressing military personnel by their rank is a mark of respect. At all levels rank is earned and those who have it from a corporal to a four star general are proud of it.

DECORATIONS:

In the British military officers are authorized to put the initials of their decorations after their name. In the Raiding Forces Series the protocol is the first time an officer is introduced in a book the initials of his decorations are listed following his name. After that for the rest of the book they are not.

In the U.S. military officers do not have the same privilege.

NICKNAMES:

In the British military nicknames are endemic. Radio operators are called Sparks, red heads are called Ginger, tall people are called Lofty but sometimes short people are called that too etc.

In the U.S. military there are a lot of nicknames but nothing like the British.

RAIDING FORCES
ONGOING OPERATIONS

OPERATION AQUATINT – The disastrous pin-prick raid on the French Coast., where SOE lost its best small-scale Commando officer KIA and the unit had been shattered so badly it had to be disbanded

OPERATION BOMBSHELL Named after pilot Pamala Plum-Martin… resulted in more than one hundred Luftwaffe and Regia Aeronautica pilots being killed (version of BUZZARD PLUCKER)

OPERATION GOLDEN FLEECE – 'Pinch' operations to capture Nazi encoding/ decoding equipment. Lt. Cdr. Flemings project aka/OPERATION RED INDIAN

OPERATION HUSKY – The Allied invasion of Sicily

OPERATION INFLUX – A British unrealized plan for an invasion of the large Italian island of Sicily as a follow-on to the anticipated success of 'Compass' in North Africa originally concocted in 1940

OPERATION LEAF EATER – Diamond interdiction program

OPERATION LIGHTFOOT – The Second Battle of El Alamein

OPERATION LOUNGE LIZARD – Remove German and Italian ships from San Pedro Harbor

OPERATION PURPLE – Obtain serial numbers from German tanks

OPERATION RED INDIAN – Cover name for OPERATION GOLDEN FLEECE

OPERATION SLEDGEHAMMER – A suicidal plan to invade France

OPERATION TORCH – Largest armada in the history of the United States to ever set sail with the intention of invading of a foreign power, it's the most ambitious, complex, high-risk amphibious operation

OPERATION WHIPCORD – A British unrealized plan for an invasion of Sicily planned in 1941

1
CASTELROZZO

COLONEL JOHN RANDAL WAS SITTING IN THE TAIL OF THE LEAD C-47 in a formation of two that was flying Captain Billy Jack Jaxx's element of the Small Operations Group (SOG) and the 575th Parachute Infantry Regiment (PIR) Rangers home from their combat jump on Port Lyautey Airfield during OPERATION TORCH. After an intermediate refueling stop, and having flown for over ten hours, they were nearing the end of what had been a hair-raising operation—even by Raiding Forces standards.

A bull session was under way with the SOG officers and NCOs gathered around. Now that they had time to wind down and decompress, everyone was relaxed and looking forward to getting back to the fleshpots of Cairo. The U.S. Army paratroopers had dubbed the ancient, elegant metropolis "Possible City"— anything was possible for a price.

From the tone of the conversation and the heightened anticipation for getting back, it sounded like everyone was planning to do some serious damage to themselves.

They were refighting their combat jump to capture the only hard-topped, all-weather airfield in Morocco at Port Lyautey. Not that it had been a tough fight— resistance had been light. However, it was a bold operation for thirty men to parachute twelve miles behind enemy lines three days *after* the invasion of North Africa began, in order to seize and hold an objective defended by an enemy force of unknown strength. All the while, their commanding officer—Col. Randal—

was leading a small company of the 10th Ranger Battalion up the winding Sebou River on board the old destroyer USS *Dallas*, in what could only be described as a mad-as-a-hatter, Charge-of-the-Light-Brigade-type race to reinforce them.

Col. Randal stuck his last custom-rolled cigar between his front teeth. Waldo Treywick had given him the cigars before he flew out for the States over a month ago. The colonel was enjoying listening to his troops tell their stories. The art of good war storytelling among soldiers is to convince your listeners you were the most scared individual present or possibly on planet Earth during the action. The men would aim for the exact opposite when telling the same tale to civilians, describing the action as "all in a day's work — it's what we do."

Fairy tales begin with "Once upon a time." War stories start out with "There I was...."

Capt. Jaxx was saying, "And, there I was . . . standing in the door of the lead jump aircraft, thinking we've done some crazy stuff, but this was a really bad idea. The plane was following the Sebou River at treetop level when we flew over the *Dallas*. All her guns were blazing, engaging targets on both banks at the same time as she was making the insane attack run to the airfield. Trees falling down, geysers of mud blowing up almost as high as the airplane—welcome to WWII. I looked down at the ship, spotted the Colonel on deck and thought, "Now, THAT'S what a *really* bad idea looks like."

Several of the SOG operators said, "Yeah — Roger that!"

Capt. Jaxx said, "He threw me a salute—then it hit me. We're going to actually do this."

Sergeant Fred Waltmier said, "I was pushing the stick, so I was crammed against the bulkhead of the lead plane and couldn't see much of anything but the line of jumpers ahead of me—we was packed in like sardines with all our gear and parachutes strapped on. I could make out a bright glow in the tail where the exit door was when the loadmaster opened it. As we crossed the IP, when the plane swooped up to jump altitude, it nearly pitched me down on the deck. I was hanging on for dear life, trying not to fall 'cause I wasn't sure I could ever get back up again.

"Everyone was shouting, "Go, go, go!" and then I was stumbling after 'em, fighting to get out the door of that C-47 before the red light come on—didn't matter . . . I was jumping. When I hit the prop blast, all I could see was tracers streaking up and like Cap'n Jaxx said, my military mind was informing me in no uncertain terms that maybe this wasn't the best thought-out plan of action.

"That's when the pucker factor kicked in big time."

Private Willie Sipowich said, "The only thing I could think of was what one of the instructors told me in jump school—'big sky, little bullet.' I was hoping that black hat knew what he was talking about."

Corporal Danny Hale said, "I like night jumps—can't see you as easy."

Master Sergeant Mack Beckwith said, "Me, I was just glad to finally hit the silk . . ."

The loadmaster made his way to the tail of the C-47. "Colonel Randal, sir, Wing Commander Dudgeon asked me to inform you our flight has been diverted to Alexandria."

LOUD GROANS MET THE ANNOUNCEMENT THE PLANES WOULD not be landing in Cairo. The C-47s were only about an hour out. R&R, rest and recreation as the military called it—or I&I, intoxication and intercourse in the jargon of the troops—was going to have to be put on hold. Why?

No one knew.

But everyone realized Raiding Forces did not divert unexpectedly without some reason. And that usually involved a high-risk mission in the dark of night—or not so dark, as the jump on Port Lyautey Airfield in Morocco had demonstrated. The troops wanted to get their debauchery started, and Colonel John Randal was impatient to check in back at Raiding Forces Headquarters and to see Lady Jane—not necessarily in that order. To say officers and men were disappointed was a major understatement.

No one was telling any more jump stories.

Since additional information would not be forthcoming until they landed, Col. Randal pushed his cut-down Australian bush hat over his eyes and dozed off. With no idea what the future would hold, he decided to get as much sleep as possible while he could.

The two C-47 Dakotas touched down at an RAF airfield outside Alexandria but did not taxi to the terminal. Following a jeep with an improvised FOLLOW ME sign mounted on the tailgate, the troop transports rolled to a remote corner of the airfield and cut their engines. A platoon of military police arrived and surrounded the planes.

It was stifling hot inside the C-47s. Col. Randal gave the order to deplane and sit on the tarmac in the shade under the wings. Not much of an improvement. No breeze.

In a few minutes, a khaki-colored Dodge staff car arrived. The Wren driver—a girl he had never met, said, "Colonel Randal, if you will come with me, sir."

The ride was silent. Col. Randal did not bother asking questions. He knew the Wren would not have any answers.

Fifteen minutes later, the car pulled up at the 10th Coastal Forces Flotilla Headquarters. Col. Randal was aware that this was where Vice Admiral Sir Randolph "Razor" Ransom, VC, KCB, DSO, OBE, DSC, maintained a small, discreet Director of Naval Operations Division (Irregular) office. While the port city of Alexandria was the main Royal Navy base in Egypt, there was no sign out front to indicate that the Admiral officed in the building. The Razor did not like to advertise—people with a need to see him knew where to find him.

Inside, VAdm. Ransom and James "Baldie" Taylor were waiting. One glance at the two of them and Col. Randal clicked on. This was no social call—not that he had expected it to be.

VAdm. Ransom said, "Time is short, Colonel. We shall dispense with the usual pleasantries and richly deserved accolades for your capture of the Port Lyautey Airfield. I want to hear every last detail at a more opportune time.

"Are you prepared to accept a Warning Order?"

It was not really a question, merely the standard preamble protocol for announcing that an assignment was about to be forthcoming. Col. Randal said, "Yes, sir."

A new mission was the last thing he had anticipated, until word the C-47s were being diverted came down. Even then, Col. Randal had been considering the possibility there might be some other reason to land short of Cairo.

Hope springs eternal.

Jim began what was not a standard Warning Order but a highly modified Frag Order—meaning it was only a fragment of the standard order. In this case, the brevity was due to a virtual total absence of target information.

"Colonel, have you ever heard of the Island of Castelrozzo? The place is spelled at least three different ways—all pronounced the same."

"Negative, sir."

VAdm. Ransom said, "The easternmost island of the Dodecanese chain in the Aegean Sea, located a little over one mile off the Turkish coast. A four-point-six-two square-mile fly speck in the Aegean Sea. Ring any bells?

"Never heard of it, Admiral."

Jim said, "Neither has hardly anyone else, except the approximately fifteen hundred islanders—a number steadily declining. The citizenry consists primarily of Greeks, with a small contingent of Italian soldiers stationed there since the Italians defeated Greece in 1941 and took control of their islands. The Turks do not claim Castelrozzo, even though it lies inside their territorial waters as a result of some convoluted settlement after the last war when they fought on the Germans' side. Even so, Turkey has the island on her bucket list.

"Admiral Cunningham, the Royal Navy Commander-in-Chief, Mediterranean, attempted to occupy Castelrozzo to use as a motor gunboat base over two years ago, but that turned into a fiasco."

VAdm. Ransom said, "I want it too. And you, Colonel, are going to capture the island for me this very night."

Jim said, "At the start of the war, Castelrozzo was a Greek possession. Then Italy invaded Greece—the two countries have been mortal enemies from antiquity. The Greeks were winning until Hitler intervened in order to prevent a humiliating defeat for his bumbling Fascist ally, Mussolini. Then Churchill made the colossal mistake of ordering in an Expeditionary Force to assist the Greeks and things spiraled out of control almost immediately. Our British troops were thrown into retreat, fell back and were evacuated by the Royal Navy— Dunkirked again.

"For our purposes, what is important to understand is that Castelrozzo only became an Italian possession after the German-backed Italians defeated Greece."

VAdm. Ransom said, "The island is something of a paradox, being located, as Jim pointed out, a little over one mile off Turkey. It has changed hands several times since the thirteenth century. Turkey has never been able to establish permanent claim—which, under modern international law, should be automatic since it is well inside the universally recognized three-mile Turkish territorial waters.

"The Turks have been natural enemies of the Greeks since the beginning of recorded history. While Turkey is glad Greece no longer controls the island, they are not enthusiastic about the Italians laying claim now. However, having declared themselves neutral, there is not much they can do about it since free right-of-passage is automatically granted to all belligerents during time of war."

Jim said, "In 1941, Admiral Cunningham decided to capture Castelrozzo to use as a base for operations west into the Aegean. The plan was for two hundred men of No. 50 Middle East Commando to invade the island, assisted by twenty-four Royal Marines—OPERATION ABSTENTION.

"Standing by off Cyprus in reserve was the First Battalion, Sherwood Foresters on board the armed yacht HMS *Rosaura*, escorted by the light cruisers HMAS *Perth* and HMS *Bonaventure*.

"The total Italian military garrison on Castelrozzo was thirty-five men. A walkover was anticipated. The fact that we did not enjoy air superiority was given short shrift."

VAdm. Ransom said, "Everything that could go wrong, went wrong fast. Faulty navigation. Bad decision making—the navy diverted the ships originally intended to supply naval gun support for the Commandos to protect a convoy. The RAF, which was supposed to attack the Regia Aeronautica airfields on Rhodes to prevent the enemy aircraft stationed there from interfering in the operation, failed to put in an appearance. The Greeks on the island went mad with joy when the Commandos and Royal Marines came ashore. They took to the streets celebrating their liberation and looted all the Italian-owned houses in a drunken orgy, throwing the beachhead into chaos.

"In a bold move no one anticipated, the Italian Navy reinforced their garrison on Castelrozzo with two hundred forty Italian Marines from the San Marco Regiment. The Regia Aeronautica put in an appearance that did not do much actual damage other than frightening one of the Royal Navy skippers to the point he lost his nerve, re-embarked the detachment of Royal Marines and departed the area. A general panic ensued.

"The British Admiral in command of the operation suddenly became ill, and the ships transporting the Sherwood Foresters decided to call it a day and sailed back to Alexandria to reorganize. The two Royal Navy cruisers supporting the operation also returned to port. Finally, the decision was made to pull out the Commandos.

"The result was a mini-Dunkirk. I have lost count of how many mini-Dunkirks our side has suffered by now. Not all our men got off the island. Some were captured. A handful swam to Turkey where they were interned.

"There was a lot of finger-pointing. Admiral Cunningham described the operation as a "rotten business." Prime Minister Churchill was livid. Naturally, the PM blamed everyone involved except himself. The Royal Navy mission planners expressed surprise at how quickly the Italians responded with a counterattack—holding their enemy in contempt once again, which is nearly always fatal.

"Now, tonight we are going to make things right. Capture Castelrozzo and keep it this time. I have my own plans for the place."

Jim said, "There is no current intelligence about the enemy forces on the island. Best estimate is at most a reinforced platoon. We believe the island is not heavily fortified.

"There is a possibility the Italian soldiers have gone native since they have been stationed on the place two years now. Personally, I would not expect such to be the case. Most of the marriages on the island are arranged, and the Greeks truly hate the Italians—so absorbing them into the community seems a dim possibility."

VAdm. Ransom said, "The tricky part is the Turks. First time around, we did not pay their sensitivities any mind. This time, the politicians have admonished us to be discreet. The Prime Minister is obsessed with the idea that we can lure Turkey into coming into the war on our side by one ploy or another and does not want to anger them.

"That said, the PM sent several of us senior officers in Middle East Command a missive that read in part, 'Now is the time in the Aegean to play high, improvise and dare . . .'

"In light of those instructions, Raiding Forces will perform a night drop by parachute on the island of Castelrozzo. Your primary objective is the Castle of the Knights of Saint John—a Crusader castle built in the Middle Ages. Government House and the mosque, a remnant from the days when the Ottoman Empire occupied the island, are currently believed to be used as military warehouses and are the only other structures of military significance.

"A MAS-boat carrying Captain "Headhunter" Hoolihan and a thirty-man troop of his Sea Squadron Royal Marines will land simultaneously with your drop to secure the harbor. My grandson, young Randy, will be standing off the island with two PT boats and the MGB 345. On board will be a company-sized party of the Durham Light Infantry who will come ashore at first light.

"A naval fire control team has been arranged for. It shall parachute in with you. The island will be covered by warships to provide naval gun support on call. I will personally be aboard one of the cruisers in overall command of the operation. Should you run into any trouble, upon request, I shall bring down enough naval gunfire to level the bloody island—you have my word of honor."

Jim said, "Once Raiding Forces captures Castelrozzo, the U.S. will not allow the American flag to fly over it. Do not put one up. Your president, General Marshall and General Eisenhower are intransigent about providing military support for Allied operations they see as ancillary to their main goal: a direct thrust aimed at the heart of Nazi-occupied Europe. Meaning they want nothing to do with anything less than a cross-Channel invasion of Enemy Occupied France staged from England.

"The U.S. chiefs are still incensed that the British chiefs did not cave to their demands to launch SLEDGEHAMMER, a suicidal plan to invade France, instead of TORCH in North Africa. There are bruised feelings and much ill will. The Aegean area of operations is where the Yanks have decided to extract their pound of flesh in the form of payback.

"Except for token Office of Strategic Services involvement and some minor naval support in the form of a few U.S. Navy-manned PT boats, we Brits are going to have to go it alone in the Dodecanese Islands.

"So, no Stars and Stripes flying from that castle that can be seen from Turkey."

Col. Randal said, "Understood."

VAdm. Ransom said, "Questions?"

Col. Randal said, "Can I take a look at a topographical map of the island?"

Jim said, "Unfortunately no, we do not have one. Very little in the way of intelligence of any kind is available, and most of it is from before the war when Air France used Castelrozzo as a civilian seaplane base. There is one captured Italian naval chart from the first invasion of the island and a handful of picture postcards. We have verbal reports from the troops who invaded the place two years ago that state it is 'mountainous'."

VAdm. Ransom said, "Air Marshal Tedder had the RAF send over a photo reconnaissance plane at first light. The developed aerial photos shall be delivered to us as soon as they arrive.

"Any other questions?"

"No, sir."

After Col. Randal departed, VAdm. Ransom said, "What do you reckon Randal is thinking right about this minute, Jim?"

"My guess, Admiral? The Colonel is wondering if we have been hitting the bottle."

2
SOLID ROCK

JAMES "BALDIE" TAYLOR LED A SMALL CONVOY TO WHERE THE C-47s were parked in isolation under tight security. Squadron Leader Paddy Wilcox, DSO, OBE, MC, DFC, was with him in the lead staff car. As was Mr. Zargo, the chief of the shadowy private intelligence/security group that supplied Raiding Forces with targeting information for its gun jeep patrols. In a second car rode Ensign Theodore (Teddy) Hamilton, OBE, *aka* "The Great Teddy"—a teenage officer who, by some accounts, was the best camouflage officer in Middle East Command. And Captain "Pyro" Percy Stirling, DSO, MC—the officer who deserved the most credit for bringing Rommel's railroads to a screeching halt, completely denying rail transportation to the Desert Fox. It was widely noted that when Capt. Stirling blew something up, it stayed blown up.

The mission to capture Castelrozzo was not as simple technically as Vice Admiral Sir Randolph "Razor" Ransom had made it sound. Tonight, the tiny airborne strike force would have to take off from Alexandria, fly approximately 350 miles due north, and locate an island the size of a postage stamp in the Aegean Sea at night. If the pilots overshot by a mile, the Dakotas would be over Turkish air space and subject to being shot down by the Turks, which would create an international incident.

S/Ldr Wilcox was slated to be the command pilot on the lead plane, even though Wing Commander Tony Dudgeon, flying the second plane, outranked him. The tubby squadron leader, who liked to wear a black pirate eye patch over one eye or the other, rotating it to "strengthen the eye muscles," had been conducting classified special operations flights for MI-6 and SOE in the Dodecanese for the last two years. A highly decorated WWI fighter ace, he had worked as a bush pilot in Alaska and Canada between the two wars.

VAdm. Ransom and Jim were obviously trying to stack the deck for the jump on Castelrozzo with as much military talent as they could. Colonel John Randal was more than a little glad to see the four officers, though it was not clear to him what their exact roles were expected to be.

Jim said, "The trucks will transport SOG to a more comfortable location. No problem about leaving your equipment here aboard the C-47s. The security detail will remain in place. Who would you like me to deliver to the Admiral's HQ to commence planning?"

Col. Randal said, "Wing Commander Dudgeon, Captain Jaxx, Lieutenants Ryder and Hays and Sergeant Major Beckwith, plus the new people you have with you."

Mission planning, such as it was, began as soon as the officers and Master Sergeant Mack Beckwith arrived at VAdm. Ransom's DDOD(I) offices. Col. Randal's team had the use of the Operations Room. The 10th Coastal Forces Flotilla people, who worked for VAdm. Ransom, had been told to "shove off," leaving the place to the Small Operations Group and attached personnel.

The jump on Castelrozzo was a mission being thrown together so helter-skelter that it did not even have a codename.

Jim gave an intelligence briefing. He sketched a schematic on a chalkboard, based on the captured Italian naval chart. There were only three targets of interest—the Crusader Castle, Government House and the mosque that had been converted by the Italians into a military stores warehouse.

As he worked, Jim said, "It is believed that the bulk of the Italian troops will be located in the castle. It is not safe for them to be out at night. The Greek islanders will kill them if they can."

As he watched the Intelligence Officer work, Col. Randal said to Ens. Hamilton, "So tell me, Stud, what's a camouflage officer doing assigned to a drop on a remote enemy island, and how did you manage to talk Jane into letting you get involved?"

Ens. Hamilton said, "My assignment is to conceal the PTs and the MAS boat before sunrise, sir. Admiral Ransom does not want them attacked by enemy air, and he says the less the Turks observe from the mainland, the better.

"As far as Lady Jane is concerned, sir, I am quite certain she shall be furious with me."

Col. Randal said, "You better hope you get killed tonight because Jane will surely murder you when we get back."

"I was thinking you might intervene on my behalf, sir."

"Not a chance."

Next, Col. Randal sought out S/Ldr Wilcox, "Flying three hundred fifty miles at night over water with a one-mile margin of error tacked on at the tail end of the flight seems pretty much impossible to me, Paddy. What's your plan?"

S/Ldr Wilcox said, "Nothing to it, Colonel. On the coast of Turkey, a couple of miles or so due east of Castelrozzo is the village of Kas. I intend to follow a flight path that takes me to Kas, then dogleg left straight to the island. No chance of overflying the Turkish coastline."

Col. Randal said, "How do you intend to find a tiny village in the dark from three hundred fifty miles out?"

"Easy," S/Ldr Wilcox said, "Turkey is a nonbelligerent. No blackout restrictions. Kas will be lit up like a beacon. Plus, it has a lighthouse just off shore. Can't miss the place, Colonel. Fly till you see the lights, then break hard left."

Col. Randal said, "Hope it works."

MSgt. Beckwith walked over. "Sir, I'm about to go take a survey of our weapons and equipment. May have had some stuff damaged in the jump on Port Lyautey Airfield. I'll re-up the troop's ammo while I'm at it."

Col. Randal said, "Have the men repack their parachutes. I doubt anyone was thinking we'd be using 'em again before turning the chutes in to the riggers after the jump on Port Lyautey Airfield."

MSgt. Beckwith said, "Yes, sir—no doubt about that. Anything else you think we're going to need, Colonel?"

Col. Randal said, "Some way to scale the castle's walls. Grappling hooks and rope. Talk to Admiral Ransom."

MSgt. Beckwith said, "Navy's got a lot a' rope. We can weld field expedient grappling hooks in one-a' their shops if we have to, sir."

"Make it happen, Sergeant Major."

Col. Randal walked over to where Jim was in conversation with Captain Billy Jack Jaxx. As he got close, he heard the MI-6 Special Operations officer say, "The last attempt to take the island was a total fiasco—with one single shining exception. The Commandos captured an Italian signals manual.

"Have your men be on the lookout for RED INDIAN material, Jack."

Capt. Jaxx said, "Roger that, General."

Col. Randal said, "I want you to plan the operation, Captain. In-flight rigging. No reserves—it'll be a low-level jump. Three targets—castle, Government House and mosque. I'll lead the attack on the castle. You decide where you're going to be, then assign Lieutenants Ryder and Hays their targets. Let them plan their individual actions on the objective.

"Once all three of you are satisfied with your plan, get back to me. We'll allocate troops for each team. Then I'll issue the Op Order to the troops."

"Yes, sir."

Capt. Jaxx was the best small-unit leader in Raiding Forces. He was also a special operations tactician of note. Having the SOG commander take charge of mission planning took a weight off Col. Randal's shoulders. It allowed him to focus on the overall operation. Kept him from being tied down working out the million details that were going to have to be resolved prior to wheels up.

Capt. Stirling approached Col. Randal. "What are you expecting from me, sir?"

Col. Randal said, "When No. 50 Commando attacked the castle, they fired three mortar rounds at it. According to Admiral Ransom, all three missed, but the Italians thought they were being bombed. Ran up a white flag.

"We don't have mortars. Why don't you work out a King-Kong-sized explosion or two. Make 'em think the entire RAF is orbiting overhead."

Capt. Stirling said, "My specialty, sir—P-for-Plenty."

Col. Randal said, "Just don't blow the entire island up, Pyro."

Jim came over. "I was in your suite at Raiding Forces HQ, briefing Lady Seaborn on the drop tonight. Noticed you left your silenced .22 High Standard behind when you departed for the States. Thought you might like to have it tonight."

Col. Randal took the pistol and strapped on the chest holster, "Thanks, General. I wasn't expecting a combat assignment when I flew out—much less two.

"Where do you plan to be tonight, sir?"

Jim said, "I shall be traveling with Mr. Zargo and the Razor. We will be flying out shortly by seaplane to link up with the navy. My guess is you can expect to see us ashore sooner rather than later."

Col. Randal said, "Try not to get killed on my watch."

Ens. Hamilton waved from the corner of the Operations Room. He was standing with Capt. Jaxx. Col. Randal walked over.

"May be a problem, sir," Ens. Hamilton said.

Col. Randal said, "What might that be?"

"I have been making a terrain study of Castelrozzo in order to determine how to best design my camouflage netting for Randy's boats. The island is mountainous, formed out of limestone with very little flora and fauna, Colonel."

"We've been checking out the aerial photographs taken this morning," Capt. Jaxx said. "I can't find a flat piece of ground big enough for a Drop Zone anywhere on Castelrozzo, sir. The best I can come up with is in a small—as in microscopic—valley with what appears to be almost vertical walls below the castle."

"So, what you're telling me is we're jumping onto an island made out of solid rock with nothing to pad our parachute landing falls—not even dirt. But that's not the problem, because you can't find a single DZ?"

Capt. Jaxx said, "Exactly, sir."

"In that case," Col. Randal said, "we'll jump right on top of our three objectives."

Capt. Jaxx said, "Sir, the castle sits on top of a mountain!"

Col. Randal said, "Plan for the castle assault party to parachute onto the side of the slope as close to the crest as possible."

"You're kidding, sir?"

Col. Randal said, "You have a better idea, Captain?"

"Negative—may have to sit this one out tonight if it's all right with you, sir," Capt. Jaxx said. "I'm nursing a bad yoga injury."

Col. Randal said, "Don't bring me any more problems like this one, Jack."

"I'll try not to, sir—the castle stick may want to jump with their reserves on, even if they can't deploy 'em."

Col. Randal said, "Why might that be?"

"Padding, sir."

"Yeah, good idea, Jack," Col. Randal said. "Get with the Sergeant Major. He's senior jumpmaster for this drop. He'll be making the castle jump."

As he was walking away, Col. Randal heard Capt. Jaxx say to the SOG officers who had gathered around him, "We're all going to die, boys."

Jack Cool.

There was not a great deal of planning to be done from Raiding Forces' perspective. The small amount of mission prep was technical in nature, Navy or Air Force details that were of no particular interest to SOG unless they went wrong. There was no reason to insert themselves in planning that was best left to the experts.

Col. Randal had long maintained a policy of not overloading himself or his troops with too many details prior to an operation. He realized not all commanders agreed with that practice, but it worked for him. He also preferred to delegate service-specific planning to others, while maintaining the right to intervene. Everyone from all three branches of the service involved on the Castelrozzo drop was a picked man. They had all worked together for a long time under difficult circumstances and respected each other's judgment.

VAdm. Ransom walked over with a Royal Navy Volunteer Reserve officer.

"Colonel Randal, I would like to introduce you to Sub-Lieutenant Trevor Montclair—a naval fire control specialist. The lieutenant and his radio operator will be parachuting in with you tonight. He has orders to flatten Castelrozzo in the event the Italians choose to put up resistance."

Col. Randal said, "We've never had a naval gunfire party attached for an operation, Lieutenant. Why don't you stick with me during planning. You can bring me up to speed on your capabilities."

"My pleasure, sir."

Within a half hour of receiving the order to draw up the operation, Capt. Jaxx briefed Col. Randal on the ground tactical plan.

"Lieutenant Ryder will jump with a party of five men and capture Government House. There's what appears to be a small parade ground with a flagpole that will serve as their drop zone. I don't think they're actually going to hit it—we'll see, sir.

"Lieutenant Hays will drop on the mosque with ten men. There's no good DZ. Clint's boys will have to jump and hope for the best. Once he secures the objective, his team will stand by to act as the SOG reserve.

"Getting the teams over their DZs for these two jumps is definitely going to be tricky, sir. The C-47 carrying Lieutenant Hays' and Lieutenant Ryder's sticks will have to conduct two drops on two individual DZs within seconds of each other. You want the pilot with the most experience dropping paratroopers flying Clint and Eddy's teams—that would be Squadron Leader Wilcox.

"For the main event, you, Colonel will lead a fifteen-man party to drop on the Crusader Castle. Once it's secured, you will consolidate on the objective and be prepared to move downhill into the harbor area in the event of any resistance from that area. Your team will also be responsible for dispatching an element under the Sergeant Major to effect link-up with Butch's Royal Marines.

"Each team leader will fire three series of red over green flares, the traditional Commando success signal, to indicate their objective has been taken. And that's about it, Colonel. Not much of a plan. Best I can do on short notice with no maps or intelligence."

Col. Randal said, "Where're you going to be, Jack?"

Capt. Jaxx said, "I'm on you, sir—for redundancy. One of us will probably break our neck on the side of that limestone mountain. If it's you, I'll be there to take charge and lead the assault. I'm hoping it'll be you, Colonel—always wanted to take down a castle."

"Good job, Jack. Brief your people," Col. Randal said. "Have the officer whose team will be dropping on the second DZ jumpmaster both teams to save time and avoid confusion on board the aircraft."

"Yes, sir."

Col. Randal began a study of the aerial photos of the Crusader Castle. As described, it was sitting on the highest point on Castelrozzo. While the fortress was of ancient primitive design and had clearly seen better days, the structure was an imposing sight for someone who had to assault and capture it with a handful of SOG operators. He had no idea how to go about it, having never actually been inside a castle.

Ens. Hamilton was walking by.

Col. Randal said, "Know anything about castles, Ensign?"

Ens. Hamilton said, "Yes, sir. Magicians often stage performances in castles for the Merlin the Magician effect on their audiences. We have to know about their architecture to take advantage of the physical design in order to enhance the effect of the show.

"Besides, I love exploring them, sir."

Col. Randal handed him a photograph. "What can you tell me about this one?"

Ens. Hamilton glanced at the picture. "Crusader design mid-1300s. This one is a ruin, sir. Looks like a pyramid with one third of the top lopped off—been destroyed and rebuilt more than once. There is an outer curtain and inner curtain, an outer gate—part of the gatehouse, an inner ward, the keep—which is the most defensible part of the castle—a barbican . . ."

Col. Randal said, "Where are the Italians going to be?"

"The bulk of the enemy troops are likely to be sleeping in the keep—as I pointed out—the most defensible part of the castle, sir."

Col. Randal said, "Get with Captain Jaxx and help him work out a scheme of maneuver to secure the place once we get over the wall."

Ens. Hamilton said, "Yes, sir. I doubt we will have to deal with a moat because those are rarely found on castles situated on top of mountains—at least not with water in them. When bone dry, a moat is nothing more than a trench."

Col. Randal said, "That's a relief."

One hour later, he issued the Operations Order.

AS THE SUN WAS SINKING IN THE SKY, COLONEL JOHN RANDAL was sitting under the wing of the C-47 Dakota troop transport with the Small Operations Group stick that was going to jump on the castle. The troops were not chuted up. Travel time to the target was three hours, so the plan was for in-flight rigging.

"Whose picture's in your pistol grip now, Jack?"

Captain Billy Jack Jaxx said, "Pamala Plum-Martin, sir. I found a year-old 1941 copy of *Esquire* magazine that had an Alberto Vargas pin-up called "Cute Trick" in it—looked exactly like Pam. When I showed her the picture, she took it to a photographer's studio, recreated the exact pose and gave it to me for my handgun."

Ensign Theodore (Teddy) Hamilton, *aka* "The Great Teddy", was studying a document he had received from Admiral Sir Randolph "Razor" Ransom—*Law of the Sea Convention*. "I can see a problem, sir."

Col. Randal, who could see a lot of problems with the work ahead of them, said, "What might that be, Ensign?"

"Article 19, sir—"Right of Innocent Passage" governing sea travel through the three-mile territorial waters of a coastal state—in this case, Turkey. The article specifies passage is 'innocent so long as it is not prejudicial to the peace, good order or security of the coastal state.' It specifically precludes military operations—to whit, 'any practice or exercising of weapons, collecting information, launching, landing or taking on board any aircraft or military device.'

"We are preparing to violate every single one of the prohibitions, Colonel."

Capt. Jaxx said, "Oh, well . . ."

There was the loud *CRAAAK* of an engine firing, then the wheezing sound of a propeller struggling to turn over. Then a second *CRAAAK* from the other engine, followed by the same wheezing. The engines finally caught, running rough, sounding like a couple of Harley-Davidson motorcycles. Soon the motors smoothed out, and the C-47 seemed more like a racehorse straining to get out of the starting gate.

Col. Randal ordered, "Saddle up."

The SOG operators and attachments leisurely climbed to their feet, shaking out their gear. The jumpers were not burdened by parachutes—which were waiting on board—but they were carrying their individual weapons, a double basic load of ammunition, extra hand grenades, pistols, knives and other items of personal equipment. Better to "have and not need than to need and not have." Every third man was issued a rope and an improvised grappling hook.

No one knew what to expect. No one seemed bothered by it. Improvise, adapt, overcome.

Capt. Jaxx said, "Well, boys, if anybody asks what you did this weekend, you can say, 'I sacked a castle'."

The RAF loadmaster signaled from the door in the tail of the C-47 for the men to begin boarding. The troops combat loaded, opposite of their jump order. Col. Randal was last to board, meaning he would jumpmaster the stick and be first out.

Within seconds of his climbing up the short metal stairs, the ground crew pulled the chocks from in front of the wheels, and Wing Commander Tony Dudgeon had the Dakota taxiing. The big bird followed the lead aircraft piloted by Squadron Leader Paddy Wilcox down the strip. The two C-47s took off into a brilliant saffron and purple sky that was quickly turning dark around the edges.

As soon as the ship was airborne, the SOG troopers—most of whom were Americans—started singing the theme song of the United States Army Parachute School, a cheerful ditty called "Blood on the Risers", sung to the tune of the "Battle Hymn of the Republic."

"He was just a rookie trooper and he surely shook with fright. He checked all his equipment and made sure his pack was tight. He had to sit *and listen to the awful engines roar AND HE AIN'T GONNA JUMP NO MORE . . ."*

Col. Randal stood up, shuffled over to the pile of parachutes they would begin strapping on in two and a half hours, climbed on top of them and went sound asleep. The men were roaring, *"Gory, gory what a hell of a way to die..."*

What seemed like about ten minutes later, Col. Randal opened his eyes, startling the loadmaster who was reaching toward his shoulder. The RAF airman, who had not yet touched Col. Randal, said, "Time to begin chuting up, sir— thirty minutes out."

In-flight rigging is a complicated process. There is more to putting on a parachute than simply throwing it over your shoulders and buckling a couple of straps. The jumper's life depends on getting it right. Especially tonight—when the drop would be too low to deploy a reserve in the event of a malfunction. The Raiders in the lead plane jumping on Government House and the mosque were not even wearing reserves.

Tension was high. They were not expecting a large contingent of enemy personnel on the island, but this was still a dangerous mission. The biggest hazard was the jump itself. Capt. Jaxx's people were hardcore professionals, fully aware that what they were about to do was high-risk.

So what? SOG never had a low-risk mission.

Col. Randal handed a chute from the pile he had been sleeping on to Capt. Jaxx. He took it and shuffled to the front of the plane—practicing the "airborne shuffle"—to keep from tripping. Paratroopers never pick up their feet when moving around a jump aircraft.

Then Col. Randal handed a chute to Master Sergeant Mack Beckwith. The tough NCO, who looked a lot like the movie star John Wayne, followed Jack Cool. They handed the two British X-type parachutes to the last men in the stick, then shuffled their way back to the tail of the airplane to pick up a couple more.

There was a subtle symbolism to the process. The commander gave the chutes to his two subordinate leaders, who gave them to the jumpers.

Using the buddy system, the SOG operators began chuting up. As soon as a man had his parachute on, he sat down. When everyone was sitting on the bench seats against each bulkhead, Col. Randal, Capt. Jaxx, MSgt. Beckwith and King went to the front of the plane and, leapfrogging each other, began conducting jumpmaster inspections. Each inspection ended with the yellow static lines snap length running over the jumper's left shoulder and hooked on the canvas handle on top of the reserve parachute. Carrying out the process in dim red light, which did not destroy night vision, on board a bucking airplane, was not easy.

Everyone was jumping "weapons exposed"—meaning they were not disassembled in canvas containers strapped to the jumper's right leg. Each rifle, submachine gun and pistol was secured to the jumper by a lanyard—the heavier weapons required two or even three. The safety cord tie downs were not standard operating procedure in all airborne units. Raiding Forces used them because they had learned the hard way that it paid to be double safe. Equipment could be ripped off by the prop blast or the opening shock of the parachute, and nobody wanted to land without every weapon they needed.

Tonight they might need their weapons quickly.

Col. Randal struggled into his parachute, then helped MSgt. Beckwith into his. Capt. Jaxx helped King. They took turns passing each other their leg straps and then giving each other a jumpmaster inspection. By the time they were finished, the loadmaster was opening the door.

The wind made a loud, unrelenting howl.

"Ten minutes, sir."

Col. Randal faced the front of the plane and saw the expectant faces of the seated paratroopers. Holding out both hands with all fingers splayed, he shouted, "TEN MINUTES!"

Wedging his canvas-topped raiding boots on both sides of the door, gripping the rim that ran around it with the tips of his fingers, Col. Randal arched his body outside the C-47. Sure enough, as promised, straight ahead was a small, well-lit village—Kas on the coast of Turkey. He did not see any sign of a lighthouse, but he could see S/Ldr Paddy Wilcox's aircraft leading the way.

Down below were whitecaps. The two airplanes were skimming across the Aegean Sea, barely above wave level. Blackshirts asleep in their beds on Castelrozzo had no idea what was coming for them.

When Col. Randal swung back inside, he could see the loadmaster speaking into his headset, talking to W/Cdr Dudgeon, but the howling made it impossible to hear what he was saying. The airman made eye contact and nodded.

Col. Randal turned to the seated Raiders and shouted, "SIX MINUTES!"

Normally at this point, he would have made another check outside the aircraft, but tonight that was not necessary. Until the two planes broke left to the island and swooped up to jump altitude, there was nothing to see of military significance or that he could use to gauge the exit.

"STAND UP AND HOOK UP!"

Tonight was a complicated jump. They were jumping blind. There were no Pathfinders marking the DZ. Castelrozzo was a tiny island. Jump too soon, and the stick landed in the Aegean on the near side. Too late and the same thing would happen on the far side.

The green light would help make the decision when to exit, but when jumping on an island, Col. Randal would make the call—not the pilot. And he would not even be able to key on the paratroopers exiting the lead aircraft to help make his decision since it would be flying to two separate DZs and not in his line of sight.

"CHECK STATIC LINES!"

Suddenly the airplane went into a power climb that seemed almost straight up, then banked hard left, almost throwing everyone to the deck. It was a madhouse inside the C-47—men shouting and cursing as everyone fought to stay on their feet. Now, they wanted to jump. Get out of the aircraft. Go kill bad guys.

"ONE MINUTE!"

Col. Randal swung back outside the aircraft. The two planes were streaking toward the island. Up ahead the castle could be seen on top of the mountain. It was an ominous sight—could this really be happening?

He swung back inside. There was not going to be any command to check equipment. Everyone was going to jump. No matter what.

"CLOSE ON THE DOOR!"

The troops surged forward, rattling their static lines shouting "GO, GO, GO..."

Col. Randal looked out, saw the green light on the wing flash on, and the castle racing toward them. When the castle was one inch off the toe of his right boot, he shouted, "LET'S GO,", made a vigorous exit, hit the prop blast, got tumbled around, all the while his brain was screaming "ONE THOUSAND, TWO THOUSAND, THREE THOUSAND . . ." Complete waste of mental energy. If the parachute failed to deploy in four seconds, there was not going to be any need to go to his reserve.

He would already be on the ground.

The chute cracked open right on cue. Col. Randal made one swing, took up a good "prepare to land" position and slammed face-first into the wall of the castle. He lay there stunned, the wind knocked out of him. Of all his operational jumps, this was about as tough a way to invade any place as he had ever done.

Fly over, jump in, take down a tiny island defended by a platoon of unwarlike Italians who had not fired a shot in anger in over two years and return home before sunrise—how hard could that be?

So far . . . pretty hard.

His ribs, injured two years before in a night drop at RAF Habbaniya, flared up in pain. It was difficult to breathe. Good thing he was wearing the reserve parachute suggested by Capt. Jaxx. The small canvas pack had padded his crash into the side of the wall—somewhat.

Col. Randal was the only man to reach the objective. He did not wait for anyone else to show up. There was no need to break out his grappling hook. The X-Type parachute canopy was snagged on something. It was not coming free. Ignoring the pain, he grabbed a handful of lines and started scaling the wall. He heard a "clink" as a grappling hook was set in place. Capt. Jaxx was climbing up his line next to him.

"I can't believe we're doing this, Colonel."

"Well, neither can I."

Capt. Jaxx said, "I don't know where everyone else is, but if the two of us can't take this place on our own, we need to find another line of work, sir."

Jack Cool.

Once they reached the top of the wall, the two crouched down in the battlement, which consisted of a defile that was three feet wide and four feet deep. It served as a protected walkway running along the top of the wall. There was no sign of the enemy stirring, but there was also no sign of any of the other SOG operators. They were either still trying to sort themselves out on the side of the mountain or they had missed it completely.

As Col. Randal was attempting to orient himself, Ens. Hamilton came scrambling over the top.

"Anyone behind you?"

"Negative, sir—the rest of the stick are scattered all over the place."

Capt. Jaxx said, "You reckon there's a guard on watch, sir?"

Col. Randal said, "If there was, he must have had pressing business elsewhere or the alarm would have been sounded by now."

The still of the night was rocked by three giant explosions—*KAAAAABOOOOOM! KAAAAABOOOOOM! KAAAAABOOOOOM!* Captain "Pyro" Percy Stirling was setting off his demolitions somewhere down the side of the mountain. It really did not matter where he placed them. The idea was to fool the enemy forces into believing Castelrozzo was being bombed.

Sounded like it was.

The simulated aerial attack was followed by shouting and yelling in Italian down in the courtyard. There was some movement visible in the dim light. Col. Randal, Capt. Jaxx and Ens. Hamilton leaned over the battlement and commenced fire.

Col. Randal was firing his new Winchester built .30 M1-Carbine that the 10th Rangers had given him. Capt. Jaxx and Ens. Hamilton were blazing away with their 9mm Beretta MAB-38 submachine guns. The three were firing magazines loaded with all tracer rounds to give the appearance of a much larger force—tracer normally being loaded one to every six rounds.

It must have worked.

From their position on the top of the wall, the trio heard the sound of panicked men shrieking and running out the front gate—trying to put as much distance between themselves and the Knights of Saint John's Castle as possible. The Italians had long been convinced that if Castelrozzo were ever invaded, the first priority of the invaders would be to reduce the fortress by gunfire from the Royal Navy or bombing by the Royal Air Force.

They were right to believe that. Except the naval fire control party was lost, having dropped down the side of the rock mountain, and were in no position to call in fire support. And there were no RAF bombers involved in this assault.

The three Raiding Forces officers ducked back down and changed magazines.

Col. Randal said, "What do you think, Jack?"

Capt. Jaxx said, "No idea, sir. No one's fighting back."

Col. Randal said, "Ready? Let's do it."

They stood up again and blazed away, in hopes of speeding any remaining enemy personnel on their exit of the premises. Down below, tracers were ricocheting all over the place but not hitting anything—there being nothing to hit.

The Knights of Saint John's Castle was abandoned.

Unfortunately for the Italians, who were in the process of conducting a highly motivated retrograde operation—meaning they were running down the mountain trail toward the harbor as fast as they could fly—Captain Butch "Headhunter" Hoolihan, DSO, MC, MM, RM was leading his Royal Marines on a speed march up the steep trail to support Col. Randal's attack. The Headhunter's Sea Squadron men had spent the last two years carrying out pinprick raids on coastal targets along the Via Balbia far behind enemy lines, operating off Lieutenant Randy "Hornblower" Seaborn's small flotilla of captured MAS boats and his Royal Navy Motor Gunboat (MGB) 345.

They were quick on the trigger.

An intense meeting engagement ensued, with all the firing coming from Capt. Hoolihan's Raiding Forces personnel. It was over in seconds. The Italians suffered three men KIA, eight WIA, and eighteen captured—virtually the entire contingent of enemy troops on Castelrozzo.

The firefight—if you could call it that—marked the end of resistance on the island. The Small Operations Group assembled in the harbor and boarded a Short Sunderland Flying Boat. Col. John Randal and SOG were airborne—destination Cairo—before sunrise.

Virtually every man had suffered some type of jump injury—ranging from scrapes serious enough to require medical attention to broken ribs, arms and/or legs. The airborne assault on Castelrozzo resulted in a 90 percent casualty rate—all directly related to the drop. Not one single wound was enemy-inflicted.

A Raiding Forces record.

3

ASSASSINATION

THE SHORT SUNDERLAND WAS WINGING ITS WAY ACROSS THE Mediterranean Sea en route to Cairo. On board the aircraft were Colonel John Randal, Captain Billy Jack Jaxx, the mercenary known as King, Master Sergeant Mack Beckwith and twenty-nine paratroopers from the Small Operations Group, primarily men drawn from the 575th Parachute Infantry Regiment (Separate) (Special) *aka* "Rangers." They were returning from invading Castelrozzo Island. Almost every man on the flying boat was injured.

The plan was to drop off Capt. Jaxx and his troops at the hospital to receive medical attention for the injuries they had suffered from their low-level combat jump on the solid rock island. Then Col. Randal, who was also banged up but not admitting it to anyone, would continue on to Raiding Forces Headquarters. A number of classified missions had been in various stages of planning and/or execution when he was unexpectedly called away to participate in OPERATION TORCH, then diverted for the jump on Castelrozzo.

He had been gone a month.

Col. Randal was asleep in the tail of the Sunderland, lying on a pile of X-type parachutes. Capt. Jaxx walked down the aisle to wake him. Jack Cool leaned down, but the Colonel's eyes flew open before Capt. Jaxx had touched him.

"Squadron Leader Wilcox needs a word with you, sir."

When Col. Randal arrived in the cockpit, the Squadron Leader was flying with his trademark black eyepatch on. The former Canadian bush pilot had perfect eyesight in both eyes. He claimed wearing the eyepatch helped strengthen his eye muscles—everyone else believed he wanted to look like a pirate.

Squadron Leader Paddy Wilcox said, "Bad news I'm afraid, Colonel. We received a signal Lady Seaborn has been shot."

It grew very quiet in the cockpit.

Col. Randal said, "Any report on her condition?"

"Negative."

With no additional information forthcoming, Col. Randal returned to the tail of the plane, climbed on the pile of parachutes and went back to sleep.

After two years of anti-guerrilla operations in the jungles of the Philippines while on detached assignment from the U.S. 26th Cavalry Regiment to the Philippine Constabulary, followed by three years of almost nonstop combat operations as a volunteer in the British Army and now back with the U.S. Army, Col. Randal did not exhibit the normal response expected of a person who had just received the news his fiancée had been shot. He did not experience highs and lows—what he felt was an absence of emotion.

Col. Randal was not proud of it.

When the flying boat landed, Brigadier Raymond J. Maunsell, who liked to be called R. J., Chief of Security Intelligence Middle East (SIME), was waiting in his staff car. A convoy of ambulances was standing by for the banged-up SOG personnel who required hospitalization. Col. Randal and Capt. Jaxx, who was limping badly, climbed in the Brigadier's staff car. With an escort of Military Police motorcycle outriders, sirens screaming, they raced through Cairo's crowded streets. MSgt. Beckwith and King followed in a police jeep.

On the way there, R. J. briefed.

"Lady Jane and Beverly were having lunch at the Gezira. As they exited the restaurant, a pair of assailants shot and killed her two Ranger bodyguards, then shot Jane. Beverly returned fire, killing one of the assassins instantly and wounding the other. Happy, Lady Jane's dog, leaped out of the Rolls waiting at the curb and attacked the injured assailant on the ground.

"Unfortunately for us, the wounded gunman died before Major Sansom was able to interrogate him. That, I am afraid to say, is the sum total of all the information available at this time."

Col. Randal said, "What about Jane?"

"My last report had her still in surgery. Before going in to operate, Dr. Milam informed me the wound is a through-and-through. X-rays indicate the bullet did not hit any bones or major organs. However, he cautioned Lady Jane had lost a significant amount of blood.

"The doctor described her condition as critical."

Capt. Jaxx said, "That's not good."

R. J. said, "Lady Jane is fighting for her life."

Col. Randal said, "Any idea who the shooters were?"

"Not at this time."

"You *will* let me know."

"Absolutely."

There was a heavy military and police presence at the hospital when they arrived. MPs surrounded the building. Major A.W. "Sammy" Sansom's Security Police were covering every entrance. Every single Raiding Forces trooper who had heard that Major the Lady Jane Seaborn, LG, OBE, RM, had been shot had come in from the field, or from duty at Raiding Forces Headquarters (RFHQ), or from leave. All were armed to the teeth. Gun jeeps with Raiders behind their machine guns had established a perimeter.

Captain "Geronimo" Joe McKoy had flown in the day before from the Gold Coast, where he had been investigating Illicit Diamond Buying (IDB). He was standing at the curb out in front of the hospital, where he had taken command of everyone and everything in sight. No visitor or staff person was allowed in or out of the hospital without first passing a series of check points. Capt. McKoy had his favorite ivory-stocked Colt .45 Peacemaker stuck in the front of his belt in plain sight, but there was nothing peaceful about him—the ex-Arizona Ranger looked like he was itching to shoot somebody.

And he was.

As the little convoy pulled in, R. J. said, "I shall return to my HQ to supervise the investigation. First priority is to ascertain who was behind the attack. My office will keep you advised of all developments, Colonel."

Col. Randal said, "Thanks."

"Be assured, SIME will not rest until we have this resolved," R. J. said.

Col. Randal said, "I want to be there when you do."

"You have my word."

Capt. McKoy ordered, "King, you and Mack go get checked out by the medicos at the front of the line. Then get back here and take charge of security. I'm headin' inside with John."

Then Col. Randal's entourage was rushed through the corridors of the hospital to a private wing where there were exclusive rooms unavailable to the general public. Admittance was strictly limited to members of the Egyptian Royal Family, military personnel in the grade of general officer, or anyone who had been awarded the Order of Muhammad Ali. They arrived at a suite that consisted of an oversized hospital room and an adjoining sitting/sleeping room with a couch that turned down into a double bed.

Col. Randal left everyone out in the hall and went in alone.

Lady Jane was out of surgery, lying on the bed, eyes closed, breathing shallowly with an IV in her arm. She looked like Sleeping Beauty. The sight did nothing for Col. Randal's morale. Not experiencing highs or lows did not mean Col. Randal lacked feelings. He did—but it was an out-of-body, cold-blooded sensation—not what is normally described as emotion.

Beverly Blackwell and Dr. Stephen Milam, the surgeon to the British rich and famous who had volunteered to serve in Egypt, were in a corner of the room engaged in a quiet conversation. The doctor had treated the commander of Raiding Forces for a gunshot wound a year previously. He considered Col. Randal something of a congenial idiot for cauterizing his wound unnecessarily with a cigar as a field expedient while on a desert patrol. Col. Randal's request for a doctor's note to Lady Jane that would give him permission to travel on light aircraft and small boats—not bothering to explain he was departing on a clandestine mission to Enemy Occupied Crete—had reinforced the doctor's opinion.

Dr. Milam said, "Lady Jane received a gunshot approximately an inch above and a quarter of an inch to the left of her navel. It was a through-and-through. The exit was no larger than the entry, leading me to believe the bullet was a full metal jacketed military round 9mm or smaller—possibly a 7.65mm.

"There are two schools of thought on how to treat penetrating abdominal wounds. The most widely accepted method is exploratory surgery to determine the extent of damage and to make sure there is no internal bleeding. Running a distant second is minimal noninvasive surgery—meaning to simply give the patient a tetanus shot, pack the wound with sulfa drugs, inject massive doses of penicillin, stitch up and wait to see what develops. Infection is the big threat. If fever occurs or other signs of hemorrhagic shock manifest themselves, then go back in.

"I prefer the less-practiced, noninvasive technique because it is not as stressful on the patient and makes for a speedier recovery. Lady Jane is in amazing physical condition with strong abdominal muscles. With a stomach wound, both of those things are a big plus in her favor. The immediate problem is that she experienced massive outflows of blood. We nearly lost her before we could begin a transfusion.

"Currently, she is in stable condition—not out of the woods yet."

Col. Randal said, "What's your prognosis?"

"Like I said, not out of the woods."

"What does that mean, exactly?"

"A lot of things can go wrong, Colonel. Lady Jane suffered a life-threatening wound. You need to prepare yourself."

Dr. Milam did not mention that the threat of gangrene and peritonitis were inherent in stomach wounds or that severe blood loss can result in permanent brain damage. Nor did he deem it appropriate to inform Col. Randal that Lady Jane would never be able to have children, preferring to discuss the matter with her privately when and if she regained consciousness and was mentally competent to carry on a cognizant conversation.

As soon as Dr. Milam departed, Col. Randal said, "Where's Mandy?"

Beverly said, "She's with Major Sansom, trying to discover who was behind the attack."

Col. Randal ordered, "Jack, go get your ankle checked out and then track down Mandy. Never allow her out of your sight. Stick tight but let her do her job. Don't shoot anybody until I get there."

"Yes, sir!"

Col. Randal said, "OK, Beverly, run it down for me."

"We were at lunch," Beverly said. "Jane and I had flown in from the States earlier this week. As we were leaving the restaurant, the Rangers met us at the door to escort us to the car that Flanigan had waiting at the curb. Two Egyptian-looking men in white linen suits walked up, shot the Rangers, and then shot Jane. All over in the blink of an eye."

"That's it?"

"That's it."

Col. Randal noted that while Beverly was clearly upset, she was not reduced to tears, nor was she exhibiting any of the adverse signs normally associated with surviving a deadly close encounter. She did seem angry, very angry.

He was impressed with the poise the former Texas beauty queen displayed under the circumstances. She seemed a lot calmer than he felt. Beverly had risen to the occasion.

"What were you two doing in the U.S.?"

"When Lady Jane was notified you were not going to be back for quite some time, she decided we should fly to California to check out the real estate Capt. McKoy and Mr. Treywick have been buying. We had a fantastic trip . . . then this had to happen."

"Let me get this straight," Col. Randal said, "two men who appeared to be locals but could have been from anywhere in the Middle East walked up and opened fire—never said anything?"

"Not a word."

"Then you took out the two gunmen?"

"Maybe one and a half," Beverly said. "Happy had the second man by the throat, which did not do him any good."

"Professional hit team," Col. Randal said. "Jane was the target. Those killers would have finished the job if you hadn't been there, Beverly."

"I have been afraid you would blame me."

Col. Randal said, "You saved Jane's life. No one could have performed any better—nobody. You recover the shooter's weapons?"

Beverly said, "Beretta 7.65s . . ."

There was a light tapping on the door. Capt. McKoy stuck his head in, "Waldo's here like you asked."

Col. Randal stepped outside into the hallway, "Mr. Treywick, I want you to escort Rocky to Oasis X. She needs to be out of harm's way. Keep her there until we have a better idea what's going on."

Waldo said, "I got an idea this shootin' has somethin' to do with those Big Four criminals we're makin' sell all the diamonds to us. I'd rather stay here in Cairo, Colonel.

"I want in on the hunt."

Col. Randal said, "Once you're confident Rocky's safe, fly back if you want to."

"Yeah, Waldo, go on ahead," Capt. McKoy said. "I won't let the payback get started until you're here."

Waldo said, "Abyssinian Rules?"

The three stood there not saying anything. Capable men and dangerous. They respected each other.

Col. Randal said, "Abyssinian Rules—full on."

Waldo said, "You make sure to tell Lady Seaborn when she wakes up that I didn't go volunteerin' to get outta town."

Col. Randal said, "I will."

Capt. McKoy said, "I'm gonna get two chairs set up outside the door here. Station handpicked men armed with 12-gauge Browning A-5s sittin' in 'em around the clock."

Col. Randal said, "Good idea."

The head nurse for the private wing arrived as Waldo was leaving.

"Colonel Randal, we have a situation, sir."

Col. Randal said, "What kind of situation?"

In her capacity as the senior matron of the VIP ward, the nurse was trained in the art of diplomacy. But the woman was rattled by the tough-looking armed personnel on high alert who had invaded her normally tranquil space.

"The flowers, sir. What would you like me to do with them?"

"What flowers?

The nurse said, "King Farouk sent a moving van full of cut flowers and potted plants to Lady Seaborn. Apparently, he bought out the entire stock of one of the local florist shops."

Capt. McKoy said, "Gotta be a lot a' shrubs."

The matron said, "If we put all the flowers in Lady Seaborn's room, she will surely suffocate."

Col. Randal said, "What do you recommend?"

"When the King made an equivalent grand gesture for one of his nieces after she had her tonsils out, we donated the flowers to the patients in the Other Ranks ward."

"Jane would like that," Col. Randal said, "A lot of my people have just been admitted. Give the flowers to them. Be sure to let the Raiding Forces personnel know they're a gift from her."

"I shall, sir."

As the matron was leaving, Col. Randal saw Lady Jane's arch nemesis, Captain Cuthbert Bowlby, RN, *aka* "Curly," Chief of Cairo Station MI-6— British Secret Intelligence Service, strolling down the hall carrying a bouquet of flowers in his arms. He was the first visitor to arrive and the last person anyone would have expected to show up.

Col. Randal said, "Lady Jane's not taking visitors. However, if you'll come in quietly, I'd like a word with you in her private sitting room."

Cuthbert said, "I am extensively trained in the art of stealthy movement."

Col. Randal handed Beverly the arrangement. He was pretty sure Jane would want to see it for herself when she woke up, as proof the spy chief had really been there. "Put this somewhere, then join us in the next room."

The two men stepped inside. Beverly slipped in a few seconds later.

Col. Randal said, "I've been on a cruise. Nothing like being at sea to give you time to reflect."

Cuthbert said, "I seriously doubt any voyage which one knows will culminate in a twelve-mile mad dash up a river infested with Vichy French collaborationists occupying both banks who likely shall be blazing away at you at point-blank range is conducive to tranquil contemplation, what!"

"Yeah, well," Col. Randal said, "I realized I don't really care what DeBeers does, what the extent of their monopoly on the world diamond market is, or how they conduct their business. Except if I catch The Diamond Company selling diamonds to Nazi Germany, I'm going to kill whoever is doing the selling and may hold the board of directors personally accountable.

"You need to make sure they know that."

The spy chief said, "A most enlightened position to take, Colonel. I shall make sure DeBeers is aware of your position."

Col. Randal said, "So, here's what's going to happen, Curly. I'll have one of my people—most likely Jim or Beverly—brief you weekly on every scrap of information we develop about DeBeers. You'll know everything we know about The Diamond Company. That way I can quit having to wonder which of my people you're trying to suborn behind my back in the name of King and Country."

Cuthbert said, "Good faith offer?"

"It is," Col. Randal said. "I don't expect you to take my word for it or to quit trying to penetrate Raiding Forces to verify if we're telling the truth—that's what MI-6 does. Just don't be so obvious about it."

Cuthbert said, "I follow orders, as do you, Colonel. That does not mean I find all of them entirely to my liking. Between the two of us—I have no personal allegiance to Sir Ernest Oppenheimer or DeBeers.

"Strictly on the hush-hush, in the event you discover any individual selling or facilitating the sale of diamonds to the Nazis directly or through a third party, my organization will assist you in liquidating them. No matter who they are or how well-connected they may be."

Col. Randal said, "I might take you up on that offer, if need be."

Cuthbert said, "We are both on the same side, Colonel. Want the same outcome. We simply serve different masters."

Col. Randal said, "I'd rather OSS in Washington didn't know I provide MI-6 classified briefings on OPERATION LEAFEATER."

"Perfectly understandable," Cuthbert said. "For my part, I pledge to do everything in my power to assist in identifying Lady Seaborn's assailants."

Col. Randal said, "When you discover who was behind the shooting, come to me first."

The SIS Chief-of-Station, Cairo, studied Col. Randal for a moment, "Never my intention to offend Lady Seaborn. Rather shocked by her reaction to my request, actually. I have something of a tin ear when it comes to dealing with women professionally."

Col. Randal said, "All's well that ends well."

Cuthbert said, "My feelings down to the ground."

Air Chief Marshal Sir Arthur Tedder, DSO, OBE, DFC, was next to arrive. He, too, was armed with a spray of flowers. Col. Randal handed them to Beverly, who was starting a list to send thank-you notes. The Air Marshal declined the offer to come in.

Col. Randal briefed him on Lady Jane's condition outside in the hall. It was short, to the point, and he did not sugarcoat her condition.

ACM Tedder said, "Trying times, Colonel."

Col. Randal said, "Roger that, sir."

ACM Tedder said, "Y-Service intercepted a German radio message I thought you might find interesting. Once Eighth Army began what is now being called the Second Battle of El Alamein, Rommel flew back to Panzerarmee Afrika HQ from Germany where he was undergoing medical treatment. He attempted to rush to the front to take command. However, en route, his command car was attacked by fighter bombers on three separate occasions. The Field Marshal was nearly killed by what was described as 'a large piece of shrapnel' that struck his automobile.

"Close air support from our side is something the Desert Fox never had to contend with in past days. Got a taste of his own medicine he clearly did not relish. The report says Rommel was shaken by the experience."

Col. Randal said, "Ronnie Gordon's been a vocal advocate for close air support, sir. As conditions in the desert began to change, he made all the difference in the world with his A-20 Havocs backing up our gun jeep patrols, sir."

ACM Tedder said, "Wing Commander Gordon ruffled quite a few high-ranking feathers along the way. Most of us senior RAF officers believed the concept of supporting the army was pure rubbish. The surprise, at least for my part, has been how keen my lads became to fly ground attack missions once they got a taste of them. Rather extraordinary—hardly the reaction I expected.

"Do not become overly attached to 'Flash Bang.' He shall not be with Raiding Forces much longer. I intend to reward Ronnie with a fighting command—A-20 converted gunships, naturally."

Col. Randal said, "While we're on the subject of deserving officers, sir, I'd like to recommend that Squadron Leader Wilcox be considered for promotion. He's been flying special operations missions to who-knows-where for SOE and MI-6 for the last year or so."

"You are not the first to mention the Squadron Leader," ACM Tedder said. "Triple ace in the last war—dripping in medals. RAF thought him too old to fly combat missions in this one. Assigned him to Air-Sea Rescue before you recruited him for Raiding Forces, if memory serves."

ACM Tedder clearly knew the officers under his command.

"Actually, sir, Paddy recruited us," Col. Randal said. "He's an innovator. When we were struggling with cross-channel pinprick raids at the beginning of the war, he came up with simple ways to do things that no one had ever thought of. He set up clandestine amphibious air bases on the islands in the chain of lakes in Abyssinia to leapfrog supplies forward to Force N. Without that, I wouldn't be here having this conversation, sir."

ACM Tedder said, "On your recommendation, I shall have orders cut promoting the Squadron Leader upon return to my office. Best part of my job is being able to reward deserving individuals. Most unusual—you looking after the best interests of one of your people during a crisis of the magnitude of Lady Jane's."

Col. Randal said, "You won't regret it, sir."

ACM Tedder said, "I want to thank you again for arranging for the supply of precision timepieces for my pilots and navigators. Forced to traffic with the Nazis. A sordid episode in my career I intend to take to the grave."

Col. Randal said, "One of my people, a Swiss national, is responsible for establishing the pipeline of watches. I don't think you're going to experience any more problems, sir."

ACM Tedder said, "You made a friend in the RAF, Colonel. When Lady Jane is recovered, I should very much like the two of you to invite me to lunch. On numerous occasions, Wing Commander Dudgeon has regaled me with his tales of derring-do during the siege of RAF Habbaniya. Interested to have the story from your perspective."

"Will do, sir."

Beverly said, "May I come too, Air Marshal? I want to hear too."

ACM Tedder said, "By all means, Miss Blackwell. Should be a rollicking good yarn—unless the Wing Commander was making it all up."

Beverly said, "I don't think he was. Not from what Mandy told me. She said the siege was a real rodeo—my words."

AN HOUR LATER, BRANDY SEABORN AND CAPTAIN PENELOPE "Legs" Honeycutt-Parker, OBE, GM, RM, arrived, running down the hallway. The two had just returned from a mission to Crete to insert one of Special Operations Executive's agents. They were in a high state of anxiety, having just learned about the shooting.

Beverly related the events of the shooting to them in the hall.

Brandy asked, "Where is John?"

Beverly said, "Inside napping on the couch in the sitting room. I think he's worried sick—not that he'd ever let anyone know. Let's tiptoe past Lady Jane. We'll wake him up."

Brandy said, "Parker, stay out here with the guards. Do not let anyone in except medical personnel. Make sure anyone seeking entrance is an actual medical staffer with ID—do not take anyone at their word."

Colonel John Randal was not in the sitting room. He was in a chair next to Lady Jane's hospital bed, holding her hand. When he saw Brandy and Beverly peeking in, he carefully placed her limp arm back on the bed and led them into the adjoining room.

Normally, it was hard to tell which woman was the happiest, Brandy or Beverly. Today was not normal. Tears were rolling down both women's cheeks.

Col. Randal said, "Jane's not sleeping. She's unconscious or in a coma. I know there's a difference. I don't know what it means."

Brandy said, "We have to wait—nothing else we can do."

LIEUTENANT MANDY PAIGE, OBE, RM, ARRIVED AND WAS MET BY Beverly Blackwell in the lobby. As the two girls walked down the hall, Mandy said, "You had not seen John in a month. When he first arrived, did you happen to hug him?"

Beverly said, "He pulled away. Only let me put my cheek against his. Why do you ask?"

Lt. Mandy said, "One whole ward in this hospital is filled up with Billy Jack's men who were injured parachuting onto Castelrozzo Island last night. Our hero, Jack Cool, is getting his sprained ankle wrapped as we speak. When we reach Lady Jane's room, I want you to give John a big hug—no matter what. Do not let him resist."

"OK."

When the two girls walked up to the door, the Lovat Scouts, who were both sporting bandages but had demanded to be allowed to personally provide security to the room, waved them in. Major the Lady Jane Seaborn was still out cold. Colonel John Randal was sitting next to the bed, holding her hand.

When Lt. Mandy and Beverly entered, the three of them moved into the sitting room. As instructed, the blond Texas beauty caught Col. Randal off guard with a full body hug. He flinched.

Lt. Mandy ordered, "Lose the shirt, John."

"What?"

"Strip. Do it or I shall have the Lovats come in here to hold you down while I take it off."

Beverly looked shocked. Col. Randal looked sheepish. Lt. Mandy looked resolute.

As he was unbuttoning his lightweight battle dress blouse, Col. Randal said, "No wonder you're such a star counterintelligence agent. Always prying into other people's . . ."

Lt. Mandy said, "Shut up, John."

When he opened the jacket, his rib cage looked like sunset over the Great Sand Sea. Truly spectacular colors. Slamming into the side of the castle had not done his ribs any good, even with the reserve parachute padding the blow.

Beverly said, "Wow!"

Lt. Mandy said, "Escort the Colonel straight to the matron, Beverly. John injured his ribs on a jump at RAF Habbaniya. Most likely they never healed properly.

"If he resists, shoot him."

Col. Randal said, "That's extreme."

Lt. Mandy said, "John, you always obsess over the care and welfare of everyone but yourself. That is a serious flaw in a commander. You need to take better care of yourself."

Col. Randal said, "I don't believe . . ."

Lt. Mandy said, "Why do you think Terry disbanded your Ranger gun jeep patrol behind your back?"

Col. Randal said, "We needed replacements."

Lt. Mandy said, "You issued orders to your patrol leaders forbidding them to do certain things, then went straight out and did them yourself. Militarily, that is a textbook example of improper command performance. You were setting a bad example for your subordinate officers and putting the troops under your immediate control at risk.

"Now go with Beverly and get medical attention, John."

As they were walking down the hall of the hospital, Beverly asked, "Did Mandy hurt your feelings?"

Col. Randal said, "I don't have any feelings."

"Mandy worries about you. We all do," Beverly said. "I know she didn't really mean the crack about 'improper command performance'."

Col. Randal said, "She could have a point. I might be guilty."

Beverly said, "You were only trying to lead from the front and maybe got a little carried away."

FOR THE REST OF THE DAY AND INTO THE NIGHT A STRING OF senior officers, dignitaries, officials, members of the Six Hundred, everyone in Cairo who possessed a title, friends of friends in the Six Hundred and people Lady Jane knew socially or had ever served with in some capacity came to the hospital. No one was allowed in unless they had a military, intelligence or police matter to discuss with a heavily bandaged—under his battle dress jacket—Col. Randal. Those allowed in were virtually all assigned to, attached to, or worked with, Raiding Forces.

Vice Admiral Sir Randolph "Razor" Ransom, back from Castelrozzo, stormed the hospital—all fire and fury—accompanied by his aide-de-camp and three Wrens. A troop of hospital staff were in hot pursuit, running to keep up. When the Admiral encountered Col. Randal outside Lady Jane's room, he said, "I never endorsed females serving in time of war—ever. Not that the girls cannot perform—they can—they've proven themselves practically indispensable.

"Hate seeing women hurt is all. Hard to take. Bad for one's morale."

Col. Randal said, "My sentiments exactly, sir."

VAdm. Ransom said, "Find out who did this to Jane and why. Then be ruthless with anyone tainted by so much as the slightest whiff of involvement."

"That's the plan, Admiral."

Doctor Stephen Milam checked in and read Lady Jane's chart while avoiding eye contact with anyone in the room. Then, seeming distracted, he departed. Dr. Milam's visit did nothing to raise spirits.

Col. Randal had the impression there was no improvement in Lady Jane's condition. There did not appear to be any medical treatment taking place. So, what did it mean?

Captain Billy Jack Jaxx and Lieutenant Mandy Paige returned to check on Lady Jane's progress and to brief Col. Randal on the status of the investigation into her shooting. They followed Beverly into the sitting room, taking pains not to make noise.

Col. Randal said, "Zero to report on this end."

Lt. Mandy said, "Nothing from us either, John. No one can identify the dead gunmen. Sammy thinks the two are likely not locals. Current thinking is they might be contract killers brought in for the job—could be from anywhere."

Capt. Jaxx, who had served as a reserve deputy for his grandfather, the sheriff of the county in Texas where he grew up, said, "Sir, my guess is the perp who ordered the hit used cutouts. Maybe a whole series of 'em for deniability. Whoever wanted Lady Jane dead would have had someone not directly tied to him go to a specialist known to be able to supply professional hitmen. The contractor took the assignment, then farmed it out to another cutout to hire the shooters.

"Makes it hard to track. All the information any of the players have is that Lady Jane's the target. None of the cutouts or shooters would snitch even if they did know something. There's never ever going to be any way to prove this case in court, Colonel."

Col. Randal said, "Not necessary."

Lt. Mandy said, "If only Beverly had not killed both . . ."

Capt. Jaxx said, "Drilled one of 'em right between the eyes, sir. Perfect head shot. The other hitman took a round in the spine at the shoulder blade level when he tried to flee. Probably wouldn't have lasted long either, but then Happy swung into action. Ripped the guy's throat out—adios."

Lt. Mandy said, "And I always thought he was such a friendly dog."

Col. Randal said, "So, what's the plan?"

Lt. Mandy said, "Sammy and his men are turning Cairo's underworld upside down. King Farouk has his Egyptian Police scouring the city. R. J. has SIME mobilized. Even Cuthbert Bowlby has his people working the streets.

"The King has posted a sizable reward for anyone who can provide the identity of the two dead assailants. A bigger one is offered for information leading to the apprehension of whoever is ultimately responsible for hiring the killers. With the kind of money the king is offering, we are going to receive a lot of false leads."

Capt. Jaxx said, "No guarantee any of that's going to work, sir. Murders don't get solved often in the Middle East. Chances are everyone involved has already been silenced by whoever ordered the hit—dead men tell no tales. One of the risks of being a contract hitman is there's a good chance your employer will have you killed after you complete the job."

Lt. Mandy said, "The Big Four have been brought in for interrogation. The consensus is that they will be key in unlocking this case. Personally, I am not so sure. Any information they provide will implicate them for not coming forward immediately to prevent the attack."

Capt. Jaxx and Lt. Mandy only stayed a few minutes before heading back to Major A.W. "Sammy" Sansom's HQ.

Lieutenant Colonel Sir Terry "Zorro" Stone, KBE, DSO, MC, arrived from Oasis X. Waldo Treywick and Captain Pamala Plum-Martin, DSO, OBE, DFC, RM—who had flown them to Cairo in one of Raiding Forces' captured Italian Ro.63s—were with him. They went into the sitting room. Brandy was on duty in the chair by Lady Jane, who had still not moved a muscle.

Lt. Col. Stone said, "All I know about what has transpired is the information Mr. Treywick provided us when he flew to the oasis with Rocky. What's the story, John?"

Col. Randal said, "Looks like a professional hit. No one knows who or why."

"One would imagine Jane to be awfully far down on the list of people in this city the Nazis or Italians would go to the trouble to assassinate," Lt. Col. Stone said.

Col. Randal said, "Mr. Treywick has a theory."

"We called a meetin' to inform the Big Four crime lords they had to sell all their diamonds to me," Waldo said. The Colonel was there and Beverly. They *was* called the Big Five until he shot one of 'em 'cause the man sounded like he didn't want to get hisself tied to an exclusive deal. The remainin' four crooks probably didn't want to either.

"They had to know about the Colonel's relationship to Lady Seaborn—everybody in the whole town does."

Lt. Col. Stone said, "But why Jane?"

Waldo said, "Maybe they was sendin' the Colonel a message."

"Sounds like something out of a D-grade gangster movie," Lt. Col. Stone said.

Capt. Plum-Martin, who had a history with the intelligence community before she began focusing on her flying, said, "You may be on to something, Mr. Treywick."

Beverly said, "When I was doing my internship at OSS Headquarters, people talked about the Mafia a lot. General Donovan has recruited some of them to use for Secret Intelligence in Sicily and Italy. One of the ways Italian mobsters deal with bad enemies is to kill someone they love.

"Make them suffer for the rest of their lives."

Waldo said, "The Big Four don't have no idea who I am, bein' in disguise. They know the Colonel—he was sittin' right there in Moe's office at the Kit-Kat Club and you don't forget somebody who shoots one-a' your associates at the negotiatin' table. They know Beverly because she was hangin' all over him. Could be *Beverly* was the intended victim, not Lady Seaborn.

"Maybe we done outsmarted ourselves?"

Col. Randal said, "Wouldn't be the first time."

"Dealin' with these crooks is worse than huntin' bad cat," Waldo said. "You can't see 'em till they're right on you. Everybody needs to stay loose, shoot first and ask questions later. If any a' our people get it wrong and take out the wrong person by mistake—well, it was just a huntin' accident."

Col. Randal said, "Terry, Red's at Mena House. Go take her to dinner but make a short evening of it. I don't want you two out on the town tonight."

"I was planning to bring you up to speed on Raiding Regiments' operations while you were away. There have been a number of developments since you left," Lt. Col. Stone said. "This last month has been the longest we have ever gone without being able to talk to each other since Raiding Forces arrived in Middle East Command."

"Brief me tomorrow. We'll be able to take our time. I want to hear everything."

"Works for me, old stick."

Col. Randal said, "Pam, you stay in one of the bedrooms in Lady Jane's suite at Mena House. Chaperone Sir Terry and Red. If you dine out tonight, eat at one of the hotel restaurants. Make sure to have a couple of your RAF boyfriends with you at all times and be in early . . . as in, way early.

"Curfew, 2100 hours sharp—that's an order."

"Yes, sir," the Vargas Girl look-alike Royal Marine pilot said. It had been a long time since anyone had bothered to give her a curfew. "Who are you planning to have chaperone me, love?"

Col. Randal said, "I think that ship has sailed, Pam."

Capt. Plum-Martin flashed a blinding smile, the first one he had seen from anyone since arriving at the hospital. Made him feel better. Something he would not have thought possible.

As soon as Capt. Plum-Martin departed, Col. Randal said, "Beverly, go find King. Tell him to report to Mena House. I want him to keep a discreet eye on Pam while she's out to dinner—they're friends. She won't mind having him on the case."

Beverly said, "King's getting stitches in a cut over his left eye right now. He'll be back here as soon as the doctor's finished. I'll tell him then."

Waldo said, "I'm headed to the Gezira to get 'em to cook up a steak for the Colonel. Brandy says she wants some roast chicken. How about you, Beverly? You got to be hungry from all that gunfightin'."

Beverly said, "Steak. Make mine burned like John's."

Col. Randal said, "Swing by the Kit-Kat Club, Mr. Treywick. Tell Moe that Rita and Lana won't be dancing until we get Lady Jane's shooting resolved. I want the girls glued to Beverly until I say otherwise."

Waldo said, "Allah help the fool trying to hurt Beverly if them two Zār priestesses gets ahold of 'em. Those girls got sharp knives and know some tricks."

Col. Randal said, "That's the idea."

Later, when the two were alone, Beverly asked, "Are you worried about me, John?"

"I am," Col. Randal said. "The Big Four all saw I enjoy your company. Makes you a prime target.

"Hanging out with me has its downside."

Beverly laughed, "And I thought going to a movie at the drive-in theater with a cowboy in a pickup truck was dangerous."

Col. Randal said, "I can see how it might be."

Beverly said, "*Do* you enjoy my company?"

Col. Randal said, "What do you think."

It was not a question, really.

THE VIGIL IN MAJOR THE LADY JANE SEABORN'S ROOM DRAGGED on like a slow-speed train wreck. Colonel John Randal or one of the women stayed by her bedside at all times. Captain "Geronimo" Joe McKoy came in from outside where he had been supervising the security detail. Captain Billy Jack Jaxx and Lieutenant Mandy Paige returned from SIME Headquarters to check in. James "Baldie" Taylor showed up from the Secret Intelligence Service's offices, where a massive investigation to identify the perpetrators was underway. Waldo Treywick came back with enough food prepared by the Gezira Club to feed everyone, to include the Lovat Scouts on guard duty out in the hall.

Captain Stephanie Fawcett-Tatum, RM, drove in from RFHQ. The tall brunette had helped nurse Col. Randal back to health after he had been shot during the "Gunfight at the Blue Duck." He was glad she arrived. Capt. Fawcett-Tatum was very capable.

She stayed at bedside with Lady Jane while the rest retired to the private sitting room to plot their next move over dinner, eaten sitting cross-legged on the floor.

Capt. McKoy said, "John, I believe we need to get all nonessential Royal Marine women and the Wrens out to Oasis X most ASAP. Don't keep any more than a skeleton crew at RFHQ. Restrict the ones stayin' behind to the compound. Ain't no sense takin' chances."

Col. Randal said, "Beverly, coordinate with Stephanie to make that happen. Have the girls flown out first thing tomorrow."

"I'm on it, John."

Col. Randal said, "Hold on. No rush, wait till we finish here."

Lt. Mandy said, "Do not dare put me on the nonessential list, John."

"Never crossed my mind," Col. Randal said. "I'm going to have King pull duty as your bodyguard starting tomorrow to free up Billy Jack. You don't move an inch without him at all times. Is that clear?"

"Perfectly."

"I mean it, Mandy. First time you go freelance, you're on the next flight to X."

"Promise, John."

"Capt. Jaxx, I want you to take King's place at Mena House in the morning. Stay off your ankle as much as possible—hang out by the pool. Keep everyone in the suite's compound at all times. There'll be guards front and back. Don't let the women talk you into letting them go to Cairo for any reason."

Capt. Jaxx said, "Roger that, sir."

Col. Randal said, "Brandy's going to want to come to the hospital from time to time. Make sure she's guarded on the trip to and from town. Whatever happens, don't let her charm you into going off on her own—she'll try."

"Yes, sir."

Brandy said, "I intend to stay right here."

Jim said, "Your decision to provide MI-6 with the information that Raiding Forces uncovers about DeBeers was a clever move. Turned a liability into an asset. Cuthbert informed me MI-6 intends to reciprocate by supplying us every scrap of intelligence related to diamond smuggling they develop."

Capt. McKoy said, "You did that, John—decided to partner up with Curly Bowlby?"

"I did."

Capt. McKoy said, "What made you change your mind?"

Col. Randal said, "Why should we care if DeBeers has a monopoly on the world diamond market? Our mission is to stop industrial diamonds from being smuggled to Germany. Keeping secrets from each other was bad for Raiding Forces."

Capt. McKoy said, "Turned a lemon into lemonade."

Waldo said, "You done it just like Joe's correspondence course says— 'the problem is the solution.' MI-6 was the problem. Now they're . . ."

Lt. Mandy said, "Maybe not. One of the theories being floated at SIME is that MI-6 was behind the shooting. With Lady Jane out of the way, there is some speculation SIS might have believed it would be easier to patch things up with John. MI-6 needs us to carry out direct action missions."

Brandy said, "My money is on Jane's worthless husband. He was a member of the British Union of Fascists before the war. Mallory may still have contacts with Italian Intelligence. You are on SIM's death list, John—for what Force N accomplished in Abyssinia."

Jim said, "I can confirm you are in fact still on the death list."

Col. Randal said, "Why would Mallory want Jane dead?"

Brandy said, "Mallory has property but very little cash. No divorce, Jane dies, he inherits."

Capt. McKoy said, "I've seen people killed for a half empty bottle a' beer. Makes the man a highly motivated candidate. Even if the Royal Navy does have him marooned on some semi-arctic island in the North Sea."

Waldo said, "I'm stickin' with one-a' the Big Four bein' behind it because they're mad at the Colonel. Maybe all of 'em conspirin' together. Those crooks can't like bein' forced to sell their inventory to one buyer exclusive and lettin' him, meaning us, set the price.

"Ain't a real good business practice."

Capt. Jaxx said, "Doesn't matter to me if the Easter Bunny did it. I'm gonna hunt down every single person involved. And kill 'em."

Jack Cool.

Capt. McKoy said, "Get in line, Jack."

2200 HOURS: RITA AND LANA ARRIVED, CARRYING LARGE CANVAS bags. A drummer from the Kit-Kat Club was trailing along behind, lugging the tall native drum he used to play the wild African beat the girls liked to dance to.

Colonel John Randal was napping in the sitting room. Beverly came in and was startled when the colonel opened his eyes before she could touch him. "John, you're going to have to go outside now."

Thinking there might be a medical emergency in progress, Col. Randal asked, "What's going on?"

Beverly said, "Rita and Lana are here to perform a Zār Cult healing ritual on Lady Jane. No men are allowed except for the drummer. You have to wait out in the hall—priestess' orders."

"Are you crazy . . ."

"The girls cured you," Beverly said, "after that lion mauled you. We've all seen those scars."

"Yeah, but that was six hundred miles behind enemy lines," Col. Randal said. "We're in a major modern hospital with a world-class surgeon on call."

Beverly said, "Will you please just go outside?"

"OK," Col. Randal said. "There's going to be trouble—the matron's not going to go for a Zār Priestess ceremony."

Beverly said, "Be a good sport—can't hurt."

Col. Randal went out in the hall and relieved the Lovat Scouts so they could step outside to smoke a cigarette. In a few minutes the rhythmic sound of the drum and the jangle of finger symbols commenced. While the noise was muted, not as wild as he remembered when Rita and Lana performed the ceremony in Abyssinia, it could be heard in the hallway.

It was only a matter of minutes before the chief matron arrived. She was not amused to discover a demonic ritual was taking place in one of *her* hospital rooms. Matters were not improved when Col. Randal refused her entrance.

The nurse stormed off in a huff.

Col. Randal was pretty sure that was not going to be the end of it. And he was right. Before long, Doctor Stephen Milam showed up.

"I was in my quarters pouring myself a dry, as in very dry, martini when the phone rang," Dr. Milam said. "I did not even have to ask who when the matron informed me a voodoo ceremony was underway in the VIP wing."

Col. Randal said, "Zār Cult."

Dr. Milam took a seat in the other chair. By now, it was clear that something was burning in Lady Jane's room, and the fumes from the unknown substance were wafting under the door. The doctor said, "Do you believe there is any chance that is legal?"

Col. Randal said, "Probably not."

"So tell me, Colonel, how does this Zār Cult business work?"

Col. Randal said, "Rita and Lana . . ."

Dr. Milam said, "Your two slaves, now feature dancers at the Kit-Kat Club?"

Col. Randal said, "They're not my slaves. The girls are Zār Cult Priestesses. They perform a ritual to drive out the evil spirits causing their patients' health problem and for a small monthly retainer, they'll keep 'em away."

Dr. Milam said, "Brilliant business model. Better than mine. Who would ever stop paying the residual?"

After a while, the sound of the drum and finger symbols stopped. Brandy came to the door. "Lady Jane woke up. Asked for her Sheba diamond. When Beverly slipped the ring on her finger, she smiled, then went back to sleep."

Dr. Milam said, "And to think of all those years I wasted in medical school."

$$4$$

NAKED DEAD WOMAN

THE NEXT MORNING, BRANDY SEABORN STAYED BEDSIDE WITH her cousin, Major the Lady Jane Seaborn, while Colonel John Randal and Beverly Blackwell took a break in the sitting room. Dr. Stephen Milam had been in earlier on his rounds. The doctor's standard-issue comment had been, "Not out of the woods yet."

Dr. Milam's cryptic report was not making anyone feel better.

Lieutenant Mandy Paige arrived shortly. Col. Randal was hoping for news of a breakthrough in the overnight search for Lady Jane's assailants. Unfortunately, Lt. Mandy had no new information. However, she came armed with a plan to try to take Col. Randal's mind off Lady Jane, if only for a moment.

It was not much of a plan, but it was the only one she could think of.

Col. Randal was reading the Cairo newspaper when Lt. Mandy arrived. A three-paragraph story appeared on Page 3 under the headline, "British Forces Occupy Castelrozzo." The news article made the operation sound routine. The writer had clearly never jumped out of an airplane at low level in the dark of night onto a mountainous island formed out of solid rock.

"Look, Beverly," Lt. Mandy said, pulling a folder out of her purse.

Beverly opened the binder to find an 8x10 glossy photo, "Who's this?"

"Gretchen von Coffenhouser—Nazi SS."

Col. Randal glanced up from the newspaper.

Beverly said, "Wow! She's beautiful."

"John shot her," Lt. Mandy said.

Beverly said, "Why would you do that, John—seriously?"

Col. Randal said, "Caught me at a bad moment with a pistol in her hand."

Lt. Mandy said, "True. An engraved 7.65 Walther PPK. Pam carries it in her purse. You have probably seen it."

Beverly said, "I have! Pam loves her pistol."

Lt. Mandy said, "So, John, the question remains—what were you doing in the hotel room of a naked dead woman with your shirt off?"

Col. Randal said, "Ahhh. . . ."

Beverly laughed. "Daddy's going to love this story."

Handing Beverly a thick file stamped SECRET in red ink, Lt. Mandy said, "Did our fearless leader ever tell you about his nocturnal adventures when he first arrived in Cairo before parachuting into Abyssinia? SOE decided to update his security clearance by having women of questionable morals attempt to entice military secrets out of him by . . ."

VICE ADMIRAL SIR RANDOLPH "RAZOR" RANSOM AND JAMES "Baldie" Taylor arrived at the hospital. The two men retired to the sitting room with Colonel John Randal. There was no immediate need for them to be there. The purpose of the exercise was to give Col. Randal something to think about besides Major the Lady Jane Seaborn. They were there in response to a phone call from Beverly Blackwell.

VAdm. Ransom led off, going straight to the main point.

"The Navy suffered more grievously during the battle for Crete than it cared to admit. Losses have continued to mount in the campaign to interrupt the Axis sea route from Italy to Tripoli. Most of our surface ships down to destroyer escort class have been pulled out of the Mediterranean by now, mainly because of the threat posed by enemy air. Attacks on Panzerarmee Afrika's supply lines that run through the Adriatic to Sicily, across the Aegean from the Greek ports of Piraeus, Kalamata and Salonica, are primarily being carried out by U.S. Navy and Royal Navy submarines.

"MI-6, using the cover names ISLD and MO-4, has continued to land and air drop agents, saboteurs and arms to local resistance groups on the habitable islands in the Aegean Sea. The intent is to lay the foundation for future uprisings."

Jim said, "A-Force, PWE, and certain other clandestine organizations that have sprung up like mushrooms in Middle East Command are also involved in the AO. To date, only limited success has been achieved, mainly because there is little in the way of sea lift and virtually no air support. All military assets are currently tied up supporting Montgomery in Libya and/or Patton in North Africa.

VAdm. Ransom said, "Long range, the plan is to raid the hundreds of tiny Aegean and Adriatic islands stretching from Turkey to the Balkans. A great many have small—meaning squad-sized—primarily Italian formations stationed on them. A few are also garrisoned by Germans from the 22nd Air-Landing Division.

"Our intention is to lay the foundation for local uprisings, to undermine the morale of the isolated enemy personnel and to cause them to be reinforced with additional Axis troops best employed elsewhere. Classic economy of force—a small number of troops ties down a large number of the enemy guarding worthless territory.

"Dudley Clarke recently established a clandestine advanced A-Force base on the Turkish coast opposite the island of Chios. He believes offensive raids can eventually be launched from there. Brigadier Clarke has also set up a schooner route through the Northern Sporades to insert agents on selected islands and bring out escapers for Mrs. Paige's MI-9. The motorized fishing caïque only make something like six knots—a slow speed operation, but all we have.

"Currently I am in the nascent stage of forming an organization called the Levant Schooner Flotilla to be commanded by Lieutenant Commander Adrian Seligman. LSF will transport our raiding parties in Greek caïques. And, it will establish secret arms and supply dumps on certain islands for future operations.

"Finally, a sabotage school is in the early stage of being established near Haifa on Mount Carmel. The idea is to train patriot Greek refugees with an eye to developing a fifth column to assist our armed forces, destroy enemy equipment and material and undermine the morale of the enemy in the Aegean.

"Colonel, I want you to take charge of planning the training curriculum for the Sabotage School. Select an officer-in-charge, supervise staffing and once the establishment is operational, command it under the umbrella of Raiding Forces."

Jim said, "If you thought Force N in Abyssinia was run on a shoestring, you will be shocked by what little is available for us in the Aegean. Virtually no air support of any kind to be had, the Royal Navy reduced to using small slow caïques to transport agents and land raiding parties. And, a mishmash of understrength units with a long history of being misused by GHQ to draw our raiders from.

"One bright spot: Mrs. Paige's MI-9 is beginning to enjoy some success."

VAdm. Ransom said, "Jim is spot-on. There is a dearth of military support. The Joint Operations Staff instructed the Admiralty to order me to take charge with an eye to stepping up raiding without offering any additional assets to accomplish the task. I have been given a mandate to set up an organization called Small Raids Incorporated. Eventually, every independent raiding unit and all naval and air assets supporting Special Operations in Middle East Command will fall under its umbrella.

"You will be my Deputy, Commander of Raiding Troops."

Col. Randal said, "What's the big picture, sir—*your* plan?"

VAdm. Ransom said, "As Panzerarmee Afrika is driven off the continent, my idea is to have you convert Raiding Forces gun jeep patrols into amphibious raiding teams. You, Colonel, will have the daunting task of amalgamating a disparate group of private armies, to include, but not be limited to, LRDG, SAS, SBS, elements of 50 Commando and PPA, into Raiding Forces. Eventually, I may be able to provide you troops from the Greek Sacred Band, which will be invaluable since the islands in the Aegean are inhabited by Greeks.

"Questions?"

"What is it you expect of me, sir," Col. Randal asked, "exactly?"

VAdm. Ransom said, "Coordinate the reorganization of the ground elements of Small Raids Incorporated, standardize and oversee training, plan raids, allocate the forces for missions, assist subordinate team commanders with mission planning and preparation—in short, you will own all things raiding-oriented. A small, joint Combined Operations type staff—consisting of RN, RAF, SOE and OSS Operations Group personnel—will be set up at RFHQ to assist you. Raiding Forces has never had the luxury of a formal staff—now you will.

"You will be in charge of troops, training, mission planning and execution. Regrettably, the U.S. Army, Army Air Force and Navy have declined to participate—choosing to view the Aegean as a sideshow not worthy of their support. However, all your offensive operations must conform to strategy agreed to by the Commander-in-Chief—a U.S. Army lieutenant general named Dwight D. Eisenhower currently headquartered on Gibraltar.

"You will need to place a Raiding Forces liaison officer at General Eisenhower's HQ.

Col. Randal asked, "Do I still have responsibility for our other commitments like GOLDEN FLEECE, RED INDIAN, PURPLE, etc., sir."

"Affirmative," VAdm. Ransom said. "Nothing changes, to include your new OSS anti-diamond smuggling/gold interdiction mission LEAF EATER. A subject we shall not mention unless you request assistance . . . which I can assure you will be forthcoming."

Jim said, "The good news is, we—meaning Small Raids Incorporated—have time to develop our plans and begin establishing forward-operating bases while Eighth Army ejects Rommel from the desert."

Col. Randal said, "Who do I report to?"

"Me," VAdm. Ransom said. "General Donovan agreed to the command structure a while back when I was in the U.S. He considers assisting my Royal Navy Operations Division, Irregular, as an OSS Special Operations function—operating on the peripheral edges of the main battle area.

"While our masters may not be in agreement on the future of the Aegean AO, Donovan has made it clear he intends for the Office of Strategic Services to cooperate with Small Raids Incorporated. He knows the Aegean AO is a pet project of Prime Minister Churchill.

"The PM's goal is to entice Turkey to enter the war on our side, which seems unlikely but worth striving for. Churchill has sold Donovan on the idea. They are convinced that driving the Nazis out of the islands will go a long way toward convincing the Turks to come in on our side. Particularly if we offer the possibility of their claiming some of the Dodecanese Islands that lie off the Turkish coast after the war, when we are dividing up the spoils."

Col. Randal said, "I'm going to have to break out a new set of maps. I don't know anything about those places, sir."

VAdm. Ransom said, "Few do. Once again, we shall find ourselves fighting a private war on the fringes of the main battle area, across vast distances, left to our own devices to conduct a campaign in places no one has ever heard of. And, no one in the conventional military establishment cares about. I can hardly wait to get started."

Col. Randal said, "You say Turkey's letting us operate from their territory or close to it. I'm *persona non grata,* sir. The Turks were pretty unhappy with me last time I was there—that going to be a problem?"

Jim said, "As far as you are concerned, all is forgiven. Turkey is neutral but cooperating with us in the same way Spain is neutral but cooperating with Germany. You killed a pair of Nazi agents spying on the Turks. One day they may decorate you for it."

VAdm. Ransom said, "Nothing is required of Raiding Forces at the moment, Colonel. The main reason for the briefing today was my desire to give you my insight and get you personally committed to the operation. My concern is that now TORCH is ashore, Raiding Forces might be snatched away if you are not fully locked into Small Raids Incorporated from the start.

"General Patton already requested you by name for the Port Lyautey mission. You were away for a month. I should not want that to become a habit."

Col. Randal said, "Count me in. There's no one I'd rather work for than you, Admiral."

When VAdm. Ransom and Jim departed, they left behind reading material—the classified after-action report on the disastrous pinprick raid on the French Coast. OPERATION AQUATINT, where Special Operations Executive (SOE) lost its best pinprick raiding officer KIA and his unit No. 62 Commando had been shattered so badly it had to be disbanded. A "Lessons Learned" Appendix was attached. With small amphibious raids in his future, the two thought Col. Randal might find it illuminating reading.

Something to take his mind off his (immediate) troubles.

Stepping into their staff car, VAdm. Ransom said to Jim, "Anyone else besides Randal, with the all the problems he is facing—Jane being wounded, supporting LIGHTFOOT, TORCH, IDB and a host of other high-priority missions—would have told us to get stuffed."

Jim said, "Most likely you muted the Colonel's response, Admiral, when you mentioned we do not have the shipping to carry out our plans."

"Rest assured I shall figure something out on the Navy side. He knows that," VAdm. Ransom said. "Randal's our best guerrilla man. What I laid out for him is amphibious guerrilla warfare and a free hand to carry it out. Based on our past association, my guess is the Colonel is already running through the possibilities—working out a reorganization plan for Raiding Forces."

Jim said, "The real purpose of the exercise today was to get the Colonel's mind off Lady Seaborn as Beverly requested. I believe we can safely say mission accomplished."

VAdm. Ransom said, "There is no military precedent I am aware of for the kind of naval combat we shall be engaging in—unless you count the Vikings. We have been handed a campaign far, far away in a remote theatre, to be fought by miniscule forces, over great distances, with a minimum of outside interference and no recognizable strategic goal.

"If the thought of that does not distract the Colonel, nothing will. It is keeping me up nights. Most intriguing military assignment I have ever been handed—raiding for raiding's sake."

Jim asked, "Off the record, strictly for my own information, what is your personal opinion of Lady Seaborn's recovery prospects?"

VAdm. Ransom said, "We have both seen men die of lesser wounds."

CHIEF WARRANT OFFICER HANK RAWLSTON ARRIVED AT THE hospital. He was there in response to a phone call from Beverly. She instructed him to give Colonel John Randal a report on OPERATION PURPLE—the mission to retrieve serial numbers off shot-up German tanks in order for the wizards at the Office of Strategic Services to calculate the number of tanks rolling off Nazi assembly lines each month. It was an operation so secret that the algebraic equation the Office of Strategic Services (OSS) mathematicians employed to make the determination had its own TOP SECRET security clearance. No one in Raiding Forces had any idea how the serial numbers collected by the PURPLE teams allowed the wizards to arrive at how many panzers were being manufactured. But apparently they were able to.

Col. Randal, CWO Rawlston and Beverly went into the sitting room.

"Afraid I left you holding the bag, Chief," Col. Randal said. "Give me a report."

"We've been flying by the seat a' our pants, Colonel," CWO Rawlston said. "What I did was I took the number of divisions in Eighth Army, which is ten, and assigned a four-jeep team to each division HQ . . . three men to a jeep. That took up all the Five-Seventy-Five men we had that flunked the Blood in the Sand.

"When a brigade reports to division they're in contact with enemy armor, one of the PURPLE teams rushes to the scene to collect the serial numbers off any knocked out German tanks before the enemy tank recovery people can get there. Problem is, them Nazis is quick to arrive and they're willin' to go to the mat for the damaged tank like dogs fightin' over a bone.

"When you explained it to me at first, sir, it didn't seem like no big deal. Just drive out and copy down some parts numbers, but that ain't how it turned out."

Col. Randal asked, "Casualties?"

"Yes, sir, three men killed and eleven wounded so far."

Col. Randal said, "Never expected that. How're the PURPLE Teams performing?"

CWO Rawlston said, "Just because them boys wasn't up to your standards for Raiding Regiment don't mean they ain't good men—they are, Colonel. Like your rules say, 'Right Man, Right Job.

"They've been gettin' serial numbers."

Beverly said, "I've been forwarding the reports to the statistical department at OSS HQ in Washington. They're pleased with what the PURPLE teams have collected. I don't believe they expected us to be up and running so fast."

Col. Randal asked, "How do you handle the independent brigades, Chief?"

CWO Rawlston said, "Don't have the manpower to station teams with 'em on a permanent basis. When they're in contact, we send 'em somebody.

"I need replacements, Colonel. Where we gonna get the men?"

Col. Randal said, "I have no idea."

CWO Rawlston said, "Don't have to be good at arithmetic to realize we're gonna run out of people before long at the rate we're losing 'em now.

"And, another thing, sir. I'm ready to get back to bein' Raiding Forces Motor Officer. I ain't cut out to be in charge of somethin' as big as PURPLE. You need to get somebody with education and a lot more rank than I got, to deal with all the big brass."

Col. Randal said, "I can make that happen. May take me a few days. Good job, Chief."

"Sorry about Lady Seaborn, Colonel."

"You and me both."

LIEUTENANT COLONEL SIR TERRY "ZORRO" STONE DROVE IN from Mena House Hotel after being summoned by a phone call from Beverly specifying his arrival and departure times. The visitation limits seemed odd to Lt. Col. Stone, but then, these were strange times. He and Colonel John Randal retired to the sitting room alone. Since Major the Lady Jane Seaborn was clearly sleeping, unconscious, or in a coma, neither officer wasted time talking about her medical condition. The two had not had an opportunity to discuss Raiding Regiment since Col. Randal had departed for the TORCH landing over four weeks ago.

A month can seem like a year when a unit is involved in high-intensity combat operations.

Col. Randal asked, "How are the patrols holding up?"

"Raiding Regiment had already been ground down before this last offensive started. Forming the 575th Ranger Regiment Patrol and bringing in RAF No. 2 Armored Car Company has been a life saver," Lt. Col. Stone said. "The Rangers turned out to be fast learners, and Squadron Leader Page and his people were experienced desert operators before No. 2 ACC converted to gun jeeps.

"That said, since you have been away, we have taken over fifteen percent casualties—six men killed, twenty wounded. Captain McKnight and Lieutenant Green among the KIA. As you know, there are no replacement officers or other ranks in our pipeline.

"Consequently, I have ordered the patrol leaders to keep their distance from the Via Balbia. The USAAF and now the RAF are engaged in strafing traffic traveling the hardball along the coast. That would be a good thing, except there have been a number of friendly fire incidents. The pilots engage anything that moves. As a result, Raiding Regiment patrols now travel only at night except in dire emergency.

"Also, I ordered the patrol leaders to use their mortars at standoff range or call in air strikes whenever possible in an attempt to reduce casualties.

"We have too many targets for the four A-20s flying out of Oasis X to handle by themselves. To take up the slack, our Seagulls have been pressed into service for ground attack. They only carry a 345-kilogram bombload—four bombs. Nevertheless, the old amphibians have been performing like thoroughbreds.

"I brought you a pile of patrol after-action reports to peruse at your convenience."

Col. Randal said, "Jim tells me General Alexander wants Raiding Forces to keep up the pressure. Personally, I'm not sure our patrols are as relevant as they were . . . what's your thought?"

"I agree, especially now that Rommel has been driven back all the way out of Egypt."

Col. Randal said, "I've been informed it could take up to six more months of heavy fighting to drive Panzerarmee Afrika off the continent. So, while our job's not done yet, we want to rethink Raiding Regiment's mission. Once the Nazis are pushed out of Libya, I don't believe jeep patrols can operate as effectively in Morocco."

Lt. Col. Stone said, "With no replacements at the rate we are currently suffering losses, six months of patrolling translates into over a hundred percent casualties for Raiding Regiment—we are done."

"Like you always say, Terry, 'it's always darkest before pitch black.' Keep patrols out. But make it crystal clear to everyone—hit and run."

Lt. Col. Stone said, "My friends in the fighting regiments tell me what the newspapers are calling 'The Second Battle of Alamein' is being fought in fits and spurts. Not always going as swimmingly as the headlines claim. Rommel is caught in a nutcracker between TORCH and Eighth Army—Yank press is calling it the 'Big Squeeze.'

"Feels like Raiding Regiment is the one being squeezed."

Col. Randal said, "I'm about to make things even harder for you, Zorro. I want Major Beauchamp and Captain Chatterhorn flown in from the desert. You won't be getting them back. Be prepared to have Captain Butterfield's Blue Patrol pulled out of Raiding Regiment and assigned to RFHQ sometime in the near future."

Lt. Col. Stone said, "Surely you jest?"

"I'm not really in a joking mood."

"Could have fooled me, old stick."

Col. Randal said, "One more thing. Send Major McCloud to take command of Sea Squadron. I'll be giving you Major Corrigan as his replacement. Send every officer in Raiding Regiment who has not attended Commando School to Achnacarry immediately.

"Also, have Major Adair fly down to discuss future Phantom operations with Admiral Ransom."

Lt. Col. Stone said, "What the devil is going on, John?"

Col. Randal said, "When Panzerarmee Afrika is finally driven out of Libya, Raiding Regiment will transition from gun jeep patrolling to small-scale amphibious pinprick raiding. Initially we'll be operating against the Dodecanese chain of islands located in the Aegean. Know much about 'em?"

Lt. Col. Stone said, "Not a bloody thing."

"Neither do I. Better break out maps," Col. Randal said. "The word is the islands are a long way from anywhere and Raiding Forces can count on less logistical support than Force N had in Abyssinia."

"One would believe that is hardly possible."

Col. Randal said, "Get used to the idea. You're going to be in command of Aegean Raiding Operations."

Lt. Col. Stone said, "The Lancelot Lancers riding boats . . . that shall be something to see. Wonder what my father, the Duke, will have to say? He detests Marines."

"Break it to him gently."

VERONICA PAIGE CAME TO THE HOSPITAL IN RESPONSE TO A phone call from Beverly to brief Colonel John Randal on MI-9 Escape developments during the time he was away. She had significant progress to report. However, the Texas cowgirl had given her strict arrival and departure times, so she kept it brief.

Veronica said, "Once Brandy had her PT boat operational, we began to make weekly runs to Crete to bring out evaders. Special Operations Executive coordinates with their operatives on the island to shepherd the men to prearranged pinpoints where they can be picked up. MI-9 brought out thirty-two soldiers, sailors, pilots and crew members while you were away.

"We are developing a close working relationship with both SOE and MI-6 to run dual-purpose missions. Brandy inserts their agents and brings out our evaders. Escape is finally in business."

Col. Randal said, "Admiral Ransom tells me you're working with Brigadier Clarke to open up an escape line into the Aegean. How's that working out?"

Veronica said, "We are only in the earliest of stages at this point. The distances are long, intelligence is sketchy, communications are almost nonexistent and the only craft we have available are called caïques—small motorized fishing sailboats we borrow from Greek fishermen. Admiral Ransom is in the process of organizing something called the Levant Schooner Flotilla—a fleet of caïques MI-9 can use to bring out escapers stranded in the islands.

"The problem is finding someone who can sail the caïques the long distances required."

Col. Randal said, "At our last briefing, you were organizing shows for pilots and aircrews to tell them how to set up Escape organizations in their POW camp if captured. How's that going?"

Veronica said, "Quite well, actually. The purpose is to teach those at risk of capture how MI-9 will be smuggling radios, compasses, maps, etc., concealed in Red Cross parcels to the prisoners. Since no one believes they will ever be captured, my idea was to put on a show starring Maskelyne the Magician to perform tricks demonstrating how our toys work and using Beverly and Mandy to keep the lads' attention."

Col. Randal said, "Sounds like a plan."

Veronica said, "Mandy is busy working with MI-5 and Lady Jane always wants Beverly to go somewhere with her. Admiral Ransom will not let me have any of his Wrens.

"Any idea on where to find showgirls?"

Col. Randal said, "There's Rocky and Rita and Lana—they'll get the men's attention."

"Perfect," Veronica said. "For once MI-9 is not taking three steps forward, then having to take two steps back. You will never know how much I appreciate your support. It has been frustrating."

Col. Randal said, "Stick with it. I've got a lot of confidence in you, Veronica."

LIEUTENANT RANDY "HORNBLOWER" SEABORN, DSO, OBE, DSC, RN arrived at the hospital from Castelrozzo. His mother, Brandy Seaborn, put her arm around his shoulder and took him into the sitting room, leaving Colonel John Randal out in the hall with the Lovat Scouts. The two were inside for a long time.

When they finally came out, Brandy said, "Love you, Randy."

Lt. Seaborn said, "I love you too, Mother. Keep me informed about Aunt Jane."

Brandy said, "I shall—nice doing business with you, Hornblower."

After Lt. Seaborn was gone, Col. Randal asked, "What was that about?"

Brandy said, "I traded Randy my brand-new PT boat for one of his second-hand MAS- boats."

"Why would you do that?"

"Top speed on a PT is forty knots. A MAS can do over fifty," Brandy said. "I prefer the extra speed. Cuts down on the time to Crete and back, allowing us to make the round trip during the hours of darkness. No German E-boat will ever be able to catch us. Moreover, the MAS has a silenced auxiliary engine. Parker and I can use it to work the boat in closer to shore for clandestine missions. There's an eight hundred-yard minimum with a PT because the American boats are so loud. The Life Boat Service Men shall not have to paddle their rubber rafts as far to the pinpoint—always the riskiest part.

"Come along some night to observe our operations."

"I will."

Lieutenant Mandy Paige dropped by for a brief visit. She seemed overwrought. Something was bothering her other than Lady Jane being wounded.

Col. Randal said, "OK, what's the problem, Mandy?"

Lt. Mandy said, "Sammy rounded up the Big Four crime lords. Egyptian Security Police are conducting interrogations. Harsh methods. The Gestapo could take lessons from them."

Col. Randal said, "Farouk's boys don't play by the same Queensbury rules our side does."

Lt. Mandy said, "MI-5 never has had any rules, much less played by them. By now, I thought I had seen it all. What the Big Four have been put through is a horror show. Will I ever again be the same girl you met at Habbaniya?"

Col. Randal said, "No—you won't."

Lt. Mandy said, "Thanks John . . . you were supposed to say everything is going to be all right."

Col. Randal said, "No one asked you to be a counterintelligence officer. When the war's over, you're never going to be the same happy girl, Mandy. That's the price for choosing to serve your country.

"Now, go find out who shot Jane."

Captain "Geronimo" Joe McKoy dropped by later. The ex-Arizona Ranger had a hard look on his face, "I ran into Mandy. She says you chewed her ass."

Col. Randal said, "That's not true."

"Yeah, well, it's what she indicated to me," Capt. McKoy said. "I was readin' a book about personal relationships one time when I was on a stakeout along the Mexican border. Had a chapter called 'Tough Love'."

Col. Randal said, "That what you came to talk to me about—tough love?"

"Hell no, I think we got us a bona fide problem, John."

"What kind of problem?"

"A 'who-done-it'—the three most dreaded words in a homicide investigator's vocabulary."

"What's that mean?"

"Detective novels and Hollywood picture shows have us crime fighters findin' clues and usin' deductive reasonin' to crack cases and track down miscreants usin' scientific investigative technique. But that ain't exactly how it's done—not in real life."

Col. Randal said, "Really?"

"Naw, what happens is, the phone rings. We pick it up. Someone on the other end tells us the name of the perpetrator. We go out, arrest 'em, throw 'em in jail—case solved. Naturally, law enforcement don't like to let on how it really works. The general public needs to feel safe in their beds at night and to have confidence in our crime-fightin' ability."

Col. Randal said, "So, what does that have to do with who shot Lady Jane?"

Capt. McKoy said, "Right now, the motive and the mastermind behind the attack on Lady Jane is unknown—a who-done-it. Contrary to popular belief, solvin' one-a' them is virtually impossible unless somebody talks.

"So far, that ain't happenin'."

Col. Randal said, "Mandy said the Big Four are undergoing interrogation. I would have believed one of them knows of—or would be in a position to find out about—every crime committed in Cairo. One of them has to crack."

Capt. McKoy said, "That's what I thought too, John. Tough grillin' like they're experiencin' will break anybody, but the result ain't always real reliable. The Big Four all understands what will happen if they get implicated in the shootin'.

"That said, the beatin' they're takin', they'll break sooner or later—bawl like baby calves. Who knows if they'll be tellin' the truth or not. One-a' the basic rules of investigatin' is never take a statement from someone who's speakin' in tongues.

Col. Randal said, "Good point."

Capt. McKoy said, "You know them boys coulda started pointin' fingers at each other. But that ain't what they're doin'. All four claim to have no knowledge Lady Jane was targeted, why she was shot, or who hired the hitmen."

Col. Randal said, "You believe them?"

Capt. McKoy said, "Ain't no honor among thieves, but those outlaws ain't turnin' on each other and that's a tell. All of 'em are offerin' up the same story. None of 'em like the idea of havin' to sell their diamonds and gold to Waldo exclusive. But they all claim to realize that after eliminatin' their competitors, like we encouraged 'em to do, they'll more than make up in volume what they lose in price.

"What Waldo done is he stabilized the market. The big crime bosses ain't got nothin' to gain by harmin' Lady Jane. Hurtin' her is bad for business."

Col. Randal said, "Then who's behind the attack?"

"No idea—this crime's got the earmarks a' turnin' into a cold case. . . meanin' it don't never get solved.

"Keep in mind, I could be wrong. The Big Four might be behind the whole deal. I ain't real firm on any a' this," Capt. McKoy said.

"Like I said, we got us a real who-done-it."

BEVERLY WAS CONTINUING TO WORK THE PHONE, SCHEDULING people to come to the hospital to brief Colonel John Randal about projects with a Raiding Forces connection.

Brigadier Dudley Clarke, the commander of the super-secret A-Force (Deception), arrived next. He walked Col. Randal down the hall so that they could have a conversation without any chance of being overheard.

"I understand the Admiral and Jim briefed you earlier today about our upcoming raiding campaign in the Aegean."

Col. Randal said, "They did."

"I shall not take much of your time today but felt it was imperative that I personally explain to you at this early stage that there is more to the operation than meets the eye. Unfortunately, unless you suddenly find yourself promoted to Supreme Allied Commander, you shall never be cleared to have complete knowledge of how vitally important it is to the war effort. You shall simply have to take my word for it."

Col. Randal said, "Considering you get paid to lie, that might be a stretch, Brigadier."

Brig. Clarke said, "I can understand how you might feel that way. What you need to know is A-Force will be involved up to its eyeballs. I want you there in charge of the tactical aspects of the operation.

"We work well together."

Col. Randal said, "I'm fully on board."

Brig. Clarke said, "Excellent . . . let's hope Lady Jane has a speedy recovery. By the way, astute of you to decide to share what information you uncover about DeBeers with MI-6. Well-played, Colonel."

Col. Randal said, "News travels fast."

Brig. Clarke said, "Yes, it does. Only one requires a Top Secret clearance to hear it. Some of us are extremely relieved this tiff has run its course."

After Brig. Clarke departed, Captain Roy "Mad Dog" Reupart, a former instructor at No. 1 British Parachute School, and Lieutenant Karen Montgomery, the Raiding Forces parachute rigger, came by to bring him up to speed on the status of the Middle East Command Parachute School they were in the process of organizing. The school had long been planned. Now the project was gaining momentum. The first class of airborne students was wrapping up.

They kept their briefing short and simple.

Ensign Theodore (Teddy) Hamilton, *aka* "The Great Teddy", appeared as the two were leaving. Beverly allowed him to peek in the door at Major the Lady Jane Seaborn, still sleeping peacefully on her bed. Fighting back tears, he gave Col. Randal a short report on the deception operations covering Eighth Army's offensive, OPERATION LIGHTFOOT. While brilliant in their simplicity and highly effective, they were not much different than all the other deceptions the boy genius had been involved with.

Waldo Treywick showed up next. He said, "Colonel, did I ever tell you about the time me and P. J. Pretorius was huntin' a remote herd a' mountain elephant that was supposed to be sportin' big ivory when the locals warned us to be on the lookout for a rogue man-eatin' gorilla?"

At this point, Col. Randal became suspicious. First chance, he pulled Brandy Seaborn aside. "Can you tell me what's happening here?"

Brandy said, "Happening?"

Col. Randal said, "One person shows up, then as soon as they leave, someone else arrives. Like clockwork. What's the deal?"

Brandy said, "Classified—if I tell you, then I shall have to . . ."

"So, it's not a coincidence?"

"Negative, handsome. No coincidence."

"What, then?"

Brandy said, "Beverly has been on the phone calling everyone she can think of, arranging times for them to arrive at the hospital and telling them how long to stay. Her idea is to keep you distracted. I do believe she is more worried about you than Jane.

"Play along . . . Beverly desperately cares."

Col. Randal said, "I can do that."

After Lt. Mandy delivered dinner to the hospital, the MI-5 girl went back to work at SIME with King. Brandy sat in the chair by Lady Jane's bed. Col. Randal and Beverly retired to the sitting room alone.

Col. Randal said, "One more time—walk me through what happened from the moment you and Jane came out of the restaurant."

Beverly said, "OK, Bannon and Clooney were waiting by the front door, armed with Thompson submachine guns. Flanigan was parked at the curb in Lady Jane's white Rolls-Royce, standing by to pick us up. We swung in behind the two Rangers, and they escorted us down the steps to the sidewalk.

"Two Middle Eastern men in off-white linen suits, wearing typical Egyptian straw hats with the brims pulled down low over their eyes walked by. Shots rang out. Bannon and Clooney went down immediately. I pulled my weapon and shot one of the bad guys. At the same time, out of the corner of my eye, I noticed Lady Jane was on the ground. By then, the second shooter had turned to run, so I shot him too.

"After that, it was chaos and hysteria. People shouting. Happy had the second gunman by the throat in full attack mode. I don't remember the details clearly—trying to staunch the flow of Jane's blood, being in the back of a screaming ambulance . . ."

Col. Randal said, "No words were exchanged?"

"Not a syllable, John."

"What pistol did you use—.32 Remington M-51 or your 9mm Browning P-35?"

Beverly produced the Browning High-Power with mother of pearl grips the master engravers at Westley Richards had perfectly matched to the engraving on the Remington pocket pistol her father had given her ten years earlier.

"My new Browning. Lady Jane and I picked it up at the shop earlier in the week."

Col. Randal said, "Did you have your hand on the pistol before the shooting started?"

"No."

"So you didn't sense any danger? Because you know to place your hand on your weapon the instant you do."

Beverly said, "You've drilled that into me a million times, John. I did not perceive any threat until the first shot was fired."

Col. Randal said, "Textbook hit. Even though the bodyguards never got off a single round, if they hadn't been there, you and Jane would both be dead."

Beverly said, "It happened so fast . . ."

Col. Randal said, "The shooters were professionals with the advantage of prior planning and the element of surprise. You're a real gunfighter. I'm proud of you."

Beverly said, "Can I put that on my resumé?"

Dr. Stephen Milam dropped by to make his evening call. When pressed, he said, "Not out of the woods yet."

5

NOT OUT OF THE WOODS

COLONEL JOHN RANDAL SNAPPED AWAKE IN THE CHAIR NEXT TO Major the Lady Jane Seaborn's bed. Beams of light were peeking through the cracks in the blinds as the sun came up. Possibly that is what woke him, but more likely it was because Lady Jane was staring at him.

She winked.

Col. Randal had a reputation for being calm under fire; however, he was decidedly *not* calm now. Lady Jane had been asleep, unconscious, or in a coma for two days, only waking up briefly during Rita and Lana's Zār Priestess ceremony. He guessed she probably wanted a drink, but then remembered you were not supposed to give water to people with stomach wounds.

What to do?

Col. Randal winked back, then dashed into the sitting room where Brandy Seaborn and Beverly Blackwell were sleeping on the couch's fold-out bed. Rita and Lana were curled up on pallets on the floor.

"Jane's awake—what do we do now?"

Beverly jumped out of bed wearing one of Captain Billy Jack Jaxx's No. 11 University of Texas Longhorns football jerseys that almost reached her knees, and ran barefoot out the door, down the hall to find a nurse. Brandy hopped up, clad in a pair of her late husband's monogrammed silk pajamas and rushed to Lady Jane's bedside.

Rita and Lana peeked in the door from the sitting room.

Lady Jane was not talking, but she was awake and alert.

Brandy immediately started kissing her on the forehead, laughing and crying at the same time. Col. Randal had never been in a situation like this, and he never wanted to be in another.

Dr. Stephen Milam hurried in, with a nurse trailing behind. He had just arrived at the hospital to begin his morning rounds when Beverly came running up to the nurse's station. The doctor began inspecting Lady Jane's bandages, while cautioning her not to try to speak.

The nurse stuck a thermometer in her mouth and then began taking her blood pressure.

Beverly returned, carrying a large glass of crushed ice and a spoon.

Dr. Milam said, "You can give Lady Jane the ice, but try not to overdo it—rub chips on her lips at first. The nurse is going to put a DO NOT DISTURB sign on the door. That way no one can blame you personally when they are not allowed in—it means what it says, Colonel."

Col. Randal said, "Understood."

"I shall have a room made available for you to use for your office. No more traipsing back and forth into the sitting room. Lady Jane needs quiet."

"Yes, sir."

Dr. Milam looked at the thermometer. "No fever, vital signs are good. Get rest, Lady Jane. We shall have you up and walking in a day or two. Then out of the hospital for home care at your Mena House Hotel suite. You are one lucky woman.

"Gave us all a scare."

Lady Jane responded with one of her patented heart attack smiles. While still lethal, it clearly required a great deal of effort. Nevertheless, it was a relief to see.

Col. Randal followed the doctor out into the hall, "What's the verdict?"

Dr. Milam said, "Not out of the woods yet."

"But you said . . ."

"*Not* out of the woods yet."

CAPTAIN PAMALA PLUM-MARTIN ARRIVED WITH CAPTAIN BUTCH "Headhunter" Hoolihan. Colonel John Randal had dispatched her to fly to Alexandria to pick him up at Sea Squadron. While the Vargas Girl look-alike pilot went in to visit Major the Lady Jane Seaborn, Col. Randal and Capt. Hoolihan retired to the office Dr. Milam had provided. The highly decorated young Royal Marine was one of his most trusted officers, having served as his enlisted number two on raids on the French coast before being commissioned in the field prior to jumping into Abyssinia with him.

Capt. Hoolihan said, "Any idea who was behind the shooting, sir?"

"Negative."

"When you do find out, Colonel, I want to be there to help take them down."

"I'll keep that in mind, Butch."

Capt. Hoolihan said, "I mean it, sir. Lady Seaborn was most generous helping me transition into becoming an officer. Far away above and beyond the call of duty. I would do anything for her—you know that."

"I do," Col. Randal said. "Now, good news and bad news. Which one do you want first?"

"Bad news, sir."

Col. Randal said, "Transfer all your troops to Raiding Regiment effective immediately. In return, Colonel Stone will send you an equal number of his people."

Capt. Hoolihan said, "Are you having me on, sir?"

"No."

"Why would we want to do something like that, sir—my command is a finely honed team?"

Col. Randal said, "I need you and Randy to bring Raiding Regiment up to the same standard of amphibious competence as Sea Squadron. The good news is, pinprick Commando raids are back in our future in a big way. We're going to begin operating against the islands in the Aegean. I'll be leaning on you big time, Butch."

Capt. Hoolihan said, "Like the sound of that, sir."

"Keep the first intake of Raiding Regiment men for two months, then transfer 'em back to Sir Terry. Plan for three sixty-day cycles. Hopefully, that should be enough time for you to work your magic."

Capt. Hoolihan asked, "What about No. 2 Armored Car Company, sir?"

"I spoke with Air Marshal Tedder. The RAF is phasing out armored car companies," Col. Randal said. "He agreed for No. 2 to be badged over to stay with Raiding Forces. Which means, Butch, you're going to have your work cut out for you. They are the only entire unit we have that's not Commando School qualified."

Capt. Hoolihan said, "Send No. 2 to me last, sir. If we do not have enough time to bring them up to speed before we commence our new phase of pinprick raids, I shall keep them under my personal command until they are fully capable."

Col. Randal said, "Get with Admiral Ransom for a detailed briefing on what the future holds. Have Roy Kidd sit in. He's going to have to do the same thing with Duck Patrol—you break the bad news."

"Yes, sir. Hate to part with my people. We have been working together for quite a while now."

"You'll get 'em back."

CAPTAIN "GERONIMO" JOE MCKOY, WALDO TREYWICK AND KING arrived as Captain Butch "Headhunter" Hoolihan was leaving. They were at the hospital to have a confidential meeting with Colonel John Randal. The office Dr. Stephen Milam had provided gave them a nice, quiet, secure place to have a conversation they would not want anyone to overhear.

Captain Billy Jack Jaxx stopped by to check on Major the Lady Jane Seaborn. He was invited to sit in after Beverly Blackwell tapped on the door and informed Col. Randal he was in the building. She came in as well.

Capt. McKoy said, "Ain't no new information about who shot Lady Jane."

Col. Randal said, "Are the Big Four still undergoing interrogation?"

"Yeah, they are. Ain't changin' their stories, givin' up any information, or turnin' on each other," Capt. McKoy said. Could mean they all cooked up a story and are sticking to it knowin' it's a death sentence if we find out they're behind the shootin'."

Col. Randal said, "You believe they're going to talk?"

"Not really—I don't. What do you think, Jack?"

Capt. Jaxx said, "Those guys have been beaten to a pulp. I wouldn't trust a word they said at this point. My grandfather, the sheriff, taught me that if you wanted good information, roughing a criminal up needed to be dished out in small doses. The Egyptian police don't see it that way."

Capt. McKoy said, "They're working those four men over in shifts because the interrogators keep wearing out."

Col. Randal said, "Can we have the Big Four released?"

Capt. McKoy said, "What you cogitatin' on, John?"

"Those men are more valuable outside working for us than inside getting hammered for something they may not know anything about."

Capt. McKoy said, "I'll talk to R. J. Tell him your thoughts. If anybody can get 'em cut loose, it'd be him."

"Good," Col. Randal said. "Now to the subject of diamonds. While I was in the States, General Donovan briefed me again on the strategic importance of stopping the flow of industrial diamonds to Nazi Germany. He insinuated LEAF EATER has a higher priority than GOLDEN FLEECE, which we have repeatedly been told takes precedence over any other operation in the war. OSS is concerned we're not be taking the mission seriously enough."

Capt. McKoy said, "Speaking for myself, I'm takin' it serious all right— only I'm not exactly real sure what the mission actually is."

Choosing to ignore the Captain's statement, Col. Randal handed a copy of a typed page he had extracted from an Office of Strategic Services "Secret Intelligence Assessment" to Beverly. It was stamped "SECRET" and contained a single paragraph. "Read this out loud."

Beverly read, "Conclusion: Only diamonds are hard enough to manufacture the millions of precision parts that are necessary for mass-producing airplane engines, torpedoes, tanks, artillery and other weapons. Only diamonds can be used to draw the fine wire needed for radar and the electronics of modern war. Only diamonds can provide the jeweled bearings necessary for the stabilizers, gyroscopes and guidance systems for submarines and planes. Only diamonds can provide the abrasives necessary for rapidly converting civilian industry into a war machine."

Col. Randal said, "OSS has determined diamonds are also reaching Germany through Spain via Tangiers."

Waldo said, "Ain't Tangiers in Morocco?"

Col. Randal said, "It is."

Waldo said, "Opened us up a whole new market when you invaded that country, Colonel."

Col. Randal said, "That's one of the reasons I want the Big Four out of jail. Tangiers is an international zone under the protection of Spain, France and the United Kingdom. However, Spain unilaterally occupied it the same day Paris fell to the Nazis . . . which can't be a coincidence.

"The U.S. has never recognized their right to do so because of Spanish sympathy for Nazi Germany. My guess is the Spanish police are aiding in—or at least turning a blind eye to—the transfer of industrial diamonds from Tangiers to Spain, then on to the Nazis. It's only nine miles across the Straits of Gibraltar."

Capt. McKoy said, "I'd say that's a good guess, John."

Col. Randal said, "OSS has a Secret Intelligence operation in place in Tangiers, headed up by a U.S. Marine major named Ortiz. We can use him as a contact. He hasn't been able to develop actionable intelligence on the diamond trade. My thought is the Big Four might have criminal ties to the area that can benefit us.

"If so, then it's Mr. Big goes to Morocco."

Waldo said, "Yeah, I'd like that, Colonel. Capture us another market. Pull in a lot more money."

Col. Randal said, "I've got some bad news to report on the money front. We were premature in converting your gold bars to cash. Gold is now trading on the Cairo black market for the same thirty times pre-war price as diamonds."

Waldo said, "You mean we coulda got thirty times more money than we did if we'd a' held on a little longer and brought the gold to Cairo instead of the States?"

Col. Randal said, "Affirmative."

Waldo said, "Went to a lot a' trouble to screw ourselves—story a' my life."

King said, "Hate it when that happens."

Capt. McKoy said, "I had a rich ol' uncle—at least he was before the Great Depression leveled him. Made a fortune buyin' up silver minin' concessions in Nevada back in the day, then sold out at the top. Put his pile into the stock market and tripled it. Lost 'er all in the Crash a' '29.

"He always told me— 'greed kills.' We've done real good, Waldo. No need to go gettin' greedy."

Waldo said, "Yeah, but with thirty times our take, we coulda bought us the entire coastline a' California, except for the parts runnin' through the big cities."

Col. Randal said, "Maybe there's a way to recover some of your lost profits, Mr. Treywick."

"I'm all ears."

Col. Randal said, "You still have a huge cache of gold coins stashed in the basement of the consulate in Kenya. Since it's illegal for private citizens to hold gold in the U.S. except in collections, General Donovan's law firm is researching how to convert that many coins into cash. The idea is to call your coins collectables. Base their value on their numismatic value, not their face value or weight.

"Coin collectors pay a lot more than thirty times face value for rare collectable coins—especially when they're gold. You can cash out."

Capt. McKoy said, "How do we get 'er done, John?"

Col. Randal said, "If we can't do it legal, OSS will do it illegal. Either way, we need to raise the money to help finance our diamond buying—leverage profits. I'll get back to you."

King said, "Cairo to Tangiers to Sierra Leone and back is almost an equilateral triangle, Chief—over two thousand miles each leg. OPERATION LEAF EATER is going to require heavy duty air travel. To reach some places will require skirting around enemy air space."

Col. Randal said, "We'll leave that problem to Tony Dudgeon. The Wing Commander's a highly experienced long-distance pilot. Air Marshal Tedder has instructed him to provide Raiding Forces priority air travel on request. He's basically our private pilot."

Capt. McKoy said, "Not just travel is goin' to be difficult. Conditions in some a' the places we're gonna have to operate in the Congo are real primitive. Wouldn't be no surprise if there actually *was* some a' those leaf-eatin' dinosaurs Waldo's been tellin' us about, roamin' around."

Col. Randal said, "How was your trip to the region, Captain?

Capt. McKoy said, "I've got most a' my folks in place all takin' a look-see. OSS has a Secret Intelligence operation goin' in Sierra Leone, but my boys ain't plannin' to have much contact with it. Don't particularly like people knowin' what they're up to.

"I'll give you a full, in-depth report when we've got more time, John. Just know this—between the five of us, and not for public consumption—we ain't gonna stop the illicit flow a' diamonds to the Nazis. Not now, not ever. It's impossible."

Col. Randal said, "I hear you loud and clear, Captain. We'll keep that estimate of the situation to ourselves and proceed at our own chosen speed as if we believe we can. Let's run through the OPERATION LEAF EATER mission statement one more time to make sure we're all on the same page.

"One, set up an off-the-books freelance enterprise sanctioned by OSS and MI-6 to infiltrate and take control of the diamond trade in Cairo—and eventually Tangiers—in order to interrupt the flow of industrial diamonds currently reaching the Third Reich.

"Two, ensure any diamond traded by any broker on the continent of Africa will be sold through Mr. Big, meaning Mr. Treywick. Those diamonds will then be resold to diamond smugglers who will attempt to transport the stones to Nazi Germany.

"Three, Raiding Forces will intercept the smugglers and recover the diamonds, which will then be resold by Mr. Big to different smugglers, who will in turn be taken down, etc.

"Four, Abyssinian Rules are in full force and effect. My verbal orders from OSS are to eliminate the smugglers with 'extreme prejudice'—Ivy League speak meaning 'kill them.'

"Five, all proceeds from the sale of diamonds will go to a private company held by certain Raiding Forces personnel—primarily Captain McKoy, Waldo Treywick, King and Beverly, as well as others to be determined. Captain Jaxx, you will also participate. However, the legalities of how you're to be paid have yet to be worked out since you're a serving U.S. Army officer.

"Upon conclusion of the war, no record of OPERATION LEAF EATER will appear in the dossier of any U.S. or British intelligence agency—it will have never happened.

"What are your questions?"

Waldo said, "Only an idiot would have any."

After the meeting broke up, Capt. McKoy strolled back to the office alone. "You know, John, if anything is too good to be true—it generally ain't."

Col. Randal said, "I've been wondering how long it was going to take for you to get around to pointing that out to me."

BEVERLY BLACKWELL CAME TO RETRIEVE COLONEL JOHN Randal. "Lady Jane is asking for you."

When they walked into the hospital room, Happy was sitting in a chair that had been pulled up next to the bed. The dog had his muzzle poked under Major the Lady Jane Seaborn's arm while she toyed with his ears with her other hand. Even without a stick of makeup, Lady Jane looked drop-dead gorgeous. Happy looked—happy.

Col. Randal said, "How did you manage to sneak him past the matron?"

Beverly laughed, "Dr. Milam wrote me a prescription that said Happy was a comfort dog."

"What's a comfort dog?"

"He claimed a medical study showed that people recovered from injuries faster if they were allowed to have their pets around."

Col. Randal shooed Happy out of the chair, sat down and took Lady Jane's hand. He was at a loss for anything to say. To date, he had exactly zero experience at initiating conversation with a woman he was in a relationship with who was suffering from a gunshot wound.

In her cut glass accent, speaking with a soft whisper, Lady Jane said, "I hear you have been playing the hero again."

Col. Randal said, "Not true. I went on a long boat ride—tell me *your* story?"

Lady Jane said, "We were walking down the steps of the restaurant to my car when shots rang out. I saw the Rangers fall and felt a shove—no pain, just a gentle push. Then Beverly opened fire and her spent cartridge cases were dancing around me on the concrete and I realized I was lying on the ground. The next thing I remember was waking up during Rita and Lana's Zār Cult ceremony."

Col. Randal asked, "How do you feel now?"

"Sore in places. I thought getting shot would hurt more. Other than being tender, I am fine—maybe a little weak."

Col. Randal said, "I don't think it always works that way."

Beverly said, "I'm going to step out in the hall to give you two some privacy. I'll be right outside the door if you need anything."

Lady Jane said, "I am ready to check out of this hospital. When can I go home, John?"

Col. Randal said, "The doctor says we can take you to Mena House as soon as he's convinced there's no chance of infection. Home care there to complete your recovery. I want you out of here too. So, don't develop an infection—that's an order."

"Aye, aye, sir."

"I believe they're going to try having you walk a few steps. We'll see how that goes. You may find out you're not as tough as you think you are."

Lady Jane laughed, but it came out as a whisper. "I shall show you, John Randal."

"You do that."

Col. Randal had pretty much expended everything he could think of to talk about at that point. He hated hospitals. He hated the smell of hospitals. He hated that Lady Jane was in the hospital. And, he wanted the two of them to get as far away from this place as fast as they could and never come back.

Finally, Col. Randal said, "I hear you and Beverly went on a trip while I was gone."

Lady Jane said, "The California coast is such a beautiful place. I love Carmel and the Big Sur. Can we live there after the war?"

There was a light tapping on the door. Brandy Seaborn opened it a crack, "May I speak to you a moment, John?"

Col. Randal went outside to find Brandy in her idea of battle dress uniform— faded khaki safari shirt, rolled up shorts and rubber-soled, canvas topped raiding boots. She had her wheat colored hair in a severe French twist and was wearing a crumpled white Royal Navy skipper's cap with the bill pulled low almost covering her eyes.

While it was universally agreed that Lady Jane was drop-dead gorgeous, Brandy was drop-dead sexy.

She said, "Frogspawn."

Col. Randal clicked on immediately.

Brandy said, "Be at the RFHQ dock at 1700 hours sharp. Do not be late."

"What the . . ."

"Tell Jane we shall be taking the MAS boat out on a shakedown cruise tonight."

"What *are* we going to be doing?"

"Sealed orders not to be opened until after we shove off."

"Give it up, Brandy."

"All you are going to get, handsome," Brandy laughed. "On second thought, I shall advise Jane about the sea trial and tell her you need a break from hanging around the hospital."

Col. Randal said, "Roger that, I do."

Brandy said, "Parker and I intend to try to set a speed record tonight—fun."

There was no smoking in the hospital. Deciding to leave the two women alone to visit, Col. Randal walked out the front door to have a cigarette. When he came back, Brandy was leaving and Lieutenant Mandy Paige was disappearing inside Lady Jane's room.

"You two aren't much help," Col. Randal said to the heavily bandaged Lovat Scouts as he pointed to the large NO VISITORS sign on the door.

The Scouts looked sheepish. Who was going to tell Lt. Mandy no? Not them.

Col. Randal went in. Happy was trying to rub noses with Lt. Mandy. Beverly and Lady Jane were laughing.

"So much for peace, tranquility, quiet bedrest and no visitors," Col. Randal said. "Mandy, if you'll quit kissing that dog, I'd like a word with you in private."

The two walked down the hall to the office. Lt. Mandy said, "Lady Jane appears to be regaining her old spirits—are you mad at me about something, John?"

Ignoring her, Col. Randal asked, "How do you feel about lying?"

"Depends—what kind of lie are you talking about, John?"

"A big one."

"How about more detail?"

Col. Randal said, "You remember the trouble we had with MI-6 over the DeBeers situation. Caused hurt feelings and mistrust in Raiding Forces. You and I worked past that."

Lt. Mandy said, "Yes, we did. You were extremely kind to me . . . in the end."

Col. Randal said, "OPERATION LEAF EATER is strictly an OSS mission. It is limited strictly Need to Know to a small select cadre. I want you in my inner circle of advisors. However, there's a problem."

Lt. Mandy said, "What kind of problem?"

"You're a serving British officer," Col. Randal said. "How would you feel about getting out of the Royal Marines?"

"Why would I want to? I love being one of Lady Jane's Royal Marines—great uniform," Lt. Mandy said. "Besides, if I resign my commission, I shall simply be drafted into some other branch of the service. All women under forty are required to serve in some capacity."

Col. Randal said. "What if you were invalided out of the Marines."

Lt. Mandy said, "I am in perfect health."

"Not necessarily," Col. Randal said, sliding a document across the desk to her.

"This claims I was wounded the day Lady Jane was!"

"Yes, it does," Col. Randal said, handing her another document.

"This is a medical report signed by Dr. Milam stating I am no longer medically fit for military service?"

Col. Randal said, "That's too bad."

Lt. Mandy said, "John, what is going on?"

"Ancillary to LEAF EATER, a small private company is being formed. It has been authorized by OSS to profit from the sale of diamonds captured from the criminals attempting to sell them to the Nazis. The diamonds confiscated will be sold to other smugglers, recaptured, resold, and recaptured and so on. The plan is to identify the individuals doing the smuggling and eliminate them, while driving up the price the Nazis have to pay for the stones we don't capture.

"I can arrange for you to be a shareholder in the company . . . provided you give up your commission."

Lt. Mandy asked, "Why not simply have me seconded to the OSS?"

"A British citizen can only be assigned to OSS on a permanent basis if they're not currently serving in their own military."

"Explain to me one more time very slowly why I would want to be a part of such a crazy scheme?"

Col. Randal said, "OSS has agreed to authorize the shareholders of the privately owned company to keep the money from the sale of the diamonds. You'll be set for life. Wealthy—in a big way."

Lt. Mandy said, "Can I continue to be involved with counterintelligence?"

"Nothing changes, except now you'll be OSS . . . a civilian drawing U.S. Army captain's pay—same as Beverly. You carry on as the Raiding Forces Chief of Counterintelligence.

"A job you created yourself, as I recall."

Lt. Mandy said, "In that case, sign me up. The increase in salary almost makes up for you so harshly informing me I would never be the same happy girl you first met at RAF Habbaniya."

Col. Randal said. "You're far more interesting as a mature woman, Mandy."

"Beautiful too?"

"Stunning."

Ex-Lt. Mandy said, "You should go on suicide missions more often if you will come back and pay me compliments like that, John."

Col. Randal said, "Maybe now you'll quit trying to be my mother?"

Mandy said, "Not a chance."

CAPTAIN BILLY JACK JAXX AND CAPTAIN PAMALA PLUM-MARTIN were waiting as Mandy Paige was leaving to visit Major the Lady Jane Seaborn.

Capt. Plum-Martin asked, "Why was Mandy unpinning her rank insignia?"

Col. Randal said, "She was wounded in the attempt on Lady Jane's life. Dr. Milam has certified her medically unfit for active duty."

"I was dining at the Gezira the day Lady Jane was shot," Capt. Plum-Martin said. "Mandy was not even in the restaurant. She and Captain Butterfield were sunning by the pool at Lady Jane's suite at Mena House."

Col. Randal said, "No kidding."

Capt. Jaxx asked, "What's going on, Colonel?"

"Mandy's joining the Office of Strategic Services."

Capt. Jaxx said, "Got it."

"Explain it to me later, Jack," Capt. Plum-Martin said.

Capt. Jaxx said, "We wanted to stop in and brief you on a BOMBSHELL we ran while you were away, sir."

Capt. Plum-Martin, the namesake of the operation to target enemy pilots, said, "Air Intelligence developed information regarding a nightspot Luftwaffe pilots were known to frequent after a hard day of flying. The bar was a converted *casa strata* located approximately one hundred fifty miles west of Alexandria. I came into possession of the intel, provided it to Jack, we developed a plan and SOG was tapped for the raid."

Capt. Jaxx said, "Five Luftwaffe and Regia Aeronautica landing grounds were within driving distance of the place with no known entertainment in between. The bar was located pretty much in the middle of nowhere, sir. There was a red-light joint on the second floor. Intelligence estimated thirty to forty pilots in the place on any given night."

Col. Randal said, "Good target."

"That's what Pam and I thought, sir. We did it the easy way. Roy Kidd and I went ashore in a single DUKW, motored out into the desert, looped around and set up a directional arrow made out of five-gallon cans half filled with kerosene, motor oil and gravel. We aimed it straight at the honkytonk, lit it off and high-tailed it back to the *King Duck* with no one the wiser."

Capt. Plum-Martin said, "Ronnie and I were racetracking overhead in the vicinity, flying A-20 gunships. We observed the indicator, rolled in and strafed the building. Two additional standard inventory A-20s armed with five hundred-pound bombs followed us in and dropped their payload at low level. Not much left of the building after we pulled out."

Col. Randal said, "Sounds like you've got air/ground cooperation down to a science."

The Vargas Girl look-alike Royal Marine pilot said, "It would be even better if you had not issued standing orders forbidding female pilots from making more than one single pass on a target. I would have liked to have made a couple more gun runs. What is the chance of you lifting that restriction, John?"

Col. Randal said, "Precisely zero."

JAMES "BALDIE" TAYLOR CAME TO THE HOSPITAL. HE AND Colonel John Randal went into conference. The Chief of MI-6 Special Operations, Middle East Command, was disgusted.

"Late-breaking development, Colonel," Jim said. "The Special Air Service was on a raid against a hard target. They were traveling by day. As darkness set in, they set up an overnight position in a wadi. What the SAS patrol did not know was that in the next wadi over there was an anti-SAS Paratroop Company, z.b.V. 250, sent out from Germany specifically to track down and eliminate the SAS.

"The German anti-SAS unit was on its first training mission to acclimate themselves after arriving in Libya. The Nazis detected the SAS. They attacked, captured David Stirling, and killed or captured virtually the entire patrol."

Col. Randal said, "You expect me to believe that story?"

Jim said, "No, but it is what the Germans are claiming. What we know to be true—Stirling is in the bag. The SAS is in shambles."

Col. Randal said, "What really happened, Jim?"

Jim said, "Like you told Dudley Clarke, Stirling was a cowboy. We both know he commanded his unit from the Long Bar here in Cairo. Planned his missions—more accurately, he reviewed the plans GHQ Operations Staff dreamed up for him—during parties at an apartment here in the city. Had no idea who all the people in attendance were, demonstrated an absolute disregard for security. Plus—and this is significant—he had been warned repeatedly about SAS's lax radio procedure—would not listen.

"The only surprise is Stirling lasted as long as he did."

Col. Randal said, "So, what now?"

Jim said, "There is gnashing of teeth and high angst in some circles because Stirling has not left behind any line of succession or other plans about what is to be done in the event he was killed or captured. Apparently never took the possibility seriously.

"The next senior SAS officer is Captain Paddy Mayne."

Col. Randal said, "Mayne . . . isn't he the SAS's highest scoring patrol leader?"

Jim said, "He is, and some claim the Captain has an almost telepathic sense for finding German targets. He has singlehandedly destroyed more Luftwaffe airplanes than most RAF fighter squadrons.

"The problem is, Mayne is possessed of a flawed psyche. He was under arrest for striking his commanding officer when Stirling recruited him for SAS. When he is back from a patrol, the man never stops drinking. When under the influence of alcohol, he becomes violent.

"There is concern Captain Mayne is not capable of holding an independent command. Dudley does not feel he can work with him. The future of the 1st SAS Regiment—or what is left of it—is in doubt."

Col. Randal said, "1st SAS Regiment?"

Jim said, "That's what Stirling had recently named it. Had his own unofficial regimental insignia—a winged dagger—some claim it is actually King Arthur's sword. A 2nd SAS Regiment is forming in England under his brother. It was hoped, by David, that it would be sent out here to form the Special Air Service Brigade—a fiction Dudley Clarke has long floated. The Phantom Major fancied himself promoted to brigadier in command."

Col. Randal said, "You didn't come here to tell me this fairy tale without some reason."

Jim said, "Stirling never set up a support element for the Special Air Service. Captain Mayne has no head for paperwork. Will you consent to providing SAS with administrative support until the best course of action has been decided as it pertains to the unit's future?"

Col. Randal said, "We can do that. I'll notify Captain Fawcett-Tatum. She'll need a point of contact at SAS. Stephanie will work out the details, but Captain Mayne has to understand that what she says goes—administratively."

Jim said, "This is a temporary fix. My guess is the Special Air Service will be disbanded in Middle East Command like most of the other units of the type. When that takes place, Raiding Forces will be able to recruit the SAS men who meet your standards."

Col. Randal said, "If we badged over the entire 1st SAS Regiment, it wouldn't make up for Raiding Regiment's recent losses."

COLONEL JOHN RANDAL WAS SITTING IN THE CHAIR NEXT TO Major the Lady Jane Seaborn's hospital bed. Exhausted from her visitors, she was sleeping quietly. He had given strict orders that no one else was to be allowed in.

To occupy himself, he was reading Appendix B of the After Action Report on the failed pinprick raid OPERATION AQUATINT that Vice Admiral Sir Randolph "Razor" Ransom had left with him. He noted the copies: Brigadier Colin Gubbins, Special Operations Executive, Vice Admiral Louis Mountbatten, Combined Operations Headquarters, Vice Admiral Sir Randolph Ransom, Director of Naval Operations (Irregular), the Admiralty . . .

The assessment of the operation was signed by I. C. Collins, GSO2 (General Staff Officer 2)—whoever that was. GSO2 Collins gave his assessment of the raid and listed twelve points . . . the lessons to be learned.

1) The risk of carrying out a frontal assault even on a supposedly lightly defended objective is considerable.

Col. Randal was aware the target was a German lighthouse on the French coast. And that 62 Commando, aka the Small-Scale Raiding Force, the unit carrying out the raid, had previously experienced success attacking a lighthouse.

The plan was to land on a very small beach farther east from the objective and climb up a narrow gully, but this opening could not be found on a very dark night and plans had to be changed. The beach landed on was defended by 75mm cannon and machine guns.

Conclusion: The assault craft must be landed on a beach where a safe and quick getaway can be affected.

A note mentioned that a beach defended by 75mm cannon and numerous machine guns appeared to be a badly chosen spot for a commando raid. Col. Randal thought that an understatement.

2) The Commandos carried an extra dory aboard the motor torpedo boat but under the circumstances it could not be used.

Conclusion: where possible, forces should go ashore in two boats.

A note made the remark that the dory lifeboat was superior to the Goatley used and two boats would have improved the Commandos' chance to escape once the raid went wrong. Col. Randal gritted his teeth. Both of these were lessons Raiding Forces had learned and reported to Combined Operations over a year prior to OPERATION AQUATINT.

3) MTB incurred too great a risk in lying so close offshore and was lucky not to be sunk.

Col. Randal did not agree with this statement. Raiding Forces preferred to carry its Raiders as close to shore as possible before launching the assault boats. This was particularly desirable when, upon completion of the raid, the raiders were withdrawing to the mother craft.

4) A plan should be made in advance where a pick-up can be effected 2–3 nights later in case some of the party get left behind.

Col. Randal could not help himself thinking, "Poor Prior Planning Produces Poor Results"—this was old news. Nothing new here. No officer should be allowed to command a raid that had not thoroughly familiarized himself with previous small-scale operations in order to learn from their mistakes.

5) MTB may have been detected as she passed within 5 miles of a point to avoid a minefield but there is no proof of this, though it is noticeable how quickly the whole stretch of coastline was alert immediately after the alarm was given.

Col. Randal thought this was irrelevant, almost silly, speculation. What did it matter if the Motor Torpedo Boat (MTB) was detected at sea? Coastal Forces ranged up and down the enemy coastline engaging in battles with German E-boats nightly. One MTB observed five miles off shore would not be enough to place the entire coastline on alert.

6) MTB on return journey crossed minefield with no mishaps.

Col. Randal wondered what lesson was learned from that.

7) The navigation throughout seems to have been excellent.

Col. Randal almost laughed out loud. Perfect navigation . . . except they landed on the wrong beach and could not find the gully the Commandos were supposed to climb up to reach the lighthouse.

8) *It is strongly recommended that as soon as possible, another raid be carried out for sake of morale. The fact must be faced that we are certain to have some mishaps.*

Col. Randal read this one with disbelief. Raids are not carried out "for the sake of morale." This kind of Armchair Commando analysis could get a lot of good men killed.

9) *Every encouragement should be given to Small Scale Raiding Force to bring their numbers back to strength.*

A note stated the unit had lost a third of its men.

There were two additional administrative notations under Lessons Learned. Col. Randal grew angry reading them. Neither was new. Apparently, the detailed reports he had provided to Combined Operations had never been disseminated to the next band of pinprick raiders formed after Raiding Forces deployed to Africa.

Dr. Stephen Milam was making his evening rounds. He came by to call on Lady Jane. "Would you mind waiting outside, Colonel?"

After what seemed like a long time, the doctor came out in the hall. Col. Randal took one look at his face and clicked on.

Dr. Milam said, "Lady Jane appears well. Her vital signs remain good. There does not seem to be any evidence of infection, but we will not know for sure for a few more days. Stomach wounds can be tricky to prognosticate.

"I believe having you here at the hospital has been helpful. Lady Jane told me she was aware you were meeting with your people in the room next door while she was sleeping. Says it was very reassuring to her. You will be instrumental in her recuperation, Colonel.

"What you need to prepare yourself for is the distinct possibility Lady Jane may never be the same again. Not everyone fully recuperates from the trauma of a gunshot wound. This one was quite serious."

Col. Randal said, "I've been afraid you might say that."

COLONEL JOHN RANDAL ASKED, "SO, MANDY, WHERE DID YOU and Dr. Milam decide you had been shot?"

Mandy said, "He thought over the left breast, an inch or two off-center, would make the boys hot thinking about it."

Clearly, Dr. Stephen Milam was getting into the spirit of the way Raiding Forces did things.

Col. Randal said, "I don't think you need help in that department."

6
PURPLE HEART

COLONEL JOHN RANDAL ARRIVED AT THE DOCK PRECISELY ON time as instructed by Brandy Seaborn. The sleek Italian MAS boat was bustling with activity. Brandy had traded her son, Lieutenant Randy "Hornblower" Seaborn, a brand-new PT (Patrol Torpedo) boat for the captured Italian MTB because it was ten knots faster, and she loved speed. Col. Randal knew quite a bit about the little warship since it was one of three *Regia Marina* craft he had discovered hidden in a camouflaged boat dock up a river off the Red Sea while conducting guerrilla operations with Force N.

MAS boat stood for *motoscafo armato silurante*—"torpedo armed motorboat"—only there were no torpedoes on this one. They had been removed to reduce weight in hopes of increasing the boat's already blazing fifty-knot speed. Besides, no one was going to allow Brandy to go hunting the German or Italian ships infesting the Mediterranean. Her only charter was to clandestinely insert or extract agents from Crete for Special Operations Executive, MI- 9 Escape or MI-6, the Secret Intelligence Service—missions known for some reason as "false nose jobs."

The normal crew of a MAS was ten sailors; however, that number had been reduced since the removal of the torpedoes and the forest of light and medium machine guns Lt. Seaborn had packed on the boat. Losing the weapons and reducing the crew also increased the boat's speed.

Brandy and her sidekick, Captain Penelope "Legs" Honeycutt-Parker, who certain members of Raiding Forces described as the best navigator in the British Army, were waiting. Col. Randal saluted the flag on the stern and requested, "Permission to come aboard?"

Brandy laughed. "Permission granted."

Walking up the plank, Col. Randal noticed GG disappearing down the hatch, going below deck. Had Brandy dragooned him to be her cook? Anything was possible with her.

He also spotted a pair of Captain Butch "Headhunter" Hoolihan's Royal Marines on board. And a pair of Lifeboat Servicemen. What was that about?

Brandy had her crew standing by, ready to cast off. The MAS boat slipped the dock as soon as Col. Randal stepped aboard. The powerful engines rumbled as the big military speedboat pulled out into the Nile.

The sun was beginning to sink, flaming golden orange in a turquoise sky. While Brandy and Capt. Honeycutt-Parker were wearing long-billed baseball caps and their standard-issue rolled up khaki shorts—it didn't take much imagination to understand why Honeycutt-Parker had been nicknamed "Legs"—it was going to get cool fast as night came on.

Col. Randal was carrying his brown leather bomber jacket with the black fur collar he had been given as a gift by the Abyssinian shifta bandit Cheap Bribe. The jacket had been a prize taken from a crashed Italian bomber. He wondered what had happened to the wily old outlaw—they had been great allies and fought a lot of battles together.

He walked up to the cockpit where Brandy was at the helm. "What happened to the light weapons?"

Brandy said, "Randy removed the guns on Father's orders. I have strict instructions to only sail by moonlight. The Razor does not believe I shall need them in the dark."

Col. Randal thought it more likely that Vice Admiral Sir Randolph "Razor" Ransom had not wanted his daughter to be tempted to find some target to use them on. Neither he nor the Admiral much liked the idea of women going in harm's way. However, WWII was being played by different rules. While both the British and the American military banned women from participating in direct combat operations, the Secret Intelligence Services (SIS), SOE, and now the OSS were using women in a number of highly dangerous roles—as spies, clandestine radio operators, and in some cases, to actually lead guerrilla bands in enemy-occupied countries. It was a full-time battle trying to keep Brandy, "Legs" Honeycutt-Parker, Captain Pamala Plum-Martin, Mandy Paige and Beverly Blackwell out of the line of fire.

A battle Col. Randal was constantly losing.

The MAS boat cruised down the river, then out into the Mediterranean. Brandy immediately went full-throttle, full-speed ahead. The powerful sixty-five-foot powerboat surged forward—screaming across the water.

Brandy said, "We have a three-hour run ahead of us. Randy told me the last time you were out with him, he ordered you to go below and take some rest. Speaking as the captain of a warship underway in hostile waters, I want you to do the same thing for me, John. You spent the last three nights sitting up with Jane at the hospital, then had meetings all day—take a break, handsome.

Col. Randal said, "That why you invited me on this sea trial tonight?"

"Not entirely—I shall have someone wake you later, then you can come up and keep me company on the bridge. If you act nice, maybe I shall let you drive the boat."

Col. Randal's relationship with Brandy was complicated. She was Lady Jane's first cousin, the daughter of VAdm. Ransom, the mother of Lieutenant Randy "Hornblower" Seaborn and the widow of a Royal Navy Victoria Cross holder decorated for his actions on a highly classified clandestine operation with Raiding Forces. The two had been drawn to each other from the moment they met. Brandy had taken him under her wing and helped him navigate the tricky waters of British upper-class society.

Brandy flirted with him outrageously.

Col. Randal thought her one of the most attractive women he had ever met. That was saying something coming from someone who grew up near Hollywood, had one of the University of Texas' Ten Most Beautiful serving in Raiding Forces and was engaged to a woman universally described as "drop-dead gorgeous." Like her younger cousin, Lady Jane, all Brandy wanted to do was to go fast and have fun. However, there might be a dark side to her. She was a trained interrogator for either Secret Intelligence or Security. Most likely MI-5 Security, an organization known to be brutal with those suspected of aiding or abetting the enemy.

Col. Randal was not supposed to know about that, but he did.

As expected, when the sun went down, coupled with the speed of the MAS boat, it cooled off fast. Brandy and Capt. Honeycutt-Parker donned oversized leather bomber jackets, courtesy of Capt. Plum-Martin, who had obtained them from one of her USAAF boyfriends. A Royal Navy Patrol Service sailor who had been on the boat since Hornblower had first put it into service led Col. Randal below to the tiny skipper's cabin.

He stretched out on the bunk and fell asleep almost instantly.

COLONEL JOHN RANDAL'S EYES CAME OPEN. THE MOTORS HAD changed pitch. Now they were throbbing. The MAS boat was heaved to. He slipped his leather jacket on before going up on deck.

Brandy Seaborn and Captain Penelope "Legs" Honeycutt-Parker were at their post on the bridge, peering through oversized night glasses.

"What's going on?"

Brandy said, "Waiting to see if Parker's navigation is as spot-on as it usually is."

"Should be," Capt. Honeycutt-Parker said.

Col. Randal asked, "How are we going to find out?"

Brandy said, "There will be a signal."

"Signal—what kind of signal?"

Brandy said, "To launch the rubber raft."

Col. Randal said, "We're on a shakedown cruise—a training mission. Why would you be launching the raft?"

"We are stationed roughly one hundred yards off a small remote beach at the bottom of a cliff on the island of Crete," Capt. Honeycutt-Parker said. "The raft is going ashore."

"What?"

Brandy said, "Signal acquired. Three dots and three dashes—away the raft."

On the bow, having heard the command, the Lifeboat Servicemen lowered the rubber assault boat—previously a life raft on a civilian cruise ship before being requisitioned for Sea Squadron use. The two LBSM climbed in and, paddling effortlessly, silently disappeared in the dark.

For the second time, Col. Randal said, "What's going on?"

Brandy said, "We are rendezvousing with the senior SOE agent on Crete, Major Paddy Leigh-Fermor. I believe you two have met. Tonight, we shall be extracting the major along with an Italian general who wishes to defect.

Capt. Honeycutt-Parker said, "Lieutenant General Angelico Carta, the commander of the 51st Infantry Division Siena."

"You're kidding."

Brandy laughed. "Negative. It is the reason we brought GG along tonight— as an interpreter in the unlikely event we need a backup to Major Leigh-Fermor. Like Raiding Forces Rules stipulate, 'It's good to have a Plan B.' For example: the two Royal Marines are to provide added security once the general arrives on board.

"We want him to remain peaceful on the return trip—no last-minute change of heart."

GG arrived at the cockpit with three steaming cups of tea, which were welcome in the chill of the night. While there were a million sparkling stars overhead, it was pitch dark.

Col. Randal said, "I thought this was a sea trial. A test. You should have informed me that we were going on an actual mission."

Brandy laughed. "Why? I wanted you to have your beauty rest. Besides, Parker and I make these runs all the time."

"You don't pick up defecting enemy generals all the time."

Brandy said, "True. We wanted it to be a surprise."

Col. Randal said, "Mission accomplished."

The tea was hot, the night cold. Time seemed to stand still. The MAS boat rocked gently. The waves slapping the side of the boat were louder than usual— or so it seemed.

The Lifeboat Servicemen should have been back by now. Had there been a betrayal? Had the Nazis learned of Lt. Gen. Carta's treachery and intercepted him? An ambush on the beach? Sitting close off an enemy shore in the dark of night on a clandestine mission, a lot of things can go through your head, most of them not good, as Col. Randal knew from long experience.

He was clicked on.

From the bow, one of the Royal Marines called out the challenge, "Happy."

From the dark came back the countersign, "Ending."

Col. Randal relaxed.

Brandy flashed a beautiful, white-toothed smile that gleamed in the dark.

Capt. Honeycutt-Parker said, "About time."

Then there were figures scrambling up the rope netting. Major Patrick "Paddy" Leigh-Fermor came on board first. He had adopted a more romantic guerrilla leader's costume since the last time Col. Randal had seen him. Long leather coat, silk cravat, silver stiletto (one of the original 500 Fairbairn Commando knives) and an ivory-handled Smith & Wesson .38 M&P revolver buckled around his waist.

Col. Randal understood the reason for the exotic wardrobe.

A chieftain of guerrillas must lead. A big part of that is showmanship. In Abyssinia, he had carried four ivory-gripped pistols and an ivory-handled riding crop with a black lion's tail as a whisk. Lady Jane had appropriated the pistol grips and riding crop when Raiding Forces arrived in Egypt and he was no longer commanding impressionable natives who expected their leader to be a "Big Shot."

Lt. Gen. Carta climbed up next, followed by the Lifeboat Servicemen. The general cut an equally dashing, if slightly tubbier, figure in Alpine uniform with spurs and plumes, sporting an astonishing number of medal ribbons on his blouse. The general was beaming with delight now that, for him, the war was over.

There was not going to be a need for the beefed-up security.

Upon being introduced to Col. Randal, the general, who had not brought his ceremonial sword, immediately offered to surrender his gold-plated, richly engraved, pearl-handled 7.65mm Beretta M-1934 pistol that had been a personal gift from Il Duce, Benito Mussolini.

Not sure of the correct protocol—Lt. Gen. Carta was still an enemy combatant even though he was in the act of coming over to the Allied side—Col. Randal declined the offer. He said, "That's not necessary, General. I simply request the weapon be unloaded for safety."

Brandy said, "GG, will you escort the general below. I am sure he is exhausted from his adventures. Put him in my cabin now that Colonel Randal no longer requires it."

Not sure how to address her, speaking in flawless English, Lt. Gen. Carta said, "Thank you, Captain. I admit to having a most arduous journey. The Nazis learned of my plans and a massive manhunt has been underway for the entirety of the trip. In fact, this very morning a Fieseler Storch flew directly overhead and dropped leaflets printed in German, Italian and Greek offering up thirty million drachmas for me, dead or alive. They fell right at our feet."

Brandy said, "Must have been a tremendous shock. You are safe now. Crash start, Parker. Let's go home."

After the Italian was below, Maj. Leigh-Fermor said, "Colonel, I would like to spend some time with you to discuss possible joint operations with Raiding Forces once we get General Carta situated in Cairo."

Col. Randal said, "Contact me at RFHQ, ask for Captain Fawcett-Tatum. Whoever answers will be able to tell you how to find her. Stephanie will schedule a time and place."

The MAS boat roared to full power and headed straight away from the pick-up point. Brandy laughed into the breeze as the big speedboat pounded for home. Col. Randal was beginning to get the idea she might be an adrenalin junky.

Brandy shouted, "I love my job."

True to her word, she let him have the wheel part way. Col. Randal had to admit the high-speed run *was* a rush.

IT WAS BEGINNING TO BE DAYLIGHT WHEN BRANDY SEABORN pulled the mas boat into the dock. Colonel John Randal was surprised to see Major the Lady Jane Seaborn's white Rolls-Royce waiting at the pier. He was not particularly surprised to see Brigadier Raymond J. "R.J." Maunsell's staff car parked next to it with Captain Cuthbert "Curly" Bowlby sitting in the back with him.

As the MAS boat warbled up to the dock, the two senior intelligence officers exited their car and walked to where the Royal Navy Patrol Service sailors were tying off. They were there to meet Lieutenant General Angelico Carta when he came ashore. Col. Randal waited until the three men departed the dock, then he saluted the flag on the stern of the boat, stepped ashore and walked over to the Rolls.

King was at the wheel. Mandy Paige and Beverly Blackwell were in the front seat with him. Brigadier General William "Wild Bill" Donovan and an older man wearing silver wire-rimmed spectacles that Col. Randal had never met before were in the back. Apparently, the chief of the Office of Strategic Services had no interest in meeting an Italian general since he had not bothered to exit the car.

King said, "Hop in, Chief."

When Col. Randal climbed in the back, Brig. Gen. Donovan said, "I flew out as soon as it was possible to get away once I received word Lady Jane had been shot. Mr. King informs me she is on the mend?"

Col. Randal said, "It was a serious wound, General. However, Jane has a brilliant surgeon who has treated her family for years. She's getting the best medical attention we could hope for. Her doctor says she's "not out of the woods yet"—whatever that means."

Brig. Gen. Donovan said, "Never fear, Colonel. When I get through cross-examining the man, we shall know more about stomach wounds and Lady Jane's recovery path than the director of the Mayo Clinic."

"Sounds good, sir."

Brig. Gen. Donovan said, "My compliments on your capture of the Port Lyautey Airfield. That one goes in the books as an OSS Special Operation, though I want you to know that we had absolutely nothing to do with planning it other than to spirit the French river pilot out of Morocco and bring him to the States in time to sail with the *Dallas.* General Eisenhower was furious when he learned what we had done. He was afraid it would compromise TORCH.

"Your success pulled OSS's chestnuts out of the fire with the General."

Col. Randal said, "Whose idea was it?"

Brig. Gen. Donovan said, "General Truscott. He had been sent to England to serve as an observer at Combined Operations Headquarters. I'm afraid Truscott, along with virtually everyone else on Mountbatten's staff, began to believe their own press about Commandos possessing superpowers.

"One thing to fool the enemy—it's quite another to fool yourself. Admiral Hewitt told me the *Dallas* had virtually no chance of making it up the Sebou River to the airfield. In his words 'a very bad plan.'"

"You made the best of it."

Col. Randal said, "Enemy resistance was light, sir."

"Nevertheless, you and the Rangers will be decorated. Capturing the Port Lyautey airfield was one of the boldest missions I've ever known of. You made the OSS proud."

Col. Randal said, "I would rather you award my medal to Captain Jaxx, sir. The jump on Port Lyautey was a long-range, highly complex airborne operation. He did a tremendous job of planning and executing it."

Brig. Gen. Donovan said, "Duly noted. Captain Jaxx was already on the awards list. I don't give one man's valor decoration to another. My guess is you do not do so either, nor would you accept one if you suspected such to be the case. I briefed the President on the operation and he wants you and two other officers in the Oval Office for a photo-op when he pins on your medals.

"Beverly, you are receiving the Silver Star for continuing the *Abruzzi* mission even after you knew your plane was not airworthy. The crash landing next to the ship was extraordinary heroism above and beyond the call of duty. Amazing demonstration of flying skill. Some, myself included, believe you should be awarded the Medal of Honor.

"I allowed you to come out to Egypt to be the OSS liaison to Raiding Forces, young lady—not to try to win the war single-handed."

Beverly said, "Wow!"

"Your Daddy is going to love the story. I intend to take a great deal of pleasure telling it to him. We have our annual quail safari coming up. He's taking a week's leave from his duties commanding the Flight School at Big Spring to meet me at your ranch."

Beverly said, "Daddy always looks forward to your bird hunt."

Brig. Gen. Donovan said, "When we reach the hospital, I would very much like to go in for a brief visit with Lady Jane. While I am so engaged, Colonel, would you have the key people you plan to employ on OPERATION LEAF EATER assemble? I want to meet, greet and provide my views on what is expected of them."

Col. Randal said, "Yes, sir."

When the Rolls-Royce arrived at the hospital, Waldo Treywick was standing out front talking to the Raiding Forces personnel manning one of the gun jeeps securing the building. Beverly escorted Brig. Gen. Donovan to Lady Jane's room. Mandy took the older gentleman in the steel-rimmed glasses to the dining room for liquid refreshment.

Col. Randal said, "Mr. Treywick, do you know where I can find Captain McKoy?"

Waldo said, "He's having lunch at the Gezira with one-a' the dancers from the Kit-Kat Club."

Col. Randal said, "How about Jack?"

Mandy said, "Inside getting his ankle taped."

Col. Randal said, "King, go pick up the Captain. If Pam's in the restaurant, bring her along with you. Mandy, you round up Jack."

King said, "On the way, Chief."

Mandy said, "My pleasure, love to see God's gift to women in pain."

Waldo said, "Sprained ankle could throw a monkey wrench into his women-chasin'."

Mandy laughed. "The girls will simply run slower."

THE MEETING WITH BRIGADIER GENERAL WILLIAM "WILD BILL" Donovan did not cover any new ground. Present were Colonel John Randal, Captain "Geronimo" Joe McKoy, Captain Billy Jack Jaxx, Captain Pamala Plum-Martin, Waldo Treywick, King, Mandy Paige and Beverly Blackwell. Col. Randal explained the roles each were slated to play in OPERATION LEAF EATER. Capt. McKoy described progress in placing his handpicked ex-law enforcement officers in the colonies to monitor illicit diamond activity. Waldo explained how the diamond trade in Cairo was being monopolized by requiring the Big Four to sell to him exclusively.

Waldo said, "We're makin' plans to take over the market in Tangiers as well."

Brig. Gen. Donovan said, "Don't waste your time. OSS does not believe enough diamonds are being funneled to Germany through Spain to make the effort worth your while."

Capt. McKoy looked at Col. Randal.

Col. Randal had absolutely no expression on his face. However, the scar on his left cheek twitched. That was a tell.

The meeting concluded with Brig. Gen. Donovan saying, "As of right now, there is no higher priority mission than LEAF EATER. Time is of the essence. I need to see immediate results in eliminating the smuggling rings—now!"

As the meeting was breaking up, Capt. McKoy said under his breath to Col. Randal, "First liar never stands a chance."

Col. Randal said, "Seems like."

A second meeting assembled as soon as the room was cleared. Present were Brig. Gen. Donovan, Col. Randal, Capt. McKoy, Waldo, King and the older man in wire-rimmed spectacles—Mr. David Smithers.

Brig. Gen. Donovan said, "Mr. Smithers is the former president of the National Numismatic Association and the owner of a chain of successful coin shops on the East Coast. He is also a currency advisor to OSS. I brought him to Cairo to brief you on a plan to legally convert the gold coins you have stored in the consulate in Kenya into U.S. dollars.

Mr. Smithers said, "In order for you to fully understand the complexities involved, I need to explain the whys and wherefores behind the little-known fact that U.S. citizens are prohibited from owning gold. During the Great Depression, there had been a wave of bank closings. To stem the tide, the Reconstruction Finance Corporation was established to stabilize the banks.

"In 1933, the RFC was required by Congress to publish the identity of every bank receiving federal assistance. The idea was transparency, but the plan backfired. When the banks' fiscal condition was made public, people saw what bad condition their financial institutions were in, panicked and started a massive run on banks nationwide that slammed them like a tsunami.

"President-elect Roosevelt was about to take office at a time the country had completely lost control over its currency. On his third day in the White House, using his war powers—highly unusual since the nation was not at war—he declared a national bank holiday. The stated purpose was to 'prevent hoarding of coin, bullion or currency.' The President chose to blame individual greed for the monetary crisis facing the nation and not the politicians who got the country into the mess in the first place.

"Since, if challenged in court the declaration would not have been upheld, FDR asked Congress to pass emergency legislation confirming the action. That happened with lightning speed, which could only mean one thing—no one voting on it actually understood the language in the bill. Incredibly, the new law contained a line that stated *The Secretary of the Treasury, in his discretion, may require any or all individuals, partnerships, associations and corporations to pay and deliver to the Treasurer of the United States any or all gold coin, bullion, and gold certificates owned by individuals, partnerships, associations and corporations.*

"And, just like that, in an action that was completely unconstitutional, Americans could no longer privately own gold.

"President Roosevelt's next executive order was shocking and totally unprecedented. He *criminalized* the ownership of gold. To fully understand what took place, you need to read: EXECUTIVE ORDER OF APRIL 5, 1933—FORBIDDING THE PRIVATE HOARDING OF GOLD COINS, GOLD BULLION AND GOLD CERTIFICATES.

"I brought copies that will be passed out at the conclusion of this briefing, for your perusal."

Capt. Jaxx looked at Col. Randal and rolled his eyes. At least one member of the LEAF EATER group had no intention of doing any extracurricular reading. Waldo's expression was that of a man nursing an abscessed tooth. Capt. McKoy had a poker face. Mandy and Beverly looked like two girls on a bad double date.

Only King seemed interested.

Mr. Smithers said, "Gold is both property *and* money. When it takes the form of nuggets, gold bars or jewelry, it is property. When it is minted by a sovereign nation to a specific weight, fineness and value as a coin, gold becomes both property and money.

"The amazing thing is, the President could as easily have demonetized gold coins and gold certificates—meaning paper bills in dollar denominations redeemable in gold held by the U.S. Treasury for the face value of the bill. Once demonetized, gold coins would have become property like fine art, and no longer subject to financial regulation. Alas . . . FDR chose otherwise.

"And that, gentlemen, is why it is illegal for a citizen of the United States to buy, sell or own gold. Which begs the question, "What are you going to do with the treasure trove of gold coins in your possession?"

Waldo said, "That's what we've been waitin' to hear."

Mr. Smithers said, "Britain, Canada, Australia and South Africa were all on the same or similar gold standard as the United States. However, none of them recalled gold coins or made private ownership of gold illegal. They merely did what the President chose not to do—demonetized it.

"Then FDR realized he might have taken a step too far and had a modest change of heart. He was an avid stamp collector. The President wanted to make an exception for coin collectors, understanding that collecting was not hoarding—he was certainly not hoarding stamps."

Waldo said, "Wasn't you some high muckety-muck in the Southwestern Cattlemen's Association's stamp club, Joe?"

Capt. McKoy said, "That was a cover story I used when Lady Jane, Pamala and me was undercover on a clandestine operation you ain't cleared to know about, Waldo."

Brig. Gen. Donovan said, "I'm confident I'm cleared, Captain. Brief me immediately following this meeting. Like to hear the story.

Capt. McKoy glanced at Col. Randal, who nodded.

"My pleasure, General," Capt. McKoy said.

Mr. Smithers continued. "The President decided he wanted his directive to differentiate between hoarding and collecting. Hoarding is a vice. Collecting and/or saving is a virtue.

"That line of thinking creates the kind of ambiguity that lawyers love. However, the wealthy Americans we want to sell your coins to, because they will pay many times the numismatic value for the opportunity to lay their hands on gold coins, generally take the position of 'why take a chance?' They do not want to risk having lawyers involved. Especially since, if they lose the case, not only do they have to pay high attorney's fees but the government will seize their coins.

"Fortunately for you, the President made a mistake. He chose to regulate gold coins as property. FDR has no authority over property rights in foreign countries.

"Since Canada is a foreign country, it has become the favorite place for rich Americans to warehouse their gold. As luck would have it, OSS has a secure site in Canada called Camp X.

"My plan is for us to fly to Kenya, clandestinely remove your gold from the U.S. Consulate and transport it across town to the safety of the British Consulate where it cannot be seized by U.S. Customs. Then I will perform an appraisal of each coin, insure them for the appraised value and have them flown aboard an RAF or Canadian aircraft to Camp X.

From there, I have already arranged for your coins to be purchased at auction by a group of U.S. buyers. The new owners will deposit their gold coins in the Canadian bank of their choice. As for you gentlemen, your cash will be wire transferred to the bank or banks of your choosing in the United States."

Waldo said, "Can we do that? Wire transfer our dough to banks in the U.S.?

Mr. Smithers said, "Nothing illegal about putting money in the bank."

Capt. McKoy said, "Our government finds out we got gold coins stashed in the basement of the U.S. Consulate they'll seize 'em?"

"In a heartbeat."

Waldo said, "How quick can we get you to Kenya?"

Mr. Smithers said, "I'm available to travel when you are."

Col. Randal said, "Captain McKoy, contact Wing Commander Dudgeon. He'll provide transport. You and Mr. Treywick need to fly out with Mr. Smithers today if at all possible."

Capt. McKoy said, "I'm all over it, John."

Waldo said, "Is treatin' gold as property a good thing or a bad thing?"

COLONEL JOHN RANDAL, CAPTAIN "GERONIMO" JOE MCKOY, Waldo Treywick, Mandy Paige, Beverly Blackwell and Mr. David Smithers were waiting in the terminal of an RAF base located on the outskirts of Cairo. Capt. McKoy, Waldo and Mr. Smithers were about to board a Liberator that would fly them to Nairobi, Kenya. Beverly and Mandy were along to keep Mr. Smithers occupied while Col. Randal had a last-minute meeting with Capt. McKoy and Waldo.

Col. Randal said, "Captain, you and Mr. Treywick arrange the transfer of the bags of coins out of the U.S. Consulate to the British Consulate. Captain McKoy, as soon as you have the gold moved, I want you to fly back to Cairo. I don't feel great having you away with the search for the men who shot Lady Jane still ongoing."

Capt. McKoy said, "I'll be burnin' daylight to get back, John."

Col. Randal said, "Good—Mr. Treywick, you travel with the coins all the way to Canada. Stay with the stash until Mr. Smithers has completed the sale. General Donovan has contacted Lady Jane's business manager in the States to be on hand at Camp X to observe the transaction.

"Once the check is in his hands, you fly back here ASAP—he'll do the rest."

Waldo said, "Yes sir, Colonel, sir."

Col. Randal said, "Don't forget to insure the gold for Mr. Smithers' appraised fair market value before you take off for the U.S. Lady Jane's bank in

Nairobi will handle that detail for you. That way if anything happens, you get your money."

Waldo said, "I ain't goin' to forget . . . don't you worry none."

Capt. McKoy said, "What do you reckon's goin' on, John—we ain't supposed to pay attention to diamonds being sold to the Nazis out-a' Tangiers? Either we're supposed to stop the diamond smugglin' or we ain't."

Col. Randal said, "You've told me from the beginning, Captain, that there's no way to stop the flow of diamonds to Germany."

Capt. McKoy said, "Yeah, but I meant we ain't goin' to get it stopped. I never said we weren't goin' to give it the all-American try. Donovan wants us to forget about Tangiers."

Waldo said, "Don't make sense."

Col. Randal said, "We're not going to ignore Tangiers. First things first. When I've got both of you men back here after all this is straightened out, we'll sit down and craft a plan. Clearly, something is not right with the original LEAF EATER mission statement we were given and there has to be a reason."

Capt. McKoy said, "We ain't had time to talk about it, John, but down in the Congo there's the Kasi River where you can sometimes find diamonds laying on the ground along the bank. The locals dig little pot holes to find 'em—they're called 'pot-holers.' The diggers sell the diamonds they find to middlemen who work the region, and no one knows who they sell 'em to—could be Nazis.

"DeBeers doesn't make a dime off those pothole stones. The General told me OSS wants us to kill every man in the chain—which would include the pothole diggers. So, the question is, has DeBeers gotten to Donovan too?"

Col. Randal said, "Have a nice trip."

COLONEL JOHN RANDAL WAS SITTING ON THE BED IN THE MASTER bedroom of Major the Lady Jane Seaborn's permanent suite at the Mena House Hotel. He had his shirt off. Beverly Blackwell was wrapping fresh dressings on his banged-up ribs. The colors were even more spectacular now than when Mandy Paige had first discovered the damage.

Earlier, Mandy and Beverly had been doing their make-up. They looked like movie stars. Now Mandy was laying out two of Lady Jane's slinkiest evening gowns.

The Big Four had been released from jail and ordered to be at a meeting in Moe's private office at the Kit-Kat Club at 2200 hours tonight. Col. Randal wanted to have a chat with them. The last time the men had met, the Big Four had been the Big Five—and that had been *before* Lady Jane was shot. The crime lords were likely not looking forward to the sit-down.

Both Beverly and Mandy were going with him.

Col. Randal said, "Capt. McKoy has informed me that native pothole diggers are finding diamonds along the Kasi River in the Belgian Congo. The stones are bought by middlemen who resell the stones to an unknown third party or parties. DeBeers does not make anything off the transactions. Raiding Forces has orders to kill everyone in the chain.

"What are your thoughts, ladies?"

Mandy said, "Sounds like a lot of poor natives trying to scratch out a living. What they are doing is only called 'illicit' because DeBeers says it is. There is nothing illegal about picking up a stone off the ground."

Beverly said, "OK, why not buy the stones from the pothole diggers? Cut out the middlemen. Then all you have to do, Johnny, is shoot Sir Ernest Oppenheimer, take over control of the DeBeers Diamond Company, and no diamonds will ever make it to the Nazis—problem solved."

Mandy said, "You *are* joking?"

Col. Randal said, "I like that plan."

Flanigan brought Lady Jane's white Rolls-Royce around. King, looking exactly like what he was, a killer in a tuxedo, held open the back door of the car. As Col. Randal slid into the back seat between Beverly and Mandy, he asked, "Can either of you even breathe in those dresses?"

Mandy said, "An acquired skill."

Beverly said, "Thank you for asking."

King climbed in the front. He was their bodyguard tonight. And would be in the meeting room.

As they drove to the Kit-Kat Club, Beverly said, "OK, we are fashionably late. When we arrive at the nightclub, Mandy, our job is to rub up against Johnny like cats."

Mandy said, "You mean the way Rita and Lana do?"

Beverly said, "Exactly. Vamping. When we're sitting at the table with the Big Four, look them dead in the eyes. Let's both of us drape our arms across Johnny's shoulders. But if he so much as twitches a muscle, carefully take your arm down—probably going for his pistol."

Mandy said, "Tonight could prove more interesting that I thought."

Beverly handed Mandy a cotton ball, "You might want to put some in your ears before we go in."

There were a lot of cars outside the Kit-Kat Club. Flanigan pulled up directly in front. King stepped out and opened the door in the back. Moe, the club's manager, was waiting at the top of the steps.

He called to Flanigan, "Park the car right there at the curb."

Moe opened the door of the club to a blast of raucous music. As usual, the Kit-Kat was rocking. The manager led the way, winding through tables to his private office. King brought up the rear. Everyone in the place, including the Hungarian dancer in the middle of her routine, turned to stare at the entourage.

Raiding Forces was well represented in the establishment tonight. Lieutenant Colonel Sir Terry "Zorro" Stone was sitting at a table with his cousin Major Baltimore "Mongo" Farquhar, MC. Captain Billy Jack Jaxx was at another table with the Jamil twins—rumored to be King Farouk's favorite belly dancers. Usually the girls chose not to perform at the Kit-Kat, preferring to perform at the upscale Egyptian Muhammad Ali nightclub. However, due to Brigadier General William "Wild Bill" Donovan being on the premises, they had been loaned out to Moe for the night. Lieutenant Clint Hays and Lieutenant Eddy Ryder, sporting bandages from the jump on Castelrozzo, were at another table with Rita and Lana. And, newly promoted Wing Commander Paddy Wilcox was at the bar, wearing his black eyepatch, chatting up a semi-nude dancer who did not appear old enough to be allowed on the premises.

As they passed Capt. Jaxx and the red-hot Jamil twins, Beverly said to Col. Randal, "That boy's eyes are definitely bigger than his appetite."

Mandy said, "Jack is going to be surprised when he finds out the twin's parents wait in the dressing room until the show is over to escort their daughters home."

Waiting for them in Moe's private office were Brig. Gen. Donovan, Brigadier Raymond J. Maunsell, Captain Cuthbert Bowlby and a badly battered Big Four. The mobster's faces were swollen to the size of pumpkins. The men looked like they were at death's door.

The bosses of the four remaining major crime families in the Middle East were fully aware of the power of the senior Allied intelligence officers in the room. Each was a law unto himself who operated with total impunity— answerable to no one. The mobsters were intimidated.

When Col. Randal arrived, the battered gangsters showed real fear.

The Big Four had assumed Mr. Big would be attending the meeting to discuss business, but there were no more empty chairs at the table. This turn of events did not seem like it was going to bode well for them. The commander of Raiding Forces had demonstrated he was not a man they could reason with.

R.J. said, "Colonel Randal requested I have the Egyptian Security Police release you men. Understand—that is the only reason you are free tonight. He would like to talk to you about the recent attempted murder of Lady Seaborn."

The Big Four all began hysterically protesting their innocence. They were panicked, or possibly they were overacting. The performance would have been comical had not the gangsters been so badly beaten.

Col. Randal said, "You men say you had nothing to do with the shooting of Lady Jane and my two Rangers—I believe you."

The Big Four fell silent.

Col. Randal said, "Hear two things. First, within the week, deliver to my headquarters the person responsible for the attack."

"Second, on my left is Miss Mandy Paige and on my right is Miss Beverly Blackwell. Both women are under my protection, which means as of now they are under yours. Should anything else happen to Lady Jane, such as a loud noise frightening her, or if Miss Paige or Miss Blackwell chip a nail, I will hold all of you men responsible. You will not like what happens next.

"Is that clear?"

The Big Four chorused assent—tinged with alarm.

Everyone in Cairo knew Lady Jane. The crime lords recognized Beverly from the last meeting at the Kit-Kat. The men had all seen Mandy observing their interrogations. The mobsters fully understood the magnitude of the threat from an officer they knew from experience was prone to precipitous action executed casually.

Col. Randal stood up abruptly and walked out of the room with Mandy, Beverly and King trailing along behind.

In the car on the ride to the hospital, where he would stay the night with Lady Jane, Col. Randal said, "We should do that cat routine more often."

Mandy said, "In your dreams."

When Col. Randal arrived in Lady Jane's room, she was sleeping peaceably. He noticed something pinned to her pillow and knew it had been left there by Brig. Gen. Donovan.

It was a Purple Heart.

7

BAD NEWS

COLONEL JOHN RANDAL, MANDY PAIGE AND BEVERLY Blackwell were in the sitting room of the private hospital suite where Major the Lady Jane Seaborn was recuperating. She was in the next room being given an alcohol bath by a nurse. When that was over, Lady Jane was going to attempt her first walk since being shot.

Mandy said, "You asked me for a report on any connection between DeBeers and the royal family. In addition to the crown jewels, the Queen has thirty-four pair of diamond earrings, fifteen diamond rings, five diamond pendants, fourteen diamond tiaras, forty-six diamond necklaces, ninety-six diamond broaches and thirty-seven diamond bracelets.

"She also has a three-carat diamond engagement ring with five lesser two-carat stones."

Beverly said, "That's a lot of rocks."

Col. Randal said, "Yes, it is."

Mandy said, "In 1940, following Dunkirk, with the war raging and England expecting to be invaded at any moment, the Chancellor of the Exchequer took the time to write to the Royal Family that 'the Queen has a patriotic duty to wear diamonds because Great Britain has such an important interest in the diamond business. The Royal Couple could be of tremendous assistance to the industry by wearing diamonds exclusively rather than other jewels'."

Beverly said, "But we've discovered the strange fact that women in the family of the director of DeBeers, Sir Ernest Oppenheimer, rarely wear diamonds."

Col. Randal said, "Really—why might that be?"

"Mandy and I have no idea."

"Has to be an unnatural connection between the Diamond Company and the royal family—or at the very least the Chancellor of the Exchequer," Mandy said. "So far we have not been able to pin it down. Let's not forget we already uncovered the fact that the Ministry of Economic Warfare's Diamond Committee was staffed entirely by former DeBeers employees drawing pensions from the company."

Col. Randal said, "Good report, ladies. Interesting. That said, from now on we're done with worrying about DeBeers, the royal family or the Ministry of Economic Warfare. Our focus is on stopping the flow of diamonds to Nazi Germany."

Beverly said, "Even if we did find something incriminating, what could we do? We're talking about the royal family."

"Exactly," Col. Randal said.

Mandy asked, "What is our next move, then?"

Col. Randal said, "Mandy, I want you and Beverly to make LEAF EATER your top-priority project. The three of us are going to constitute the big picture element within the operation. I can't be here all the time. When I'm gone, you girls will be my eyes and ears. I want you sitting in on every transaction in Cairo where diamonds are bought or sold or any meeting about diamonds, no matter how insignificant. If one of you can't attend, the one who does needs to disseminate the information gained to the other at the first opportunity . . ."

Brandy Seaborn stuck her head in the door, "Girls, can you excuse John and me for a moment."

It was not a question. Brandy was not smiling. Col. Randal clicked on.

When Beverly and Mandy were gone, Brandy said, "Dr. Milam called. He is about to have a conversation with Jane and wanted me to be present. After we wrap up, you can come in if Jane feels up to it."

"I see."

Brandy said, "You should wait outside in the hall with the girls."

When Col. Randal stepped out of the door of Lady Jane's hospital room, Mandy said, "What is going on, John?"

At that moment, Dr. Stephen Milam breezed by and went inside without stopping to chat as he usually did.

Col. Randal said, "I have no idea. The doctor wants a word with Jane in private."

Dr. Milam was in the room for what seemed like a long time. Then he left, stone-faced, and hurried down the hall. They could hear Lady Jane sobbing when the door opened.

Brandy walked out, looking pale. As a rule, people do not normally turn white . . . that's only in storybooks. However, her golden tan had definitely turned white. "Jane would like to speak to you, John."

Col. Randal went in to find Lady Jane sobbing, tears streaming down her cheeks. As he reached the bed, she handed him her promise ring. "Here. Take this. I never want to see it again."

"Are you breaking up with me?"

Lady Jane sobbed. "Doctor Milam informed me I shall never be able to have children. I am so sorry, John. It would be terribly unfair of me to hold you to your pledge now."

Col. Randal took Lady Jane's hand and slipped the Sheba diamond back on her finger. "You've already been shot once. Take this ring off one more time without a damn good reason—I'll shoot you again."

"You would, too," Lady Jane said, laughing through the tears. She was on an emotional rollercoaster. She had not expected this response.

Most men who found themselves in a similar situation might have second thoughts.

"I love you, John Randal."

"Don't make me do it."

Lady Jane laughed, "One gunshot wound at a time is quite enough, thank you."

There was nothing more to be said. Lady Jane's new reality had arrived. Keep calm and carry on.

Easy enough to say.

Outside in the hall, Brandy was explaining the news. In the middle of her explanation, they heard the distinct sound of Lady Jane laughing. Loud enough to be heard through the door.

Beverly said, "OK, so Jane's happy?"

Brandy said, "What could she possibly be laughing about?"

Mandy said, "With those two, anything can happen when John is around."

Switching into her PT boat skipper mode, Brandy ordered, "Now hear this. Consider everything revealed here Top Secret. Need to Know. No one needs to know.

"You two banged-up Scouts—do you read me?"

"Yes, ma'am," the Lovat Scouts chorused. Lady Jane's latest development was more medical information than they bargained for.

Col. Randal came to the door, "Jane's decided she's ready to give walking a try. You ladies better stand ready. I'm fairly sure this isn't going to end well."

Lady Jane was sitting up on the side of the hospital bed, eager to get started and movie-star glamorous in her white silk robe. After three steps, she quit laughing. Two more and it took all of them to maneuver her back to the bed.

Beads of perspiration dotted Lady Jane's upper lip from the effort. She said, "That was fun."

Col. Randal said, "Oh yeah—you're real tough."

COLONEL JOHN RANDAL AND CAPTAIN BILLY JACK JAXX WERE sitting in the Pan American VIP lounge with Brigadier General William "Wild Bill" Donovan. The General was waiting to board his Pan Am Boeing 314 flight to Washington. Capt. Jaxx and Mandy Paige had been escorting the director of the Office of Strategic Services around Cairo all morning, paying courtesy calls on the offices of the British intelligence organizations headquartered in the city. Wild Bill was highly social, adept at "pressing the flesh," and he thoroughly enjoyed meeting and greeting the key players in Middle East Command.

The senior British intelligence officers tended to view Brig. Gen. Donovan as a good-natured, highly decorated, politically connected amateur. They had no intention of allowing him into the inner sanctum of Secret Intelligence (SI) unless specifically ordered to by higher headquarters in London. That, they were reasonably certain, was not going to be forthcoming except in rare, isolated cases where their masters needed something from Wild Bill.

Brig. Gen. Donovan said, "We have alarming reports coming out of the Congo about illicit diamond smuggling activity in the colony. OSS has SI operatives in place stationed out of Léopoldville. Reports indicate the Belgian colonists are not in step with the exiled government in Great Britain. Apparently, greed and corruption are rampant. Local government officials appear more interested in lining their pockets than defeating the Nazis."

Col. Randal said, "We ran into a similar problem in the Gold Coast when Raiding Forces was staging for OPERATION LOUNGE LIZARD. The British Colonial Office and the Regional Military Commander not only had no interest in pursuing the war, but they even attempted to prevent Raiding Forces from carrying out our orders."

Brig. Gen. Donovan said, "Captain McKoy briefed me on the mission. A story straight out of Hollywood—stuff of legends. Too bad only those possessing a Need to Know will ever hear the tale. I would like you to give a talk to my staff about LOUNGE LIZARD next time you are in Washington. My people need to hear what a handful of dedicated men and women operating a long way from home can accomplish when they put their hearts into it."

Col. Randal said, "Yes, sir."

Brig. Gen. Donovan asked, "Is there anything I can do for Raiding Forces when I return to my office?"

Capt. Jaxx said, "M1 Carbines—my boys have all checked out the one the 10th Rangers issued Colonel Randal. They'd like to have 'em if possible, sir."

This was not an entirely accurate statement. The U.S. troops' reaction to the .30 M1 Carbine was mixed—some liked it, some not. With the U.K. troops, it was love at first sight.

Brig. Gen. Donovan said, "I'm not familiar with the M1 Carbine. Be glad to look into securing an allotment for Raiding Forces—see what we can do, Captain."

Col. Randal said, "I'd like you to make sure Mr. Treywick gets back to Cairo as soon as possible. He needs to be here masquerading as Mr. Big. We're ready to start ramping up LEAF EATER, sir."

Brig. Gen. Donovan said, "I'll personally keep tabs on the progress of both the sale of the gold coins and the money transfer. My law firm will handle the legalities—dot the i's and cross the t's. Now, I know you're running LEAF EATER out of Cairo because it's the major diamond trading center in Africa, but don't neglect the stones being smuggled out of the Congo . . ."

As they were watching the big Pan American seaplane taxiing for takeoff, Col. Randal asked, "Jack, did General Donovan mention the Belgian Congo when you and Mandy were squiring him around town?"

Capt. Jaxx said, "Yes, sir. That's a Rodge. When we were with him in the car. But now that I think about it, the General never discussed the Congo with any of the people Mandy introduced him to."

Mandy said, "That's right."

Col. Randal asked, "Ever say anything about Tangiers?"

Capt. Jaxx said, "Just the one time to you, sir."

"What's your takeaway?"

Capt. Jaxx said, "I'd say Wild Bill has brought the Congo up at least a half dozen times in my presence, sir. The General said all the diamond mines in South Africa have been shut down for the duration. Now there was only one other source of industrial diamonds in the interior of tropical Africa—the Belgian Congo."

Col. Randal said, "So . . . ?"

"Seems like General Donovan wants Raiding Forces to get the word to concentrate on the Congo without giving us a direct order," Capt. Jaxx said. "He did not appear the least interested in Tangiers—why might that be, sir?"

Col. Randal said, "I have no idea."

CAPTAIN PAMALA PLUM-MARTIN, THE VARGAS GIRL LOOK-ALIKE Royal Marine aviator, arrived in the office Dr. Stephen Milam had provided Colonel John Randal at the hospital. As usual, she looked like she had stepped right out of the pages of *Esquire* magazine.

Capt. Plum-Martin said, "I am taking you to lunch, love. Lady Jane gave me permission as long as I keep my hands off of you. Time to have some fun."

Col. Randal said, "Let's do it."

Flanigan drove them to the Gezira.

They were shown to their table in the very back behind a palm, where Col. Randal could have classified conversations in plain sight. Captain Billy Jack Jaxx was at the bar chatting up a USO entertainer—the reigning Miss Nevada. Veronica Paige, Mandy's mother, the head of MI-9 Escape, was dining with Brigadier Dudley Clarke. Lieutenant Colonel Terry "Zorro" Stone and Red were at another table, having just arrived.

As they came past, Lt. Col. Stone said, "Our meal has not been served. Would you like for us to have it brought to your table so we can join you, old stick?"

Col. Randal glanced at Red. He was well aware she was not able to spend much time alone with her boyfriend. He said, "Why don't you enjoy your lunch, then come back later for dessert with us."

Red rewarded him with a fabulous Clipper Girl smile. She knew from experience that when Col. Randal and Zorro got together, all they did was talk to each other.

Lt. Col. Stone said, "Splendid."

As they were taking their seats, Capt. Plum-Martin said, "Nicely done, John—Red certainly thought so."

Col. Randal said, "What makes you think I didn't want to keep it the two of us?"

Capt. Plum-Martin said, "Even better, love."

They had been friends since the days when she was Major the Lady Jane Seaborn's driver and Raiding Forces was failing in their attempts to learn how to paddle Goatly dories through the surf. The two had been on a number of high-risk missions together. There was deep, mutual respect between them.

Capt. Plum-Martin said, "Ronnie has been given the Special Duties Wing. Straightaway, he grounded me from flying A-20 gunships. Did you have anything to do with his decision?"

"Negative—the wing commander say why?"

"Ronnie claimed he has enough A-20 pilots now and ATA flyers were never intended to be flying combat in the first place."

Col. Randal said, "Good for him."

"John!"

"You know I've never been in favor of you and Beverly flying ground attack missions."

"True."

"Don't worry," Col. Randal said. "Raiding Forces is about to have a change of scenery. We'll be operating in the Aegean. Piloting our amphibians will keep you busy. Can't be many airstrips where we're going."

"Probably not."

"Check in with Admiral Ransom. He'll provide more details. With Wing Commander Gordon out of the picture and Paddy flying who knows where, your services are going to be in demand."

Capt. Plum-Martin said, "There are hundreds of tiny islands dotting the Aegean. Too many for them all to be heavily defended. Should be the Happy Hunting Ground for small-scale raiding."

"We'll see," Col. Randal said. "Until the Admiral briefed me for the jump on Castelrozzo, I couldn't have found the Dodecanese Island chain on a map."

James "Baldie" Taylor appeared at the table, wearing the uniform of a major general. "Might I have a word with you, Colonel?"

The two stepped back to the corner for more privacy.

Jim said, "I am preparing to fly to Morocco to observe U.S. military operations in North Africa. Initial reports indicate General Eisenhower's Allied Force is not performing well. Particularly the green U.S. troops. For his part, Monty's Eighth Army is not exactly covering itself in glory either."

Col. Randal said, "Before we flew home from North Africa, General Patton told me 'the troops were bad and the officers worse' during the initial TORCH landing. I'll be interested to hear your report when you return, General."

Jim said, "Fortunately, the U.S. Army Chief of Staff, General Marshall, and virtually the entirety of the President's military advisors—to include Generals Eisenhower and Patton—failed to have their way. Instead of Morocco, they wanted to land in France and drive on Berlin. If the U.S. Army struggled against second-rate Vichy French forces, there is no doubt what would have happened if they had attempted to make an opposed landing against battle-hardened German troops."

Col. Randal said, "The part of the invasion I observed was certainly disorganized."

"All the U.S. Army needs is time in combat," Jim said. "North Africa is the perfect place to audition generals, identify the best field-grade battle commanders and allow the troops to gain battle experience fighting a modern mobile enemy. Rommel's caught in the 'Big Squeeze,' a vise between Montgomery's Eighth Army and Eisenhower's Allied Force.

"Hitler's days in Africa are numbered."

Col. Randal said, "As per your instructions, I'm initiating plans to begin winding down our gun jeep operations."

Jim said, "We can confer on what is next for Raiding Forces in detail when I return. Right now, I wanted to stop by for another reason. While you were away for TORCH, I was in the States performing my liaison duties between OSS and MI-6.

"I had an opportunity to talk to the senior SIS officer stationed in the U.S., a Canadian code-named Intrepid. We discussed the recent flap between Raiding Forces and MI-6 over DeBeers. My intent was to make it perfectly clear that spying on you is unacceptable because a harmonious relationship between our two organizations is vital for future operations.

"Intrepid was in complete agreement. He needs to be able to work with the Office of Strategic Services. A tiff over a commercial company like DeBeers does not do anyone any good."

Col. Randal said, "Roger that."

Jim said, "MI-6 is sensitive to the appearance that a British company is trading with Nazi Germany. To counterbalance the charge, Intrepid was instructed to research U.S. multinational corporations to discover if any of them are guilty of the same kind of crime. Except, is it a crime if the heads of both governments know what is taking place and allow it to continue?"

Col. Randal said, "Don't ask me, General."

"I have a file six inches thick you can peruse, or I can brief the quick and dirty version."

"Give me a break, General."

Jim said, "The following account is classified Top Secret—Need to Know. No one in your sphere, with the possible exception of Donovan, has the requisite need—and that means *no one*. Clear?"

Col. Randal said, "Crystal."

"Intrepid's report is styled Actions by U.S. Multinational Corporations Post Pearl Harbor. One: Chase Bank in Paris is conducting banking business with the Nazis in enemy-occupied France with the full knowledge of the firm's home office in Manhattan. Two: Ford trucks are being built under license for the Wehrmacht in France with authorization from its Dearborn, Michigan, headquarters. Three: The president of ITT flew New York to Madrid to Bern to help improve Hitler's communications system. Four: While gas rationing is in effect in America, Standard Oil is shipping fuel to Germany from South America through Switzerland.

"These are documented facts. Treating with the enemy is treason. I have always been under the impression anyone who did was given a last cigarette, the option of a blindfold, stood against a wall in front of a firing squad, then shot."

Col. Randal said, "That's what I thought too, General. Let's stay on mission. Nothing's going to interfere with our relationship."

Jim said, "We can let somebody else worry about the politics of allowing private companies to get away with putting profit over national interest. See you upon my return. We have a great deal of interesting work ahead of us."

When Col. Randal sat down at the table, Capt. Plum-Martin said, "Jim certainly seemed serious."

Col. Randal said, "The clash between MI-6 and Raiding Forces over DeBeers still has him on edge. May be a while before the dust settles."

Capt. Plum-Martin said, "Lady Jane was defending you, John."

"I know she was."

"Not many men have a woman who would stand up to the British Secret Intelligence Service over a perceived slight to their lover. You and Lady Jane have a very special relationship. I envy you two."

"I saw your name on the list Jane gave General Donovan to apply for dual citizenship."

Capt. Plum-Martin said, "A fresh start in America after the war does sound tempting. What do you think of the idea?"

"Jane wants to live in one of the most beautiful parts of California. Nothing I'd like better than for you to be in the same area—give it some thought, Pam."

Capt. Plum-Martin's eyes flashed pleasure. "Jane and I shall talk. I have always liked you, John—now I *really* like you."

Lt. Col. Stone and Red joined them.

Col. Randal said, "Raiding Forces is transitioning to Castelrozzo to begin small-scale raiding operations against targets in the Aegean. The U.S. is not on board with committing to the AO—national politics are involved. That being the case, my thought is we're going to need a British officer in command."

Lt. Col. Stone said, "Probably not a bad idea, old stick, politically speaking—a subject which I know nothing about."

"As I've already explained," Col. Randal said, "you're it. Turn over the Raiding Regiment to the officer you feel is most qualified."

Lt. Col. Stone said, "That would be Major Pelham-Davies."

"Negative, he will be forming a Sea Squadron-type unit serving under you."

Lt. Col. Stone said, "In that case, Mongo gets the nod. Not only is he the most experienced armored cavalry officer we have, but Baltimore has proven to be a tremendously capable patrol commander."

"Your call," Col. Randal said. "Fly to Oasis X for a change of command. Be back here as soon as possible. Set up shop in Alexandria with Admiral Ransom. We need to start planning for what I suspect is going to be a long campaign. As usual, you can count on almost nothing in the way of support."

Lt. Col. Stone said, "Raiding the islands may prove extraordinarily interesting. The Aegean has been an area of military adventurism since the abduction of Helen of Troy in 1100 BC.

Col. Randal said, "The Trojan War."

Miss UCLA, his high school English Literature student teacher, had assigned him to do a report on it, probably hoping it was the one subject on her list he would actually research. Col. Randal had not thought about his student teacher in a while.

He wondered what had happened to her.

Capt. Plum-Martin asked, "Helen of Troy . . . was she a real person?"

Lt. Col. Stone said, "Possibly—archeological digs have turned up evidence that tends to support the legend."

Col. Randal said, "We're going to need a background briefing on the Aegean AO."

"I shall scrounge up an expert on the Dodecanese somewhere. Be forewarned, it is a complex story," Lt. Col. Stone said. "Virtually impossible to follow and I am only talking about the last fifty years or so. Nevertheless, one needs to hear it in order to have an idea what a witches' brew of convoluted politics, ancient hatreds and territorial ambitions we shall be diving into.

"Homer called the Aegean 'the wine dark sea'—blood dark would have been a more apt description."

Capt. Plum-Martin said, "One day soon, as the war marches on, we shall have to abandon Oasis X. Sad. I love the place."

Red said, "I do as well—always look forward to spending my layovers there."

Col. Randal said, "Terry, any truth to the rumor you broke up Ranger Patrol because you had come to believe I was too reckless?"

Lt. Col. Stone looked his commanding officer and best friend in the eyes and lied. "I needed the men."

MANDY PAIGE AND BEVERLY BLACKWELL CAME RUSHING INTO the restaurant, causing a stir as they hurried toward Colonel John Randal's table. People turned to stare. So did Captain Billy Jack Jaxx. Miss Nevada did not much care for the officer she was having a drink with checking out other women.

Mandy said, "We have to leave, John. The mobster who ordered Lady Jane's assassination has been cornered by Egyptian police in Alexandria. They are standing by for you to arrive before going in."

Beverly said, "The Hudson's being refueled. We're flying, Pam."

Col. Randal stood up, knocking over his chair. "Let's go."

Lieutenant Colonel Sir Terry "Zorro" Stone said, "I am coming with you."

Col. Randal said, "Negative. You fly up to X, turn over command to Major Farquhar. Come straight back and get started on your new assignment."

"Wilco."

Col. Randal said, "Beverly, see if you can tear Jack away from the girl at the bar."

As Col. Randal and party raced out of the Gezira, Beverly dashed over to Capt. Jaxx, who was standing with one foot on the brass rail, dazzling the USO entertainer with tales of derring-do—some of which were actually true.

"Police have the gangster who set up Lady Jane surrounded in Alexandria. Wheels up in one-five, Jack."

Capt. Jaxx threw his glass down so hard it shattered. He was at a dead run in three steps. Jack Cool had forgotten all about his sprained ankle.

Miss Nevada was in shock. No one had *ever* left her standing at the bar.

Capt. Jaxx had not even bothered to say good-bye.

Major A.W. "Sammy" Sansom, chief of Cairo Field Security, was waiting outside with a police escort. Col. Randal and the three girls piled into the Rolls with Flanigan. Capt. Jaxx climbed in with Maj. Sansom and the little convoy was off, sirens screaming. They raced through the crowded streets of Cairo en route to the RAF airfield on the outskirts of town. The airfield was used by Raiding Forces to ferry troops to and from Oasis X when they were given leave.

There was an assemblage waiting at the Hudson. Brigadier Raymond J. "R.J." Maunsell was standing next to his staff car. Captain Roy Kidd, MC, and the two Lovat Scouts were holding rifle cases that contained their scoped 7X57 Rigby rifles. Snipers might be of use, bandaged or not. King was on hand, as was Ensign Theodore Hamilton, *aka* "The Great Teddy." Three of the Big Four were there, so battered they were painful to look at. The fourth crime lord was on the scene in Alexandria. He had discovered the identification of the gangster who had issued the order for Lady Jane to be murdered.

Captain Pamala Plum-Martin and Beverly ran up the metal steps to the plane, went into the cockpit and immediately began their preflight. Everyone started boarding. One of the Big Four had been beaten so badly during his interrogation by the Egyptian Security Police that he needed assistance walking to his seat.

A jeep came tearing up, driven by Master Sergeant Mack Beckwith, who jumped out to join the line of passengers. He had a pile of gear with him, including his cherished .30 Colt Monitor—a locally chopped Browning Automatic Rifle. The tough NCO also brought an M-1 rocket launcher, *aka* "Bazooka," with six high explosive antitank (HEAT) rounds he had swiped from the 10th Ranger Battalion.

The Hudson's right engine backfired, and the prop began wheezing as it started to turn over. Then the left engine followed suit. Both were soon whirring in perfect synch.

Capt. Plum-Martin's ex-LRDG navigator—who always flew with her—slammed the door to the passenger compartment shut. The Hudson was cleared for takeoff and began to taxi. Col. Randal sat in the front-row aisle seat with Mandy next to him by the window. R. J. sat in the aisle seat directly across from him so they could talk during the flight. Capt. Jaxx sat directly behind Col. Randal so he could lean forward to listen in on the conversation.

R. J. said, "We received a phone call from one of the Big Four. He informed my office that the individual who had placed the contract on Lady Jane was a second-tier criminal operating out of Alexandria. This information came from one of the Big Four crime lords who was in the city supervising the search there. He received a tip from an informant who hoped to collect the reward money for information leading to the capture of the person or persons behind the attempt on Lady Jane's life.

"Alexandria's Police Department personnel responded and surrounded the mobster's residence. King Farouk was informed of the development by telephone and ordered out the local army commander. He deployed his Field Security Police. Admiral Ransom arrived shortly with a detachment of Royal Marines detailed from a Royal Navy cruiser docked in the port. Now there is a small army ringing the place, standing by waiting for you to arrive on scene before they storm the building."

Col. Randal asked, "Any information on why Lady Jane was targeted?"

"Not at this time."

"We need the perpetrator taken alive."

R. J. said, "That order had been issued to all the on-scene commanders. It is imperative to discover the motive for the attack. Whoever is behind the assignation is a dead man—but we do not want him dead quite yet."

Flight time to Alexandria was less than an hour, but it seemed to take forever. A convoy of taxi cabs was waiting for them at the airfield when the Hudson touched down. Everyone disembarked immediately.

A leather-faced Egyptian who introduced himself as Major Gamal was on hand to escort Col. Randal's party to the scene. Speed was of the essence. The Egyptian Army's primary task was the repression of civil unrest, and it had a reputation for brutality. The concern was that they would jump the gun, charge the building, and kill everyone inside.

On the way, shouting to be heard over the screaming of the police car leading the taxis, Col. Randal ordered, "Mandy, you're on me. At no time are you to get out of my sight."

"Yes, sir."

Mandy was clearly of a mind to lead the charge with the Egyptian Army herself.

Col. Randal said, "We're observers on this one."

Mandy said, "Not what I wanted to hear you say."

The convoy pulled up to the mobster's impressive mansion. It was located at the beach on the west side of town behind a high wall. The criminal may have been "second tier," but that did not mean he was not fabulously wealthy from his felonious pursuits.

Red lights were flashing from a fleet of police cars, ambulances and firetrucks. Troops in full battle gear were ringing the place with Vickers .303 caliber machine guns and 3-inch mortars spaced all around. Three armored cars pointed their machine guns at the mansion. A battery of towed 75mm howitzers was pulling in when Col. Randal's entourage arrived. With King Farouk taking a personal interest in the operation, the Egyptians were in no mood to fool around.

Their taxi stopped approximately fifty yards away from the front of the compound. The giant gate, which was closed and chained shut, was notable for its elaborate iron work. Men could be seen peering from a rock guardhouse positioned on the left side of the driveway. How many were inside the post was impossible to tell.

Another taxi arrived with five slightly hungover Duck Patrol Raiders who were in town on a three-day pass. The men had heard about what was happening, grabbed their gear and rushed to lend a hand.

Vice Admiral Sir Randolph "Razor" Ransom was standing with a party of Royal Marines, Alexandria Police Department and Egyptian Army officers. They were studying the mansion through their field glasses. Two men in suits could be observed on the roof of the main building, looking back at them through their own binoculars.

Col. Randal stepped out of the cab. He, R. J. and Mandy, true to her orders to stay close, walked over to join VAdm. Ransom and his party.

Col. Randal said, "Admiral, will you request that the army advise the mortars and 75s to stand down until we can consult with the Egyptian ground commander and come up with a plan? Colonel Stone is going to want to use the place for his HQ once we've got this situation sorted out."

VAdm. Ransom said, "I was in the process of doing that when you arrived."

The cab carrying Capt. Plum-Martin and Beverly arrived. Col. Randal ordered, "Mandy, go tell them to stay with you, meaning me. Under no circumstances are you three to enter the compound until I give the word."

Mandy said, "Wilco, I hear you, John—loud and clear. Quit worrying about me."

VAdm. Ransom made introductions to the senior Egyptian officers present, "Colonel Randal, this is General Moustafa, the commander of the Alexandria Military District, and Colonel Zaher, the commander of Field Security Police."

Col. Randal said, "How many people are believed to be inside?"

Gen. Moustafa said, "Eight to ten, to include women. At this time of day, children would be attending school. We have no information about preschool age toddlers."

Col. Randal asked, "What's the plan, gentlemen?"

"The original scheme was to mortar the house to pin down those inside, use artillery to breach the walls, then go in with my Field Police attacking simultaneously from all four sides," Col. Zaher said. "With the preservation of the main building a priority, we shall have to rethink."

Col. Randal said, "Mind if I make a few suggestions?"

Gen. Moustafa said, "By all means, Colonel, your reputation precedes you. My orders from the King are to the effect that if you arrived in time, you are to command the assault."

"This is an internal Egyptian operation. I am only here in an advisory capacity. However, I do have recommendations for your consideration."

Gen. Moustafa said, "In that case, Colonel Zaher will lead the assault. He would welcome your ideas."

The expression on Col. Zaher's face indicated that might not be the case— the part about welcoming ideas.

Col. Randal said, "One of my people can neutralize the guardhouse at the gate from here. My Lovat Scout snipers can drop the two suits standing on the roof of the house. I have no objections to using the artillery to breach the walls— under tight control not to fire on the mansion proper."

Col. Zaher said, "Strict orders will be given."

"Do you believe one of your mortars is capable of dropping a single HE round inside the compound to signal the assault without hitting the main building?"

Col. Zaher said, "Yes, we shall select our most proficient crew. The house will not be harmed. Except possibly for minor shrapnel damage to the exterior walls."

"In that case, my men will take out the guard post and the two men on the roof simultaneously," Col. Randal said. "When the guardhouse explodes, your mortar team will fire one round of high explosives inside the compound. When it detonates, the rest of your mortars need to begin following up the HE with smoke rounds. Then your Field Security Policemen should begin the assault.

"If it were me, I'd ram the gate with an armored car—your call."

Col. Zaher said, "A sound plan, Colonel."

Col. Randal said, "One other thing—the honor of capturing the compound and all outbuildings goes to you and your people, Colonel. However, I'd like to suggest you consider allowing Admiral Ransom's Marines to take down the main house. They are highly trained at clearing rooms in tight spaces."

Gen. Moustafa nodded.

"As you wish," Col. Zaher said. The Field Security Police commander was not overly happy that the Royal Marines were participating in the ground assault, but he had orders to cooperate.

Col. Randal said, "Prisoners will immediately be brought outside by the Marines and turned over to your men for interrogation. No reason to be gentle on my behalf. I do want information concerning why Lady Seaborn was targeted."

Col. Zaher's sinister smile indicated that this was the part of the plan he was most pleased to hear.

The biggest drawback to the operation was that none of the Royal Marines or Capt. Jaxx knew what the criminal they were after looked like. All the house assault team had to work with was his name—AAANI, which meant "ape" in English. None of the Big Four were in any condition to go in with the Marines to make the identification.

Capt. Jaxx disappeared. Minutes later, he returned pushing a wheelchair borrowed from one of the ambulances. He told the Big Four, "I need a volunteer."

Jack Cool.

Col. Zaher briefed his subordinate leaders on the change of plans.

Col. Randal issued a Frag Order. The troops gathered round, sitting on the ground cradling their weapons. Everyone was intent.

"On command from Captain Kidd, Sergeant Major Beckwith will light up the guardhouse with a HEAT round from his bazooka. Simultaneously, you Lovat Scouts will eliminate the two men on the roof of the house. Then the Royal

Marines will make entry into the compound following the Egyptian Field Police, who will breach the gate and flow in, taking down all the outbuildings—your mission is to peel off and set up a perimeter around the house.

"Traveling behind the Marines will be Captain Jaxx's entry team, consisting of Captain Kidd, Sergeant Major Beckwith, King, the Duck Patrol Raiders and the Lovat Scouts."

Not exactly how Col. Randal had explained it to Col. Zaher.

"The entry team will pass through the Marines, enter the house and take everyone inside into custody—alive if at all possible. In the event a firefight breaks out inside, you Marines will stand ready to assist upon request.

"Trailing behind the assault element will be one of the Big Four in a wheelchair pushed by Ensign Hamilton. He'll be able to identify our target. When he does, immediately separate the individual from the other prisoners. We'll be subjecting the bad guy to an immediate interrogation before transporting him back to Cairo.

"I'll be traveling with Captain Jaxx's entry team.

"Once the main house is secure, a Marine guard will be posted on all entry points. Do not let anyone that's not a member of Raiding Forces inside. Mandy, when the all-clear is sounded, you take charge of searching the house—priority to LEAF EATER material. Remain here in Alexandria until the task has been completed to your satisfaction. Captain Plum-Martin, you and Beverly will assist in the search; however, we'll be flying out before dark, so your time here is limited.

"Admiral, do you have anything, sir?"

"Negative—other than I shall enter the compound with Ensign Hamilton."

Col. Randal said, "In that case, people—what are your questions?"

There were no questions.

A "Frag Order" was exactly what the name implied—a fragment of an Operations Order prepared in haste because of exigent circumstances. This one cut straight to the Concept of the Operation paragraph. Col. Randal wondered what he had left out that should have been covered. At the last minute, he had Ens. Hamilton exchange his 9mm Beretta MAB-38 for MSgt. Beckwith's .30

Colt Monitor. He would find the much shorter submachine gun more maneuverable inside the mansion.

Col. Randal ordered Ens. Hamilton, "Cover the windows in the front of the house before you advance with the wheelchair."

Ens. Hamilton said, "Sir!" Clearly, he hoped a target would present itself.

Col. Zaher walked up. "My men are ready when you are, Colonel."

Col. Randal said, "On your command once the guardhouse blows."

MSgt. Beckwith placed his bazooka on his shoulder. Capt. Jaxx inserted the rocket in the back and said, "UP."

Col. Randal said, "Do it."

MSgt. Beckwith knelt down and aimed the bazooka. He glanced over his shoulder to make sure no one was standing behind him in danger of being struck by the back blast, then touched the rocket launcher off. The guardhouse disintegrated.

Capt. Kidd ordered, "On one—three, two, one."

The Lovat Scouts fired on the men in the suits on the roof of the mansion, both shots sounding like a single round. The two guards dropped. They lay on the roof, not moving.

Col. Zaher raised his hand above his head, and chopped it down, while blowing a silver whistle he was wearing on a lanyard around his neck.

THUUUUUNK!

A high explosive mortar round launched out of the tube, arched high in the air out of sight, then came almost straight down and pre-detonated on the tile roof of the mansion. That was not the plan. While the shell had not penetrated the structure, it could not have done the morale of anyone inside the house any good. Col. Zaher's jaw clenched, and his angry expression guaranteed someone was going to pay for the errant round at a later time and place.

The battery of mortars began dropping smoke rounds into the compound. Soon the mansion was completely engulfed in a stark white cloud. Col. Zaher spoke into a field phone that ran to the three 75mm guns spaced around the walls. The howitzers opened from point-blank range, knocking down part of the walls along the sides and at the back of the compound.

Col. Zaher fired a red star cluster from a flare pistol, signaling his troops that the ground attack was about to begin.

Like clockwork, everything happened at once.

The Egyptian Field Police charged through the holes punched in the walls by the 75s. The Royal Marines' dog trotted after an armored car as it crashed into the iron gate. Once through, they raced toward the mansion. Capt. Jaxx's entry team came hard on their heels.

Col. Randal trailed along behind the Raiders with King. Ens. Hamilton followed, pushing the wheelchair.

The action did not last more than a minute. The occupants in the main building had been terrorized when they were surrounded by the Alexandria Police, who they knew were working in conjunction with the Egyptian Army. When the inhabitants saw the antitank rocket pulverize the guard post, everyone inside the mansion rushed out the back door into the arms of the Egyptian Field Security Police who arrived in position before the Royal Marines could surround the house.

Col. Randal and King walked inside and waited in the magnificent main room, while the Raiders went through the building. This place was almost as fantastic as the one Raiding Forces had captured in Cairo. Egyptian criminals knew how to live.

Capt. Jaxx came down the spiral staircase, "All clear, sir. Roy's not happy. This bad guy doesn't have a gun collection like the other one."

King was searching for the bail-out luggage the inhabitants intended to take with them in the event they had a chance to make a run for it. He was hoping to find a stash of diamonds like the last time. Nothing.

He found the bags packed and ready to go, but no money or jewels. Possibly everyone inside realized escape was not likely once they saw the compound surrounded. Could be they had not bothered to take the money or diamonds out of the safe. Now the problem was where to find the lockbox.

Col. Randal went to the door and signaled Mandy the all-clear to begin her search. The three girls entered, oohing at the opulence. It was clear—crime *did* pay—until it didn't.

Ens. Hamilton arrived inside, pushing one of the Big Four in the wheelchair. VAdm. Ransom and Brig. Maunsell were with him.

Col. Randal said, "Wheel your charge around to the garage out back where they're holding the prisoners, Ensign. As soon as your man identifies our target, bring him back here and turn him over to R. J."

"Sir!"

"Go with him, King."

VAdm. Ransom and R. J. strolled up the stairs for a look at the rest of the mansion. Col. Randal signaled Capt. Jaxx to go with them. A lot of closets and possible hiding places still had not been thoroughly checked out. Someone could be hiding inside with a weapon.

Why take a chance?

Mandy said, "We should start on the top floor and work our way down to the basement. To thoroughly search this place is going to take days. One thing is for sure, I have no worries about not having enough time to bring extra clothes or makeup. Plenty of everything a girl would ever need in this place."

Col. Randal said, "Ladies, if anything strikes your fancy, it's yours."

King was back in a few minutes, "You are not going to believe this, Chief. The Security Police stripped the prisoners, six men, five women. They had already cavity-searched the men and were getting ready to start on the women by the time we arrived. Those idiots slit the throat of all the men, including our target individual.

Col. Randal said, "You're kidding."

"Negative."

Col. Randal said, "Cavity searches produce anything?"

King said, "Oh, yes—count on a haul of diamonds to rival our last find."

Col. Randal said, "Get back out to the garage. Don't let any of the Security Policemen leave. I'll ask Admiral Ransom to instruct General Moustafa to have every man who's been in the garage searched.

"We want all the jewels."

King said, "Never trust the Egyptians. For all we know, King Farouk ordered the mob boss we flew here to take to be silenced."

Col. Randal said, "I don't."

VAdm. Ransom and R.J. came back down the stairs. "I shall have a platoon of naval construction engineers on site within the hour to tear this place apart. Far too big a project for Mandy and a handful of Raiders by themselves."

R.J. said, "Suits my size are in the master suite . . ."

Col. Randal said, "Be my guest."

8
ZARGO

COLONEL JOHN RANDAL AND CAPTAIN "GERONIMO" JOE MCKOY were in the private office Doctor Stephen Milam had made available at the hospital in Cairo. Capt. McKoy had arrived about the time Col. Randal had finished taking Major the Lady Jane Seaborn for her morning walk. Her spirits were high, and she was making progress. Able to go a little farther each time.

Capt. McKoy said, "One-a' the Big Four fingered the crook who allegedly put out the contract on Lady Jane?"

Col. Randal said, "Roger."

"A bunch-a' you piled on the Hudson and hightailed it straight to Alexandria. The Egyptian Army had the perpetrator's place surrounded. The Razor and an Egyptian general were on scene. Everybody had strict orders to take the perp alive."

"That's right."

Capt. McKoy said, "The assault went in. All the bad guys and the women surrendered without resisting. You brought in one-a' the Big Four to point out the man you was lookin' for. Only the Egyptian Security Police murdered all the men by the time he got there—in minutes?"

"That's about it."

Capt. McKoy studied the tip on one of Waldo's long, thin cigars he and Col. Randal were smoking. "So, what does that say to you, John?"

Col. Randal said, "Seemed too easy."

"So, you're thinkin' maybe the Big Four fingered the wrong guy to get you off their back. Maybe knock off a competitor. Kill two birds with one stone?"

Col. Randal said, "They're convinced I'm no longer looking for whoever put out the contract on Jane."

Capt. McKoy said, "Let's let 'em hang on to that thought. Meanwhile, we'll keep diggin' until we find out for sure what really did happen. I ain't plannin' on lettin' anyone involved in the attack on Lady Jane and the murder a' her two Ranger bodyguards go scot-free. One thing's for sure ... somebody on the Egyptian side in Alexandria was in the pay a' somebody else or those prisoners wouldn't-a' got themselves rubbed out the way they did."

"Who might that be, in your professional opinion?"

"Don't know yet," Capt. McKoy said. "Most likely that Egyptian general's palms got greased. The question is who greased 'em and why."

Col. Randal said, "Tell me about your trip to Kenya."

"Wasn't a whole lot to it. We waltzed into the U.S. Consulate with written orders from General Donovan authorizing us to pick up some Top Secret stuff OSS had stored in the basement. No problem. The Marine guards helped us haul the crates containin' the gold coins up the stairs and load 'em on a truck—no questions asked.

"We drove over to the British Consulate where we was safe from U.S. authorities confiscating the gold. Cuthbert Bowlby had let 'em know in advance we was comin', so the Brits gave us a room to work out of and left us alone. Took that appraiser three whole days to get 'er done—examined every single coin with a jeweler's glass, gradin' 'em."

Col. Randal said, "How much?"

"Three point two million."

"You and Waldo are big rich."

"Yeah, well, when we got the number, we altered the plan some," Capt. McKoy said.

"In what way?"

Capt. McKoy said, "Now, when Waldo gets the money from the legal sale of the gold coins in Canada, he's headin' straight to New York's diamond district where diamonds are still goin' for the prewar price and spend it all on high-grade sparklers. Then he's comin' back to Cairo as fast as he can and we'll sell 'em on the black market to smugglers for thirty times the prewar price—which is the goin' rate out here.

"The money from that sale is gonna be the capital we'll use to bankroll LEAF EATER. The best part is, we'll still end up with the diamonds later on. After we take 'em away from the smugglers, we sell 'em again when they try to run the stones to Turkey for transshipment to Germany."

Col. Randal said, "Sounds like you've got things under control."

Capt. McKoy said "We're gettin' there."

Beverly came to the office, "Time to change your dressings, Johnny."

Col. Randal stood up, sat on the edge of the desk and began unbuttoning his blouse. Beverly laid out fresh bandages. As soon as the shirt was off, she began unwinding the old compress.

Capt. McKoy said, "Whoa! Must-a' been some drop on that Castelrozzo. Those ribs a' yours are sportin' colors I never saw on a live man before."

Beverly laughed, "Me either. Not even bull riders."

MR. ZARGO ARRIVED AT THE HOSPITAL, HAVING BEEN summoned to meet with Colonel John Randal. The mercenary spy chief was in town on business. Every six weeks to two months, he visited Cairo to touch base with the various intelligence agencies and exchange information.

Col. Randal said, "What do you know about the island of Castelrozzo?"

Mr. Zargo said, "The easternmost island in the Dodecanese chain. It is located a little over a mile off the coast of neutral Turkey. The British invaded the island in 1940 and occupied the place for two days. Then the Italians counterattacked and recaptured it.

"Why do you ask?"

Col. Randal said, "Ten nights ago, I jumped on Castelrozzo with Captain Jaxx and a team of SOG operators. Admiral Ransom is planning to have Raiding Forces initiate small-scale raiding operations into the Aegean in the near future. The island will be our base of operations."

Mr. Zargo was a master at concealing his true thoughts; however, he could not hide his interest in Castelrozzo. The Aegean Islands were claimed by Greece. However, because the Nazis had intervened in the war between Italy and Greece, forcing the Greeks to capitulate, the Italians now occupied them.

Mr. Zargo was a Greek.

Col. Randal said, "You held a commission in the Hellenic Army?"

Mr. Zargo said, "I did."

Col. Randal said, "A one hundred-man detachment from the Greek Sacred Band is being attached to Raiding Forces. The troops are composed primarily of former officers who volunteered to serve in the ranks as private soldiers. Initially, I intend to use them at Oasis X running gun jeep patrols. Eventually they will take part in raiding the islands.

"I need a commander."

Mr. Zargo said, "I would sell my soul for the opportunity to fight the Italians in Greek waters."

"That won't be necessary. You are my first and only choice. You'll find your new command in Alexandria."

Mr. Zargo said, "My former rank was colonel. If that poses a problem, I will gladly serve in any grade."

Col. Randal said, "Not a problem for me."

Mr. Zargo said, "Since I shall be commanding a company-sized element and serving under you, the rank of major will do nicely—Major Zargo.

"I like the sound of it."

Col. Randal said, "Zargo—I never asked before—is that a pseudonym like your operatives use?"

"The Nazis will retaliate against my family should they learn my true identity."

Col. Randal said, "I can see why they would. Move your troops to Oasis X as soon as possible, Major—coordinate with Captain Fawcett-Tatum for transport. I plan to start drawing down on the Raiding Regiment patrols operating from there. As soon as you're fully operational, I'll pull out what's left. From that point on, you'll own the place until Admiral Ransom calls for you to join him on Castelrozzo."

"I am indebted to you, Colonel, as I have never been to any man," Maj. Zargo said. "Never once have I allowed myself to dream that such an opportunity would ever be possible. Coming out of the shadows to lead a unit of my countrymen in the fight to take my country back—mere words cannot express my emotions."

Col. Randal said, "You'll have one hundred volunteers with varying degrees of military experience. Get rid of the men who don't meet your standards. Pick officers from the pool in the ranks or bring in any outsider you choose. Recruit experienced NCOs or promote from within. Organize your command to your personal satisfaction, keeping in mind the ultimate goal is long-range, pinprick raiding from small boats."

"Would it be possible for my Greeks to be made a permanent formation of Raiding Forces—not merely attached?"

Col. Randal said, "Don't see why not."

Maj. Zargo said, "In that case, we shall call ourselves Greek Sacred Squadron, Raiding Forces—GSSRF. I have already decided on a unit motto. Like to hazard a guess at what it will be?"

"I have no idea."

"Beware of Greeks bearing gifts."

Col. Randal said, "I like it."

He had never realized Maj. Zargo had a sense of humor.

BEVERLY BLACKWELL STROLLED INTO THE OFFICE. COLONEL John Randal was cleaning the Remington M-51 .380 pocket pistol she had given him. The little handgun was arguably the best of its type ever made.

Beverly said, "I told Lady Jane I was jealous Pam got to take you to lunch. She said I could take you out too, if we promised to bring her back her favorite meal."

Col. Randal said, "We can agree to those terms."

In the car, Beverly entertained Col. Randal with a story the way Lady Jane always did. "Daddy graduated from the University of Texas—played football.

Always flies to every football game. Naturally, he was in the stands the night Billy Jack ran the punt back one hundred and two yards against Baylor, so I had to introduce him after the game.

"Daddy thinks Billy hung the moon. They have been corresponding by V-mail. Jack sent him the swimsuit photo of Brandy he took out of his plexiglass pistol grip when he replaced it with the Vargas art tribute shot of Pam—he rotates photographs. Now Daddy wants to volunteer to ferry an Air Transport Command airplane out here to Egypt to meet her."

Col. Randal said, "Can't blame him."

Beverly laughed, "We can never let that happen."

The Gezira was packed. Captain Billy Jack Jaxx was at the bar chatting up one of Red's Clipper Girl flight attendant friends in town on a layover. Captain Pamala Plum-Martin was dining with an RAF wing commander. Captain "Geronimo" Joe McKoy was at another table with one of the dancers from the Kit-Kat Club. Mandy was there as well, with Captain Duke Slater.

Col. Randal made eye contact with Mandy as he and Beverly made their way to a table in the back behind a palm. She and Capt. Slater stood up and followed them to their table in the back of the restaurant.

Capt. Slater had joined Raiding Forces with the initial contingent of the American Volunteer Group. He was the longest-serving U.S. Army officer in the unit, although technically a civilian at the time he arrived. In a command crammed full of outstanding officers, he was one of the best.

The captain had flown in from Oasis X on orders from Col. Randal.

When the four were seated at the table, Col. Randal said, "What are you doing in town, Mandy? You're supposed to be in Alexandria."

Mandy said, "Terry flew in after turning over his command to Mongo Farquhar. He took charge of the search of the gangster's house since it's going to be his headquarters. I hopped a flight back here."

Col. Randal said, "How was it going when you left—find anything?"

Mandy took a small black velvet pouch out of her purse, "Only these diamonds in a safe. There was a fair amount of gold as well. Terry plans to send it on by truck. I have a feeling we are not doing a very good job of locating where the mobsters we have taken down are hiding their assets."

Col. Randal said, "You could be right. Talk to R. J. about your hunch. Turn the packet over to Capt. McKoy."

He reached in the pocket of his faded battle dress jacket and tossed Capt. Slater one of Waldo's cigars, rolled up in a sheet of paper.

Col. Randal said, "Orders promoting you to major."

Maj. Slater said, "This is unexpected, sir."

Col. Randal said, "Save the cigar for later. Mandy doesn't like the smoke."

Mandy said, "True—in this case I can make an exception."

Beverly laughed. "Congratulations, Duke—I thought the tradition was for *you* to give *us* cigars."

Col. Randal said, "Afraid there won't be time for a celebration. You're taking command of Sea Squadron effective immediately. Admiral Ransom is about to initiate raiding operations in the Aegean Sea. You will be in command of Raiding Forces' first element to deploy to the area.

"I want you in Alexandria before the end of the day—report to the Razor."

Maj. Slater said, "I thought Major Pelham-Davies had taken command of Sea Squadron, sir."

Col. Randal said, "Change of plans."

Maj. Slater said, "In that case, I'm out of here, sir—skip lunch. I'll get you a cigar later, Beverly. I'm keeping this one."

Mandy and Beverly chorused, "Bye, Duke."

Brigadier Dudley Clarke, the commander of A-Force, the primary Allied deception organization worldwide, came back to the table. "A word with you in private, Colonel?"

Col. Randal stood up, and the two moved back to the corner where they could talk in plain sight of the dining room with no risk of being overheard by anyone.

Brig. Clarke said, "Raiding Forces is about to commence operations in the Dodecanese Island chain which, starting now, are codenamed MANDIBLES. I wanted to stop by to tell you in person that A-Force has an interest in the area. In future, if a few of the missions you are tasked to perform do not seem to make sense, bear in mind there is a bigger game in play that may not be obvious down at the tactical level."

Col. Randal said, "This isn't the first time we've had this conversation, Brigadier. I'm not sending my people on meaningless raids. And, I'm not sending 'em on any mission that a single pass by an A-20 gunship could accomplish."

"What might appear unimportant to you at the tip of the sword may have far-reaching implications in another theatre at a later time and place outside your sphere of knowledge," Brig. Clarke said. "You know I would never ask you to sacrifice your Raiders needlessly."

Col. Randal said, "Actually, I don't, Brigadier—you've ordered SAS on raids no one returned from for little or no gain in the past."

Brig. Clarke said, "Understand this, then—the small-scale operations carried out by Raiding Forces in the Aegean will be vital to the war effort long-term. Save tens of thousands of American lives when the Allies eventually invade Europe, even though your President and the Allied Forces commander, General Eisenhower, refuse to accept that outcome as a military fact.

"The U.S. chooses to believe we British are playing at postwar Imperial politics."

Col. Randal said, "I don't play politics when it comes to my troops."

"Fair enough. I stopped by to tell you one thing . . . and this is classified above Top Secret, with no one having the Need to Know," Brig. Clarke said. "While the Razor is to be in command of the theatre and Raiding Forces is to be the controlling headquarters for all military personnel and units, both of you will, in fact, be working for me.

"Over time, I hope to be able to arrange the transfer of the remnants of the SAS, SBS and LRDG to Raiding Forces. Unfortunately, all together they will not total more than a handful of troops. Once again, Colonel, you will find yourself fighting a distant private war over an enormous area of operations with limited means—only this time you shall be playing at pirates."

When Col. Randal returned to the table, the girls were too well-schooled in the concept of Need to Know to ask what Brig. Clarke had wanted. So he told them—sort of.

"The Brigadier expressed his heartfelt desire for me to know that raiding the Dodecanese Islands will be a major contributing factor in winning the war."

Mandy asked, "Do you believe him?"

Col. Randal said, "All up, Raiding Forces and attachments will be less than four hundred effectives—no, actually I don't."

Beverly said, "OK, love Dudley—don't think I would trust him very far."

Mandy said, "Very perceptive, Beverly."

Beverly said, "John and I are having a lunch date. No more war talk. We're supposed to be having fun."

Mandy said, "If you believe I am about to go away and leave you two alone, you are crazy."

Beverly laughed. "Knew that was too much to hope for."

Col. Randal said, "The brigadier mentioned something else—Y-Service intercepted a cable from Germany containing urgent instructions to its consulates in Angola and Mozambique to purchase seven hundred thousand carats of diamonds."

Beverly said, "Don't have a clue what that means in pounds."

Col. Randal said, "Three hundred eight—I asked."

Mandy, having picked up some of Beverly's slang, said, "Wow!"

COLONEL JOHN RANDAL AND MAJOR THE LADY JANE SEABORN were in the sitting chamber adjoining her hospital room. Now she was making rapid improvement. Even so, Dr. Stephen Milam was yet to come off his prognosis of "Still not out of the woods yet."

They were waiting for the doctor to make his afternoon rounds.

If Lady Jane passed muster on his visit, agreed to hire a private nurse and promised to come to the hospital once a week for a thorough checkup, she could move to her suite at the Mena House Hotel. Lady Jane was beside herself at the prospect.

Lady Jane said, "Wish the doctor would hurry up. My tan is fading. I look like a corpse."

Which was not true. Corpses, as a rule, are not generally drop-dead gorgeous.

While they waited, Col. Randal was glancing through his old, hard-used copy of *The Commando Pocket Manual* he always carried. There was a brief introduction that described the training at Achnacarry—home of the famed Commando Castle. " . . . *tuition follows a carefully prepared syllabus with all the specific skills crucial to raiding.*"

Col. Randal thought, "That sounds painless. Scientific training. My recollection is less science and more up the hill and down the hill, in the rain, all night, no food."

"*Volunteers for special service will learn and be tested day and night in all weathers, in physical fitness, outdoor survival training and living off the land...*"

Col. Randal remembered there had been a scandal about the 'living off the land'—Raiding Forces students fishing the streams using hand grenades and poaching the local red deer.

" . . . *field craft and patrolling—the art of moving troops across country unheard and undetected, small-unit tactics, reading and compass work, weapons training to include enemy small arms up to light mortars, unarmed and close quarter combat with knives to include silent killing, explosives and demolitions, signaling, rope work and the Tarzan course, rock and cliff climbing, amphibious assaults, small-boat handling, river crossings and first aid.*"

Col. Randal made a mental note to have Captain Roy "Mad Dog" Reupert organize an amphibious warfare refresher course using the *Commando Pocket Manual* as the basis of the curriculum. Sea Squadron to attend initially, then the remainder of Raiding Forces before they deployed to the Aegean. It had been a lifetime since many of the men had gone through Achnacarry. Battle skills have to be used or they get lost. Gun-jeep patrolling and small-scale amphibious raiding require two distinctly different skill sets.

Back to the manual . . . Maj. William Fairbairn was quoted, "*In war, your attack can have only two possible objectives: either to kill your opponent or to capture him alive.*"

Lady Jane interrupted his reading. "You are not talking to me, John. I need you to keep my mind off what Dr. Milam is going to say about leaving the hospital."

Col. Randal closed the manual and slipped it in his pocket. "How's this, I have a mission for you. And if you accept, you can't carry it out from here or from Mena House. So, get well fast."

She laughed, "What is my mission?"

Col. Randal said, "Sea Squadron will be relocating to Castelrozzo to use as a base to carry out amphibious raids into the Aegean. Eventually, the bulk of Raiding Forces in Middle East Command will relocate to the island. Your mission, if you accept it, is to go there, identify suitable space to set up RFHQ Advanced Base Aegean to include barracks for the troops—then make it happen."

Lady Jane said, "Perfect! You know I love these types of projects—I accept my mission. What can you tell me about the island?"

"It's small, only four square miles, with virtually no vegetation because it's solid rock. A cliff rises out of the sea on the north side, with the bulk of the houses starting at the water's edge and running partway up the side of the slope. Before the war, Castelrozzo belonged to Greece, so I think you'll like the architecture."

"Sounds lovely."

Col. Randal said, "The island was bombed by the Italians in 1940 and that, combined with a declining population—many of the people have left the island for the bright lights in the big cities of Turkey or Egypt—means quite a few of the villas have been abandoned. You'll have a lot of properties to choose from, but they may need major renovation."

Lady Jane said, "Sounding better and better. I shall bring in an architect. The Razor can find a Royal Navy construction engineer to manage the project or we can hire a civilian."

Col. Randal said, "Turkey is only a mile or so off the north shore. If you can locate a non-military type boat, you should be able to find a lot of what you need over there instead of having to ship it in from Cairo. You'll have to check on neutrality regulations governing how a Royal Marine officer can go about visiting.

"I have no idea what the rules are."

Lady Jane said, "I am excited."

Col. Randal said, "Have to get past Dr. Milam first."

CAPTAIN BILLY JACK JAXX SHOWED UP AT MAJOR THE LADY JANE Seaborn's hospital room. Commander Ian Fleming, RNVR, was with him. The debonair Royal Navy Intelligence Officer had flown in from his office in Room 39, *aka* the "Zoo", at the Admiralty. The two were shown to the sitting room, where Colonel John Randal was waiting for Dr. Stephen Milam with Lady Jane.

For once, Lady Jane was not feeling all that sociable. Being on pins and needles, she was wanting only Col. Randal to keep her company.

Cdr. Fleming said the code word to trump all code words—"GOLDEN FLEECE."

Col. Randal clicked on.

Cdr. Fleming said, "Only recently, it has come to the attention of Royal Naval Intelligence that the Germans have installed a radar station on the tiny island of Kupho located off the southeast tip of Crete. Tonight two platoons from B Company, 11th Royal Marines and the Small Operations Group, Raiding Forces—sailing aboard two Royal Navy destroyers out of Alexandria—are going to raid the island, destroy the radar station, capture certain components of the equipment, and recover the safe believed to be in the office of the German commandant. It is hoped RED INDIAN material will be discovered in the strongbox once it is brought back to Cairo and cracked open.

"You, Colonel, are to command the operation—questions?"

"What do we know about Kupho?"

Cdr. Fleming said, "There is good news and bad news. Which would you like first?"

"Bad news."

Cdr. Fleming said, "Nothing is known about the enemy garrison. We know very little about the topography of the island—not even a suitable map. The good news is, Naval Intelligence in Alexandria was able to locate a Cretan who claims to be a native of Kupho, one Antonopoulo. He has agreed to serve as your guide—unfortunately, the man is currently residing in a jail cell, locked up for being a security risk.

"He likes to brag, and it was feared he might compromise tonight's mission."

Col. Randal said, "Jack, how long's it going to take to have your team assembled?"

Capt. Jaxx said, "My men are required to stay at RFHQ or within the city limits of Cairo and check in by phone every two hours. SOG will be ready to go, wheels up, in the next ninety minutes, sir."

Col. Randal said, "You coming with us, Fleming?"

"I would prefer to stay here with the ravishing Lady Jane," Cdr. Fleming said. "However, duty calls. I shall be aboard one of the destroyers, observing."

Col. Randal said, "Good—I want Admiral Ransom overseeing the navy end of things in Alexandria. Any problems with that?"

Cdr. Fleming said, "I shall put in a call to him immediately."

Col. Randal said, "I'll be at the airfield by the time your SOG people assemble."

Dr. Milam arrived. Col. Randal went out in the hall, where Beverly was impatient to learn whether or not Lady Jane was being released from the hospital. The two Lovat Scouts seemed like they wanted out as well. Everyone was sick of the place.

King walked up.

Col. Randal said, "SOG has been alerted for a raid later tonight. You and the Scouts stand by ready. As soon we get the doctor's report, we're moving out."

King said, "Let me go organize replacement bodyguards for Lady Seaborn, Chief, and an armed escort for her to Mena House."

Col. Randal said, "Roger."

After what seemed like an interminable wait, Dr. Milam cracked the door. "Colonel."

When he stepped inside, Lady Jane was sitting on the side of the hospital bed. One look and Col. Randal knew it was good news—she was beaming. There had been no guarantee that would be the case.

Dr. Milam said, "Afraid we are losing our most glamourous patient. Here is the drill, Lady Jane—Mena House, private nurse, bed rest, dine in, no travel except to come for a checkup once a week. And no strenuous activity—you *do* *understand* what I mean, Colonel."

Col. Randal said, "Affirmative."

Lady Jane asked, "Can I lay out by the pool?"

Dr. Milam said, "Only short periods in the sun—no overheating. Stay under an umbrella most of the time. If you promise to have Beverly tanning with you, I shall consider making house calls."

After that, things moved fast. Mandy arrived. She and Beverly took charge of checking Lady Jane out of the hospital. Flanigan brought her Rolls around to the front of the building. Two Rangers replaced the Lovat Scouts.

Lady Jane was excited and disappointed at the same time, "Be safe, John. I want you back all in one piece to keep me company until Dr. Milam lets me off the leash."

Col. Randal said, "If I understood Commander Fleming correctly, I'll see you tomorrow."

Lady Jane said, "You better."

A jeep was waiting for Col. Randal. King and the Lovat Scouts piled in the back with their gear and headed to the departure airfield. By the time they arrived, SOG team members had already converged on the landing strip, having commandeered taxis, private automobiles, and even the odd motorcycle. One Raider showed up in a police car—minus the policeman.

Cdr. Fleming said, "Never saw anything to match this show in my life. These men have their blood up, what!"

Capt. Jaxx said, "I put out the word to the 575th Rangers who jumped on Castelrozzo, sir. Most of 'em made it. Some of our guys went AWOL from the hospital."

Col. Randal said, "Conduct a quick inspection. Anyone you believe not physically capable of making the raid, send 'em back."

Two USAAF loadmasters were penciling in manifests for the pair of C-47s that were already firing up their motors for the hop to Alexandria. King grabbed Col. Randal's gear out of the jeep and threw it over one shoulder. He tossed him the little M-1 Carbine.

Master Sergeant Mack Beckwith was making a head check. Then he verified the number with the loadmasters and said to Col. Randal, "Good count, sir."

Col. Randal ordered, "Let's go."

The flight to Alexandria did not take long. There was an air of expectancy on board both aircraft since they were flying into the unknown. Lieutenant Colonel Sir Terry "Zorro" Stone was waiting in a staff car alongside three U.S. Army "deuce and a halfs"—two-and-a-half-ton trucks—to transport the Raiders. Major Jeb Pelham-Davies, DSO, MC, and Major Taylor Corrigan, DSO, MC, were with him. Lt. Col. Stone was in town to confer with Vice Admiral Sir Randolph "Razor" Ransom.

The two Raiding Forces majors were not sure why they had been ordered there.

Col. Randal filled them in on the ride to VAdm. Ransom's headquarters. "I know you two were recently given new assignments; however, there's been a change of plans. Duke Slater will be taking command of Sea Squadron. Both of you will be tasked with raising two additional Sea Squadron-type outfits and transitioning our gun jeep patrols into amphibious raiding teams.

"I have no idea what the final TO&E of your new commands will look like, or if Sea Squadron as presently configured will even work in the Dodecanese Islands. Get with Admiral Ransom for his input. You can count on my help as much as possible during the organizational stage—keep me in the loop."

Col. Randal had just handed them a complex task. One he would have liked to undertake himself. Maj. Pelham-Davies glanced at Maj. Corrigan. Both officers knew there was zero possibility that Col. Randal would be able to restrain himself from getting involved with the organizational planning.

They were fine with that.

WHEN THEY ARRIVED AT 10TH MOTOR TORPEDO BOAT FLOTILLA Headquarters, Col. John Randal and his Small Operations Group officers went straight to the suite of offices where Vice Admiral Sir Randolph "Razor" Ransom maintained a low profile as Director, Naval Operations Division

(Irregular), at Headquarters Command Center. They found VAdm. Ransom standing in front of a giant wall map, talking to a Royal Navy intelligence officer, the company commander of B Company, 11th Royal Marine Battalion, and two of his platoon leaders.

Col. Randal noted that the Razor did not have the demeanor normally associated with happy campers—he did not like surprises on short notice with limited intelligence.

VAdm. Ransom made the introductions, keeping them in accordance with Raiding Forces' Rules for Raiding—'Short and Simple'. "Gentlemen, this is Colonel Randal. He will be in command of the landing party tonight. Introduce yourselves after young Lieutenant Nelson from the Office of Naval Intelligence—which is in damned short supply, meaning virtually nonexistent this day—gives you his assessment of the objective.

"Then, Fleming, if you want to chime in . . . or not."

VAdm. Ransom had already chewed a strip off the special Intelligence Officer for springing the raid on him with no advanced warning.

Lieutenant Tyrone Nelson, RN said, "Kupho Island lies off the southeasterly tip of Crete. The two are separated by a narrow channel. Not much is known about the place. RAF sent over a reconnaissance aircraft this morning—a Martin Baltimore that was making smoke to appear like it was crashing, so it could only make one pass. Unfortunately, the sky was overcast—low-level fog. No useful photos were obtained.

"Here is what we know. Kupho is a small island with a hill dead center in the middle. A single dirt track runs from the beach on the south side up the hill. On top is a lighthouse and a small building complex. Most likely the radar station is located there.

"Naval Intelligence has determined by classified means that there is a safe in the commandant's office. It may contain certain sensitive information. The purpose of the exercise is to capture the material in the safe.

"The general idea is to land the two platoons of B Company, 11th Battalion, Royal Marines, under the command of Captain Tisdale-Peterson and the Small Operations Group, Raiding Forces, under Captain Jaxx on the south shore of Kupho. They will advance up the trail to the summit of the hill, secure the HQ complex, and destroy the radar station and the lighthouse. SOG will enter the headquarters and conduct a search for classified information and locate the safe known to be in the building.

"Following the search, everyone will move down the hill, re-embark on the destroyers and return to base. The strongbox is to be brought back to Alexandria, where it will be opened by an expert.

"Commander Fleming . . . ?"

Cdr. Fleming said, "I want to reiterate—Colonel Randal is in command of all ground forces. The Marines are to seize the military crest and set up a defensive perimeter around the top of the hill. SOG will clear the HQ complex and perform certain other classified tasks."

VAdm. Ransom said, "Colonel."

Col. Randal said, "Captain Tisdale-Peterson, I want you to develop a scheme of maneuver for your Marines and present it to me in the next thirty minutes. Capt. Jaxx, same thing for SOG.

"Lieutenant Nelson, locate a suitable area for us to conduct a rehearsal. I want to be walking through the actions on the objective within the hour.

"Right now I need to confer with our native Kupho guide."

Lt. Nelson said, "He is in the brig, sir."

Col. Randal ordered, "Get him out—now! Let's go, people."

As the conference was breaking up, VAdm. Ransom said, "Colonel, I would like to introduce you to Lieutenant Commander Nigel Clogstoun-Willmond. He commands a unit called the Combined Operations Pilotage Parties, or COPP for short. No one is exactly sure what he does—something called 'beach reconnaissance.'

"After several false starts out here in Middle East Command, the Commander managed to find his way to me. I am assigning the COPPs to Raiding Forces. Take him along tonight. See if he can make himself useful."

Col. Randal asked, "Know anything about Kupho, Commander?"

Lt.Cdr. Willmond said, "Never heard of the place, sir."

"Stick with me," Col. Randal said. "After you have heard what Captain Tisdale-Peterson and Captain Jaxx come up with, you tell me if there is anything you can contribute tonight.

"We'll have plenty of time later to talk about what COPP's role in Raiding Forces will be."

Lt.Cdr. Willmond said, "Tonight sounds like it has all the elements of a three-ring circus, sir."

Col. Randal said, "That is a fact."

Capt. Jaxx walked over, "There's no way I can draw up SOG's actions on the objective, sir. Not enough information. Besides, when we get there, it's not going to be what we think now."

Col. Randal said, "I realize that, Jack. Get with Tisdale-Peterson to coordinate your plans. Let the Marines flow through the objective to secure it, follow on close with SOG, hit your target, make a search, grab the safe, then get out of there—some variation of that."

"Yes, sir. Poor prior planning produces . . ."

Col. Randal said, "Yeah, I know."

Lt. Nelson arrived back with their trusty guide Antonopoulo. He introduced him to VAdm. Ransom and Col. Randal. "The idea is for Commander Willmond and Antonopoulo to go in first by dinghy, spy out a good landing place, then flash a signal to the cutters containing the Marines and SOG to come ashore."

Sounded like a reasonable enough plan, though this was the first Lt.Cdr. Willmond or Antonopoulo had heard it.

Col. Randal watched as the two platoons of B Company, 11th Battalion Royal Marines and SOG walked through their scheme of maneuver for the attack on the lighthouse, radar station and building complex. There was not a hill available. The Marines and Raiders ran through the attack in slow motion at a walk on flat ground to familiarize everyone with what was going to be expected of them in approximately six hours when the troops did it for real.

By any stretch of the imagination, this was winging it.

There was the usual confusion the first few run-throughs. That was to be expected. Finally, once the troops had the movement down, Col. Randal had everyone fall in around him and take a knee. He briefed again the actions on the objective as worked out by Capt. Tisdale-Peterson and Capt. Jaxx.

"Tonight, I want you to go in screaming like banshees. Strike fear into the heart of the bad guys. Safe on their island, they will not be expecting to be attacked. Every one of you needs to have one magazine loaded all tracer to increase the shock value during the assault.

"When we land, a four-man SOG team led by Mr. King will go up first to eliminate any sentries at the top of the dirt track and to act as guides. Then you Marines will go up in a column of platoons abreast, squads in file, First Platoon on the left, Second Platoon on the right. The remainder of SOG will be in trail bringing up the rear. As you Marines near the crest, you will be met by the guides at the top, who will be holding red filtered flashlights to signal you to deploy to the left and right of the track as rehearsed.

"When he is satisfied you are in position, Captain Tisdale-Peterson will fire a flare from his Very pistol to signal the attack. When you Marines reach the crest, Captain Tisdale-Peterson will fire a second flare, which will be the signal to pause, shift your fires to the left and right, as rehearsed, in order for SOG to pass through and assault the objective. At that point, on voice command from Captain Tisdale-Peterson, you Marines will push past SOG to the far side of the hilltop. Once the objective is secure, radar destroyed, demolitions placed in the lighthouse and buildings searched, SOG will pull back down the track. At that time, you Marines will fold in and follow them down the hill in reverse order. We will board the cutters, return to our respective destroyers and sail for home.

"Captain Tisdale-Peterson, take charge of your Marines and move them to the assembly area, preparatory to loading. Captain Jaxx, take charge of SOG and fall in after them.

"Move out."

AS SOG MOVED PAST, CAPT. BILLY JACK JAXX SAID, "SORRY, SIR, no matter how hard we tried to keep it short and simple, the actions on the objective still turned out pretty complicated."

Colonel John Randal said, "It's either going to work or it's not. Stay loose and ready to improvise."

Capt. Jaxx said, "Roger that, sir."

Two Hunt class destroyers were standing by at the pier. First Platoon, B Company, 11th Battalion Royal Marines, and the Small Operations Group boarded one. The Second Platoon and Capt. Tisdale-Peterson's command party boarded the other. VAdm. Ransom was on hand to see them off with Captain "Pyro" Percy Stirling. The captain had been flown in from Oasis X to supervise demolitions.

Col. Randal said, "Glad you made it, Percy. Go ahead and board."

Capt. Stirling said, "I understand we have another lighthouse tonight, sir."

Uh-oh!

Vice Admiral Sir Randolph "Razor" Ransom said, "Godspeed, Colonel."

Col. Randal saluted, then, without a word, joined Cdr. Ian Fleming and Capt. Jaxx on board one of the Hunt class destroyers. Events had moved so fast he did not even know the ship's name. Nor had he met the ship's captain, which was not the best of ways to embark on a raid and was probably in violation of half a dozen principles laid down in his *Commando Pocket Manual*.

Cdr. Fleming said, "Time to go get a RED INDIAN."

Easy enough for him to say. Cdr. Fleming was not going ashore on an island no one but their guide knew anything about. And he was not going to attack an enemy position whose troop strength was unknown. If the defenders were battle-hardened German sky soldiers from the 22 Air-Landing Division, they were not going to roll over.

Tonight could end very badly.

From the moment the destroyers slipped the pier, the mission began to take on an air of unreality. Raiding Forces was used to having targets of opportunity sprung on it. On their first early cross-channel raids against enemy-occupied France, navigation was an almost insurmountable problem. But at least the Raiders knew what to expect would be waiting at their objective, even if they failed to find it.

Col. Randal took the opportunity to have a brief conversation with Lieutenant Commander Nigel Clogstoun-Willmond, "I see you're wearing the DSO ribbon. Tell me your story."

Lt.Cdr. Willmond said, "No one knew what to do with COPP—not understanding what beach reconnaissance meant. They put me in a submarine and shipped me off to inspect the beaches on Rhodes in anticipation of a full-blown invasion of the island.

"Silly fools in MEHQ awarded me the nation's second highest valor decoration for riding around in a submarine looking through a periscope. My team is trained to *swim* ashore and survey the beaches up close and personal. Then, to turn the sublime into the ridiculous, we never actually invaded Rhodes."

Col. Randal had better luck with Antonopoulo, who boasted, "Kupho—I know the hills, the beaches, the tides, the rocks, every inlet, every pebble, every current like the back of my hand."

Cdr. Fleming said, "Deuced lucky to have that man along this night, quite!"

Col. Randal was not so sure.

Following an uneventful high-speed run, the destroyers stood off Kupho. The night was quiet. Lt.Cdr. Willmond and Antonopoulo were rowed ashore in a dinghy by a rating, there being no Sea Squadron Lifeboat Serviceman in Alexandria available to go on the raid. For once, the Cretan needed no warning to maintain silence.

Out of the night, the darker silhouette of the island rose ahead of them. Lt.Cdr. Willmond whispered to the local expert, "We are getting close. What course do we steer?"

No response.

"How should we steer?"

In broken English, Antonopoulo said, "Me no know. Never been this place before."

"What?"

"Me no know. We go home now. Please we go home."

Antonopoulo was blubbering.

Lt.Cdr. Willmond said, "We shall take you home right enough. Have you bloody well shot, you liar."

He slipped over the side of the dinghy and swam in to inspect the beach. By sheer dumb luck, it was as good as any he could expect to find. Back to the dinghy, Lt.Cdr. Willmond flashed his torch out to sea.

Col. Randal and his men were in cutters, standing by to begin the pull to shore. When he saw the signal, he ordered, "Let's go."

The boats swished in, the sailors paddling furiously. King leapt out and disappeared up the track with his party—the two Lovat Scouts and a 575th Ranger, Pvt. Zeke Swearington, who was a crack pistol marksman. All four were armed with silenced .22 High Standard handguns.

The Royal Marines and SOG fanned out on the beach. Col. Randal glanced at the lime green hands on the Rolex Lady Jane had given him over three years ago. He marked the time. Ten minutes later, he ordered Capt. Tisdale-Peterson, "Move out."

The Marines snaked up the track. It was steep, though luckily not very far to the top. The red-filtered flashlight came into view. Capt. Tisdale-Peterson deployed his platoons to the left and right.

Col. Randal noted the Royal Marines were moving extremely well in the dark—the mark of professionals. Suddenly, machine guns opened from the top of the hill, the bullets cracking overhead. Tracers arched out to sea. The enemy was alert, but they were firing on the destroyers and the rounds were all high above the Marines and SOG Raiders.

Col. Randal and Capt. Jaxx continued up the track until they made contact with King and his team. The Very pistol flare went off. The Marines began screaming and firing their weapons as they advanced uphill, triggering a round off every time their left foot hit the ground. Their tracers lit up the night and it did seem like a million madmen were going in for the kill.

Which was the idea.

Capt. Jaxx inched his men forward, making sure not to advance past the assault line. Then the second flare went off, indicating the Marines were on the crest. Capt. Jaxx shouted, "Follow me, boys!"

SOG went in with all guns blazing and, unlike the Marines who were primarily armed with bolt action .303 Mark III Enfield rifles, they were carrying an assortment of automatic weapons, .30 caliber Johnson Light Machine guns, cut-down .30 caliber BAR's, 9mm Beretta M-38 submachine guns and sawed-off 12-gauge Browning A-5 semi-automatic shotguns. There were even a few .45 caliber M1-A1 Thompson submachine guns.

The small, built-up complex became a beaten zone, smothered by fire.

The Marines quickly silenced the machine gun positions along the crest of the hill. Their grenades were thundering. A few were muffled—the sound solid and ugly when they went off inside sandbagged bunkers. Detonations flashed one after another, painting the objective in a strange, disjointed blue-white light that made the troops' movements appear herky-jerky.

Resistance was light to nonexistent.

SOG swept across the objective, screaming as they went, executing their attack with parade ground precision, employing fire and maneuver combined with "violence of action" as laid down by the instructors at the Commando Castle.

Col. Randal ordered, "Your turn, Percy."

Capt. Stirling and two of his Railroad Wrecking Crew Patrol people moved toward the radar station and the lighthouse, carrying huge backpacks of explosives they had muscled up the hill. "Pyro" Percy had a reputation when it came to blowing things up. His presence tonight did not bode well for the bad guys' materiel and equipment.

It probably was not going to do much for their morale either.

Col. Randal arrived at the enemy Command Post with the action swirling all around. Capt. Jaxx was there. All the enemy headquarters personnel inside were dead or dying from the grenade Jack Cool had prudently tossed inside before going in to spray the place with his 9mm Beretta MAB-38 submachine gun.

They located a big, heavy, steel safe.

Capt. Jaxx asked, "How are we supposed to get that to the boats, sir?"

Col. Randal said, "Roll it down the hill. We don't care if what's inside gets banged up. That's Fleming's problem."

Capt. Jaxx said, "Roger that, sir."

Time seemed to be standing still when, in reality, it was screaming by. The objective was a tiny place, but there were a number of tasks to be performed before they could withdraw. The Royal Navy destroyers had to be well away from Crete before daylight.

Capt. Jaxx went to check on his troops.

Col. Randal looked around inside the enemy Command Post (CP). There was nothing much of interest. He did note that the enemy personnel were in fact

Germans, wearing the red and white striped insignia of the 22nd Air-Landing Division. Fortunately, there had not been very many of them stationed on Kupho.

Capt. Jaxx returned, "We're up, sir. Capt. Stirling has his charges placed. He intends to wait until we have withdrawn to ignite the fuse lighters.

"I've detailed a security team to stay with him."

Col. Randal said, "Start moving your men down to the beach."

Things started happening fast. SOG leapfrogged back, then began moving down the track. Col. Randal joined Capt. Tisdale-Peterson, who was waiting beside the trail, where he had established his command post to monitor his troops as they passed by on the way down to board the cutters.

Col. Randal said, "When you hear Capt. Stirling shouting 'Fire in the Hole,' you might want to have your troops step up the pace. There's a lighthouse fueled by acetylene on top. You're about to experience a Captain "Pyro" Percy Stirling masterpiece—a life-altering experience."

"Yes, sir."

When Col. Randal arrived on the beach, everything was orderly. Head counts were being taken. Master Sergeant Mack Beckwith was overseeing the SOG personnel. Capt. Tisdale-Peterson's Company Sergeant Major was supervising the Royal Marines.

Four SOG operators were manhandling the safe they had rolled end over end down the trail. The Raiders got it loaded onto one of the cutters. Col. Randal and Capt. Jaxx planned to be in the same boat with the strongbox.

Cdr. Fleming and his masters back at home in Naval Intelligence Division, MI-6 and the codebreakers at Bletchley Park were most likely standing by in high anticipation, eager to discover if the codes contained inside the safe were for the unbreakable four-wheel Enigma device, as they had reason to believe. The codes could be a war-changing event.

Only Col. Randal, the Raiders and the Marines were not cleared to know about that.

Capt. Stirling arrived. He announced, "Last man."

MSgt. Beckwith said, "We've got a good count, Colonel."

One of the Royal Marine corporals walked up, "Captain Tisdale-Peterson sends his compliments, sir. All Marine personnel are assembled, accounted for, boarded on their cutters and standing by for your orders, sir.

Col. Randal said, "Inform your captain it's time to get the hell out of Dodge."

The Marine sergeant had no idea what that meant. "Sir!"

The row out to the destroyers seemed to take forever. As a cutter arrived, the troops on board began climbing up rope loading nets to the deck. Then the boat was hauled up by ropes manhandled by sailors on board the ship.

Col. Randal and Capt. Jaxx scrambled up the net on the port side of the destroyer. Once on board, they leaned back over the side to watch their boat being hoisted up. Cdr. Fleming was there to greet them.

Night suddenly turned into day. Kupho seemed to have exploded—the entire island. The three-story tank of acetylene powering the lighthouse went up in the mother of all fireballs. The magnitude of the detonation was indiscernible; it was like the sky was being ripped apart and set on fire. The sight was as frightening as it was awe-inspiring. Especially if you had never witnessed anything like it before.

It seemed like the world was coming to an end.

Ignoring the fireworks, Cdr. Fleming said, "Where is my safe?"

Col. Randal pointed down at the cutter being hauled up.

At that moment, one of the hauls carried away. The sailor who was pulling it, startled by the suddenness of the flash over Kupho, let go of the rope. The cutter tipped. Then it dangled, stern down, plowing the waves as the destroyer gathered way.

The safe in the stern sheets rolled out, smacked the water, and sank.

9

CARD GAME

COLONEL JOHN RANDAL WAS LYING ON A CHAISE LOUNGE BY THE private pool at the suite Major the Lady Jane Seaborn kept at Mena House Hotel. Beverly Blackwell, in her black French-cut swimsuit, was lying next to him. Brandy Seaborn and Lady Jane were in the pool, floating on air mattresses. Rita and Lana had been playing badminton, but now they were throwing a tennis ball for Happy to chase.

Lady Jane was pretty much ignoring her doctor's orders.

Beverly said, "OK, General Donovan sent you an "Eyes Only" message. Since I decode all incoming OSS traffic, I know what it says. All the spy-versus-spy stuff doesn't work out in actual practice the way the people back at HQ in Washington imagine it does."

Col. Randal said, "What's it say?"

"OSS intercepted a message from the German consulates in Angola and Mozambique stating that they weren't able to buy the seven hundred thousand carats of diamonds in their districts as instructed by Berlin."

Col. Randal said, "That's too bad."

"OSS has concluded that the only place the Nazis can obtain the quantity of industrial diamonds it requires is the Belgian Congo because their mines are still producing," Beverly said. "General Donovan wants an update on the status of Raiding Forces' intentions to go there and initiate anti-diamond smuggling operations."

Col. Randal said, "You've seen all the classified messages. Been in the room or been briefed on every conversation I've had with the general about diamonds. What's your estimate of the situation?"

Beverly said, "General Donovan is totally obsessed with the Belgian Congo."

"Yeah, and I have no idea why that might be."

Beverly asked, "Is it true that the safe you raided Kupho to capture fell overboard and sank?"

"Roger that."

Beverly said, "Ian saw what happened?"

"Looking straight at the cutter when it went down."

Beverly laughed. "I would have loved to have seen his face."

"Wasn't happy," Colonel Randal said.

Beverly reached into her bag and extracted a small box. She took out a silver pin. "Lady Jane had these made for me—my WASP wings. They resemble USAAF pilot's wings but have a diamond shape in the center to symbolize the shield carried by Athena, the Goddess of War."

Col. Randal said, "Wasp?"

Beverly laughed. "No, Johnny, Women's Army Service Pilot—WASP. These wings aren't officially authorized for issue yet, so Lady Jane had her jeweler make this pair from a pattern Daddy sent her. He knows Jackie Cochrane, one of the WASP founders."

Col. Randal said, "Jane marches to her own drum. Doesn't much like to wait around for orders to be cut once she decides to do something. How many sets of wings does that make you qualified for?"

Beverly said, "Four—my British Parachute Wings, U.S. Jump Wings, British Air Transport Auxiliary Wings and U.S. Army Women's Service Pilot's Wings. I'm going to do like you and not wear decorations, but I love my wings. I'm going to wear all of 'em at the same time, one on top of the other."

Col. Randal said, "I like that plan."

Brandy climbed out of the pool, came over and lay down on the lounge on the other side of Col. Randal.

She said, "Father tells me Raiding Forces will be relocating to Castelrozzo, preparatory to commencing operations into the Aegean. Small heavily armed parties raiding tiny islands. Transported in fast boats."

Col. Randal said, "That's what he tells me too."

Brandy said, "I want in."

"Negative."

Brandy began oiling her perfect golden legs. "Why not?"

Col. Randal said, "You and Parker won't be in the mix—it's not happening."

Brandy said, "I have a fast boat. Parker is the best navigator in Middle East Command—you need us, John."

Col. Randal said, "I say again, hear me loud and clear—negative. Your mission is to insert or extract agents for SOE or rescue evaders for Veronica Paige's MI-9."

Brandy said, "You have never been able to say no to me."

"There's always a first time. I don't want you hurt. Jane getting shot was the last straw."

Brandy said, "Are you aware that Jane never had to be in a war zone—and that includes England. Turned down a perfectly safe job in Washington, D.C. as the social secretary for the British Ambassador to be with you. Jane was well aware of the risks of being here in Egypt, and so am I."

Col. Randal said, "Never knew that."

"Pam and Beverly get away with flying combat missions on the flimsy excuse they work for SOE or OSS. Mandy works the dark underbelly of Cairo every day as a counterintelligence agent for SIME," Brandy said. "Veronica recently completed parachute training so she can be qualified in the event she needs to parachute in someplace to arrange the extraction of evaders. Women are actively participating in this war—but we have to fight our own military for the right to do our part."

Col. Randal said, "Pam and Beverly have been grounded from flying ground attack missions."

Brandy said, "I shall go over your head for authorization if you make me."

"That's your prerogative. Get yourself killed. Won't be on my conscience."

Brandy said, "When I do reach out for permission, you know you shall not be able to stay mad for long—you love me."

"That's true," Col. Randal said. "Who're you planning on going over my head to?"

Brandy laughed. "I have no idea. No one understands Raiding Forces' chain-of-command. Not even you."

Beverly said, "When you figure out how to go over Johnny's head, Pam and I want to know. It's not fair of him to bench us."

Brandy handed Col. Randal her bottle of oil, "Do my back, handsome."

Col. Randal said, "Love to."

Captain Roy Kidd walked out to the pool. He and Col. Randal took chairs under one of the umbrellas Lady Jane was supposed to be sitting under. Capt. Kidd said, "You wanted to see me, sir?"

Col. Randal said, "Report to Colonel Stone in Alexandria. Major Slater is taking over Sea Squadron. We'll be raising two more Sea Squadron-type units. You commanded Duck Patrol longer than anyone, so your input will be invaluable during the reorganization.

"Create the job you want for yourself while you're at it, Roy."

Capt. Kidd said, "Outstanding, sir!"

Col. Randal asked, "That a new pistol in your chest holster?"

Capt. Kidd said, "Yes, sir. Jack knew how much I liked Lugers, but they aren't reliable enough. He asked King to have a Swiss Army 9mm Lahti L-35 Valmet—an improved cold weather P-08—shipped to me from Switzerland through Spain to Cairo. The Finns used 'em in their Winter War with Russia.

"Never jams."

Col. Randal said, "I'd like to fire it when there's time. Right now, get yourself to Alexandria. Take Sergeant Major Mikkalis with you. 'March or Die' has spent as much or more time with Duck Patrol as you have."

"Yes, sir."

Mandy Paige came out to the pool in her swimsuit, looking like Lady Jane's younger sister. Captain "Geronimo" Joe McKoy arrived shortly after. He took the chair Capt. Kidd had vacated under the umbrella and broke out a couple of Waldo Treywick's custom-rolled cigars.

Col. Randal said, "Donovan is impatient for us to commence operations in the Congo. You have any thoughts?"

Capt. McKoy said, "I do, John."

Col. Randal looked over to the chaise lounges and made eye contact with Mandy. She said something to Beverly. The two girls stood up, walked over and took seats under the umbrella.

Capt. McKoy said, "My men have been workin' the Belgian Congo pretty hard and they've got an idea what's goin' on. I told you about the river where the locals dig shallow holes and find diamonds. The way it works is the natives dig 'em. Then they sell 'em to middlemen who in turn sell the stones to smugglers who slip 'em out of the country. What happens after that I don't really know . . . but it doesn't matter much.

"Our plan is to become the middlemen and cut 'em off at the pass."

Mandy said, "We purchase the diamonds from the pot holers for a song. Then we transport the stones to Cairo where we sell them for an outrageously inflated price on the black market to smugglers. Then we chase down the smugglers and recover the diamonds when they try to move them out of the country.

"Pretty clean business model, Captain—quite the entrepreneur."

Capt. McKoy said, "Well, it ain't goin' to be as easy as it sounds. My boys believe the middlemen could actually be Nazi undercover agents who might not take our steppin' in and buyin' up all the stones lying down. The Belgian Congo Colony is a cesspool a' war profiteering—corruption with the earmarks of some downright treason. The colonial authorities are corrupt. The military, well, they ain't even an organized body a' men, being a bunch-a' thugs in uniform. We ain't gonna be able to count on help from them or from local law enforcement.

"The Chief of Police in Léopoldville is alleged to be the kingpin of the whole diamond smugglin' operation."

Beverly said, "I thought the Belgians were on our side."

Capt. McKoy said, "Where diamonds get involved, the deal gets real complicated real quick. Ain't no sides to it exceptin' the money side. Don't matter who occupied your mother country—Nazi Germans or moon men."

Mandy said, "The diamond smuggling ring is not going to be pleased when we start buying up all the stones and corner the market."

"Not a problem," Col. Randal said. "Orders from the top are to shoot the smugglers out of hand."

Mandy said, "When we do, we will be destroying the middlemen's clients. Probably not going be happy either. Especially if they actually are in the pay of the Nazis."

Capt. McKoy said, "Could get downright Western."

Col. Randal said, "Let's bring in Dick Courtney to set up a clandestine security force to protect our buyers. Harry grew up in Africa. He was in the Gold Coast Border Police when I recruited him for Raiding Forces during OPERATION LOUNGE LIZARD."

"Dick's a good man," Capt. McKoy said.

"OK, so we'll be buying sparklers in Cairo, Tangiers, and along some remote river in the Congo," Beverly said. "Daddy says it's the heart of darkest Africa."

Capt. McKoy said, "He ain't wrong about that."

Beverly said, "Diamonds have to be graded to establish the price. How are we supposed to know what to pay for 'em?"

It was a good question.

Mandy said, "Preston lived in Paris working for Cartier before the war. He knows everything there is to know about jewelry. Pres will have an answer for us."

Col. Randal said, "Track down Captain Butterfield—get him in here."

Major Zargo arrived poolside. Capt. McKoy departed for town. Mandy went inside to call RFHQ to locate Captain Preston Butterfield III and have him flown to Cairo. Beverly went back to her chaise lounge to work on her tan.

Col. Randal said, "What are you doing here, Major?"

Maj. Zargo said, "The Sudan Defense Force is transporting my Greek Sacred Squadron to Oasis X by truck as we speak. There are two officers in the city I have an interest in recruiting. While I was here, it seemed an opportune time to obtain your approval for our Table of Organization."

Which reminded Col. Randal, he needed to talk to Major Jack Merritt about his intentions for future employment now that Raiding Forces was leaving the desert. Officially, he was assigned to the Sudan Defense Force. Maj. Merritt was near the end of his two-year tour with the SDF.

Col. Randal said, "Let's hear what you've come up with."

Maj. Zargo said, "I have decided to organize my command into three 'Commandos,' each identified by the first letter of a Greek God. M for Mars, C for Chaos and K for Kratos—the God of strength and power. No enemy will ever be able to determine our true numbers based on those unit names alone."

Col. Randal said, "That is a fact."

"I have been considering your generous offer to arm and equip my men with U.S. Army-issue weapons and equipment. The Greek Sacred Squadron will be pleased to accept. We request your permission to adopt enemy weapons or other items of equipment we deem suitable for our purposes."

Col. Randal said, "Absolutely. You have a free hand. Tell me what you need. I'll try to make it happen."

Maj. Zargo said, "It was very insightful of you to allow my refugee Greeks to form their own unit instead of trying to integrate them into existing Raiding Forces formations piecemeal as replacements. We are about to embark on a long fruitful endeavor together, Colonel."

"I thought we were already on one."

Maj. Zargo said, "Not such as this."

After he left, Col. Randal joined Mandy and Beverly on a lounge.

Mandy said, "'Beware of Greeks Bearing Gifts.' Hilarious motto. Mr. Zargo is full of surprises."

Beverly said, "Scares me."

Col. Randal said, "He scares me too."

Brigadier Raymond J. Maunsell, who liked to be called "R. J.," arrived. He and Col. Randal took seats under the umbrella.

R. J. said, "I wanted to drop by and check on Lady Jane. Appears to be enjoying her escape from the hospital. Not certain that floating on a raft in the pool was exactly what the doctor had in mind when he released her, but she certainly seems to be having fun."

Col. Randal said, "You didn't drive all the way out here to see Lady Jane poolside, R. J."

"You might be wrong. This pool has the best scenery in Cairo."

Col. Randal said, "There is that."

R. J. said, "I do have one thing, Colonel. Well, actually two, to discuss. As you know, my Security Intelligence Middle East is a labyrinth of highly classified agencies. One of them, separate and apart from MI-6, is Secret Intelligence."

Col. Randal said, "I've never asked what you do exactly, R. J. However, I am aware of your SI work."

"I understand Raiding Forces is making plans to relocate, at least in part, to Castelrozzo."

"We are."

R. J. said, "SIME would very much like to place an observation post on the island. Never hurts to keep tabs on the Turks. One can always hope they will eventually enter the war on our side—possibly, possibly not."

"Not a problem," Col. Randal said. "Let Captain Fawcett-Tatum know RFHQ needs to support your people. She'll take care of 'em."

"Eventually, I shall be wanting to place agents on some of the other Dodecanese Islands all the way up to the Adriatic Sea. Can I count on you to help make that possible as well?"

Col. Randal said, "You can."

"Always a pleasure, Colonel."

Col. Randal said, "Anytime—I don't say that to everyone, Brigadier."

R. J. said, "I know."

Major Clive Adair, the Phantom Squadron Commander, showed up shortly after R. J. left.

Col. Randal said, "Raiding Forces is in the process of winding down operations at the Oasis."

Maj. Adair said, "A pity. I have enjoyed my tour being the 'Mayor' of X."

Col. Randal said, "Your new assignment is to be the Mayor of Castelrozzo—dramatic change of scenery, Clive."

Maj. Adair said, "Castelrozzo?"

Col. Randal said, "It's the easternmost island in the Dodecanese chain in the Aegean Sea. You'll be working with the Greek inhabitants. We're going to need your Phantom operators to set up long-range communications for our raiding parties, who'll be operating against the islands west in the Aegean."

Maj. Adair said, "I have no idea where Castelrozzo or the Dodecanese Islands are located, Colonel."

Col. Randal said, "Neither did I before we jumped on the place. Report to Admiral Ransom in Alexandria. He'll get you wired in on what's in store for the future. We are going to need Phantom's long-range communications."

Next to arrive was Major A. W. Sammy Sansom, Chief of Cairo Security Police. He waved at Mandy, his counterintelligence protégée, then took a chair under the umbrella with Col. Randal.

Maj. Sansom said, "You called, Colonel?"

Col. Randal said, "Tell me what just happened in Alexandria."

"There were five major crime lords operating in Egypt. You shot one of them," Maj. Sansom said. "Two unknown assailants attempted to murder Lady Seaborn. The remaining four crime lords were rounded up and harshly interrogated by Egyptian Security. You gave them seven days to find out who ordered the hit . . ."

Col. Randal said, "I know all that."

Maj. Sansom said, "In the murky world of Middle Eastern crime, if one major player is killed or sent to prison, another takes his place. Unlike in America where crime bosses often continue to run their criminal empires from behind bars. When the Big Five was reduced by one, it was only a matter of time before another criminal stepped up.

"There is the possibility the man in Alexandria who put himself forward was not acceptable to the Big Four."

Col. Randal said, "Really?"

"Quite likely, actually."

Col. Randal said, "And that's all you know?"

"I laid out the facts with one possibility," Maj. Sansom said. "We may never ascertain what transpired—to whit, if the man who ordered the assassination of Lady Jane is dead or not. The Big Four will never tell."

Col. Randal said, "Thanks for dropping by."

"If any new information develops, you will be the first to know, Colonel."

"Thanks."

Maj. Sansom said, "I have an undercover job in the works. Your two slave girls would be extraordinarily useful to set a honey trap. Do I have your permission?"

Col. Randal said, "Rita and Lana are not my slaves. Talk to Mandy. If the girls agree, I want her to be their handler."

"Mandy was already penciled in for the assignment," Maj. Sansom said.

After the security policeman left, Lady Jane swam over to the shallow end of the pool and walked up the steps, squeezing the water out of her mahogany hair. She came over to the umbrella. As usual, Col. Randal had trouble remembering to breathe in and out when she was in his immediate proximity.

Lady Jane said, "We are supposed to be relaxing, having fun celebrating my prison break. All you have been doing is sitting in meetings or flirting with Beverly. Enough. I require personal attention—bring it, stud."

Lady Jane had clearly been picking up on Beverly's Texas slang.

Col. Randal said, "That's a sexy little scar on your stomach."

Lady Jane said, "Not nearly as sexy as yours where the lion tried to eat you."

Col. Randal wondered if she had any idea of the effect she had on him.

COLONEL JOHN RANDAL WAS IN THE MASTER BEDROOM OF THE suite Major the Lady Jane Seaborn kept at Mena House Hotel. He was studying a map. Lady Seaborn was reclining on the bed wearing oversized white silk pajamas, idly leafing through a copy of *Hollywood Reporter* looking at the photographs of movie stars. She was thinking she might have overexerted herself this afternoon, though wild horses would not have been able to drag that admission out of her.

The two were enjoying each other's company.

Col. Randal had a ruler. He measured the distance from Alexandria to Castelrozzo and compared it to the scale on the map—342 miles. That was a long way by ship, considering the Royal Navy did not have enough surface transports to handle their own needs. Not much chance the navy would support some crazy special operation on a tiny island no one had ever heard of.

While Castelrozzo was only a mile or so off the Turkish coast, it was in the middle of nowhere. There were good points and bad points to its isolation. The good was the Germans and Italians would most likely not go to very much trouble to attack the place since Panzerarmee Afrika had been pushed out of Egypt. The bad was that the island would be difficult to supply unless some arrangement could be made with the Turks to purchase non-military items that did not violate their neutrality.

That might prove tricky. Col. Randal searched for some other place to stage supplies. The best he could locate was Paphos, located on the western coast of Cyprus. He measured the distance—186 miles. Still a long way, but better. He was pretty sure Vice Admiral Sir Randolph "Razor" Ransom had already done this calculation and reached the same general conclusion he had.

Sea Squadron could establish a rear echelon base at Paphos to shuttle supplies to Castelrozzo. He measured the distance to Alexandria—284 miles. Paphos had a port. The map did not indicate if it had an airstrip or not. Col. Randal needed to check that out.

Being able to fly supplies to Paphos, then offload them onto a ship for the trip to Castelrozzo would make supplying the island a lot easier. Even so, the logistics were going to be more difficult than supplying Oasis X, which could be reached by Major Jack Merritt's Sudan Defense Force convoys traveling overland. Raiding Forces was transitioning to a navy war.

The idea was going to take some getting used to.

For the past two and a half years, Col. Randal had been commanding units that rode mules or gun jeeps. The Sea Squadron navy consisted of three PTBs— actually two, since Admiral Ransom had shanghaied one of them for his personal use—an MGB, a MAS boat and a Landing Craft Tank (LCT). By any standard, it was a mongrel outfit.

Four small boats in a big sea. And, the Axis had air superiority.

The LCT was too slow for long-range raiding because of the need to make the round trip to and from the target during the hours of darkness. There was not likely going to be a need to transport Duck Patrol's gun jeeps to the Dodecanese islands—some did not even have roads. Royal Navy Volunteer Reserve Acting Provisional Sub-Lieutenant Skipper "Warthog" Finley was not likely to be satisfied with a rear echelon assignment commanding what he was sure to describe as a "banana boat" now that he had a taste of commanding a warship.

Col. Randal knew he was going to have to deal with that problem. What to do?

Beverly tapped on the door, "Mr. Treywick is here."

Lady Jane said, "Can you bring chairs in here? I would love to hear about Waldo's trip."

Col. Randal said, "Can do."

Captain "Geronimo" Joe McKoy, Captain Billy Jack Jaxx, King and Mr. Treywick came in, carrying chairs. Beverly Blackwell and Mandy Paige climbed on the bed with Lady Jane. Col. Randal closed the door. This was a private diamond interdiction meeting.

Col. Randal said, "We need a cover name for this group."

Lady Jane said, "Why not CARD GAME?"

Capt. McKoy said, "Pretty good, Lady Jane. Won't make anyone suspicious. Somebody might be inclined to believe you've had yourself a little secret intelligence experience."

Lady Jane rewarded him with one of her heart attack smiles. She had served in both MI-6 and SOE. Both intelligence organizations had sent her to practically every spy school they had to keep her occupied and out of danger, having no intention of using a high-profile member of the aristocracy on clandestine missions.

Col. Randal said, "Tell us your story, Mr. Treywick."

Waldo said, "I flew to Canada on a Royal Canadian Air Force C-47 transport with all them bags a' gold coins. Donovan came up and we met at what the OSS is callin' Camp X—I think they copied our Oasis X some. Wild Bill wanted to make sure everything went all right and it did.

"The coin auction off went smooth as silk. All done over the telephone. The cash was wired to one-a' the banks in New York that Lady Jane's man recommended.

"As soon as the money was in the bank, I flew to New York. Mr. Harry Winston, the world-famous jeweler, met my plane and escorted me to the Diamond District—he's an advisor on the OSS payroll. Harry supervised the purchase of a bag a' sparklers for us to resell back here on the black market."

Waldo reached into the pocket of his tailor-made suit—for an ex-slave, former ivory poacher who had bummed around the worst parts of Africa most of his adult life, he wore his money well. He pulled out a velvet bag and tossed it on the bed next to Lady Jane.

She picked it up and poured out a stream of glittering stones.

Lady Jane said, "Well done, Mr. Treywick."

Waldo said, "Red walked me around customs onto a Flyin' Clipper with those in my pocket and here I am."

Col. Randal said, "Nice job, Mr. Treywick. Did General Donovan have anything for us?"

Waldo said, "Not really . . . other than the man is hot to trot for us to get LEAF EATER goin'. Brought up the Belgian Congo more 'n a couple a' times. Seems real interested in the place for some reason."

Capt. McKoy said, "He mention Tangiers at all?"

Waldo said, "No, but I did. Got to be a good market for us. Donovan didn't have much to say about it—don't make sense."

Col. Randal said, "Nothing about LEAF EATER makes sense."

Lady Jane said, "What do you mean, John?"

"Why would OSS focus on the diamonds flowing out of the Congo and Cairo but not Tangiers? Why would Donovan allow us to take control of the black market in diamonds, sell them and keep the profits?"

Capt. McKoy said, "Lettin' us keep the cash money has been botherin' me from day one."

Capt. Jaxx said, "Donovan is bribing us to guarantee our silence—forever."

Waldo said, "I, for one, am perfectly willin' to keep quiet as a church mouse but what is it I'm supposed to be keepin' quiet about?"

Capt. McKoy said, "If it's a bribe, like Jack says, it's big money. Serious money. None of this deal adds up.

"We've got to be missing somethin'."

Lady Jane said, "Agreed. But allowing CARD GAME to keep the proceeds is not part of it. OSS has created the textbook-perfect, off-the-book, self-financing, clandestine operation. LEAF EATER buying and selling diamonds does not cost OSS, the U.S. Army or any other government agency anything. No one cares about the money because it does not officially exist."

Capt. McKoy said, "You ain't wrong there."

"One more thing, LEAF EATER is a 'black operation,' Lady Jane said. We may never discover its true purpose. There is the possibility the operation has *nothing* to do with diamonds."

Brandy tapped on the door, "Captain Butterfield has arrived."

Col. Randal said, "Send him in."

Captain Preston Butterfield III, the commander of Blue Patrol, walked in carrying a chair. Captain Pamala Plum-Martin had flown him in from where his patrol was operating deep inside Libya. He had no idea why he was in Lady Jane's bedroom. It was the last place he imagined he would end up when the Vargas Girl-looking Royal Marine pilot plucked him out of the field and flew him to Cairo.

Col. Randal said, "We have an operation you're uniquely qualified to advise us on, Captain. First, I have to ask, are you willing to volunteer for an assignment which will require you to join an American unit so secret even its initials are classified?"

Capt. Butterfield said, "Not if it means I have to leave Raiding Forces, sir."

Col. Randal said, "It won't."

Capt. Butterfield said, "In that case, yes, sir. Perfectly willing. Sign me up."

Col. Randal said, "Welcome to the Office of Strategic Services. I'm the senior OSS Special Operations Officer in this part of the world—that's classified. From time to time, elements of Raiding Forces carry out OSS missions, but they are never aware of who they're working for."

Waldo asked, "Ain't you gonna swear him in like you did me and Joe?"

Capt. McKoy said, "That was a joke, Waldo."

Col. Randal said, "I'm going to give you the short version of a complex story, Preston. We'll fill you in on the details later. First, I need to know—can you appraise diamonds?"

Capt. Butterfield said, "Yes, sir. When I was living in France, I worked for Cartier in Paris after my family cut me off for being a playboy. I was supposed to be there to study French instead of going to Harvard. Rich parents do that to force their children into line. Not me. I landed a job and kept right on partying. The boyfriends of the dancers at the Folies Bergère were my best clients—Hollywood's A-list.

"Cartier liked having an American on their staff. They sent me to school to learn diamond grading and appraisal. It's not all that complicated. All you have to do is master the 4 Cs.

"Then the Russians invaded Finland . . ."

Col. Randal said, "A river runs through the heart of jungled Africa. Along a certain stretch, diamonds are found on the banks or in shallow holes dug by the local natives—they're called 'pot holers.'

"The natives sell the diamonds to buyers who sell them to smugglers. The smugglers somehow manage to secretly move the stones out of Africa to sell to the Nazis.

"How would you put a stop to that program?"

Capt. Butterfield said, "I'd buy the diamonds from the pot holers direct, sir, cut out the middlemen buyers, which would dry up the supply for the smugglers to sell to the Nazis—disrupt the system."

It did not go unnoticed in the room that he outlined the same plan as Capt. McKoy had drawn up.

Col. Randal said, "How difficult would it be to make that happen?"

"All we would have to do is set up a network of buyers, sir."

Col. Randal asked, "Can you arrange for qualified diamond buyers on the scale we need? Men capable of operating in a hostile jungle environment?"

Capt. Butterfield said, "You're talking about the Belgian Congo—we knew about the pot holers at Cartier before the war. Only difference, sir—in those days the smugglers were making illicit diamond sales to jewelers and cutting out DeBeers.

"The Diamond Company was furious. There was talk of hiring an army of mercenaries to put a stop to it. The chairman of the board, Sir Harold

Oppenheimer, believes any diamond found anywhere in the world belongs to DeBeers.

"The way the system in the Congo works is the middlemen buy the diamonds from the pot holers for virtually nothing—as in pennies. You don't need sophisticated diamond appraisers to do that. All you need is money. The trick will be to pay a few cents more than the middlemen are paying so that the natives sell all of their stones to us.

"You realize, sir, once we start, there's going to be a war."

"Col. Randal said, "I intend to have Captain Courtney set up a security force to deal with that contingency."

Capt. Butterfield said, "I would have thought you might have preferred the services of my ex-French Foreign Legionnaires in Blue Patrol for the job, sir. Once you start cornering the diamond market in the vast remoteness of the Congo, things are going to turn ugly fast.

"Hard men and extreme measures will be required."

Col. Randal said, "I have another assignment for you, Captain."

BRANDY TAPPED ON THE DOOR AGAIN AND OPENED IT A CRACK, "Veronica is here to see you, John."

Colonel John Randal stepped out into the living room. Veronica Paige, Chief of MI-9 Escape, had just arrived—she worked for him. He clicked on the instant he saw the look of urgency on her face.

Veronica said, "MI-9 received a priority request from Admiral Cunningham, Commander-in-Chief, Mediterranean Fleet, to extract an evader in hiding on an island in the Aegean. Approximately eighteen months ago, the submarine *Perseus* went missing off the island of Aetos. The admiral is anxious to find out the cause of its loss and learn any information that might prove useful about why the sub disappeared.

"We have learned through our network of informers that one able-bodied seaman managed to survive and swim ashore. He has been hidden on Aetos ever since by the local Greek islanders. Our information is that the sailor is not in good health.

"In light of the fact Admiral Cunningham is anxious to recover him, I drove to Alexandria and spoke with Admiral Ransom's staff. The Razor's operations officer informed me Admiral Ransom and Lieutenant Seaborn were at sea en route to Castelrozzo aboard MGB 345.

"Since that would be the best place to stage a rescue attempt from, I caught the first flight back to Cairo and came straight here. I would dearly love for MI-9 to do this favor for Admiral Cunningham. We would be making a friend in a high place."

Col. Randal said, "How far is Aetos from Castelrozzo?"

Veronica said, "Approximately two hundred and thirty miles."

Col. Said, "Any idea how big the island is?"

"Slightly less than thirty square miles."

Col. Randal said, "Signal Admiral Ransom I'll be arriving at Castelrozzo with a SOG team later this evening. Ask him to have Lieutenant Seaborn standing by to provide transport to Aetos. Contact Major Zargo and tell him we need a Greek speaker who is willing to land ashore and help pinpoint the location of the evader.

"Inform Pam we need a Walrus ready to fly—now."

Veronica said, "I want to go along to observe, Colonel."

Col. Randal said, "It's your mission."

Veronica said, "From the moment I rode up to your HQ at RAF Habbaniya—the day Mandy was injured—I knew you were a man worth being associated with."

Col. Randal said, "That's not true. You said, 'I thought you would be bigger'."

Veronica laughed. "Only because of the stories Mandy was telling me—made you sound about seven feet tall."

Col. Randal went back in the master bedroom, "Jack, round up an eight-man SOG team. Beverly, get with Pam. We're flying as soon as you two can get to the dock and complete your preflight. Destination, Castelrozzo."

The meeting broke up quickly after that.

Col. Randal said, "Captain McKoy, you and Mr. Treywick give Captain Butterfield a full briefing on LEAF EATER while I'm away. We'll continue this conversation when I get back. Set a meeting with the Big Four—I don't need to be there. Time for Mr. Big to introduce the Captain as the man who'll be establishing the price for what we'll pay for diamonds here in Cairo."

After everyone cleared the room, Col. Randal said, "What did you mean LEAF EATER might not have anything to do with diamonds?"

Lady Jane said, "It's complicated. I shall explain when you return. Take care, John."

Beverly and Capt. Jaxx left first in one of the Mena House Hotel cars. Capt. Plum-Martin was to meet her at the dock. Col. Randal, King and Veronica were right behind in Lady Jane's Rolls-Royce. They had a long way to go and time was short.

Lieutenant Clint Hays, Lieutenant Eddy Ryder, Master Sergeant Mack Beckwith, the Lovat Scouts and two SOG operators were already assembled when Flanigan pulled up. MSgt. Beckwith had thought to bring Col. Randal's 9mm Beretta MAB-38 submachine gun, as well as his Brixia 45mm shoulder-fired mortar. He saw no reason not to be prepared.

Col. Randal said, "Thanks, Sergeant Major."

There was only one hiccup. Major Zargo had not been located. There was no Greek speaker from his Sacred Squadron at the pier.

Veronica said, "I am fluent in Greek."

Col. Randal said, "You were always going to figure some way to go ashore. Did you even *try* to find Maj. Zargo?"

Veronica said, "Not very hard."

Col. Randal ordered, "Load up."

The troops had barely taken their seats in the Walrus before Beverly, in the left seat because Capt. Plum-Martin had been flying earlier in the day, was taxiing for takeoff. Everyone on board did what experienced military types do when the opportunity presents itself—went to sleep.

Col. Randal's eyes came open after what seemed like only a few minutes but was in fact over two hours. The pitch of the engine had changed. Beverly was preparing to land in the bay at Castelrozzo.

The Walrus splashed down and taxied up to the beach. Ensign Theodore Hamilton, *aka* "The Great Teddy", was waiting to put a camouflage net over the airplane. The idea was to maintain as low a profile on the island as possible— not that they were fooling anyone. Especially not the Turks.

The troops disembarked and were immediately led to MGB 345. Vice Admiral Sir Randolph "Razor" Ransom was standing by at the gunboat with his grandson, Lieutenant Randy "Hornblower" Seaborn. He wanted a word with Col. Randal as the troops loaded on board.

VAdm. Ransom said, "You will only have a short time to be ashore on Aetos. Randy has to be well away before sunrise. The Italian Air Force has control of the skies in this part of the world. Do not take the threat lightly, Colonel. The Regia Aeronautica is very aggressive in the Dodecanese."

Col. Randal said, "Roger, sir."

THE SEA WAS GLASSY SMOOTH WHEN MGB 345 SLIPPED OUT OF the bay and into the open waters. The sun was going down in spectacular colors. It seemed entirely too picturesque to be departing on a dangerous mission. However, with little actionable intelligence and no knowledge of enemy forces on Aetos, that is exactly what they were doing—extremely high risk.

As MGB 345 pounded toward the sunset, Col. John Randal asked, "How long's it going to take to get there?"

Lieutenant Randy "Hornblower" Seaborn said, "Approximately six hours, sir."

Col. Randal said, "Seems like old times, Hornblower."

Lt. Seaborn said, "A pleasure for us to be working together again, sir. I have put in a lot of sea time since our first missions out of Seaborn House. Maybe we will not be flying by the seat of our pants quite as much this time around."

Col. Randal said, "Don't count on it. Your grandfather has his sights set on raising merry hell in the Aegean. Only I don't know what that means, exactly."

Lt. Seaborn said, "Neither do I, sir."

Veronica Paige joined them on the bridge. She was a talented equestrian who loved riding fast and the feel of wind in her hair. The Chief of MI-9, Escape, was clearly enjoying herself.

Col. Randal said, "Do you have a small pistol for your purse?"

Veronica said, "I have never been issued one."

Col. Randal produced his Browning M-51 .380. "Put this in your handbag in case of emergency. It's a present from Beverly—so whatever happens, don't lose it—I want it back. Try not to have to shoot anybody tonight."

Veronica said, "I am quite capable with a pistol."

"You're turning out to be almost as much trouble as Mandy."

Veronica laughed. "I shall take that as a compliment."

"It was."

Going below to rack out, intending to conserve his energy for who-knew-what was ahead, Col. Randal stretched out on a bunk across from Capt. Billy Jack Jaxx. "Do we have any pocket pistols left over from the collection at the crime boss's house?"

Capt. Jaxx said, "Yes, sir. Roy's got 'em."

"Remind me to give one to Veronica when we get back."

"Do you think there's any chance Mrs. Paige might consider posing for a picture for my pistol, sir?"

Col. Randal said, "I wouldn't press my luck, Jack."

Lieutenant Clint Hays, Lieutenant Eddy Ryder, Master Sergeant Mack Beckwith and King came down the narrow aisle and knelt on the deck between the two bunks. They were there to attend a brief leader's conference.

Capt. Jaxx said, "Any idea what's expected of us tonight, Colonel?"

Col. Randal said, "Aetos is approximately thirty square miles in size, so it's not exactly tiny. Reportedly a small Italian garrison is on the island. Also, it's my understanding there's a long-range radio station.

"The plan is to land on a beach three miles east of the town of Vourvoulos. We'll slip ashore and pick up an evader for MI-9. He's a Royal Navy sailor who escaped from a submarine lost at sea well over a year ago. There's a chance SOG won't even need to leave the boat."

Capt. Jaxx said, "That's it, sir?"

Col. Randal said, "I just brought your team along as Plan B in case something develops."

Everyone found a place to stretch out and in short order, the Raiding Forces contingent on board MGB 345 was sound asleep again.

Col. Randal's eyes came open when the pitch of the engines changed. He was sitting up by the time the sailor that Lt. Seaborn sent down to wake him arrived. MGB 345 had switched to its auxiliary engines for silent running, which meant they were off Aetos.

When he came up on deck, Col. Randal was immediately struck by the fact that it was an incredibly beautiful star-studded night. The lime green hands on the Rolex Lady Jane had given him read 0013 hours. Right on schedule, give or take a few minutes.

In the distance, the silhouette of the island began to swim into view. Aetos looked like it was floating on the water. MGB 345 purred steadily in toward the beach.

Veronica, who had spent the trip in Lt. Seaborn's cabin, was already on the bridge. For a woman getting ready to go ashore on an enemy-held island in the dark of night, she seemed remarkably composed. The Chief of MI-9 was studying Aetos through a pair of Royal Navy night glasses.

Col. Randal said, "Nice job, Randy. You found it."

Lt. Seaborn said, "Had a lot of practice lately, sir."

Veronica said, "I see the signal."

Capt. Jaxx arrived on the bridge.

Col. Randal said, "I'll be going ashore with King and Veronica. You stand by. If I signal the letters JC with my red filtered light, land your SOG team."

"Yes, sir."

Two sailors lowered a rubber assault raft over the side. A Lifeboat Serviceman followed it down and held it against the side of MGB 345 while Col. Randal, King and Veronica climbed in. At this point, the motor gunboat was standing only a hundred yards offshore. The moon was up, which flew in the face of conventional wisdom about when to schedule a clandestine naval operation; however, it made visibility less of an issue.

In no time, the raft was nosing up on the gently sloping beach.

There was only one person waiting to greet them—two were expected.

Veronica immediately initiated a conversation.

While she and the man were talking, Col. Randal said, "King, do you speak Greek?"

King said, "I understand the language better than I speak it."

Veronica said, "Colonel, we have a problem. My evader has been held in hiding in the attic of a house in Vourvoulos for nearly eighteen months. Because of the inactivity, he is too weak to walk the three miles to our location. Our contact has arranged for a donkey to ride but we have to go to the house in Vourvoulos where our man is hiding to retrieve him."

Col. Randal said, "Ask for a complete report on the location of all the bad guys."

Following an exchange, Veronica said, "There are forty Italian soldiers in their barracks in the town. Their commanding officer is sleeping with his mistress at a private residence nearby. Outside of town is the radio station I mentioned to you earlier. It is usually manned at night by two or three signalmen."

Col. Randal walked to the water's edge where the Lifeboat Serviceman was waiting. "Inform Lieutenant Seaborn there's going to be a delay—at least two hours."

"Sir!"

After flashing the signal to land the Raiders, Col. Randal spent the waiting time interviewing the Greek guide through Veronica as interpreter. When the rubber raft arrived, Capt. Jaxx and his SOG operators stepped out. MSgt. Beckwith handed Col. Randal his Brixia 45mm shoulder-fired mortar and pack with forty rounds in it.

Capt. Jaxx said, "Plan B reporting for duty, sir."

Col. Randal ordered everyone to gather around, explaining, "Our evader is too weak to walk, so we have to go retrieve him and bring him back on a donkey. While we're at it, let's pay a call on the Italian troop commander who is in a private residence with his girlfriend—it's on the way. Lieutenant Hays, you and Voight will drop off at the house, wait until you hear the sound of gunfire, then go in and capture him—make your way independently to the pickup point on the beach.

Lt. Hays said, "Yes, sir—Voight, you're on me."

Col. Randal said, "I'll drop off next at the troop barracks with Captain Jaxx, the Lovat Scouts and Komansky. We'll wait thirty minutes before we initiate our attack.

"That should give the guide, Veronica, and Sergeant Major Beckwith time to reach the house where the evader is standing by. They'll retrieve him and make their way back to the Extraction Rally Point on their own.

"King, you and Lieutenant Ryder will continue to march, following the main street north to a small hill on the far side of Vourvoulos, where the radio station is located. Take out the radiomen and destroy the signals station—Capt. Jaxx, redistribute the explosives to King and Lieutenant Ryder. After you take down the signals station, traveling independently, you three men move overland to the Extraction Rally Point.

"There's a curfew after dark. Anyone out tonight is a bad guy—act accordingly.

"Questions? No? We're moving in zero five. Let's do this."

Navigation was no problem. The party merely had to skirt the beach until they came to a pier and follow the road into town. King led out on point with the guide setting a fast pace, moving almost at the double time.

The mercenary had his 9mm Beretta MAB-38 submachine gun slung over on his back and was carrying his silenced .22 High Standard in both hands at the high port. Not that King expected to encounter anyone—friend or foe. The curfew kept civilians inside.

The Italians knew the Greeks hated them with a red-hot passion. The soldiers stayed inside after sundown for their personal safety. The Greeks would kill them if provided the opportunity.

Besides, in the two years the island had been occupied, there had not been one single enemy action of any kind. Military discipline suffered as a consequence. The likelihood of sentries being posted was virtually zero.

King halted the patrol. He whispered to Col. Randal, "Road straight ahead."

Everything was quiet. They watched a few minutes. Nothing.

Col. Randal whispered, "Move out, King."

Everyone except the guide was wearing rubber-soled, canvas-topped raiding boots. They made no sound on the cobblestone roadway. Raiding Forces ghosted into Vourvoulos.

Now the guide was walking with Col. Randal right beside him. He grabbed his arm and pointed to a house. Lt. Hays and 575th Ranger Private Dean Voight peeled out of the column and moved toward it.

King stepped off again, moving deeper into the town. Vourvoulos was under blackout restrictions. That did not stop the Greeks from burning oil lamps and candles behind their curtains. Occasionally a sliver of mellow yellow light could be seen through a crack.

After what seemed like a long, long time, but was in fact only a few minutes, the patrol came to the troop barracks. The building was a two-story rectangular frame structure that had been constructed on a vacant lot by the Italians using local labor.

Col. Randal pulled Veronica close, "I'm dropping you off here. You know what to do. Stick to the plan. See you at the boat."

Veronica whispered, "We could have sneaked in, picked up our evader, and slipped away home with no one the wiser."

Col. Randal said, "Nobody asked you to come along, Mrs. Paige. Next time, provide an interpreter—like I ordered you to."

King moved out with the remainder of the patrol.

Col. Randal huddled with his people in the shadow of the barracks. "Capt. Jaxx, you and Komansky move around and take up station at the back door. Fenwick, you're on the right side of the building, and Ferguson, you take the left. I'll be at the front.

"The signal to commence fire will be me putting a 45mm round through one of the front windows. We outnumbered by about ten to one. If the Italians get out of the building, we're in real trouble—light 'em up.

"On my command 'Rally,' everyone meet me here in the street. We'll travel down to the pier, then along the shore to the MGB.

"Move out."

Col. Randal stayed in the shadows and inspected his weapons while the rest of the team worked their way into position. He had his 9mm Beretta MAB-38 submachine gun, his silenced .22 High Standard pistol, 9mm Browning P-35 pistol, one 1911 Model 38 Super pistol and his 45mm Brixia light mortar modified to be fired from the shoulder. The 45mm grenades were in a backpack. He opened it so they were easily accessible—the idea being for him to be able to fire, eject a round, reach for a new one, load, bring the weapon back to his shoulder and launch another round without ever taking his eyes off the target.

The front door opened. An Italian soldier walked out, sat down on the steps, and lit a cigarette.

WHIIIIICH, WHIIIIICH, WHIIIIICH. The silenced .22 High Standard did not make a sound louder than a match being struck. The Blackshirt was dead before the second two rounds struck him. Col. Randal holstered the pistol, picked up his 45mm Brixia, glanced at the Rolex again, and fired a round through the open front door.

KAAAAABOOOOOM!

Windows on the ground floor shattered. An air raid siren began wailing somewhere. Men inside the barracks were screaming and shouting. Each of the SOG operators threw a hand grenade at a window, Scouts Fenwick and Ferguson were aiming for the second story. Submachine guns and chopped .30 BARs opened, sounding like a thunderstorm bursting.

The automatic weapons fire was continuous, perfectly disciplined and—in the still of the night—loud. There were only four Raiders, but they packed a lot of firepower. Up and down the street, panicked people could be heard yelling through the open windows of their houses as they ran for the nearest bomb shelter, which in most cases was their basement. Most of the citizenry and all the enemy military believed Vourvoulos was under air attack.

Col. Randal was firing methodically. He quickly developed a rhythm. He worked the downstairs floor of the troop barracks with 45mm rounds, then shifted his fire to the second level. His mortar rounds and the hand grenades being thrown by the SOG operators were shredding the interior of the structure with metal splinters.

After a while, the screaming coming from inside the barracks subsided. Col. Randal kept pumping rounds into the building. The ground level began to smolder. Then one of the walls started burning.

When he reached down, there was not another 45mm mortar shell. His pack was empty. Col. Randal felt surprised because it seemed like he had only been firing on the building for a minute or so. There was no way he could have depleted his entire supply of Brixia rounds, but he had.

Now the bottom floor was awash in flames. The fire was beginning to spread to the second level. As he watched and wondered how he had been able to fire so fast, the wooden barracks burst into a blazing inferno.

Because of the curfew, the Vourvoulos Volunteer Fire Department did not respond. The Greeks hated the Italians. They could put out their own fire.

In the distance, the radio station exploded.

Col. Randal shouted, "RALLY!"

The team assembled in the light of the roaring flames in a matter of seconds. Capt. Jaxx was jubilant. "That's what I call a takedown."

Col. Randal led the men down to the pier, turned left, then jogged along the shoreline. When they got to the MGB, Col. Randal found it hard to believe they were the last to arrive at the Extraction Rally Point.

The news was bad.

Lt. Hays reported first, "The Italian commander dived out a second-story window and escaped in the dark before we could make it upstairs, sir. He got away, sir."

King said, "When we entered the radio station, one of the Italians fired a single round from his pistol. Lieutenant Ryder was struck in the heart. He was dead before hitting the floor, Chief."

Eddy Ryder was one of the best and brightest junior officers in Raiding Forces. His troops respected him and everyone liked him. His loss was a crushing blow.

Col. Randal felt the absence of feeling he always experienced when one of his men was killed. He was not proud of it. But it was always the same.

Veronica said, "Our guide was hit in the stomach by a stray bullet on the way out of town. We managed to get him on the donkey with the evader. He needs immediate medical attention."

Col. Randal said, "Let's get the hell out of Dodge."

The Greek died on the row out to MGB 345.

10
YUMMY

COLONEL JOHN RANDAL WAS SITTING ON THE EDGE OF THE private pool at the suite Major the Lady Jane Seaborn kept at Mena House Hotel, dangling his legs in the water. There was a small crowd at the pool today, mostly women. Lady Jane, Brandy, Mandy and Beverly were on rafts arranged like a pinwheel, with their heads together so they could talk. Captain Penelope "Legs" Honeycutt-Parker was on a lounge on one side of the pool and Rikke "Rocky" Runborg was in one on the other side, chatting with Captain Pamala Plum-Martin. Rita and Lana were at the far end, face-down on lounges with the straps to their swimsuit tops unsnapped. They would not want tan lines to show when they were dancing at the Kit-Kat Club. Captain "Geronimo" Joe McKoy and Waldo Treywick were sitting in the shade of one of the umbrellas, smoking a couple of Waldo's custom-rolled cigars.

King came out of the suite with Commander Ian Fleming. He led the commander over to where Col. Randal was sitting, and then went back inside. Col. Randal stood up and walked with Cdr. Fleming to sit under the umbrella with Capt. McKoy and Waldo.

Waldo offered the suave naval officer a cigar, which he declined.

Col. Randal took one and stuck it between his teeth, unlit.

Across the way, Happy was tugging on one of Rita's dangling straps.

Cdr. Fleming was hoping for an invitation to join the fun; however, because Lady Jane's pool party was mainly for her girlfriends, one was not forthcoming.

Realizing this was a private Royal Marine event, he decided to state his business and shove off.

Cdr. Fleming said, "I dropped by to inform you that the documents you brought back from Aetos are priceless. Not the quality of what we hoped to find in the safe on Kupho, but still a significant treasure trove. My masters at the Admiralty have signaled me to convey their heartfelt appreciation."

Col. Randal said, "I lost one of my best officers obtaining them."

"Colonel, had Naval Intelligence known in advance you were going to attack the signals station on Aetos, they would have ordered you to execute the mission even if it cost a hundred men," Cdr. Fleming said. "The recovery of one critical document or piece of signals equipment can make it more than worth the sacrifice, so we have to take the risk.

"You are not cleared to know the details contained in the documents. However, knocking out the long-range radio station alone will result in countless Royal Navy lives saved, and who knows how many priceless ships."

Col. Randal said, "If Raiding Forces continues taking losses at our current rate, it won't be long before the outfit is broken beyond repair. Tell *that* to your masters at the Admiralty."

Cdr. Fleming said, "I shall—by the way, Y-Service intercepted a message from Crete you might find amusing. Seems a battalion of the 22 Air Landing Division stationed on the eastern tip of the island witnessed the lighthouse on Kupho go up. They reported to their division HQ that a volcano had erupted.

"Never bloody dawned on me that any man-made demolition could result in an explosion that extraordinary. Enjoy your afternoon, Colonel. A pleasure to see Lady Jane back to being her old self again."

Capt. McKoy and Waldo walked him out, intending to pour themselves a drink at the bar inside.

Shortly after they left, Captain Billy Jack Jaxx arrived poolside with the reigning Miss Nevada. Capt. Jaxx had called ahead to ask for Lady Jane's consent to bring a date. He was trying to get back in the USO entertainer's good graces after having left her standing at the bar at the Gezira.

Jack Cool was Lady Jane's favorite—permission granted.

Capt. Jaxx escorted Miss Nevada over. "Colonel, I'd like to introduce you to Vegas. People call her that because of the town she's from in Nevada—Las Vegas."

The USO entertainer was slim, dark tan, dark hair, dark eyes, big smile, white teeth—skintight swimsuit.

Vegas said, "Billy Jack has told me all about you."

Col. Randal said, "Yeah, like what?"

Vegas said, "All those scars—a souvenir of a one-night stand with a beautiful Nazi SS woman in the heat of passion."

"Jack said that?"

"Must have been a hot date."

Col. Randal said, "Be advised, Jack Cool's the type your mother warned you about."

Vegas said, "Yummy!"

Captain Preston Butterfield III walked out to the pool with Capt. McKoy and Waldo. His arrival had been eagerly anticipated. All the women—to include Rita and Lana, as soon as they got their tops back on—abandoned their lounges or got out of the pool and headed for the umbrella where Col. Randal was sitting. They pulled chairs up around the table. Capt. Butterfield was about to give a demonstration on how to grade diamonds.

It did not hurt that the captain looked like the dreamy-eyed Legionnaire staring off into the great unknown on a French Foreign Legion recruiting poster.

He was very good with women.

Capt. Butterfield said, "You may have heard of the four Cs—cut, color, clarity, and carats. Lady Seaborn has been so gracious as to allow me to use her diamond as a training aid, and I understand we have loose stones as well."

Lady Jane took off her ring and handed it to him.

Capt. Butterfield said, "Cartier, where I was employed before the war, grades diamond cuts as 'Cartier best grade, ideal cut, very good cut, good cut, and poor/fair cut.' The company never carries any stones graded poor/fair. Fewer than fifteen stones out of every ten thousand diamonds examined will qualify as Cartier best grade.

"The diamond cut is the most important feature to consider when establishing the value of a stone. When diamond cuts are made with the correct proportions, light is returned out the top of the diamond. Gemologists refer to the top or crown as the 'table.' The purpose of a high-grade cut is to gather and reflect the maximum light possible. The end result is brilliance, fire and sparkle.

Capt. Butterfield took out a jeweler's glass, screwed it into his eye and studied the Sheba diamond. "If cuts are too deep, light escapes out the side of the stone. Too shallow and it leaks out the bottom. Light performance is measured by the three factors I've already mentioned: brilliance, fire and sparkle.

"I have no idea by whom or when Lady Seaborn's diamond was cut. While it's called the Sheba diamond, the provenance on the stone is sketchy. I understand Colonel Randal obtained it in Abyssinia, which was Sheba territory. However, there's no historical evidence the queen of Sheba ever existed. If she did live, it would have been at least four hundred years before the first diamonds, as we know them today, were being cut.

"However, we don't know everything, and some of the ancient artisans were equal to or superior to modern-day craftsmen. Besides, it makes a great story. How many girls have a magnificent diamond named after a legendary queen whose fiancé shot dead the previous owner?"

The women all laughed.

"If you look closely, you will observe Lady Seaborn's stone blazes like it has a tiny bolt of lightning trapped inside. The sparkle almost blinds the eye. Without a doubt, the cut would be rated Cartier best grade.

"One of the finest examples of an artisan's work I've ever seen."

Capt. Butterfield passed the ring around.

"Diamond color is the second most important characteristic to consider when evaluating a stone. There are six categories on the color chart. We are getting into the weeds when we start talking about grading colors. Suffice to say, the top-rated diamond color is, in fact, virtually colorless—extremely rare. The higher the grade, the less color there is and the more expensive the stone.

"The Sheba Diamond is Cartier best grade white—no color.

"Now, that said, color can be a good thing. Only one in every ten thousand diamonds possesses natural color. The more intense the color, the rarer and more valuable the stone. Colored diamonds can be even more valuable than white diamonds. However, color is first and foremost a matter of personal taste—some people like it, some don't.

"When it comes to diamonds, ladies, money is not everything. Beauty is what counts—buy—or better yet, have your boyfriend or husband buy—what *you* like, not what some clerk in a jewelry store tells you is more valuable."

The women nodded.

"The next C is clarity. It's the least important factor when grading a stone. Most diamonds have microscopic inclusions or blemishes. What is important to remember is to select a stone that does not have any imperfections that can be seen through the crown without magnification."

Col. Randal noted Capt. Butterfield diplomatically chose not to point out any imperfections in the Sheba diamond.

"Last, but certainly not least, is size. And, as we all know, size is what it's all about when it comes to diamonds. What most people don't realize is that the term 'carat' refers to a stone's weight . . . not how large it is."

After Capt. Butterfield had spent half an hour discussing the various aspects of gemology, demonstrating with the stones Waldo had brought back from New York, most of the women drifted back to the pool. Lady Jane, Mandy and Beverly stayed, in the event the conversation might turn to CARD GAME.

Which it did.

Capt. McKoy said, "You know your sparklers, Preston."

Waldo said, "I always thought bigger was better."

Capt. Butterfield said, "Usually it is; what most people want is a lot of flash for little cash."

Col. Randal said, "Impressive performance, Captain."

"Smoke and mirrors, sir. Most people can't tell the difference in diamonds from two inches out," Capt. Butterfield said. "Individual stones wisely selected by a trained professional can be an excellent investment.

"Jewelry, on the other hand, once you buy a piece, it's like a new car—value goes down the minute you walk out of the shop. My guess is the Big Four will be bringing us a combination of jewelry and loose stones."

Capt. McKoy said, "Yeah, that's kinda what we figure's gonna happen. Probably we're gonna need to break down the jewelry to get the diamonds. Concealability bein' a real important factor for smugglin'."

Capt. Butterfield said, "My guess is you don't get to be the head of a major crime family by being stupid. The Big Four will most likely have everything appraised before they bring it to me. That means I'll need to come up with a reasonably accurate number to ensure my credibility."

"Maybe not as much as you'd imagine," Capt. McKoy said. "Those crooks are gonna expect us to cheat 'em some—wouldn't respect us if we didn't.

"Keep in mind, Preston, we're buyin' stolen jewelry or loose diamonds from criminals who don't have any choice but to sell to us. We'll be selling to brokers who are desperate to get their hands on product to smuggle to Europe.

"Some a' them stones is gonna end up in the hands a' the Nazi Germans unless we do somethin' about it, which takes fair business practice completely off the table."

Capt. Butterfield said, "So, you don't need me to actually appraise the stones—you only want me to set the price we're willing to pay?"

Waldo said, "You're a fast learner, Cap'n. Might be a future for you in crime."

Col. Randal said, "When you grade the diamonds, set aside the best of the best. We may not sell those."

Lady Jane said, "Marvelous. We should keep them."

Capt. Butterfield said, "I was going to suggest you consider something like that. On the other hand, you need to bear in mind, sir—diamonds are in a screaming seller's market. It's a bubble and it can't last forever.

"When LEAF EATER has run its course, you do not want get caught with a big inventory of rocks on your hands."

Col. Randal said, "Point taken."

"When the war's over, DeBeers is going to crack down hard on what they consider rogue diamond merchants, meaning anyone not working for them,"

Capt. Butterfield said. "Any jeweler anywhere in the world caught buying a consignment of stones from anyone besides an accredited agent of the Diamond Company will be blackballed for life.

"Never able to purchase another diamond from DeBeers—ruined financially."

Capt. McKoy said, "DeBeers plays hardball."

Col. Randal said, "Not as hard as we're going to."

Beverly and Mandy went back to the pool.

AS CAPTAIN PRESTON BUTTERFIELD III WAS LEAVING, HAVING made a date with Mandy for dinner, Major the Lady Jane Seaborn stopped him for a brief conversation. He took out a small pad from his breast pocket, jotted something down, tore the page out, folded it in half, then handed it to her. She opened it, smiled, and returned to her lounge.

Captain Billy Jack Jaxx left to join the girls at the pool.

Captain "Geronimo" Joe McKoy studied the end of his cigar, and said, "John, I've been doin' a little cogitatin'. You confident Dick Courtney's the right man to head up our security force in the Congo?"

Colonel John Randal said, "Why do you ask?"

"Nothin' against Dick—he's one-a' the best officers we've got," Capt. McKoy said. "Just—he's sorta a Boy Scout. The Congo's the bad part a' the world, wild and wooly with all the hair on.

"Ain't gonna be no Geneva Convention in the jungle, if you get my drift."

Col. Randal asked, "Who do you suggest?"

Capt. McKoy said, "Don't know offhand. I'd say Mike Mikkalis, but the Sergeant Major ain't gonna take the job. King would be real good, but you probably don't wanna give him up. Besides, after all that trouble with MI-6 over DeBeers, we probably best stick to Americans for as much a' the LEAF EATER field work as we can."

Waldo Treywick said, "Cap'n Butterfield could do it. May be a jewelry salesman, but he's tough cookie. Too bad we need him here in Cairo."

"I don't have anyone else," Col. Randal said.

Capt. McKoy said, "Might be Butterfield knows some American still servin' in the French Foreign Legion who'd like to volunteer?"

"Ask him. You're in charge of LEAF EATER in the jungled parts of Africa. You pick who you want, Captain."

Capt. McKoy said, "Waldo's not wrong about Butterfield. For an East Coast Ivy League playboy, he's seen hard duty. We can use him for more than just appraising diamonds."

Waldo asked, "Like what, Joe?"

"Once our merchandise gets in the hands of the traffickers, we're gonna need somebody reliable to run 'em to ground, recover it for us and eliminate the smugglers as per our orders from OSS. Captain Butterfield's the perfect fit for that job."

Col. Randal said, "Exactly."

As the two were getting up, Col. Randal said, "What about Frank Polanski for the Congo assignment?"

"Yeah, he'd be good," Capt. McKoy said. "Experience in the Marines during the 'Banana Wars.' Set himself up as a mercenary in Abyssinia before hooking up with us in Force N. I'll have a word with him."

Quoting Raiding Forces Rules, Waldo said, "Right Man, Right Job—I should-a' thought of Frank. He ain't squeamish."

Vegas walked by, talking to Beverly and Mandy, ". . . the Miss Nevada title's not as impressive as it sounds. Only thirteen towns in the whole state were big enough to enter contestants . . ."

Major Baltimore "Mongo" Farquhar, the commander of the Lancelot Lancers Raiding Regiment, meaning the Lancelot Lancers Yeomanry—the smallest cavalry regiment on the British Army's reserve list—arrived. He had been slated to take the place of his cousin, Lieutenant Colonel Sir Terry "Zorro" Stone, as the commander of the Raiding Regiment. That changed when the Greek Sacred Squadron arrived sooner than expected.

Maj. Farquhar took a seat at the table under the umbrella.

Col. Randal said, "Thanks for coming, Major."

Maj. Farquhar was a highly popular, extremely capable commander. He was known for saying '*etc.*' as many times as possible in any given sentence. Mongo was also a natty dresser. Today, he was impeccably turned out in a tailored uniform with a non-regulation silk houndstooth scarf at his throat.

Col. Randal said, "Raiding Forces is undergoing a re-organization. Eventually, your Lounge Lizards will be employed as amphibious raiders. Until then, what I want you to do is contact the 1st Airborne Division and make arrangements to have your people trained to land their gun jeeps by glider."

Maj. Farquhar was so astonished by the order that he did not say "etc." even one time. "By Jove, Colonel, I was not aware it was remotely possible to land a jeep by glider, what!"

Col. Randal said, "Apparently it is."

Maj. Farquhar said, "Where would one find the 1st Airborne Division, sir?"

Col. Randal said, "I have no idea. Somewhere in North Africa. Arrange for transport for your gun jeeps through Captain Fawcett-Tatum. She'll help once you find out where you're going.

"I want regular reports about the progress of your training."

"Sir!"

As Maj. Farquhar was leaving, Beverly walked out of the suite carrying an envelope that had just arrived by messenger.

Beverly said, "Incoming congratulatory messages. Do you want to read them or would you rather I do it for you?"

Col. Randal said, "Summarize 'em."

"The first is from Admiral Cunningham, 'Well-done . . . skill, daring, bold execution, decisive leadership . . . look forward to . . . future small-scale naval operations'."

"That's nice."

Beverly said, "Brandy told me her father and the Chief of Naval Operations Mediterranean Fleet are like competitors. Admiral Ransom has enjoyed rubbing Admiral Cunningham's nose in our capture of Castelrozzo."

Col. Randal said, "I never knew they were rivals."

Beverly laughed. "That's what you have me for—scandal."

"Make sure you're reporting it—not causing it."

"John . . . !"

Col. Randal said, "Tell Mandy I said for you two to quit making Miss Nevada feel so inadequate about her looks."

Beverly laughed again. "Hard not to love you, Johnny."

"Who's next?"

"Brigadier Menzies, chief of British Secret Intelligence Service: '. . . latest coup . . . impressive . . . high hope . . . long-standing relationship . . . water under bridge . . .'"

Col. Randal took the cigar from between his front teeth and shook his head. It was going to be a long time before the DeBeers controversy blew over. "Anybody else?"

Beverly said, "You're not getting into the spirit of these compliments. Two more to go. Rear Admiral Godfrey, Chief of Naval Intelligence Division—Ian's boss: '. . . hauled chestnuts . . . great job . . . bold action . . . Fleming advises you are our best hope . . . GOLDEN FLEECE'."

Col. Randal said, "I've never eaten a chestnut in my life."

Beverly laughed. "I don't think I've ever even seen one—OK, our last congratulatory message for today is from Brigadier General Donovan, OSS: '. . . bold . . . daring . . . made us proud . . . advise . . . provide . . . additional support . . . en route your location . . . inspect Castelrozzo . . .'"

Col. Randal said, "Reply to General Donovan: 'Send one hundred men who have completed basic ordnance training ASAP. Failing that, PURPLE will have to stand down. Raiding Forces needs the 575th Rangers currently being used for the assignment released back to my command for duty in the Aegean.'

"You understand what PURPLE is?"

Beverly said, "I do—the teams Hank Rawlston organized to lift the serial numbers off damaged or destroyed enemy tanks so OSS can estimate how many of them the Germans manufacture per month."

"Very good."

Beverly said, "Hope you don't mind my asking, but are you totally devastated by Eddy getting killed?"

Col. Randal lied. "I am."

"He was a nice boy. I liked him a lot."

Col. Randal said, "The war doesn't stop when one person goes down, no matter who it is."

It came out sounding more heartless than intended.

Beverly said, "That's so cold."

"I know."

When Beverly went inside to send Col. Randal's request to OSS Headquarters, Capt. Jaxx came over to the table. "I'm going to need a replacement officer, sir."

"I don't have anyone to give you."

"There's a couple of the 575th Ranger lieutenants who might work out, sir."

Col. Randal said, "Negative, Jack. You can't have 'em."

"Sir, I'm. . . ."

Col. Randal said, "At the rate things are going, we might not be able to afford SOG much longer. You've got the best men in Raiding Forces concentrated in one small unit. When we make the move to Castelrozzo, it may be time to spread the talent around."

"Colonel, SOG has to be on call to handle special intelligence missions like GOLDEN FLEECE/RED INDIAN and I need another officer."

"I know that, Jack, so figure out where you're going to find one—improvise, adapt, overcome, stud."

Capt. Jaxx said, "One of the 10th Ranger Battalion people handled himself pretty well at Port Lyautey Airfield—Lieutenant Chase Starrett."

Col. Randal said, "See if Lieutenant Starrett is interested. The only way this works is if Starrett volunteers for OSS. The 10th Rangers can't refuse the transfer if he does."

"Maybe we should send Beverly to Morocco to recruit him—guarantee success in advance."

Col. Randal asked, "Will Miss Nevada be making an appearance on your pistol grip sometime soon?"

"Affirmative, sir."

After he left, Mandy came over and took Jack Cool's chair. "Mother told me you said she was turning out to be as much trouble as I am."

"Roger, I said that."

"She also claims you snapped at her."

Col. Randal said, "Your mother made it impossible for me not to let her go ashore. Then in the middle of the mission, she decided she didn't care for my handling of the tactics. Pretty sure she blames me for Lieutenant Ryder's death."

"I doubt she blames you for Eddy. But you did turn a clandestine MI-9 rescue into a full-blown Commando raid," Mandy said. "You tend to do things like that on occasion, John."

Col. Randal said, "Once we learned we had to go into town to retrieve the evader, everything changed."

"Why?"

"There was no way I could *not* attack the barracks. If the alarm had been raised at any point, the bad guys could have stood to, given pursuit and wiped out our entire team," Col. Randal said. "Trying to capture the senior Italian officer on the island was a free shot, since the patrol had to walk right by the house where he was in bed with his mistress.

"The long-range radio station was a strategic target—I don't get to decide to pass on those."

Getting up to leave, Mandy said, "I shall talk to Mother. She is under the impression you may be angry at her."

"Not true—I'm probably her biggest fan."

BRANDY SEABORN CAME OVER AND SAT DOWN. "HAD A CHANGE of heart yet about letting me operate off Castelrozzo, handsome?"

Colonel John Randal said, "No, but you are right about the speed advantage. Your boat would have improved our time to and from the target during the hours of darkness. Did you hustle your son?"

Brandy laughed. "Me . . . do something like *that*?"

"Yeah, you would."

"I know you want my MAS boat at Castelrozzo, if for no other reason than because you like to have me around."

Col. Randal said, "That's true. Feel free to visit the island any time."

"This conversation is not over."

Ignoring her, Col. Randal said, "I learned a few things on our first mission. Island raiding is going to take some adjusting to. There's more to it than meets the eye."

"Parker and I have been conducting a map study of the Aegean. There are a great many tiny islands," Brandy said. "Not all of them are inhabited. Most are in sight of another island in the chain.

"Since the Luftwaffe and Regia Aeronautica have control of the skies, Raiding Forces can only operate Randy's MGB, my MAS boat or the PT boats under cover of darkness. Since Castelrozzo is on the extreme eastern end of the Dodecanese Islands, that is a problem.

"What it means, in practical terms, is having to travel to the island you intend to raid and land the raiding party ashore. Then, in most cases, the boat will have to make a high-speed run to the nearest uninhabited island before sunrise, camouflage itself and lay up during the following day. As soon as darkness sets in, the boat can return to pick up the Raiders."

Col. Randal took the cigar out from between his teeth, "Are you saying my men will be required to spend a full day on an island with no possibility of being extracted in the event things don't go well? Even if they take casualties or the bad guys show up for one reason or the other and land reinforcements?"

"Exactly."

"That's not good."

"Problem only intensifies the deeper we penetrate into the Dodecanese," Brandy said.

"What about staging from some other island farther west?"

"Not a good idea to move the Raiding Forces Forward Operating Base closer to islands where the Germans and Italians have airfields. Even worse, islands deeper in the Aegean are vulnerable to invasion by an Axis amphibious landing force or even a paradrop by the German 22 Air Landing Division," Brandy said. "Plus, we can expect highly aggressive patrolling by Kriegsmarine E Boats and Regia Marina MAS boats the closer we get to their home ports.

"Considering all those threats, resupplying and sustaining a more westerly Forward Operating Base from Castelrozzo becomes problematic."

Col. Randal asked, "You and Parker figure all that out by yourselves?"

"Not that hard."

Col. Randal said, "How would you like to be my Naval Operations Officer?"

Brandy laughed, flashing a Cartier best grade quality smile. "Nice try, handsome. Not a chance. My plan is to wear you down until you cave in and let me have my way. You can never resist me—not for long."

"Why are you trying so hard to get yourself killed?"

"Why are you?"

At that moment, Vice Admiral Sir Randolph "Razor" Ransom, Brandy's father, walked out of the suite to the pool area and headed for Col. Randal's umbrella.

"Hello, Father," Brandy said, as she stood to leave.

Col. Randal said, "Wait. Tell the Admiral what you just told me. I'd like to hear his reaction."

Brandy ran through her recital again. VAdm. Ransom listened intently.

"I am afraid Brandy is spot-on in her estimate of the situation, Colonel. Of all the threats she points out, enemy air controlling the skies over the Dodecanese creates the most dangerous problem. Neither the U.S. nor Royal Navy is willing to risk capital ships in the Aegean Sea because of it.

"We will be fighting what amounts to a small-scale, hit and run, navy guerrilla war, primarily at night, with nothing bigger than patrol boats. We are going to have to fight with what we have, not what we need," VAdm. Ransom said. "The Royal Navy does not possess the resources to provide us additional small craft and the U.S. Navy has discovered how valuable their PTs are in the Pacific. No more Lend Lease patrol torpedo boats any time soon as previously hoped.

"The Aegean AO has the lowest priority of any theatre in the war."

Brandy said, "What is your plan, Father—you always have one?"

VAdm. Ransom said, "The Levant Schooner Flotilla, which I described to Col. Randal earlier. When we were evacuating Crete, we had to use any bottom that floated. Even a fleet of caïques—which are Greek fishing schooners—were pressed into service.

"Recently, the Royal Navy has turned half the caïques they have over to Special Operations Executive. The other half has been reconstituted as the Levant Schooner Flotilla and assigned to me, in my capacity as Director of Naval Operations Irregular—Small Raids Inc. In turn, I am detailing the LSF to Raiding Forces."

Brandy said, "You are to have your own navy, John."

Col. Randal said, "I keep hearing that, but I don't even know what a caïque looks like, much less how to run a flotilla, sir."

VAdm. Ransom said, "In the past we had boats, but a shortage of crew, particularly officers, to man them. Now, so many of our ships have been sunk trying to interdict the supply of Rommel's troops by sea from Italy, we have sailors on the beach unemployed with no ships to assign them to. I have precisely the man to command the LSF for you—Lieutenant Commander Adrian Seligman—mentioned him to you before, as I recall."

Brandy asked, "You found someone willing to command a decrepit fleet of Greek fishing boats?"

VAdm. Ransom said, "Affirmative. Right Man, Right Job. Before the war, Seligman dropped out of Cambridge to spend two years circumnavigating the globe in a two hundred fifty-ton French fishing barkentine—accompanied by a small crew, his seventeen-year-old wife and a piano. Not long ago, he skippered a tanker, the *Oilshipper,* down the Turkish coast bound for Russia. Extraordinary sailor, top-notch navigator, he is something of an eccentric—should fit right in with Raiding Forces' band of cutthroats."

Col. Randal asked, "Lieutenant Commander Seligman commands the LSF and Raiding Forces supplies his rear echelon headquarters support and has the use of the caïques to transport raiding parties?"

"Lieutenant Commander Seligman works for you—takes Raiding Forces where it needs to go when it needs to go," VAdm. Ransom said. "All requests for the employment of any or all of the LSF—for any other mission in support of another agency—goes through you for approval."

"We can do that, sir."

"Unless, of course, I require a caïque or two for some task."

Col. Randal said, "Understood, Admiral."

"I shall have Commander Seligman report to you in the next day or two. He can give you a tour of LSF. Show you how the caïques are being modified to his specifications."

VAdm. Ransom left to check on the progress of the three motor launches under construction, which Brandy had rejected as being underpowered for her taste. They were months from being ready for sea trials.

Col. Randal asked, "Ready to trade your MAS boat for a caïque? I might rethink my no-combat policy."

Brandy laughed. "Top speed of eight knots, possibly less if the wind dies—dream on."

Col. Randal made eye contact with Beverly. She immediately returned to where he and Brandy were sitting. "Do you have any idea where to find Teddy?"

"He's staying at Shepard's Hotel."

"See if you can reach out for him."

Beverly said, "On the way."

Col. Randal turned back to Brandy. "Have you ever seen a caïque?"

"I have, and they do not have much to recommend—slow and ugly."

"Describe one."

Brandy said, "The average caïque is a motorized sailboat about thirty feet in length designed for fishing, weighs twenty tons or so, and for wartime service can be managed by a crew of five—the skipper, a stoker, a coxswain, a gunner and a wireless operator. There is no wheelhouse, which means whoever mans the tiller has to stand out in the open in all weather. The craft are usually powered by a twenty horsepower Bolinder diesel engine—which are fairly noisy for stealthy inshore work. The holds, which are designed to store the catch, can carry six or seven of your fully armed and equipped Raiders, provided they do not mind the smell of fish."

Col. Randal said, "When you're not rescuing evaders or working for SOE, I'm going to count on you to advise me on how to best employ our caïques."

"Love to."

Beverly came out of the suite. "Ensign Hamilton is on the way, Johnny."

Col. Randal said, "Brandy, when Ted gets here, I want you to sit in on our conversation."

As she was going back to the pool, Brandy said, "Aye, aye, sir."

Col. Randal made eye contact with Mandy. She came over to the table. "Couple of things for you ladies. We're missing something about LEAF EATER, and I want to know what it is. You two go to the library tomorrow and research the Congo. I want to know everything being exported from the colony."

Beverly asked, "Anything specific?"

"I have no idea," Col. Randal said. "Don't let anyone in the library know what you're doing. We don't want the word to get out that we're looking at the Congo."

Mandy said, "There's no security at the Cairo Public Library. If we find something, we can steal the book."

"How do you know about security at the library? What were you doing there?"

Beverly said, "Lady Jane has had us researching Castelrozzo. She's really excited that Raiding Forces is setting up a base on the island."

"Really," Col. Randal said. "Learn anything interesting?"

Mandy said, "Nothing except a convoluted history impossible to follow."

Col. Randal said, "On another subject—we need to find Teddy girls his own age to go out with. He's been hanging out at the Kit-Kat Club with Billy Jack."

Beverly laughed. "The captain is definitely a bad influence. I'm not sure how old Theodore is. He told me eighteen."

"He lied," Mandy said. "Teddy may be seventeen by now. Terry's father, the Duke, turned a blind eye to the army's age requirement and gave him a commission in the Lancelot Lancers nearly two years ago."

Col. Randal said, "You need to find him someone."

"There is a secondary school for the children of the expatriate families stationed in Cairo before the war started. The older girls would be about his age," Mandy said. "They should love to meet a decorated teenage war hero."

"Well, see what you can do."

Beverly said, "Maybe we can arrange for him to give a talk at the school. The Great Teddy can talk about camouflage, do magic tricks, wear his medals. He'll get the girls."

When Beverly and Mandy went back to the pool, Rita and Lana came and took their place. Col. Randal said, "What have you two troublemakers been up to?"

Big smiles. Naturally they would not speak to him because of a Zār Priestess vow they had made in Abyssinia. Col. Randal had not realized how much he missed having them around. The three had spent a lot of time together.

Rita and Lana were easy to talk to since all his conversations were one-way.

Brigadier Dudley Clarke put in an unexpected appearance. The commander of A-Force (Deception) sat down at the table. Rita and Lana vanished as silently as they had come.

Brig. Clarke said, "I drove straight here after a meeting at Grey Pillars. A decision has been reached on what to do about the Special Air Service now that David Stirling is in the bag. The unit will be split, with two-thirds of the men going to a Commando-type formation called the Special Raiding Squadron under the command of Major Paddy Mayne.

"The remainder of the men will be transferred to an amphibious raiding outfit called the Special Boat Section under Major the Lord George Jellicoe. The SBS troopers came out to Egypt trained to conduct beach reconnaissance missions from canoes. Typically, the staff at 'Muddle' East Command Headquarters, Operations Division, assigned them to the Special Air Service where they were employed as desert raiders in jeeps.

"Eventually, the plan is for the SBS to be attached to Raiding Forces, once Lord Jellicoe has completed its reorganization."

Col. Randal said, "How many men are we talking about?"

Brig. Clarke said, "A little over fifty. Possibly more later on."

"I'll take what trained men I can get."

"Here is what I require from you in return," Brig. Clarke said. "There is an island. A rather large one. There are three airfields located on it. In the near future, I need Raiding Forces to land a pair of ten-man parties by submarine and another ten-man party by parachute to attack the aircraft stationed on the landing grounds."

Col. Randal asked, "Are the airfields located near the coast?"

"Negative, the two parties landing by sea will have a five-day approach march, traveling at night and laying up by day. The parachute party will be able to land within a three-day—or should I say night—march to their target. A Royal Navy submarine will extract all three parties after they make their way to separate beaches following their attacks on the airfields.

"The name of the island is classified and will only be revealed immediately prior to the mission."

Col. Randal said, "You want three teams of Raiding Forces personnel, possibly augmented by the Special Boat Section, to invade a large, enemy-held island, travel three to five days to the objective without being discovered, attack it, and then spend another three to five days exfiltrating to separate pick-up points on the coast where they may or may not be met by a submarine?"

Brig. Clarke said, "That is the plan."

"You'd better go spring David Stirling out of his German POW camp so he can take on this assignment, Brigadier," Col. Randal said. "I've told you before—we don't do missions that a single pass by a flight of fighters can accomplish just as effectively. And we don't do big islands where our teams have to make an approach march for days before reaching their targets— submarines have a bad habit of not showing up."

Brig. Clarke said, "I was afraid this was going to be your response. Expected it, actually. In that case, do not be counting on the SBS men anytime soon. We shall have to divert them to raid the airfields."

"You do that."

Brig. Clarke stood up to leave. He was not entirely displeased with Col. Randal's response. It was essentially a one-way mission. Brig. Clarke knew Raiding Forces "Rules for Raiding" included: "Plan missions backward (know how to get home)."

He had not mentioned to Col. Randal that the raids were an A-Force deception to cover OPERATION HUSKY—the Allied invasion of Sicily. The teams conducting the raids would accomplish their mission even if they were all killed or captured.

He did not care which unit carried out the mission.

ENSIGN THEODORE HAMILTON, *AKA* "THE GREAT TEDDY", arrived. Brandy Seaborn came over and sat down. Beverly walked by and kissed Teddy on the forehead.

Colonel John Randal said, "Thanks for coming, Ensign. Admiral Ransom was here earlier and informed me that Raiding Forces would be using caïques for transportation to and from our objectives in the Aegean. Brandy has agreed to advise me on certain nautical matters when she's not zipping around in her speedboat rescuing evaders for Mandy's mother.

"She explained that a caïque is a slow, partially sail-powered Greek fishing boat. And says the boats will have to hide at unoccupied islands by day and continue their mission by night. My question to you: can you camouflage them? They will need to be safe from observation by enemy air and passing German and Italian patrol boats."

Ens. Hamilton said, "Yes, sir. I have been running tests at Castelrozzo for Admiral Ransom."

Col. Randal said, "How're you going to make a tall mast on a sailboat disappear?"

Ens. Hamilton said, "Sir, as we have discussed before, the purpose of military camouflage is not to make an object disappear, it is to make it look like something else. Many of the islands in the Aegean are characterized by rugged cliffs by the sea with jagged rocks jutting out of the water. I have developed a net that can be placed over the mast that will make it look exactly like a natural rock spire sticking up next to an island.

"Sir, I am also working on a technique of draping the nets when the caïques anchor off a sheer cliff that make the boats conform to the slope."

Col. Randal said, "You believe it will work?"

"It's virtually impossible to distinguish one of the camouflaged caïques from the air. To a passing boat, they are indistinguishable from a matter of feet. This has turned out to be one of the easiest assignments I have ever been handed as a Camouflage Officer, sir."

Brandy asked, "You can hide my MAS boat?"

"Yes, ma'am."

"I want a demonstration, Ensign."

Col. Randal said, "So do I. Set it up."

Col. Randal made eye contact with Capt. Jaxx. He came over to the table after Brandy and Ens. Hamilton had departed. "What's your takeaway from our raid on Aetos, Jack?"

Capt. Jaxx said, "We're going to be fighting in built-up areas even if they're small, sir. Probably always outnumbered. And, we won't have the massed firepower of our gun jeeps."

"Exactly the conclusion I've come to," Col. Randal said. "I'm going to designate you to be the training officer during our transition from desert patrolling to amphibious raiding. Find some place to start conducting drills on small-unit tactics in a built-up area.

"Get with Capt. McKoy. The two of you find some way to increase the lethality of an eight- to ten-man raiding party. You're going to need to be creative."

Capt. Jaxx said, "Yes, sir!"

Major the Lady Jane Seaborn came over, dripping wet mahogany hair swept back, "Vegas looks lonely, Jack."

Capt. Jaxx took the hint and made himself scarce.

Col. Randal asked, "What was in the note Captain Butterfield gave you—his phone number?"

"The appraisal of my ring—almost the exact value Harry Winston placed on it for insurance purposes in New York when Beverly and I were there. Preston knows gemology. He shall be a valuable asset for LEAF EATER."

"How much?"

Lady Jane laughed. "I shall never tell. You would ask for it back."

Col. Randal said, "I don't think so."

11

THREE ISLANDS

COLONEL JOHN RANDAL AND MAJOR THE LADY JANE SEABORN were in the master bedroom of the suite in the Mena House Hotel. The Great Pyramid could be seen in the moonlight out the glass wall on one side of the room. According to archeologists, the pyramid had been built over a period of twenty years with a massive, quarried stone being put in place every twenty minutes.

Col. Randal had his doubts about that.

Lady Jane was reclining on the bed, wearing a glamorous black silk nightgown. Col. Randal was in an overstuffed chair reading a classified stack of documents describing the origins and operations of the Special Air Service and the advent of the Special Boat Section in Middle East Command.

He was hoping to be impressed.

That was not turning out to be the case. What he was reading was a case study in bad leadership and misuse of a valuable military asset by rear echelon planners who had no concept of small-scale operational art.

For example, the Special Air Service was parachute qualified—the sales pitch made by Brigadier Dudley Clarke to Middle East Command Headquarters (MEHQ) was what convinced MEHQ to authorize formation of the unit. However, the SAS made only one operational jump the entire time Lieutenant Colonel David Stirling commanded the regiment.

It was a complete disaster.

Col. Randal understood that units like the Special Air Service and Raiding Forces would never win a war, even if they could strike by land, sea or air quickly and be gone. At best, a campaign of small-scale raids could force an enemy commander to disperse and tie down valuable troops guarding places that were never going to be raided.

Until they were.

The Special Air Service had fallen victim to its own legend. Most of what had been written about the SAS in the newspapers or shown in Movietone news reels was pure fantasy. The same thing had happened with Raiding Forces' *Jump on Bela*—pulp fiction.

From the file, it was apparent that while the SAS had its share of successes, a high percentage of its missions were disasters. That did not mean the men of the SAS were not bold and daring. They were. It was not the troops' fault that their unit was the textbook example of mismanagement—commander absent partying in Cairo while armchair Commandos at MEHQ planned impossible missions and then compromised those missions by confiding their brilliant ideas to colleagues, who bragged about their inside knowledge of upcoming raids to their cronies in every bar in town.

Lady Jane said, "You are wearing a grim expression."

"SAS never stood a chance. MEHQ selected their targets, spelled out the actions on the objective and set the date and time of attack. Then the Operations Division staff who drafted the raid plan failed to maintain basic operational security. I knew about the problems with their commander, but I had no idea about all the staff meddling."

"You sound dispirited, John."

"I'm not, but I'm beginning to realize it would be delusional to believe that anything Raiding Forces does will make the slightest difference to the big picture."

Lady Jane said, "Look on the bright side. Who knows when one of our raids might produce some war-winning piece of intelligence?"

"Well, it certainly won't be the men and women of Raiding Forces who know. When we go on a GOLDEN FLEECE/RED INDIAN, all we're cleared to know is what item of equipment we're expected to bring back. We have no idea what it means."

"What is really bothering you, John?"

Col. Randal said, "Seems like we're going 'round in circles. Originally, we were amphibious pinprick raiders, then we were mountain mule cavalry raiders, then desert gun jeep raiders. Raiding small islands is going to require an entirely different approach. We're not set up for it."

Lady Jane said, "Reorganizing Raiding Forces and developing tactics for a new theatre of operations is your long suit. Improvise, adapt, overcome—that's what you always tell people."

"Yeah, but I've always had some idea what I was doing."

Lady Jane laughed, "When I first met you in the Blind Eye Pub, Raiding Forces could not paddle their Goatley dories without tipping over."

Col. Randal said, "That's true."

"You will figure it out. You always do."

"Not much help from other amphibious raiding units. The Special Boat Section after-action reports seemed to offer the best chance of finding useful 'lessons learned.' Problem is, the SBS has never actually gone on any small-scale amphibious raids."

Lady Jane laughed. "Typical—what did you expect to find, a diagram of a table of organization chart telling you how to reconfigure Raiding Forces?"

Col. Randal said, "Well, that would have been helpful."

He read a document marked "MOST SECRET: Agreement reached with Combined Operations for two hundred Commandos all ranks to be assigned to SAS. An attachment ordered, 'Dispatch earliest possible by air to Cairo two Small Scale Raiding Force officers with experience of amphibious operations to assist SAS initiate seaborne raiding operations'."

There was nothing to indicate they had arrived.

Another document said, "SAS to form D squadron under the command of Major the Earl George Jellicoe as a sea-born element of the regiment . . ."

While another said, "Initial element of fifty Commandos from the now disbanded Small Scale Raiding Force previously attached to Special Operations Executive to be amalgamated into D Squadron, Special Air Service."

Problem was, there was no longer an SAS—D Squadron had ceased to exist.

The one conclusion Col. Randal gleaned was that cross-Channel pinprick raids on the enemy-occupied French coast were a thing of the past. The units tasked with performing them were being broken up and shipped out piecemeal to the Middle East Command.

He doubted the two hundred Commandos would ever arrive. The fifty men from SOE's Small-Scale Raiding Force would probably never show up either. However, the thought occurred to Col. Randal that maybe it was time to bring the company of the 575th Parachute Infantry Regiment (PIR) stationed at Seaborn House in England back to Egypt.

They had experience carrying out pinprick Commando raids.

Col. Randal decided that if the only conclusion his reading had led him to was the idea to bring home the 575th PIR troops, then it was time well-spent.

On another subject, a set of orders in the folder announced the winged dagger cap insignia with the motto: "Who Dares Wins" had been approved for wear by the 1st Special Air Service Regiment.

Col. Randal knew the SAS had been wearing the badge for nearly a year. There were competing theories about the dagger. Some said it was a Fairbairn Fighting Knife. Others claimed it was King Arthur's sword, Excalibur.

No one was going to know for sure now. Lt. Col. Stirling was a POW. He had never worn the SAS badge—officially.

Raiding Forces had a silver and black shoulder flash in the shape of a scroll. The unit had never adopted its own cap badge. The Raiders wore the scroll stitched on their berets over a pair of parachute wings. Officers wore the scroll over their rank insignia.

Col. Randal said, "Since we'll eventually be absorbing the SAS, do you think we should adopt their 'Who Dares Wins' cap badge?"

Lady Jane said, "No—the 1st Special Air Service Regiment has passed from the scene in Middle East Command. Take their men, not their history. Besides, I love wearing the RAIDING FORCES flash on my beret."

Col. Randal said, "Good point."

BEVERLY BLACKWELL TAPPED ON THE DOOR, "MESSAGE FROM Admiral Ransom."

Colonel John Randal said, "Come on in."

Beverly walked in, wearing one of Captain Billy Jack Jaxx's old No. 11 UT football jerseys she used as a sleeping shirt, "I decoded it for you."

"What's it say?"

Beverly read, "ABC has requested DDOD(I) destroy the long-range radio stations located on the islands of Kalos, Mikros and Omorfos at the earliest possible date. Signed Ransom, Vice Admiral, RN."

ABC was Admiral-of-the-Fleet Andrew Browne Cunningham, Commander-in-Chief, Mediterranean Fleet. Not a man known to have a sense of humor or suffer fools lightly. When he wanted a thing done, he wanted it done *yesterday*, as did the Razor.

Col. Randal asked, "Did Admiral Ransom say where the islands are located?"

"Negative."

Lady Jane said, "Go ask Brandy if she knows."

Brandy arrived in her silk robe, carrying a rolled-up chart of the Aegean Sea. She spread it out on the floor. Beverly weighted down the corners with an ashtray and three of Lady Jane's magazines.

Col. Randal said, "You know anything about these three islands?"

Brandy said, "No, we shall probably need a magnifying glass to find them."

Col. Randal, Brandy and Beverly were down on their knees trying to locate the targets. Finally, they located four islands forming a chain. Kalos was fifty miles north of Aetos, which Raiding Forces had already raided. Mikros was thirty miles south of Aetos, and Omorfos was twenty miles south of Mikros. The four islands formed a rough north–south picket line across the entrance into the Aegean Sea from the east.

Once the islands were located, as Brandy had predicted, they did look like fly specks on the map. It was clear that what were described as long-range radio stations were, in fact, also naval observation posts (OPs). No capital warship was going to be able to enter the Aegean from the east—meaning Egypt/Cyprus—during daylight hours without being spotted. The long-range radios would allow their position to be immediately reported to the Kriegsmarine or Regia Marina, or worse, the Luftwaffe or Regia Aeronautica.

Col. Randal said, "Pretty clear ABC intends to black out the eastern end of the Dodecanese by knocking out the remaining three islands in the picket line."

Brandy said, "My guess is Admiral Cunningham wants us to strike quickly before the opposition understands the situation and reinforces the three remaining islands."

"Mine too," Col. Randal said.

"We may have a situation, John," Brandy said.

"What might that be?"

Brandy said, "We have to stage from Castelrozzo. The only patrol boat presently at the island is Father's PT. All of Randy's squadron are either in dry dock or operating far up the Libyan coast in support of Eighth Army. You shall need at least three boats if you plan to attack all of the islands simultaneously."

"We have to hit them at the same time, or reinforcements will be rushed in to the ones we haven't attacked."

Col. Randal said, "Ten hours from here to Castelrozzo in your MAS boat. It's late for you to get started tonight without arriving at the island in full daylight. Shove off tomorrow evening. We're going to need you to transport aviation gas on deck.

"Beverly, you and Pam fly SOG to Castelrozzo in a couple of the Walruses. Once there, top off one of them from the cans on Brandy's boat. We'll use it to raid one of the islands.

"Is that do-able?"

Beverly said, "No problem, Johnny. We can fly the mission—tell me which island."

"Brandy will decide which ones the PT and MAS boat can reach fastest. You take the one that's left."

Brandy laughed. "I knew you were going to need me, handsome. Never dreamed it would be this easy."

Col. Randal said, "I don't have any choice. The bad guys aren't stupid. My guess is they've already figured out our next move.

"We have to get there first."

"I have a lot to do to make ready to put to sea," Brandy said. "Will you have Flanigan drive Parker and me to my boat's berth tonight?"

Col. Randal said, "He'll be ready when you are."

Beverly asked, "OK, what do you want me to do right now?"

Col. Randal said, "Call RFHQ and have SOG put on alert. Track down Pam and let her know she'll be flying. I know Jack's out with Vegas. If he calls in, tell him he doesn't need to be here until 0800 hours tomorrow but to stop drinking. I don't want Jack Cool hung over.

"Where's Mandy?"

"She has a date with Preston."

Col. Randal said, "When you talk to Mandy, tell her we need to try to gather as much intel about our targets as possible."

Lady Jane said, "I can help."

Col. Randal said, "You're not getting off that bed."

"I don't believe we're going to find much information about Kalos, Mikros or Omorfos. Not even an accurate census count. Unless MI-6, SOE or SIME have something," Beverly said. "When we were at the library doing research on Castelrozzo, we looked up some of the other Dodecanese Islands for fun. One we read about had five different names over the years but there wasn't a single sentence describing the place."

Col. Randal said, "Call Captain Fawcett-Tatum. Tell her to contact the Razor's Intelligence Officer and have him send over every stick of intel he can lay his hands on about our targets. Tomorrow, you and Mandy work the intelligence services and see if they have anything."

Beverly said, "I'll call the Admiral's Intelligence Officer personally as soon as you turn me loose here."

"Double check with RFHQ to make sure Lieutenant Hays gets notified of the alert. He'll have to command one of the three raids. I need him wired in on the planning from the start."

"Clint usually stays at the Continental. If he isn't in his room, I'll instruct the front desk to give him a message to call me when he comes in," Beverly said.

Col. Randal asked, "Where's King?"

"He's having dinner with Pam in the Mena House Hotel Restaurant."

Col. Randal said, "Don't call them back here, but have Rita or Lana carry a message with instructions to see me after their meal."

The restaurant was a block up the street from Lady Jane's suite.

Brandy said, "We should probably find out who is available to skipper Father's PT boat. I recommend Randy be flown in, if he is not already at Castelrozzo."

Beverly said, "I'll check."

"Ask Major Zargo to select three of his Greeks who are fluent English speakers to serve as our interpreters," Col. Randal said. "And find out if any of his Sacred Squadron people know anything about our three islands. Have them flown here tomorrow."

Beverly said, "Anything else?"

"Not for now," Col. Randal said.

There was a knock on the front door of the suite. Beverly jumped up to see who it was. They were not expecting guests. She came back with a U.S. Navy officer in tow—Lieutenant Douglas Fairbanks Jr., USN—the movie star.

Lt. Fairbanks said, "I was having dinner with Brigadier Clarke at his residence when Admiral Ransom phoned to inform me you had something interesting in the works I might want to observe. I drove straight here. My impression was the Razor meant a Commando raid.

"Wasn't expecting a pajama party."

SMALL OPERATIONS GROUP BEGAN TO ASSEMBLE AT RAIDING Forces Headquarters the next morning. Colonel John Randal issued a barebones Warning Order to the SOG officers and NCOs, Brandy Seaborn, Captain Penelope "Legs" Honeycutt Parker, Mandy Paige and Beverly Blackwell.

Lieutenant Douglas Fairbanks Jr. observed. The movie star had carried out several off-the-books peacetime clandestine intelligence missions in South America for President Franklin D. Roosevelt, managed to obtain a commission in the U.S. Navy prior to Pearl Harbor even though he was too old, pulled a tour at sea, been transferred to England to serve on board the carrier USS *Wasp* on one convoy to Malta, and been on a cruiser on the disastrous convoy PQ-17 to Russia, which lost twenty-four of its thirty-five ships. Lt. Fairbanks was then detailed to observe at British Combined Operations Headquarters before being recruited by the Office of Strategic Services.

He had spent the last six months attending various British amphibious raiding schools in Great Britain and Scotland, working with Commander Ian Fleming at the Naval Intelligence Division, and observing A-Force in Egypt. He had also assisted Ensign Theodore Hamilton, *aka* "The Great Teddy", on certain camouflage projects in support of Montgomery's Eighth Army.

Brigadier General William "Wild Bill" Donovan wanted Lt. Fairbanks to develop a Naval Special Operations component for OSS.

The Warning Order was issued to the Small Operations Group and all attachments.

Col. Randal said, "Situation: Enemy Observation Posts/Radio Stations located on the Dodecanese Islands of Kalos, Mikros and Omorfos pose a threat to naval forces operating in the Aegean Sea.

"Mission: SOG and attached personnel, broken down into three self-contained raiding teams, will simultaneously attack and destroy the long-range radios located in the enemy OPs on all three islands.

"Execution: SOG and attachments will relocate to Castelrozzo Island to stage for the raids.

"Lt. Hays will command Team A, consisting of eight Raiders plus a Greek-speaking officer to attack the OP/Radio Station on Kalos tomorrow night. Team A will be transported to their target island by a MAS boat under the command of Mrs. Brandy Seaborn.

"Captain Billy Jack Jaxx will command Team B, consisting of eight Raiders plus a Greek-speaking officer to attack the OP/Radio Station on Mikros tomorrow night. Team B will be transported to their target island by PT boat—skipper not designated at this time.

"I will command Team C, consisting of eight Raiders plus a Greek-speaking officer to attack the OP/Radio Station on Omorfos tomorrow night. Team C will be transported to their target island by a Walrus amphibian aircraft piloted by Captain Pamala Plum-Martin, with Beverly Blackwell acting as her copilot.

"Individual team composition is yet to be determined. There will be an officer's call immediately upon conclusion of this Warning Order to resolve the question. Sergeant Major Beckwith will announce team lists immediately following the officer's call.

"A Warning Order is intended to tell you only the basics—Who, What, When and Where. You may have noticed I was not able to cover all those items. Raid Team leaders—don't be expecting much more information when I issue the Operations Order. No intelligence about these islands is available.

"Organize heavy on firepower with a designated demolitions man. I expect us to be outnumbered. Go in fast, hit hard and pull out ASAP.

"Officer's call starting now—Sergeant Major, you and King attend.

"Questions—save 'em for later. Fall out."

The troops headed to their barracks to check their gear, draw ammunition, etc. The officers gathered around Col. Randal.

"Captain Jaxx and Lieutenant Hays—you get first choice on team members. The Sergeant Major's traveling with Lieutenant Hays. King's on me—same for my Lovat Scouts Fenwick and Ferguson. Select the men you are most comfortable working with.

"Don't worry about Team C. I'll take whoever's left—there's no second string in SOG."

As the selection process began, Col. Randal and Lt. Fairbanks stood off to one side smoking cigarettes.

Lt. Fairbanks asked, "Where do you want me, sir?"

Col. Randal said, "I thought you might like to observe either the PT or MAS boat in action tomorrow night."

"Actually, I would rather see how you insert a Commando party by seaplane, sir. Novel idea. Never knew that was possible."

"No problem."

Lt. Fairbanks said, "When I was in London, I ran into an old pal of mine from Hollywood—told me to look you up when I came out here."

Col. Randal said, "Who might that be?"

"David Niven—said you two had worked together on the very first Commando raid. He has gotten himself married now, but David still went to great lengths to tell me you 'poached his bird'—meaning Lady Jane."

"Still browned off about it."

Col. Randal said, "You'd have to ask Jane about that."

Lt. Fairbanks said, "Brigadier Clarke told me essentially the same story—he's still peeved as well."

"Talk to . . ."

Lt. Fairbanks said, "I did, sir. Lady Jane's response was to flash a heart attack-inducing smile and show me her ring. Hope my wife never sees the Sheba diamond."

"I got a good price on it," Col. Randal said.

Master Sergeant Mack Beckwith began calling off names from his clipboard.

King walked over, "We're good, Chief, team's fine."

Col. Randal said, "Have you met Lieutenant Fairbanks? He wants to travel with Team C. Like to observe Commandos deploying from an amphibious aircraft."

The tough Merc, clearly unimpressed with the idea of an A-list movie star joining them on a raid, said, "Have you introduced him to our pilots?"

Col. Randal said, "Why don't you do that?"

"Follow me, Lieutenant," King said. "You are in for a surprise."

Capt. Jaxx walked over. "Any chance of us getting any intel on the islands, Colonel?"

Col. Randal said, "Negative, Admiral Ransom informed me the navy is using charts made by the HMS *Spitfire* in 1852."

"We've been on some crazy stupid missions, sir," Capt. Jaxx said. "But no one's ever ordered us to take down point-type targets and not been able to tell us where to find them once we land ashore or what the opposition is expected to be. Someone's not playing with a full deck, if you ask me."

Col. Randal said, "You're not wrong."

Captain "Geronimo" Joe McKoy arrived with Waldo Treywick.

Capt. McKoy said, "You ain't fixin' to sneak off on a mission without tellin' me about it, are you John?"

"I'm not sneaking," Col. Randal said. "Mr. Treywick needs to meet with the Big Four tonight or tomorrow night to introduce Captain Butterfield as our diamond appraiser. Then, you two have to fly to Tangiers. Time to start putting a plan in place for LEAF EATER in North Africa."

Capt. McKoy said, "Waldo can handle that on his own. Ain't nothin' to the meetin' with the Big Four. Beverly's got him an OSS contact in Tangiers—guy named Ortiz, ex-Foreign Legion. She's using him to recruit some lieutenant from the 10th Ranger Battalion for Billy Jack."

Waldo said, "Yeah, I can handle it. No problem if Joe wants to go with you, Colonel.

"Negative," Col. Randal said. "You're both on mission."

Capt. McKoy said, "Billy Jack told me you was wantin' some heavier firepower for small foot mobile raidin' parties. What if I was to show you a prototype wonder weapon that could provide that in a big way?

"You'd let me go along on this operation to test her out in the field, right, John?"

Col. Randal said, "If there was ever an example of what happens when a camel gets his nose under the tent . . ."

"I ain't no camel. But I do have somethin' affectionately called the 'Stinger.' It's a daisy."

"A Stinger?"

Capt. McKoy asked, "You remember Roy Dunlap?"

"No."

"He's that sergeant in the U.S. 303rd Ordnance Regiment—Company D, which works on small arms. Modified those BARs we sent him to Colt Monitor specs. We traded a bunch a' our captured stuff for some weapons he had a while back."

Col. Randal said, "Now I remember."

"You're aware there was some a' us U.S. Marshals attached to the Marines down in Nicaragua during the banana wars."

"I am—that where you won the Medal of Honor?"

Capt. McKoy said, "No, it ain't. But I got to know a lot of Marines and some of 'em are still on active duty."

"Is this story going anywhere?"

"One ol' Gunny wrote me a letter from Pearl—that's in Hawaii where the Japs bombed. He said a Para-Marine out there was doin' some work on lightweight .30 caliber M2 Aircraft M1919 Brownin' Machine guns. They're called ANM2s—designed to be the tail gun for primarily amphibious airplanes," Capt. McKoy said. This Para-Marine has been takin' 'em off crashed planes and modifyin' 'em for his paratroop battalion because they need more firepower against human wave banzai attacks in the jungle.

"The ANM2 is one third lighter than the regular M1919—some parts bein' made out of aluminum. He sawed the barrel off to twenty-four inches, fixed a box on it to hold a hunnert round belt a' 30 caliber ammo, changed out the butterfly trigger for one off a M-1903 Springfield rifle, took off the double-handled spade grip and replaced it with the pistol grip off a spare M1 Carbine stock. Weighs twenty-five pounds all up fully loaded, ready to go.

"A man can stand upright and lay down walkin' fire while he advances.

"Roy made one up for me built on the specs the Gunny sent but all the substitution parts came off captured Italian rifles. Ain't much to look at, but shoots to beat the band—cyclic rate is 1350 rounds per minute which is three times as fast as the standard .30 cal. M-1919 mounted on a tripod."

Col. Randal asked, "You have one of these Stingers?"

Capt. McKoy said, "I do."

"Team C, that's mine. Talk to King—he'll designate an assistant gunner for you. Don't get killed on my watch—I mean it, Captain."

Capt. McKoy said, "You have always been a reasonable man."

"I'm going to quit trying to keep people who have no business being there out of harm's way. You, Pam, Brandy, Mandy, Beverly . . ."

Capt. McKoy said, "Probably a good idea, John—lot less stressful."

Vice Admiral Sir Randolph "Razor" Ransom walked over. "Admiral Cunningham is sending his personal Catalina for you to use as you see fit. ABC is not what one would describe as a philanthropist. The C-in-C is invested in seeing the chain of RS/OPs taken out.

"You shall have to use your pilots because the ferry crew has a regulation rest period after the long flight here. Are your two Amelia Earharts qualified?"

Col. Randal said, "Yes, sir. I'll check to see if they prefer a Catalina to the Walrus for the mission."

VAdm. Ransom said, "Find me two seats for the trip to Castelrozzo. Randy will be arriving here anytime now. He needs to fly out to skipper my personal PT boat."

Col. Randal said, "Yes, sir."

Captain Hawthorne Merryweather pulled up in a taxi. The Political Warfare Executive (PWE) officer stepped out lugging a canvas bag and a well-traveled 9mm Beretta MAB-38 submachine gun—it had been a brand-new capture, still in cosmoline, when Col. Randal had given it to him while he was serving with Force N in Abyssinia. He looked like a happy porpoise.

Col. Randal greeted him. "Haven't seen you in a while."

Capt. Merryweather said, "Been stuck working with Montgomery's Eighth Army Headquarters, sir. Escaped that mob—the Razor requested my presence most immediate."

"Glad you're back. Why don't you go visit Jane at Mena House? She'll be happy to see you."

Capt. Merryweather said, "Actually, I was hoping to catch a ride to Castelrozzo, sir."

Col. Randal said, "Why might you want to do that?"

Capt. Merryweather said, "PWE, through the good offices of Admiral Ransom, ordered me to set up shop on the island, provided I could obtain your permission, sir. From Castelrozzo, I can trifle with Germans, Italians and even the Turk's minds. Gave up on trying to win any hearts back in Abyssinia."

"Go see Brandy."

He wondered how the PWE officer was going to wrangle a spot on the raid. There was a zero percent likelihood Capt. Merryweather would not try.

Capt. Plum-Martin and Beverly came to see him in response to a summons from a messenger he had dispatched to where the two Walruses were docked. The blondes were wearing identical tailored black flight suits tucked into their yellow crocodile peewee cowgirl boots. The girls may have been getting ready to fly a combat mission, but they could see no reason not to look good while doing it.

Capt. Plum-Martin said, "You wanted to talk to us?"

"Admiral Cunningham is sending Raiding Forces a Catalina PBY," Col. Randal said. "The pilots won't be allowed to fly the mission due to Royal Navy regulations regarding rest periods between flights, so you're still up. You ladies tell me if you want the Catalina or our amphibians?"

Beverly said, "The PBY has two engines as opposed to one for the Walrus. Safer for long flights over water. It's fifty mph faster with a range of over two thousand miles as opposed to six hundred for a Walrus."

Capt. Plum-Martin said, "Crew of ten. We only need the radio operator, flight engineer and tail gunner. With Team C on board, we will still be at normal load, meaning we can fly at max cruising speed."

Col. Randal said, "You're planning to use your ex-LRDG navigator tomorrow night?"

Capt. Plum-Martin said, "Never leave home without him, love—when I fly."

Beverly said, "We can make the hop direct to Omorfos from here at RFHQ. No splashing down in the bay at Castelrozzo. Can't be sure who's watching from Turkey."

Col. Randal said, "You need to get one of our pilots to fly the Razor and Randy to Castelrozzo."

Beverly said, "I'll notify the duty pilot at RFHQ."

Capt. Plum-Martin said, "Keep the movie star out of my cockpit once we take off. I have an ironclad rule against married men.

Beverly said, "Commander Fairbanks believes in the Foreign Country-Hundred Mile Rule."

Col. Randal said, "What's that?"

Beverly laughed. "Daddy always says it doesn't count if it's in a foreign country or over a hundred miles away."

As the two pilots departed to get their gear out of the Walrus, Col. Randal went in search of MSgt. Beckwith. He found him with Capt. McKoy, inspecting one of the ugliest weapons ever devised—the Stinger. All the parts appeared to have been cobbled together, then bolted on—and they had been.

Col. Randal said, "Sergeant Major, a word."

"Yes, sir."

The two walked off a short distance so they could talk in private.

Col. Randal said, "I assigned you to Team A."

"Yes, sir."

While always prepared to carry out his orders in an efficient military manner, the senior U.S. Army NCO in Raiding Forces was not pleased with the assignment. MSgt. Beckwith believed it was his duty to accompany Col. Randal in the field or wherever military duties were performed. He took the responsibility seriously.

Col. Randal said, "We're not having this conversation."

MSgt. Beckwith said, "No, sir."

"This is Lieutenant Hay's first independent command. He's drawn a bad card having to raid a target we have zero intelligence on. I need you on Team A to give him a little added confidence."

"Can do, sir."

Col. Randal said, "I'll tell him the reason is because Captain McKoy has a new machine gun he wants to demonstrate, and my team already has Lieutenant Fairbanks strap-hanging."

"I'll look after the lieutenant," MSgt. Beckwith said. "He's a good officer, sir."

"Thanks, Sergeant Major."

MSgt. Beckwith said, "If you don't mind me saying so, Colonel, somebody planning this operation has got a screw loose."

"You got that right."

After speaking to MSgt. Beckwith, Col. Randal went in search of Lieutenant Clint Hays. He wanted to spend as much time as possible with the young officer before Team A's departure. Leadership takes many forms. A commander showing interest in one of his junior officers is one of the best.

He found Lt. Hays with his team, getting ready to test fire their weapons. Test firing is the only way to know for sure if a particular weapon works. In military terms, it is officially "not good" to discover a submachine gun or pistol is malfunctioning at the point in time you are trying to shoot someone with it.

Col. Randal pulled Lt. Hays aside while Team A continued assembling their weapons after cleaning them. He said, "How's it going, Lieutenant?"

"Fine, sir."

Col. Randal offered him one of Waldo's custom-rolled cigars. This was a first, one Lt. Hays did not fail to note. Nor would he forget it.

"I've attached Sergeant Beckwith to Team A because Captain McKoy talked me into letting him go with my team to try out a new belt-fed light machine gun. I've also got Lieutenant Fairbanks . . ."

Lt. Hays said, "I'll be glad to have him, sir."

"How many missions have you been on with SOG?"

"Lost count, sir."

Col. Randal said, "I'm expecting big things from you, stud."

"I won't let you down, sir."

Mandy arrived at RFHQ. She had spent the morning in Cairo visiting every intelligence agency in the city. No one had any information on the three islands targeted. She had uncovered one piece of disturbing news to report to Col. Randal.

Mandy said, "Troops from the 22nd Air Landing Division arrived on Aetos Island two days after your raid. Acting on orders from the division commander, General Muller—nicknamed the Butcher—the Germans publicly executed every male on the island over the age of fourteen. The general consensus among the intelligence specialists I talked to is that no quarter will be given in our war in the Aegean.

"The Greeks will slaughter the Italians if they have the chance. The Germans will slaughter the Greeks, and we will slaughter the Germans, the Italians and the odd Greek collaborator."

Col. Randal said, "So be it."

VICE ADMIRAL SIR RANDOLPH "RAZOR" RANSOM BRIEFED THE Situation and Mission paragraphs of the Operations Order. The three teams were gathered in the Operations Room of Raiding Forces Headquarters. Everyone was paying close attention. If there was one thing the troops respected, it was tough professional commanders. The Razor had won every valor medal Great Britain possessed—most of them more than once—and he was as hard as homogenous steel.

Raiding Forces liked him.

The Admiral gave a simple, no-nonsense explanation of what the three teams were tasked to accomplish. He explained why the mission was important. Later, each of the three team leaders would brief their men on their individual targets based on what little they had to work with. The maps available were not much more than schematic diagrams, and there was no intelligence on enemy forces.

VAdm. Ransom said, "Crete, Scarpanno and Rhodes form the Axis 'Iron Ring', blocking the entrance to the Aegean Sea. Enemy air operates off fields located on Crete and Rhodes. The Luftwaffe and Regia Aeronautica pose the biggest threat to our surface fleet. The enemy needs advance notice of our ship movements in order to coordinate a concentrated air attack.

"Out in front of the three big islands are three tiny islands—Omorfos, Mikros and Kalos—forming a natural picket line. Located on each of these islands is an enemy observation post equipped with long-range signals equipment. They provide the Axis the early warning it needs.

"Small Operations Group is to raid all three islands tomorrow night to destroy the radio stations. When you accomplish your mission, you blind the Axis Powers and disrupt their ability to communicate sightings of our naval forces operating in the constricted waters of the Aegean.

"By your actions, untold ships and the lives of countless sailors will be saved."

Colonel John Randal replaced VAdm. Ransom in front of the Raiders.

"Execution . . ."

12
COSTARRED

LIEUTENANT RANDY "HORNBLOWER" SEABORN'S LEND LEASE Patrol Torpedo Boat (PT) and his mother Brandy Seaborn's captured MAS departed for Castelrozzo two hours before sundown. To increase speed, neither boat was armed with torpedoes. However, now that their mission was to operate in the Aegean where German E-Boats roamed, both had recently undergone significant upgrades to their deck armament and Brandy was being allowed to carry guns on her boat again.

Captain Billy Jack Jaxx's Team B sailed on board Randy's boat. Colonel John Randal had a last-minute pang of doubt about letting those two hard chargers go off on their own as the PT cleared the dock. Lieutenant Clint Hays' Team A was on Brandy's MAS. The two boats would travel together as far as Castelrozzo. The following night, they would make their way independently to Kalos and Mikros.

Team C would fly direct from the dock outside Raiding Forces Headquarters to Omorfos, which negated the need of having to haul aviation fuel to Castelrozzo on the MAS boat. Col. Randal's men had an extra night and day to rest and conduct mission prep before flying out.

Major the Lady Jane Seaborn arrived from Mena House Hotel in time to see the boats off. She ordered a special meal laid on for Team C. Then, exhausted from over-exertion and clearly not recovered yet, Lady Jane retired to her third-floor suite to rest before dinner.

Col. Randal ordered Team C to do the same—stand down. Experience had taught him to have his troops store as much energy as possible before a mission.

Besides, disassembling, cleaning and reassembling weapons could only be done so many times. Once test fired, it was best to leave them alone. After the men had checked all their equipment for the one hundredth time—they would continue checking and rechecking right up until the moment the Catalina landed at Omorfos—Team C racked out.

There was nothing else to do. Meaningful rehearsals were not possible. No one knew where the objective was located or what they would find when the Raiders reached it. The plan for all three teams was the same:

1.   Land.
2.   Attempt to make contact with someone who lived on the island, using the Greek speaker from the Sacred Squadron to make the contact.
3.   Have the local islander lead them to their target.

Failing that, logic dictated that a radio station/observation post would be located on the highest point on a given island. The teams would land ashore, and if unable to secure a guide, climb the highest hill they could find. It might work.

When Col. Randal explained Plan B to Lady Jane, she looked at him incredulously. "Are you having me on?"

Lady Jane had attended virtually every school MI-6 and SOE sent their field agents to. The drop-dead gorgeous Royal Marine was a veteran of her fair share of stumbling around the English countryside in the dark of night on training exercises, disoriented and trying to get her bearings. She knew the drill.

Col. Randal said, "Could be the worst fallback plan ever."

Lady Jane laughed. "Your idea?"

"I'm not proud of it," he said.

"I've heard Special Operations have caused more disruption to our side than it ever has the enemy," Lady Jane said. "Raids requiring more advance planning and organization than one of Montgomery's full-dress battles."

Col. Randal said, "Not for the raids on Kalos, Mikros and Omorfos. There's more prior planning being put into the dinner you're having for Team C tonight."

Flanigan knocked on the door to the master bedroom. "Admiral Ransom to see you, sir."

Col. Randal walked out into the living area. "Evening, Admiral."

Vice Admiral Sir Randolph "Razor" Ransom said, "I came by to inform you I will be traveling with Team C when we fly out tomorrow night."

Col. Randal said, "That's fine, sir. You can keep Lieutenant Fairbanks company on board the Catalina while we carry out our mission."

"Negative, I shall be going ashore with Team C."

"Sir . . ."

VAdm. Ransom said, "Captain McKoy requires an assistant machine gunner for his Stinger—whatever that is."

"Are you serious, sir?"

"We are on the cusp of a new island raiding campaign I am to command because the Aegean theatre of operations has been classified as Irregular—not even granted official status by the U.S.," VAdm. Ransom said.

"The politics are not my concern. My problem is a total lack of understanding of what raiding the hundreds of islands is going to involve.

"I need to get on the ground and see for myself."

Col. Randal said, "Understand—this is it, Admiral—one time only. Don't get killed on my watch, sir."

"McKoy said that is what you told him as well."

"The difference is, sir—I know I'm not going to be able to keep Captain McKoy from going on raids in future. You're another matter, Admiral. Ask again, and I'll contact Admiral Cunningham."

V. Adm. Ransom said, "I believe you would. Fair enough, Colonel."

AS DAWN WAS BEGINNING TO BREAK, THE MAS BOAT AND THE PT boat pulled into the bay at Castelrozzo. Ensign Theodore Hamilton, *aka* "The Great Teddy", was standing by with work crews to camouflage the two craft. His goal in life was to become a professional illusionist. For the last two years, he had been getting a lot of practice staging magic tricks designed to fool the Germans and Italians. Within a few minutes, the two boats appeared to be part of the shale beach.

For all intents and purposes, they had disappeared.

Ens. Hamilton liked to point out that the overriding goal of camouflage was not to make something disappear. The idea was to make it look like something else. Harmless.

Teams A and B slipped ashore and changed into Greek garb. Like the two patrol boats, they became—if not invisible—at least of no interest to anyone in Axis pay who might be watching through a high-powered telescope from Turkey. Captain Billy Jack Jaxx and Lieutenant Clint Hays checked with Vice Admiral Sir Randolph "Razor" Ransom's Director of Operations Division (Irregular), Advanced Headquarters Castelrozzo, to inquire if there was any new intelligence on Kalos and Mikros

There was not.

Lieutenant Randy "Hornblower" Seaborn and his mother, Brandy, remained at the dock to supervise the refueling of their boats. Mechanics were standing by to perform engine inspections. The two boats needed to be in tip-top mechanical condition for the voyage.

Both had prototype Elco Thunderbolt gun turrets retrofitted on their bow to be used in action for the first time. Each Thunderbolt boasted a pair of 20mm Oerlikon automatic cannon and six .50 caliber M-2 Browning machine guns. One gunner controlled all eight weapons at the same time. Additional twin-mounted .50 caliber M-2 Browning machine guns were bolted on anywhere space could be found.

The Axis owned the day because their airfields on Rhodes, Kos and Leros gave them command of the air. However, small ships of the Royal Navy could fight it out with the Kriegsmarine E-Boats and Regia Marina MAS boats on an equal footing under cover of darkness. It was hoped the added weaponry on the PT boat and the MAS boat would not be needed—stealth being paramount for small-scale Commando raids. If a chance encounter occurred, any Axis craft engaged was in for a nasty surprise.

The Thunderbolt turret had been invented by a mad genius.

At Raiding Forces Headquarters and on Castelrozzo Island, the day dragged. Standing by to go was always hard duty. Some said the waiting was the worst part of a mission. No matter how many raids anyone had done, waiting on it was always the same—like running your fingers down a chalkboard.

No matter how much rest the troops got, everyone still felt exhausted.

Lieutenant Douglas Fairbanks Jr. was entertaining Team C with his inexhaustible stable of tales about his Hollywood salad days. The son of the most famous true-action movie star who had ever appeared on film—and an actor of almost equal stature in his own right—it seemed like he knew every famous person, particularly the world's most beautiful women, on three continents. The Raiders just wanted to hear about who was sleeping with whom.

That was perfectly fine with Lt. Fairbanks. A swashbuckler in the boudoir as well as on the silver screen, the movie star-turned-U.S. Navy officer had an endless series of stories not suitable for publication. An unlikely number involved accidental encounters with women turned on by whips and chains but it was always all a big laugh.

He was more than willing to share.

ON CASTELROZZO ISLAND, TEAMS A AND B WANDERED AROUND the town. A few men climbed up to inspect the Crusader castle they had jumped on not all that long ago. Others tried to make the acquaintance of the local Greek girls.

Because so many men had left the island to escape the Italian occupation or join the Greek military forces in exile, there were a lot of bored women. The girls seemed excited to learn Raiding Forces was coming back to stay. Their strict Greek Orthodox Church-going mothers? Not so much.

Finally, at long last, the sun began to sink. In Egypt, Team C began to file on board the Catalina. Every member of Raiding Forces who was at RFHQ at the time gathered to see them off. Mandy Paige, the female contingent of Royal Marines, and all the Wrens were in the crowd. Major the Lady Jane Seaborn was there, trying hard not to cry—women of her class were trained from birth not to show any emotion in public except joy. Usually calm and cool, she seemed more emotional since being shot.

Brigadier Dudley Clarke, A-Force, Brigadier Raymond J. "R. J." Maunsell, SIME, and Cuthbert Bowlby, SIS, drove down from Cairo. The intelligence community had a great deal of interest in the Aegean Campaign. The three senior officers all had long-range plans for the AO. With Cairo fast becoming a backwater, the war in Middle East Command was rapidly transitioning into a new low-intensity phase.

Colonel John Randal was last to board. He hated the good-byes. Always had.

He made his way to the cockpit where Captain Pamala Plum-Martin was the command pilot with Beverly Blackwell as her co-pilot. The ex-LRDG navigator had moved back to the navigator's workstation for the duration of the flight. Col. Randal strapped himself into the vacant seat.

"Let's do this."

Capt. Plum-Martin announced over the intercom, "Prepare for takeoff."

The big Catalina began to cruise down the Nile out into open water. The engines increased their pitch to a full-throated roar. The plane began its long takeoff run, picked up speed, then gradually lifted into the air.

Col. Randal relaxed immediately, exactly the opposite of what anyone who had never commanded a combat operation would have thought possible. It was always the same. Once the mission was underway, the stress of planning, organizing, and dealing with a million and one problems fell away. Now all he had to do was take it easy and let the pilots do the work. Prior to making the final approach to the target, he would dial back in.

At that point, there would be plenty to worry about.

Normally, Col. Randal spent the time en route to the target running over every detail of the mission again and again. Not tonight. He did not have enough information for the mental gymnastics to be meaningful. Team C was going to land, go ashore, wing it from there—kill bad guys and come home.

It was often said in military circles that no plan survives the first shot. In Col. Randal's experience, most plans started unraveling by the time you shoved off from your point of departure. Tonight he was confident in the pilots and confident in his Raiders and their ability to adjust to whatever was found on Omorfos.

Still, intelligence about enemy forces would have been nice.

On Castelrozzo, once it was full-on dark, Teams A and B began boarding their respective boats. Everything went smoothly. The SOG operators were old hands at moving on and off all types of small craft.

On the MAS boat, Lieutenant Clint Hays reported, "All troops loaded and below deck, Skipper."

Brandy said, "Hang on tight, Clint. We were running at reduced speed on the way here to maintain station with Randy's boat. Now we will be traveling independently.

"Stand by to fly."

Lt. Hays said, "I'll pass the word."

He thought the MAS boat *had* been flying.

Lt. Hays had crafted a very basic plan. The map of Kalos contained very little useful information. It did show where a scattering of houses was located, indicating the only vestige of a town on the island. One mile north of the village was what appeared to be a beach.

His concept of the operation called for the MAS boat to put his men ashore on the beach. The Greek-speaking guide provided by Major Zargo would walk to the village and attempt to locate someone to guide Team A to the enemy RS/OP. After finding an islander willing to help, Aleksy—only first names were being used by the Greek Sacred Squadron interpreters—would return, pick up Team A, and they would follow the local to the objective.

As plans went, it did not get much simpler than that—except they did.

LIEUTENANT RANDY "HORNBLOWER" SEABORN AND CAPTAIN Billy Jack Jaxx had come up with an idea so barebones that it made Lieutenant Clint Hays' scheme of maneuver sound like Einstein's theory of relativity. Their plan was so simple that the two young officers had taken the precaution of not telling anyone, even their own men, what they intended to do until the PT boat departed Castelrozzo for Mikros.

Once the PT boat was well underway, Capt. Jaxx briefed Team B.

"Mikros only has one town. It's called Mikros. Not much imagination naming places among the locals on our island. The map doesn't indicate a beach within five miles of the village. That means a ten-mile forced march round-trip—not counting the distance to the RS/OP, however far that might be.

"What we know is that most of the islanders in the Aegean support themselves by fishing. Common sense dictates there should be a pier for fishermen's boats at a seaside village like Mikros. What Lt. Seaborn and I propose is for the PT boat to slip in and tie off at the dock. Our Greek speaker will step off, snatch some sleeping fisherman out of his caïque and politely invite him to guide us to the objective.

"Vitalis, our Greek Sacred Squadron guy, has a big sharp knife, so cooperation is pretty much a given."

Team B laughed.

Capt. Jaxx said, "SOG ain't a democracy, boys, but what the hell—let's take a vote. All in favor of a ten-plus-mile forced march, raise your hands.

"No—all in favor of the pier? Skip the forced march?"

Every hand shot up.

Capt. Jaxx said, "Next stop, downtown Mikros."

IN THE PASSENGER COMPARTMENT OF THE CATALINA PBY, Lieutenant Douglas Fairbanks Jr. was still regaling Team C with tales of bedroom swordsmanship. He had been in the arms of every beautiful actress they had ever lusted after at the Saturday matinee while growing up in their hometowns. Up front in the cockpit, Colonel John Randal was beginning to run through the next moves he had to make. His plan was not much more complicated than those of Team A and B.

The direction of the prevailing breeze on Omorfos was a known. This was significant. Captain Pamala Plum-Martin was going to approach the island into the wind—meaning it was blowing toward the PBY. It was hoped the draft would diffuse the sound of the aircraft engines.

Col. Randal said, "Pam, when we get back, I want you and Beverly to set up tests so we can find out how much sound abatement there really is from landing into the wind. We don't want to count on something that might not be happening."

Capt. Plum-Martin said, "Wilco."

Like the other two islands, there was only one town indicated on Omorfos. It was labeled "Oia." However, since there was also a town by that name on Aetos Island, scene of their last raid, the name was suspect.

Not that it mattered.

Omorfos, like the other two islands being targeted tonight, had been formed by an ancient volcano. There was a steep hill that looked like a miniature mountain jutting up. Presumably the RS/OP would be on or near the top.

There was no guarantee of that, so a local guide was a necessity.

Unlike the other two islands, Omorfos had a number of beaches located at varying intervals all the way around it. Finding a place to come ashore was not going to be a problem. Team C had Vice Admiral Sir Randolph "Razor" Ransom attached tonight, and his presence was a consideration. The Admiral did not routinely train to go on forced marches. Col. Randal thought it best for the PBY to land as close to Oia as possible.

Capt. Plum-Martin and Beverly picked a beach fairly close to the village but far enough away so the airplane would not be heard by Oia's inhabitants—they hoped.

Col. Randal said, "Looks as good as any to me."

Which was about as militarily scientific as throwing darts at the map.

If tonight were a graded field training exercise, Team C would have already flunked.

The Catalina was going to touch down and motor right up to the shore. This might not have been the best idea since anyone out violating curfew along the beach would come across the plane, but it made disembarking—and especially re-embarking—easier and faster. Once a raid is complete and it's time to go home, fast is good.

Col. Randal was willing to take the risk.

NO ONE PLANNED IT, BUT THE TEAMS ARRIVED AT THEIR TARGETS in sequence—A, B, C.

On the MAS boat transporting Team A, Captain Penelope "Legs" Honeycutt-Parker came up from below where she had been double checking her navigation.

"Stay hard on our present course. Approximately fifteen minutes out."

Lieutenant Clint Hays went below and gave his men the order to move up on deck and prepare to disembark. Tension spiked in anticipation. The troops were all seasoned veterans. They had worked together for a long time, going all the way back to their Panama Canal Zone days in the 1/575th Parachute Infantry Regiment, when the unit was known as "Jungle Rangers."

Everyone knew their job. The troops trusted their lieutenant. Team A was ready to make it happen.

The night was fairly dark but not pitch-black. Brandy reduced speed. In the distance, a shadow darker than the rest of the night seemed to have come into view. The trick was to not look directly at it—use peripheral vision instead. That helped, but not as much as the instructors teaching night vision classes liked to claim. A further reduction in speed. Now the island was definitely in view and the MAS boat was gliding though the water, carried by its own momentum.

Brandy reversed engines, and the fast patrol boat came to a gentle stop a stone's throw from the beach. Team A was over the side in knee-deep water. The troops charged ashore, went into the prone and set up a half-perimeter defense with the Aegean lapping at their backs.

Aleksy moved out immediately in the direction of the village with the intent of finding a guide. At this stage of the operation, the only thing anyone else could do was to wait. Team A was hoping no one, meaning an enemy patrol, came walking along the beach.

On the MAS boat, the crew was closed up at Battle Stations.

Every wristwatch worn by Team A and the crew of the MAS boat seemed to have broken at the same time—the hands were not moving. The watches worked fine. It was time that was warped.

Happened on every mission.

In less than thirty minutes, Aleksy appeared, bringing someone with him. The Greek Sacred Squadron interpreter had stumbled across a fisherman who was in a boathouse repairing his nets less than a quarter of a mile up the beach. The man readily agreed to take Team A to the RS/OP.

Lt. Hays said, "Ask him how many bad guys are here."

Aleksy said, "He told me there are six Italian signalmen stationed on Kalos. They are terrified of the Greeks. All of them stay at the radio station for mutual protection when the sun goes down. There is supposed to be a curfew in effect, but since the enemy never comes down off the mountain at night because they are afraid of getting knifed, everyone ignores it."

Lt. Hays said, "Sergeant Major, have the men ready to move out in zero five."

Master Sergeant Mack Beckwith said, "Wilco, sir."

Lt. Hays waded out to the MAS boat, "We're traveling as soon as I get back to the beach, Mrs. Seaborn. There are only six Italians and we know where they are. We'll take out the RS/OP as planned.

"I'll fire a red flare to let you know it's us when we're on the way back."

Brandy said, "Godspeed, Clint."

TEAM B REMAINED ON THE PT BOAT WHILE VITALIS WALKED UP the rotting plank pier to a caïque tied off there. The boat looked old enough to have sailed with Columbus to discover the New World. The Sacred Squadron trooper disappeared down the hatch into the cabin.

Shortly, he came back on deck with another man and walked back to where Captain Billy Jack Jaxx and the rest of Team B were waiting on a high state of alert.

Vitalis said, "This man says the Italians have eight soldiers stationed on Mikros. The radio station is located at the top of the hill about a half mile from the town. Exactly as we thought it would be."

Capt. Jaxx said, "Where do we find the bad guys?"

"Four of the Italians are on duty at all times. The other four sleep in a house near the edge of town on the way."

Capt. Jaxx asked, "Ever go out at night?"

Vitalis said, "Nowhere for them to go. All the single women are spoken for. Besides, an Italian venturing inside a Greek pub for a nightcap on this island would be committing suicide."

"OK, boys," Capt. Jaxx said, "we'll patrol through town. When we get to the house where the four off-duty Blackshirts sleep, we'll drop off Harwich and Malarkey, armed with their BARs. One of you take the front and the other the back. Don't let anyone leave the building—if they try, light 'em up.

"Is that clear?"

Private Fred Harwich and Private Joe Malarkey both said, "Clear, sir."

Capt. Jaxx said, "The rest of Team B will continue to march to the objective. We'll kill or capture the signalmen located there, search for any RED INDIAN material, place explosive charges on the radio, then come straight back. When we arrive at the house, we'll kill or capture the Italians inside, continue on to the dock, board the PT and sail for home.

"Questions?"

There were no questions. This was a small-scale raid in the extreme. Everyone knew their job and was ready to get to it.

Capt. Jaxx said, "Lieutenant Seaborn, you might want to post a couple of your Blue Jackets at the end of the pier with submachine guns while we're gone."

Lieutenant Randy "Hornblower" Seaborn said, "Aye, aye."

He did not say 'sir.' A Navy lieutenant is equal to an Army captain. Technically, by date of rank, Hornblower outranked Jack Cool.

Team B moved out in a loose file formation.

CAPTAIN PAMALA PLUM-MARTIN SAID, "TWENTY MINUTES."

Colonel John Randal said, "Alert the troops."

Capt. Plum-Martin spoke into the intercom, "This is the captain speaking. We will be arriving at your destination in twenty minutes. On behalf of myself and Beverly Blackwell, our co-pilot for tonight's trip to Omorfos Island, thank you for choosing Raiding Forces Airlines. We hope you have enjoyed your flight.

"Lock and load."

In the passenger compartment, Lieutenant Douglas Fairbanks Jr. stopped one of his bodice-ripping stories in mid-sentence. Those men sleeping were instantly awake. Everyone rechecked their personal equipment for the one hundred-and-first time.

Captain "Geronimo" Joe McKoy said to his assistant machine gunner, "Showtime, Admiral. You stick with me."

Vice Admiral Sir Randolph "Razor" Ransom said, "Roger, Joe."

Col. Randal left the pilot's cabin and came back to the passenger compartment. He walked down the aisle, speaking to everyone as he came past. One of the troopers said something that was hilarious, and the troopers all laughed.

Thirty seconds later, no one could remember what it was.

When he finished his informal inspection, Col. Randal pulled King aside, "Go with our Greek speaker, Stavos, when he sets off to find a guide. Get back as soon as possible. Let's execute this mission and go home fast."

King said, "Can do."

Col. Randal said, "My guess is we're going to end up having to negotiate a steep incline to reach the RS/OP. When we arrive at the foot of the hill, we'll halt the patrol and redistribute the .30 caliber machine gun ammunition the Razor's carrying. I'll carry the Stinger for Captain McKoy. You stay on point when we move out again. Call a halt below the military crest so I can hand the machine gun back over to the Captain, and the Admiral can get his ammo back."

"Negative, Chief," King said. "You're already carrying the Brixia, a pack full of 45mm rounds and your Beretta submachine gun. The Lovat Scouts can hump the Stinger and the spare ammo. Last thing we need is for you to be huffing and puffing when we reach the objective."

Col. Randal said, "Fair enough."

Two Lifeboat Servicemen were inflating a rubber raft. It was not clear at this point if it would be needed to transport Team C ashore. Capt. Plum-Martin intended to run the nose of the Catalina up onto the beach if she could. The amphibian was purpose-built to be able to do that.

Capt. Plum-Martin came on the intercom, "Take seats, fasten your safety belts and prepare to land. I have Omorfos in sight. Five minutes to splashdown."

LIEUTENANT CLINT HAYS HAD HIS TEAM A IN A FILE FORMATION with Master Sergeant Mack Beckwith supervising the point element, consisting of Aleksy—the Sacred Squadron interpreter—and the fisherman acting as their local guide. The tough NCO did not speak one word of Greek, so he had no idea what the local and Aleksy were whispering to each other.

Lt. Hays moved up to the front of the column. "Aleksy, we need to completely skirt the town. I want to scale the mountain and come in on the target from the rear."

"Yes, sir."

Lt. Hays dropped back and whispered to MSgt. Beckwith, "Lead out."

MSgt. Beckwith whispered back, "Moving now, Lieutenant."

The night was pleasant. However, the going was rough. Volcanic rock made for poor footing.

A strange feature of Kalos Island was that the "mountain" was, in fact, an escarpment . . . which meant there was a sheer side and a sloping side. The steepest incline to the top of the mountain was from the sea. The back side gradually fell off to the central part of the island. Lt. Hays was not aware of the feature because Raiding Forces did not have contour maps or aerial photographs of the islands its three teams were operating against tonight. He was merely trying to arrive on the objective unannounced and unexpected.

Which are good things when conducting a raid.

Lt. Hays was a natural leader. His troops were comfortable with him in charge. There was zero reluctance to follow him into action. As a result, Team A was making the movement to contact with the ease of a training exercise.

Up ahead, the objective came into view. There was a dull glow at what was most likely the peak. From where Team A was making its approach march, the climb appeared to be approximately five hundred to eight hundred feet. Following the local guide as he looped around, Lt. Hays was more than a little pleased to discover the terrain at the point he intended to ascend the hill formed an escarpment rather than a cliff, making for an easy climb.

The wind was blowing hard. Other than that, there was not a sound. Team A began working their way up the slope.

As per the plan, Aleksy passed the guide back down the column until he came to the last man. The fisherman had done his part. Lt. Hays did not want him to get in the way once the assault went in. Additionally, he did not completely trust the Greek not to give their presence away by exuberance. He issued orders for the guide to be kept with the patrol until the firing started. Then he could go.

Why take a chance?

The higher Team A climbed, the bigger the glow at the top grew. Soon it became apparent it was created by oil lamps inside a pyramidal tent. The RS/OP was right where the fisherman had said it would be.

On the highest terrain feature.

Lt. Hays brought Team A on line twenty-five yards from the tent. He was positioned in the center. After looking left and then right to make sure everyone was ready, he brought his 9mm Beretta MAB-38 submachine gun to his shoulder and commenced fire.

Every man in Team A instantly emptied a full magazine into the target—Beretta MAB-38s, Colt .30 Monitors, .30 M-1941 Johnson light machine guns and one .45 cal. Thompson submachine gun. The sound was like a thunder squall breaking. A concentrated cone of fire shredded the tent.

No one inside could have survived. That did not stop Lt. Hays from moving up to the flap that served as the entrance and tossing in a pair of U.S. Mark 2 fragmentation grenades.

He shouted, "Grenades!"

Everyone in Team A hit the dirt.

The four-second fuses seemed to take five minutes to go off, but then, that was always the case. *WHAAAAAM! WHAAAAAM!*

The instant the second grenade went off, Team A was on its feet, charging inside the tent. Dead and dying enemy soldiers littered the floor. Flames were beginning to lick the canvas sides of the tent from one of the oil lamps that had exploded.

Lt. Hays ordered unnecessarily, "Demo!"

Corporal Jeff Stillingworth, the designated demolitions man, was already placing his prepared charges on the radio.

The rest of the search party quickly tossed the tent for RED INDIAN material. They scooped up anything near the radio that had writing on it. Since SOG members were only cleared to know what to look for—not what it meant—Team A had no idea if anything they found was of any intelligence value.

Lt. Hays ordered, "Light it off."

Cpl. Stillingworth shouted, "Fire in the hole!"

There was a short sixty-second fuse on the explosives. Team A moved out smartly, wanting to put as much distance between themselves and the demolitions as possible. So far things had gone like clockwork.

Lt. Hays intended to keep it that way.

Standing off the beach, the MAS boat waited for the Raiders to return. A sailor appeared in the cockpit—not wanting to have shouted, "Skipper, enemy E-Boat off the stern port side!"

Brandy looked to the rear and saw a German torpedo boat sliding in alongside. It could be the enemy craft had been on patrol, spotted the Italian MAS boat and decided to pull in, stop and visit to break the monotony of a long night on patrol. Possibly the crew wanted to barter foodstuffs because the E-Boat was not at Battle Stations manning its weapons.

Brandy called softly, "Guns."

"I see them, ma'am," said Guns, one of the highest scoring antiaircraft gunners in the Royal Navy before he transferred to Raiding Forces to become the 20mm gunner on Col. Randal's jeep in Ranger Patrol. Because of his skill with weapons, he was manning the Elco Thunderbolt Turret—two 20mm Oerlikon fast-firing cannon and six .50 caliber Browning M-2 machine guns all firing as one.

The Thunderbolt Turret had more firepower than most fighter aircraft.

The MAS boat had a buzzer controlled from the cockpit that was used to signal the gunners on board when to commence fire. In order to give Guns the chance to bring his Thunderbolt guns to bear, Brandy delayed the order to commence fire until the German torpedo boat was completely alongside. A move that took nerves of steel.

The rest of the gunners on the forest of M-2 Browning .50 caliber machine guns mounted on the MAS boat were nonchalantly waving at the German sailors ready to swing into action the second the buzzer sounded.

Brandy touched the button. Guns commenced fire. The concentrated weapons in the Thunderbolt turret exploded into life. The roar was more like a gigantic deep buzzsaw yawning than the sound of gunfire.

Guns deftly painted the E-Boat from bow to stern in a single sweep, leaving it a shattered mass of kindling. One second the little Nazi warship was one of the deadliest small craft afloat. The next, everyone above deck on board was dead.

Just like that.

Guns was so fast and deadly that most of the other gunners on the MAS boat did not have a chance to open. Caught by surprise in the intense blizzard of fire, no one on the German E-Boat got off a single round. The Royal Navy sailors were shocked at the devastation they had wreaked in such a short amount of time.

The Thunderbolt was a monster.

Brandy crash-started the engines and pulled off a short distance to give her crew room to have a better angle to engage the E-Boat, then she pushed the gun buzzer again. Her thought was to have the E-Boat searched for Red Indian Material when Lt. Hays returned.

This time when the buzzer sounded, all the gunners concentrated on the area below deck where there might still be enemy survivors. When the sailors ceased fire, the E-Boat had been reduced to matchsticks. Shot to shreds.

The purpose of the exercise was for the enemy not to be in any condition to engage the Raiders in a prolonged firefight when Lt. Hays sent a search party below to investigate the radio room. Team A needed to be well away from Kalos before sunrise because Axis air controlled the sky.

The last thing Brandy wanted was to be caught at sea in broad daylight.

TEAM B WAS TIPTOEING UP THE ONLY ROAD THROUGH THE TOWN. The Greek fisherman was leading the way. Vitalis' long, sharp knife had not been necessary. The patrol was ghosting along like phantoms. There are few things spookier than creeping through an unsuspecting village occupied by enemy personnel in the middle of the night.

While there was a blackout in effect, the Italians did not bother to enforce it. To do so would have required them to venture out at night, which was something they were afraid to do. Since there was no electricity on Mikros, the houses showing light were using kerosene lamps. They provided a mellow yellow glow.

Captain Billy Jack Jaxx was third in the column behind Vitalis, the Greek Sacred Squadron interpreter, who was following the fisherman. It was a tiny village. In only minutes the patrol came to a halt at the house where the four off-duty Italian signalmen rotated spending the night.

By design, Private Fred Harwich and Private Joe Malarkey were walking behind Capt. Jaxx in the column. Jack Cool grabbed both men by their web gear and pulled them in close.

He whispered, "Harwich, you take the back. Malarkey, you stay here in front. If anyone moves inside, both of you toss in a concussion grenade in case there are any civilians in the house. Should anyone try to exit, shoot 'em.

"Clear?"

"Clear, sir."

"If anyone tries to exit *before* we take out the RS/OP, use your silenced .22 High Standards.

"Is that clear?"

"Clear, sir."

One of the advantages of using SOG personnel for the missions tonight was that they all routinely carried silenced weapons—and were skilled at using them. It would not end well for anyone attempting to enter or leave this house tonight.

The remainder of the Team B column moved out. Their rubber-soled raiding boots made no sound on the cobblestone road. Actually, it was more of a cobblestone path, since there was not a single motorized vehicle on Mikros.

Once out of town, the pace picked up. Then the slope steepened until Team B was speed marching up a forty-five-degree incline. A faint glow came into view at the top. Soon the patrol was approaching the light created by kerosene lamps inside a large cylindrical tent.

An Italian soldier stepped outside to smoke a cigarette. He was a rear echelon soldier who had spent the last two years stationed on a tiny island where everyone hated him. As he was lighting his cigarette, he saw Team B arrive. While not an elite fighting trooper by any stretch of the imagination, the Blackshirt did draw his Beretta sidearm and manage to get off the first round. *BAAAAANG!*

While it was only a .380 round, in the still of the night it sounded like a 500-pound bomb. There went the element of surprise. Once lost, it could never be regained.

Displaying remarkable survival skills, the fisherman acting as the Team B guide dropped to the ground, leaving Vitalis and Capt. Jaxx face-to-face with a very scared, armed Italian soldier. All three immediately engaged.

Vitalis was armed with a .45 caliber Thompson submachine gun. Capt. Jaxx was carrying a .30 caliber Colt Monitor — chopped BAR. For the second time, the Italian soldier fired and missed. Capt. Jaxx and Vitalis fired and did not miss.

The heavy burst from the pair of automatic weapons blew the Blackshirt off his feet.

Without waiting for orders, the rest of the patrol rushed up, came on line and opened fire. The tent was caught in a withering vector of steel-jacketed rounds. No one inside shot back.

MSgt. Beckwith threw a U.S. Mark 2 fragmentation grenade inside the open flap.

"Grenade!"

Everyone hit the dirt.

WHAAAAAM!

Then Team B charged inside to conduct a hasty search. The three remaining enemy signalmen were dead or dying. Demolitions were placed on the radio. Wanting to get back down to Harwich and Malarkey as fast as possible, Capt. Jaxx ordered, "Do it, Fontain."

Corporal Micky Fontain, the demo man, shouted, "Fire in the hole."

Not waiting around to see the results, Team B started double-timing down the hill. They were halfway to the bottom when they heard firing.

By the time the Raiders arrived on the scene, the engagement was all over. The shooting had started when an enemy soldier had run out the front door, alarmed by the distant sound of automatic weapons coming from the direction of the RS/OP.

Capt. Jaxx made a quick estimation of the situation. He decided against entering the house. The odds were against anything of intelligence value being inside. And he could think of no good reason to risk one of his men on a pointless search.

To cover the withdrawal, Capt. Jaxx ordered, "Everyone pick a window. On my command, chunk in a grenade. Then move out smartly."

After allowing time for his people to get in place, Capt. Jaxx shouted, "DO IT NOW!"

There was the sound of tinkling glass being shattered, then Team B was running through the village, the patrol forming up on the move. Silence not being an issue, the troops were laughing like mad men. Behind them, the grenades were thundering. Tonight had been a classic example of improvisation, skill, teamwork, stealthy movement, immediate reaction and combat experience—all brought to bear on an ill-disciplined, unsuspecting enemy.

The ill-prepared Italians never had a chance.

ON OMORFOS ISLAND, COLONEL JOHN RANDAL WAS STANDING ON the beach with Lieutenant Douglas Fairbanks Jr., waiting for King and Stavos, the Greek Sacred Squadron interpreter, to return with a guide. The Catalina PBY was a few yards out, bobbing gently in the waves looking like a prewar picture postcard depicting exotic air travel of the rich and famous.

At the last minute, Lt. Fairbanks had demanded to accompany the patrol, which had not been part of the plan.

Captain Pamala Plum-Martin mouthed, "Please."

Rather than debate the issue, Col. Randal said, "As long as you promise not to stop to sign any autographs."

He already had Vice Admiral Sir Randolph "Razor" Ransom and Captain "Geronimo" Joe McKoy along. One more strap-hanger—why not? Besides, Lt. Fairbanks had brought his own .45 caliber Thompson submachine gun.

Col. Randal hoped he knew how to use it.

Lt. Fairbanks said, "Niv said you were a great guy, Colonel."

Col. Randal guessed he meant Major David Niven—another A-list actor assigned to Phantom in London.

King and Stavos reappeared. They had with them, of all things, a Greek Orthodox Church priest. The cleric was talking a million miles a minute.

Col. Randal asked, "What's he going on about?"

Stavos said, "He wants a submachine gun to go kill the Italians occupying the island."

"The priest does?"

Stavos said, "He says they are all murderers, rapists, sodomizers and molesters of small children . . ."

"Tell him negative on the submachine gun."

King said, "The priest informed us there are ten enemy personnel stationed on Omorfos. Two German stiffeners and eight Italians. They do a five-on and five-off rotation with one of the Nazis on each shift. Generally, stand a twenty percent alert—meaning one man awake at all times."

Col. Randal said, "Where's the RS/OP?"

King said, "Located on the hill behind the town. The off-duty enemy troops live on the second story of the bank in the village. The priest says it is easier to go straight to the hill from here and bypass the town."

"How far?"

Stavos said, "About a mile. He claims it is steep."

Col. Randal said, "King, have the Lifeboat Servicemen report back to Pam. Tell her to stand by ready. We're moving on the objective as soon as you return."

King said, "Roger, Chief."

Col. Randal had Team C pull in on him. "We're traveling cross-country to the RS/OP to avoid the village. The idea is to take out the target and head home without the enemy garrisoned in the town knowing we've been here until we're airborne and gone.

"Costello, put a forty-five-minute fuse on your demolitions."

Corporal Danny Costello, the demo man for Team C, said, "You got it, sir."

Col. Randal said, "Saddle up, we're moving in zero five."

King came back.

"Let's go," said Col. Randal.

The terrain was favorable, gently sloping the farther inland they traveled. Team C was marching fast—almost at the double. It was dark with no moon out. Without warning, the point element slammed into a sheer cliff face.

The patrol had arrived at the foot of the hill.

The priest had said it was steep. The mother of all understatements. From where Col. Randal was standing, the hill looked like Mount Everest. Straight up for a thousand feet.

Actually, it only seemed straight. However, it was a thousand feet or so above sea level. A long way to the top.

Neither Capt. McKoy nor VAdm. Ransom protested when the redistribution of the Stinger and the spare ammunition took place. Both men were highly experienced combat veterans. They knew it was the right thing to do.

The climb was not going to be easy, even without the weight.

Capt. McKoy whispered, "Nobody explained it to me like this, John."

Col. Randal whispered back, "Yeah, well, they didn't explain it to me like this either."

Lt. Fairbanks whispered, "We have to scale *that*?"

A quick patrol reorganization was necessary as well. King, because he was from Switzerland and the most experienced climber, remained on point. The two Lovat Scouts from the Scottish Highlands were moved up behind him. Col. Randal came next with Stavos, VAdm. Ransom, Capt. McKoy and Lt. Fairbanks—who was wishing for a stunt double right about now. The rest of Team C followed. The priest passed to the rear of the column because there was no longer any need for a guide.

Col. Randal gave the command. "Move out."

It was a tough climb. Not technically challenging, but steep. At times they were virtually crawling. There were a lot of sharp, volcanic rocks to make things more difficult, and the approach had to be silent.

The good news was no one at the top of the hill would be expecting anyone to approach from cliffside. Not that they would be expecting anyone to approach at all. No one had, not since one local entrepreneur had decided to haul some ouzo up the trail from the village one night shortly after the Axis Forces occupied the island. He was hoping to sell it to the troops manning the radio station.

Not knowing the countersign when challenged, he had been summarily shot.

Team C snaked its way up. As planned, when King reached the military crest—just below the top—he halted. The Lovat Scouts gave the Stinger and the extra .30 caliber ammunition back to Capt. McKoy and VAdm. Ransom.

Col. Randal and King crawled up to the top of the crest to take a peek at the objective. All they could see was a GP pyramidal tent—U.S. Army's nomenclature for a large general purpose. The canvas glowed from the oil lamps inside, and some light spilled out from the open entry flap.

King went to bring up the rest of Team C. Silently and carefully they moved into position, with two men sealing off the trail back down the hill to the village.

Capt. McKoy was standing on one side of the entry flap with the Stinger on its sling over his shoulder, holding it by its improvised Italian Carcano pistol grip. VAdm. Ransom was standing close behind him with a belt of .30 caliber ammunition ready for a fast reload. Lt. Fairbanks was on the other side, well back, holding his .45 caliber Thompson submachine gun to his shoulder, pointed at the interior of the tent.

Col. Randal and King stepped inside with their silenced .22 High Standard Military Model D pistols at the ready. A German Feldwebel smoking a cigarette was on duty sitting in a folding canvas chair at the desk holding a radio. Four other men, presumably Italian Blackshirts, were sleeping on cots.

WHIIIIIICH, WHIIIIIICH. Col. Randal shot the Nazi in the back of his whitewall-shaved head. The German slumped over on the desk. He never made a sound.

Then he and King both began firing on the sleeping Italian soldiers. The series of silenced .22 pistol shots—no louder than a match striking—came fast and furious, like a swarm of silent bees. None of the enemy made it off their cots.

The tent was secure less than five seconds from the time they stepped inside.

King stepped to the open flap. "Clear."

The search party entered and began collecting anything that might be of intelligence value. Other than a code book and a few papers, there was not much of interest. Col. Randal picked up the dead Nazi's P-08 Luger off the desk, racked the slide enough to eject the round in the chamber and handed it to Lt. Fairbanks.

"Souvenir of your Raiding Forces mission."

Lt. Fairbanks said, "Thanks, Colonel—what I would not give to play this scene in a movie someday."

Capt. McKoy said, "Son-of-a-buck—never even got to fire my Stinger."

Col. Randal said, "Maybe next time."

AFTER WORKING THEIR WAY BACK DOWN FROM THE OBJECTIVE without anyone falling and killing themselves, Team C made their way to the Catalina in short order. Movement back on the flat ground was a relief. The PBY had been taxied around and was backed in close to the shore so the Raiders could wade out to board.

Colonel John Randal said, "Let's get the hell out of Dodge."

Lieutenant Douglas Fairbanks Jr. said, "I costarred in that one."

13
LAID BACK AS A SNAKE

COLONEL JOHN RANDAL WAS SITTING IN THE MESS HALL located on the ground floor of Raiding Forces Headquarters, drinking coffee with Captain Billy Jack Jaxx and Lieutenant Clint Hays. The Team A and B leaders were giving him reports on their raids—an informal debriefing. The kind he liked best. One thing was becoming clear from the "Lessons Learned" on the first four missions. Small islands in the Aegean were soft targets. They were manned primarily by homesick Italian soldiers who had been isolated for years, surrounded by a close-knit population of Greeks who hated them.

Even when German stiffeners were present, lethargy still set in from the daily grind of nothing ever happening—until it did. In every case, the element of surprise—coupled with violence of action—had stunned the enemy.

Col. Randal was beginning to see possibilities. The small islands were exactly the kind of target he was looking for. Raiding Forces could arrive at a time and place of their own choosing, unannounced and unexpected in the dark of night, concentrate overwhelming combat power on a point-type target, then be gone.

The ability to count on the support of the local Greek islander population made the Aegean Area of Operations the ideal place to conduct small-scale raids. Transportation and small-unit leadership were both going to be key to success— the same as it had been with desert gun jeep patrolling. While getting to and from the objective might prove challenging, Raiding Forces had the best small-unit leaders in the business.

Just not enough of them.

Col. Randal said, "Good job. You two studs made it look easy."

Capt. Jaxx said, "What would have made all of our raids a pushover would have been basic actionable intelligence. We all had to develop our own intel once we arrived. That might not always work out so great, sir."

"There has to be some way to solve that problem, Colonel," Lt. Hays said.

Col. Randal said, "Right now, we're limited to a couple of PTs and MAS boats. There are a lot of islands."

Lt. Hays said, "Another thing to think about, sir—the population on most of the islands is so small, a newcomer's freedom of movement will be severely limited. Might be setting ourselves up to be ambushed if the bad guys spot a new face and get suspicious."

"Good point," the colonel said.

Capt. Jaxx said, "Clint and I'll work on it. Has to be something we can do to keep from going in blind, sir."

"Keep me in the loop."

Col. Randal walked upstairs to the third-floor suite that he and Major the Lady Jane Seaborn occupied. When he arrived, he walked outside onto the landing, where he found Captain Pamala Plum-Martin sitting on King's desk and talking to the Merc. Col. Randal said, "You need to see me, Pam?"

The Vargas Girl look-alike Royal Marine said, "Negative."

"Right—carry on," Col. Randal said.

The door had hardly closed behind him when King tapped and opened it."Chief, someone from 15th Army Group to see you."

Col. Randal had never heard of 15th Army Group and he had not been expecting a visitor. "Send him in."

A trim lieutenant colonel sporting "General Staff" insignia walked in, carrying a roll of papers under one arm. Col. Randal clicked on. Arrivals bearing maps were not paying a social call.

"Lieutenant Colonel Marvin Woodbine, sir."

Col. Randal said, "What can I do for you, Colonel?"

Lt. Col. Woodbine said, "I work for General Patton's Seventh Army. It's assigned to the 15th Army Group under General Sir Harold Alexander. General Patton sent me here on a matter he considers of some urgency, sir."

"What might that be?"

The last time Lieutenant General George S. Patton had summoned him to discuss something urgent, he had ended up on the destroyer *Dallas* sailing up the Sebou River twelve miles behind enemy lines to attack the Port Lyautey Air Field three days into OPERATION TORCH.

Lt. Col. Woodbine said, "Everything we are about to discuss is classified Top Secret. It cannot be repeated. No one outside this suite possesses the Need to Know."

Col. Randal said, "Lady Jane's in the bedroom—does she count?"

"No, sir. However, I do have a get-well-soon card from the General for Lady Seaborn. He ordered me to hand-deliver it personally."

"Soon as you finish this 'urgent matter', I'll make that happen."

The two officers stepped into the small briefing area off the living room. Lt. Col. Woodbine said, "General Eisenhower was still wrapping up the Tunisian Campaign, which I am confident you are aware did not go well . . . except that we won, when he received a directive from the Combined Chiefs to begin planning for his next assignment, OPERATION HUSKY.

"In turn, Eisenhower tapped General Patton to command all U.S. troops—meaning the Seventh Army. HUSKY is the occupation of a large, enemy-held island which will remain unnamed right up until we actually invade it. The major maneuver units involved are Montgomery's Eighth Army and Patton's Seventh Army.

"On receipt of the orders to begin preparation for HUSKY, before handing off to General Patton, Eisenhower assembled an ad hoc team of air and ground planners and dispatched them to Cairo—called the Cairo Group. Their assignment was to rough out a scheme for the use of airborne forces for HUSKY. Because there was not one single parachute-qualified officer on 15th Army Group's staff at the time, none were in on the planning."

Col. Randal took out one of Waldo's custom-rolled cigars and stuck it between his front teeth, unlit.

"Since they had no idea what they were doing," Lt. Col. Woodbine said, "the Cairo Group referred to a pair of outdated British plans to use airborne troops for a drop on the same target as their model. The first, OPERATION INFLUX, was originally concocted in 1940, with the second, OPERATION WHIPCORD, planned in 1941.

"The two proposed drops were ambitious, considering there was not one parachute battalion in the entire Middle East Command at the time. Since the British did not have an established airborne doctrine to guide them in those days, the INFLUX and WHIPCORD planners were winging it like the Cairo Group. We've got ourselves a true-life example of the blind leading the blind, sir."

Col. Randal said, "Sounds like."

"As you are probably aware, sir, the British tend to view paratroopers as Airborne Commandos," Lt. Col. Woodbine said. "INFLUX and WHIPCORD both called for dropping penny packets of parachutists all over the place. Therefore, it should come as no surprise that when the Cairo Group finished their work, they had developed a similar plan.

"To their credit, Eisenhower's staff rejected it out of hand. The Cairo Group was sent back to the drawing board. This time they outdid themselves. The 82nd Airborne Division was to make a mass drop directly onto the invasion beaches to engage the enemy defensive system before the sea-born troops of the 1st Infantry Division stormed ashore.

"Even officers like me, who have never jumped out of an airplane and have no intention of ever doing so, knew that idea was insane, sir. The Cairo Group was disbanded. General Eisenhower was so unimpressed that several of the officers in it were relieved of duty and shipped home.

"Then word got around that the British 1st Airborne Division was slated to take the lead in the drop, with the 82nd Airborne playing a supporting role. To add insult to injury, it was learned that the British paratroopers were to be transported in United States Army Air Force C-47s, sir.

"General Ridgway, the 82nd's CG, blew his stack.

"By now, 15th Army Group had an 'Airborne Advisor' assigned, Major General Frederick "Boy" Browning, the United Kingdom's senior parachute officer. Rumor soon got around that he intended to make a power grab to take command of *all* the parachute troops the Allies have on this side of the Atlantic.

"Would you happen to know General Browning, sir?"

Col. Randal said, "Never met the man. Lady Jane is acquainted with his wife, Daphne du Maurier. Wrote *Rebecca*, I believe. Chose the wine-red beret for British Airborne Forces because it matches the shade of her favorite claret."

"Not exactly the background information I was hoping for, sir."

Col. Randal said, "This is a classified briefing. Need to Know. You quote me to anyone, I'll have you shot by that mercenary you met out front or will do it myself—understood?"

"Without question, sir," Lt. Col. Woodbine said.

Col. Randal said, "According to Lady Jane's friends who know him well, Boy Browning is an egotistical, overly ambitious self-promoter. Personally, I don't understand how a general managed to command British Airborne Forces without ever actually having taken any of them in harm's way.

"Browning's not even jump-qualified."

Lt. Col. Woodbine said, "That's the conclusion General Patton came to after meeting with him, sir. Georgie piled into the fray, backing General Ridgway. Battle lines were drawn along national interests.

"Almost immediately, another fight erupted over allocation of C-47 troop transports. There are only three hundred sixty planes available to fly the HUSKY mission because of crew shortages. That's not enough to drop the 1st Airborne and the 82nd Airborne simultaneously in one lift. Monty and Georgie both wanted all the Dakotas.

"The feud began to spiral out of control.

"Finally, sir, General Eisenhower decided to step in and have 15th Army allocate the troop transports. He gave two hundred fifty of the C-47s to the 82nd. That's only enough to drop the 505th Parachute Infantry Regiment—reinforced by one battalion of the 504th—on the first night of the invasion.

"Which means the penny packets of paratroopers are still penny packets . . . only bigger."

Col. Randal said, "Lovely."

"That's where you come in, Colonel."

SOMEWHERE IN TUNISIA

COLONEL JOHN RANDAL WAS UNDERNEATH THE WING OF A United States Army Air Force C-47, leaning back against the British X-type parachute Raiding Forces Chief Rigger Captain Karen Montgomery had dropped off for him. The Royal Air Force referred to the plane as the Dakota. The USAAF called it the Skytrain. For reasons that were never clear, most people tended to go with C-47 or Dakota.

No one called the troop transport a Skytrain.

In approximately six hours, the 575th Parachute Infantry Regiment (Special) (Separate), the Rangers, was going to take off for a three-hour flight to a drop zone in Sicily. Calling the 575th a regiment was a stretch. It consisted of 1st Battalion 575th Parachute Infantry Regiment made up of composite seventy-man A, B and C Companies and the 10th Ranger Battalion (Airborne)(Provisional)(-). The minus being one company that was detached, guarding 15th Army Group's Headquarters.

The two battalions had never worked together before, with the exception of B/10th Rangers. Under Col. Randal's command, it had sailed up the Sebou River on the destroyer *Dallas* to capture the Port Lyautey Airfield. Small Operations Group, led by Captain Billy Jack Jaxx, had jumped on the runway to support the attack.

That was the only time elements of the two outfits had met.

To further complicate things, the 1/575th had to be completely reformed. Its troops had been scattered throughout Raiding Forces and needed to be pulled off their current assignments and reconstituted as ad hoc parachute infantry rifle battalion for OPERATION HUSKY. It was a testament to the men's ability to be flexible and focus on the mission in front of them that they were able to make the transition virtually on the move to the assembly area.

Major Duke Slater had been commanding Sea Squadron when tapped to be the battalion commander of the 1/575th. 'A' Company was commanded by Captain Billy Jack Jaxx of SOG. 'B' Company was commanded by Captain Roy Kidd, who was leading Duck Patrol when the call came. 'C' Company was commanded by Captain Preston Butterfield III, who had been in Cairo organizing a group of tough former French Foreign Legionnaires from his Blue Patrol to be on the clandestine team to recover the LEAF EATER diamonds after they had been sold to smugglers when he received the temporary change of mission.

Neither the 1/575th's battalion commander nor any of the three company commanders had ever served in the battalion previously.

The 10th Ranger Battalion (-) was under the command of Major Jack Dance. Except for its B Company, it had never been in combat. The bulk of the battalion had spent its time overseas guarding Lieutenant General Dwight Eisenhower's Tunisian Allied Force Headquarters and/or pulling sentry duty at one or another of the POW camps scattered around North Africa.

The 610 men of the 575th PIR would be the first troops in, leading the way in the first Allied invasion of Fortress Europe—the tip of the sword.

Following them would be an air armada of C-47s from the USAAF 52nd Troop Carrier Wing, transporting 3,400 paratroops of the 82nd Airborne Division, 505th Regimental Combat Team under the command of Colonel James "Slim Jim" Gavin, making its combat début.

The 505th RCT was to drop on a ridge known as Piano Lupo, north by northeast of the coastal town of Gela. Col. Gavin's mission was to block enemy efforts to rush reinforcements to Patton's Seventh Army's landing beaches where the U.S. 1st Infantry Division would be coming ashore.

The 575th PIR was to drop nine miles northeast of the 505th RCT. Col. Randal's assignment was to secure a 300-foot long concrete slab bridge over a large intermittent stream, (currently dry), that was a tributary of the Gela River. The steep, deep banks of the streambed created the perfect antitank ditch. In addition, there was a road junction leading to the bridge. Any enemy vehicle attempting to counterattack in the direction of the 1st Division's, 16th Infantry Regiment's assault on the easternmost beach near the town of Gela would have to cross the concrete bridge to negotiate the obstacle. In military terms, the Axis Forces would be channelized into a choke point.

Tactically, that is a bad thing.

However, if the slab over the riverbed was not secured, the opposing forces would be able to rush to the scene of the invasion during the first critical hours of Seventh Army coming ashore. Lieutenant General George S. Patton recognized the importance of keeping enemy fighting vehicles off his beachhead.

The bridge was the reason he had called on Col. Randal. He did not have anyone else to capture it. The remainder of the 82nd Airborne Division had already been committed to either land by sea or drop in to reinforce the 505th RCT on the night of D+1.

On paper, the 575th PIR appeared to be full strength.

The question in Col. Randal's mind was, could a hastily thrown together, undermanned, lightly armed, parachute infantry regiment—meaning a half strength battalion—be able to accomplish the mission?

No one knew the answer.

Various specialist units had been showing up to be attached for the mission ever since the 575th PIR had arrived at the departure airfield. Two medical teams from the 307th Medical Company (Airborne), a platoon from the 307th Engineer Battalion (Airborne)—which was a little confusing since both sported the same number identifier, a detachment from the 82nd Airborne Signals Company to help establish commo with the U.S. 1st Infantry Division and the 82nd Airborne, plus a pair of jump-qualified U.S. Navy Fire Control Teams.

Provided one or both of the parties of naval forward observers reached the bridge and could establish radio contact with the fleet offshore, the big guns of the navy could be called down in support. Col. Randal assigned one team to the 10th Ranger Battalion and the other to the 1/575th.

Captain "Dynamite" Dick Coogan arrived from Raiding Forces Headquarters near Cairo with a demolitions team made up of men from his Railroad Wrecking Crew II Patrol. They were late, having been on an operation when the 575th PIR departed.

A tall lieutenant sporting crossed cannon artillery insignia on his collar reported in. The artillery officer saluted. Military etiquette did not call for returning salutes from a reclining position. In fact, it did not address the subject at all. But Col. Randal was not disposed to get up.

He gave a sort of casual wave in acknowledgement.

"Who might you be?"

"Lieutenant Issacs, sir. Commanding Officer E Battery, 376th Parachute Field Artillery. We've been attached to the 575th for the drop tonight. Understand you can use help fighting tanks."

Col. Randal said, "No one has mentioned enemy tanks, but we'll take all the help we can get. What can you do for me, Lieutenant?"

Lieutenant Christopher Issacs said, "E Battery consists of four 75mm howitzers, sir. We load out one gun per C-47 with ten parachute artillerymen on board. I was only able to bring three guns. Our fourth is in ordnance down for maintenance."

"I've never seen a pack 75s air dropped. How's that work?"

Lt. Issacs said, "We break the gun down into its major component parts. Those go out the door first and then my artillerymen follow. The trick is to find all the pieces once we land, sir."

Col. Randal pulled out a fuzzy aerial photo, "This is a concrete slab bridge over a dry tributary to the Gela River. We'll be jumping on Drop Zone T located right about here. You drop in, do your Easter egg hunt, assemble what guns you can and place your battery where you believe best to deny the enemy access to the bridge.

"Don't let anything across."

Lt. Issacs said, "Anything else I need to know, sir?"

"Negative—stand to your guns."

Lt. Issacs was used to detailed Operations Orders about the size of a phone book for the training jumps he had made with the 82nd Airborne Division at Fort Benning. He asked, "Are you sure you're not leaving anything out, sir?"

Col. Randal said, "Oh, I forgot. The challenge is 'George' and the countersign is 'Marshall'."

Lt. Issacs said, "Colonel, do you mind if I point out this operation sounds a little loose?"

"I don't mind at all."

Master Sergeant Mack Beckwith took Lt. Issacs to Air Operations to learn which planes his battery was assigned to for the drop. Col. Randal ordered him to specify that E Battery, 376th Parachute Field Artillery, was to be transported by the most experienced pilots with the best navigators.

The pack 75s needed to be dropped as accurately as possible.

Lt. Issacs asked, "Is Colonel Randal always so laid back before a mission? Prior to the jumps I've made with the 82nd, the senior officers run around like chickens with their heads cut off."

MSgt. Beckwith said, "Sometimes the Colonel catches a few Z's, which is what you need to be doing as soon as you get the chance, lootenant."

The two had not been gone long before another jeep pulled up to the C-47. A stocky captain dismounted, then lifted his gear out of the back. He walked over and saluted.

"Captain Ragsdale, sir. I've been assigned by Colonel Gavin to be the 505th's Regimental Combat Team's liaison officer to the 575th."

Col. Randal responded with a nonchalant salute. "Really?"

Capt. Delbert Ragsdale said, "Yes, sir."

"Sit down, Captain—give me a rundown on the 505th. Then I'll have someone show you how the X-type parachute works. You ever jump one?"

"Negative sir, never heard of an X-type chute."

Col. Randal said, "You're going to like it. Not much opening shock. Has a quick release system.

"Tell me about your regiment."

"The Five-O-Five—where to start, sir. I'm an excess officer assigned to the division prior to it shipping out," Capt. Ragsdale said. "That's why I have the honor to be selected as the regimental liaison officer—I didn't have a job. What I'm about to tell you are my personal observations since the division landed in this hellhole called North Africa. Consider them for what they're worth.

"Please keep everything I say confidential, Colonel."

Col. Randal said, "I can do that."

"Heat, flies, and sand. More heat, flies, and sand. In your food. In your hair. Down your neck. Can't sleep. No showers for weeks. After all the months that the 82nd has been living under conditions you would not inflict on a stray dog, it's ready to fight somebody, sir.

"The 82nd Airborne is the finest division in the U.S. Army—though it has yet to see combat. The Five-O-Five is the best regiment in the division. Colonel Gavin is the best regimental commander." Capt. Ragsdale said.

"Having said that, all is not sunshine and happiness in the Five-O-Five. The regiment has outstanding troops. The officers, well, there is an undercurrent difficult to put your finger on. For example, the regiment has three battalions. Col. Gavin relieved the 2nd Battalion's commander two weeks ago on what some believe was a flimsy excuse. The battalion's new commander, Major Alexander, has only been in the army a little over two years.

"Meanwhile, the 3rd Battalion is commanded by Major Krause—known as 'Cannonball.' He's a loudmouth blowhard. His officers don't respect him. They make no bones about it, don't try to hide their contempt—everyone in the division feels the same way. Why he still has his job is a total mystery.

"The 1st Battalion is commanded by Lieutenant Colonel Gorman. The men call him 'Hardnose' for cause. The Colonel's a strict disciplinarian, but he's a really great guy. Cares about his troops. Leads from the front, sir.

"They say he's the first military parachutist to jump from ten thousand feet.

"As for the company grade officers, sir, so many have been relieved for one infraction or another—those in place now are the best of the best."

Col. Randal said, "So, what are you planning to tell Colonel Gavin about me?"

Capt. Ragsdale said, "As soon as you release me, sir, I'm going to go report you're so calm about our jump tonight that you're taking salutes from the prone position."

King took Capt. Ragsdale in search of the Raiding Forces Chief Rigger, Capt. Montgomery, to issue him an X-type parachute.

Before they were out of sight, another jeep rolled up to a screeching stop. The vehicle was being driven by a big, good-looking pilot with eagle rank insignia on his collar and pilots' wings on his chest. He gave the impression of being in charge of everything and everyone in sight—or maybe it was he did not care who was.

Colonel Sam Houston Blackwell—friends called him "Bronc"—shouted, "This the Five-Seven-Five? I'm looking for the CO."

Col. Randal said, "That would be me."

"I'm the commander of the Provisional Troop Carrier Group out of Big Spring Army Airfield. We'll be dropping your boys tonight," Col. Blackwell said. "Hop in, let's go to the head shed and I'll fill you in on the route we'll be flying."

Col. Randal said, "Sounds like a plan."

As the jeep roared off, the pilot stuck out his giant-sized paw, "Bronc Blackwell."

Col. Randal felt his hand getting swallowed up, then crushed, "John Randal."

"You're John Randal?" Col. Blackwell turned to stare.

"Affirmative."

Col. Blackwell looked at him in disbelief or possibly disappointment, "*The John Randal—my future son-in-law?*"

Col. Randal said, "Well, I don't know about that last part."

"I'm Beverly's daddy. Little girl writes me three to five V-mails a week. Types 'em so she can squeeze more words on those little bitty forms. Beverly has never mentioned any boy to me more than twice in her whole life.

"Writes something about Johnny in almost every letter. I've been trying to figure out how to divide up the ranch."

Col. Randal said, "Beverly talks about you all the time."

"Glad to hear that. Thinks you walk on water, J. R. Hate to have to be the man who's gonna get you killed tonight."

"Let's try not to, Bronc."

Col. Blackwell said, "I command the flight school at the U.S. Army Airfield in Big Spring, Texas—C-47s. We're cranking out pilots as fast as we can get 'em dual-engine qualified. There ain't enough transport drivers on the planet to meet the worldwide demand. But pilots are not the real problem—it's navigators.

"My graduates can fly 'cause we teach 'em—and I mean *right*. But I'm not in charge of training navigators. The ones they're certifying these days in the school on the other side of the airfield have trouble charting a course from their barracks to the chow hall."

Col. Randal said, "Always a problem for Raiding Forces—finding places."

"Here's the deal, J. R. I was sitting in my office one day when a Top Secret message from an old polo playing buddy a' mine, Georgie Patton, landed on my desk," Col. Blackwell said. "He wanted to know if I could get over here to

Tunisia real fast with enough people to crew fifty C-47s. Said he could scrape up planes if I could bring aircrew to fly 'em on a mission of short duration. So I rounded up fifty unassigned navigators who had just graduated, got a hundred of my pilot instructors and senior student pilots—one to fly left seat and one co-pilot, loaded 'em on a dozen of the flight school's Dakotas and we took off for WWII.

"I figured it was some kind of resupply deal for a big push or something. Nobody told me we were going to be dropping paratroops at zero dark thirty on a heavily defended, enemy-held island after a three-hour flight over open water before we get to our initial point. My boys probably won't be able to find Sicily—much less your DZ."

Col. Randal said, "I don't expect to hit the drop zone—try to put us out over dry land."

"We'll give it our best shot. Here's the plan," Col. Blackwell said. "We take off here and fly direct to Malta. They'll have the island lit up like a Christmas tree for us—understand, there's more searchlights per square foot than any other piece of ground in history, so it'll make one spectacular beacon. We hit Malta, then dogleg left for the run in straight to Sicily and your DZ about an hour out."

Col. Randal said, "That's good."

"You may actually be as cool in the face of death as Beverly claims—or you don't give a damn, Johnny. Which one is it?"

Col. Randal said, "I can't fly an airplane—that's your job. You've already informed me your people won't be able to execute the mission as planned. That means adjusting to the situation once we're on the ground.

"I'll get dialed in then."

Col. Blackwell said, "Beverly mentioned you were about as 'laid back as a snake.' You plan on biting anybody tonight?"

"Not until we get to Sicily."

THE DEPARTURE AIRFIELD WAS A BEEHIVE OF ACTIVITY, AND IT would get busier as Station Time got closer—jumpers on board belted in their seats thirty minutes prior to takeoff. Manifests were being typed, parachutes issued, inspected. When there was a deficiency, one of Captain Karen Montgomery's Royal Marine riggers working with the 575th and/or riggers on loan from the 82nd Airborne working with the 10th Rangers, would move in and make the fix. Jumpers were being assigned to their plane—called a chalk. Each chalk was in a serial of planes for the air movement to the drop zone. Jumpmasters were taping the doors of the aircraft they would be jumpmastering to eliminate sharp edges, tugging on the steel cables that the jumpers' static lines would be hooked up to, checking to make sure they were firmly attached and inspecting the "towed parachutist retrieval mechanism"—a canvas strap with a snap hook on the end.

If a jumper's canopy became entangled and the paratrooper was being towed behind the aircraft, there were two scenarios. In the event the towed parachutist was conscious, the man was to put one or both hands on his helmet. In that case, the jumpmaster would cut him free and the jumper would activate his reserve parachute—to land who knew where. In the event the trooper being towed was not conscious and did not put one or both hands on his helmet, then the jumpmaster and the USAAF loadmaster would hook up the towed parachutist retrieval mechanism, meaning the canvas strap, and try to muscle the trooper back on board.

Everybody—jumpmasters, loadmasters, pilots and every single one of the paratroopers jumping tonight sincerely hoped neither of those two options occurred on board their aircraft.

Trucks came around with extra bandoliers of ammunition and grenades for anyone who wanted to carry more. Every officer and NCO was issued a flare pistol and a dozen flares. Every man in the 10th Ranger Battalion and 1/575 PIR was issued five flares. Finally, everyone jumping tonight was issued a mine, Mark 1, Anti-Tank—weight 10 pounds, in a canvas carrying bag.

There was no explanation concerning the flares or the mines—just "take 'em."

Certain items of clothing and equipment differentiated between the 10th Ranger Battalion and the 1/575th PIR. The Raiding Forces men were wearing locally made, lightweight, faded green safari suit battle dress uniforms with big pockets everywhere, including on the thighs of the pants. The 10th Rangers were wearing khaki jumpsuits which—unknown to them—had been modeled in part on the battle dress uniform Col. Randal was wearing when he visited the U.S. Army Airborne School at Fort Benning, Georgia.

The 10th Rangers sported tall brown Corcoran jump boots. The 1/575 had on their canvas-topped, rubber-soled raiding boots.

The 10th Rangers were armed with an assortment of standard TO&E weapons for parachute infantry—.30 M-1 Garand rifles, .30 M1 Carbines, M1-A1 .45 Thompson Submachine Guns, .30 Browning Automatic Rifles and crew served .30 Browning M-1919 Browning Light Machine guns.

The 1/575th was armed with 9mm Beretta M-38 Submachine guns, chopped .30 BARs and .30 M-1941 Johnson LMGs. There were a few .45 Thompson submachine guns and .30 M1 Carbines.

Troops from the two battalions managed to find time to do what soldiers like to do—mingle and compare uniforms, weapons and equipment.

Colonel Sam Houston Blackwell invited Colonel John Randal to bring his battalion and company commanders to his pre-mission briefing so they could be introduced to the USAAF aircrew who would be flying them. The commander of the Provisional Troop Carrier Group that had flown in from Big Spring, Texas, insisted the commander of the 575th Parachute Infantry Regiment say a few words. He wanted his pilots and crew to hear from the commander of the paratroops they would be dropping tonight.

Col. Randal said, not entirely truthfully, "Colonel Blackwell has informed me you men were handpicked to fly this mission. Two things: First, make sure to keep your air speed down when you green light the jumpers on your ship. When my boys hit the silk, we don't want people losing equipment from excessive opening shock or experiencing blown panels due to you pilots trying to get the hell out of Dodge a little early. Second, everyone jumps. Do not—I say again, do not—bring anyone home. If you can't locate the DZ, put your jumpers out over land—anyplace.

"It's an honor to be flying with you tonight—good luck, gentlemen."

At 1800 hours, Col. Randal issued his Operations Order to the assembled 575th Regimental Combat Team. He kept it short and simple, as stipulated in

Raiding Forces Rules. Half the troops in his command were combat veterans—the rest having never heard a shot fired in anger.

Too much detail would only be confusing.

Besides, moments before taking the stage, he had received word from Col. Blackwell the winds over Sicily would be 30 mph gusting to 45 mph. Anything over 13 mph was rated excessive for parachute drops. All the detailed planning, coordinating and assembling for an airborne operation of this magnitude was going to go down the tube the minute the 505th RCT and 575th PIR went wheels up.

Maj. Duke Slater and Maj. Jack Dance, his two battalion commanders, would issue considerably more detailed Operations Orders to their respective battalions upon conclusion of Col. Randal's briefing. Then each company commander would issue his own Operations Order to their companies. And the platoon leaders would issue theirs to their platoons.

The 575th was going to be told everything it needed to know—almost.

Unknown to anyone in Lieutenant General George S. Patton's Seventh Army was the fact that the officers and men taking part in OPERATION HUSKY were being lied to. G-2 Intelligence briefers stated in every briefing and/or printed Enemy Forces Intelligence Summary handout that there were no German combat units stationed on Sicily. That was not true.

The wizards at Bletchley Park had intercepted and decoded signals transmitted by the Nazi Hermann Göring Fallschirm-Panzer Division that confirmed not only was the elite parachute-tank division on the island, it was located in the immediate proximity of the 505th RCT and the 575th PIR's drop zones. Allied Force Commander Lieutentant General Dwight Eisenhower, had been forced to make a hard strategic decision: he could not risk exposing the fact that the Allies had cracked the German Enigma Code by revealing knowledge of the presence of the Nazi combat units on Sicily to the troops who would be carrying out the invasion.

Officers and men had been promised they would be fighting Italians with low morale.

Col. Randal was standing on a six-foot platform, looking down at his troops gathered around on the tarmac. He said, "Well, men, I guess you're wondering why I called you here."

As usual, this brought a laugh, even from the Raiding Forces personnel who had heard him say it before. Tension ratcheted down. If the Colonel was not worried, why should they be?

"Situation: The bad guys are on Sicily. We're in Tunisia. In a few hours, we jump on Sicily.

"Mission: Our mission is to parachute onto Drop Zone T nine miles east of Gela. Once on the ground, you will move independently to our Assembly Point at the objective—a concrete slab bridge over an intermittent tributary of the Gela River. We are to secure the span until relieved by the 16th Infantry Regiment of the Big Red One, attacking overland from the beach east of the town of Gela.

"Execution: Each of you has been issued an M-1 anti-tank mine and five flares. Your individual assignment is to deliver those items to the Assembly Point. The first officer or NCO who arrives at the AP will immediately put up a flare and continue putting one up every five minutes. The flares will be a signal the rest of the Five-Seven-Five can rally on. When you arrive, immediately hand over your flares to whoever is performing the signaling.

"Concept of the Operation: The first men to reach Assembly Point will cross over the bridge and move inland until coming to a Y road junction. Those troopers will place their mines, blocking the junction. Then they will return and take up defensive positions in their assigned company areas to cover the obstacle with fire. As more troopers arrive at the AP, they will continue to move across to scatter their mines along the roadway, leapfrogging back until there is a carpet of antitank mines from the road junction all the way across the span.

"Don't let anyone or anything prevent you from delivering your flares and placing your mine. We're going to seize that bridge and hold it at all costs until relieved. Now you know what I expect of you.

"Is that clear?"

Six hundred-plus men of the 575th PIR shouted, "CLEAR, SIR!"

COLONEL JOHN RANDAL MET WITH MAJOR DUKE SLATER AND Major Jack Dance under the wing of the C-47 he would be jumping. The two battalion commanders were impatient to get back to their battalions, so he kept it brief. Time was running out to coordinate with their company commanders; however, both officers wanted this last-minute meeting with their boss before wheels up.

Col. Randal said, "Nothing is going to go right tonight. Don't expect it to. Some of the pilots flying us haven't graduated from flight school yet; the navigators are inexperienced; and the winds over the DZ are going to be thirty mph gusting to forty-five mph. Tie down every piece of equipment your jumpers are carrying, then tie it down again—I want redundancy.

"There's no chance of finding the externally dropped bundles with the excessive winds. Instruct your troops not to waste time looking for 'em. We can send out recovery parties after the sun comes up.

"Tell your people to land, drop their chutes, and go. I'll see you in Sicily. Let's do this."

The 1/575th would take off first, the idea being to have veterans on the ground before the follow-on 10th Rangers arrived. The order was A Company, E Battery, 376 Parachute Field Artillery, B Company, then C Company. At his own request, Colonel Sam Houston Blackwell, *aka* Bronc, who would be flying the lead plane in the lead serial, would be transporting Captain Billy Jack Jaxx—the two were friends.

Since Jack Cool would be jumpmastering the drop on board his plane, leading the stick out the door, he would be the first U.S. Army soldier of the war to invade Fortress Europe. Col. Randal would be traveling in the lead serial carrying the 10th Ranger Battalion, which would put him in the middle of the air armada.

Col. Blackwell stopped by in his jeep, clearly enjoying the organized chaos taking place all around the airfield. He said, "Don't worry about my boys. It's the 52nd Troop Carrier Wing carrying the 82nd Airborne that's going to be the problem. I trained most of their pilots, but they've had six months overseas to pick up bad habits.

"The word is, they haven't been getting in much practice flying formation. Holding station in a big formation is difficult in daylight. It's almost impossible at night on radio silence, lights out, in a high wind, and while getting shot at."

Col. Randal said, "Get us there. It doesn't have to be pretty."

Col. Blackwell said, "I'm going to put my planeload of jumpers out at approximately 2400 hours, right on the DZs. If things go according to schedule, the Five-O-Five and Five-Seven-Five will be on the ground a half hour before moonset. I detailed my best pilot instructor to fly your chalk. You're in good hands. We wouldn't want Beverly to be a widow before she got married."

"I think you're confused about our relationship, Bronc."

"Happy landing, J. R."

Normally at this point, the men in Col. Randal's stick would chute up and be given a jumpmaster inspection. That would not happen tonight. Everyone would carry their parachute on board. Then one hour out from the drop zone, they would perform in-flight rigging, working in two-man teams helping each other get into their parachutes.

Once everyone was chuted up, Col. Randal's jumpmaster inspection would take place while the C-47 flew on toward the DZ.

Master Sergeant Mack Beckwith said, "Station Time in ten, sir."

Col. Randal glanced at the Rolex that Major the Lady Jane Seaborn had given him a lifetime ago. "Load up."

On board the Dakota would be King, the two Lovat Scouts, MSgt. Beckwith and eleven Rangers from B Company . . . all veterans of the Port Lyautey drop. The makeup of the stick was no accident. Major Jack Dance, the 10th Ranger Battalion commander, was intentionally surrounding his boss with men who had served with him previously.

Col. Randal had expected MSgt. Beckwith to jumpmaster another planeload tonight, but the senior NCO insisted on jumping his plane. It was the Sergeant Major's prerogative.

Col. Randal was last to board, standing alone on the tarmac in the event some late-breaking development required his attention. A jeep raced up with a staff major from the 15th Army in the passenger seat. He was wearing judge advocate corps insignia. Col. Randal had never met the man before. The major hauled a cram-packed duffel bag out of the back of the jeep and dragged it over to where he was standing.

"These are your regulations covering the establishment of POW camps in Sicily, sir."

Col. Randal said, "Put 'em on the plane."

King leaned down from the door and hauled the big canvas bag full of documents inside.

As soon as the staff officer drove off, Col. Randal said, "King, when we're over water, ditch that duffel bag."

"My pleasure, Chief."

Col. Randal waited until the C-47's engines were running smoothly. Then, taking one last look around the airfield, he struggled to climb aboard because of all the equipment he was carrying. Inside the aircraft the Rangers were laughing and joking, trying to downplay any possibility they might be experiencing the pre-jump jitters.

Col. Randal shouted, "Is everybody happy?"

The troopers roared, "HELL, YES!"

You could have cut the tension with a knife.

14
IF ANYTHING CAN . . .

COLONEL JOHN RANDAL GLANCED AT HIS ROLEX. THE C-47 HAD been flying for two hours. It was almost time to make their dogleg at Malta for the run in to their drop zone on Sicily. He stood up and started putting on his parachute. Master Sergeant Mack Beckwith assisted him from the rear, saying, "Right leg strap, sir—left leg strap, sir."

Col. Randal would bend down, take the proffered leg strap and snap it into the quick release device on his chest. Once he landed, all he had to do was pop off the safety clip, twist the round turn buckle until the flat side was up and hit it with his fist; then the straps would be released and the parachute harness would fall free. It only took seconds. The British quick-release system was the best in the world.

The 1/575th was jumping British X-type parachutes with the QRS.

Unfortunately, the U.S. Army had chosen not to adopt it. Men in the 505th Regimental Combat team and the 10th Rangers jumping standard-issue U.S. Army T4 parachutes tonight were going to pay for that decision with their lives. They had to either unbuckle their thick canvas straps one at a time or cut them loose with the switchblade jump knives they carried in the zippered collars of their jump jackets. Not an easy thing to do if you are being dragged due to high winds, have landed in water or you are being shot at.

As soon as Col. Randal was chuted up, he instructed MSgt. Beckwith, "Have the troops begin inflight rigging. I'm going up to the cockpit to talk to the pilot. We should have made our turn by now."

The C-47 was fighting a 35mph headwind. The plane seemed at times to be bucking. The wild ride complicated movement and made inflight rigging a challenge.

Col. Randal did a modified "airborne shuffle"—sliding forward without picking his boots off the deck of the aircraft. Not picking up his feet reduced his chances of tripping, losing his balance and falling down. Tonight the buffeting of the Dakota was so violent that one paratrooper after another was lifted off his feet and thrown against the bulkhead from time to time—airborne shuffle or not.

Made things interesting.

What Col. Randal found when he reached the cockpit was not good. The pilot and co-pilot were sweating bullets, and the navigator was mumbling to himself. Out the windscreen there was nothing but darkness.

What they should have been seeing was the lit-up island of Malta putting on a spectacular light show with over a thousand searchlights aimed skyward. Nothing. They were lost.

The C-47 Dakota was racing through the sky. Headed toward—where? Col. Randal kneeled between the pilots, looking out over their shoulders and listening to them debate the situation. The strong winds aloft had blown the armada of troop transports—or at least parts of it—off course.

The air fleet was stacked in flights of Vs, three ships each. Up front somewhere in the first plane piloted by Colonel Sam Houston Blackwell, *aka* Bronc—Beverly's father, Captain Billy Jack Jaxx was leading the way with his A/1/575th. Were they disoriented too?

Col. Randal was flooded with the sensation of rushing into danger combined with the great unknown of what was ahead, while being responsible for commanding a regiment of paratroopers who were getting ready to jump behind enemy lines. It was a heady feeling. One that no other U.S. Army officer besides Colonel James M. "Slim Jim" Gavin, traveling a half hour behind with his 505th Regimental Combat Team, had ever felt.

Tonight's mission was the largest parachute operation attempted by Allied Forces to date. And it was not going well. Because the pilots were on strict radio silence, they could not call anyone to help clarify the situation.

From the left seat, the pilot, Captain Wallace Mossberg said, "We're overdue to make the dogleg to the left, sir."

Col. Randal said, "How do we miss a one hundred twenty-five square mile island?"

Capt. Mossberg said, "First, you miss Linosa, the two square mile island, which was supposed to be a checkpoint to let us know we were on the right flight path, sir."

The night previous, Captain Butch "Headhunter" Hoolihan had landed a party of his Sea Squadron Royal Marines ashore from the HMS *Nubian* to capture the Italian garrison on Linosa. His mission was to have bonfires blazing all over the tiny island as beacons for the C-47s to steer by. First was to be a flyover by a wave of fifty planes carrying the 575th Parachute Infantry Regiment, followed by the main force of 250 planes with the 505th Regimental Combat Team on board.

That was not happening.

Not feeling charitable at this point in what was a clearly deteriorating operation, Col. Randal said, "What did you do in civilian life before you joined the Army and decided to fly airplanes?"

Capt. Mossberg said, "I'm a commercial pilot for Pan Am, sir."

Col. Randal said, "Lovely."

"I believe we should make our break to the left now, Colonel."

"Do what you think best, Captain. I'm going to conduct my jumpmaster inspection, then I'll be back. Try hard to find Sicily—really not interested in jumping on Italy tonight."

"Yes, sir," Capt. Mossberg said. "Flying's a lot more fun when there's a stewardess sitting in your lap and no prospect of getting shot at."

Col. Randal said, "I can see how it would be."

Back in the passenger compartment, the troops were chuted up and had returned to the bench seats running down the length of the C-47. Starting with the first Ranger to jump, Col. Randal began his inspection. He had each trooper stand up, one at a time. Starting with the trooper's helmet, Col. Randal went to work, touching everything like a Braille reader.

Taking his time but not wasting any, he worked his way down to the reserve, then ran his palms under the jumper's leg straps. Then he had the Ranger turn around and started all over again with the helmet at the back. When finished, Col. Randal traced the yellow static line over the jumper's right shoulder to where the snap length was attached to the canvas carrying handle on the top of the reserve parachute. When satisfied there were no deficiencies, he slapped the paratrooper on the helmet, indicating he was good to go.

"See you on the ground, Johnston."

"Airborne, sir!"

Then he moved to the next man. Col. Randal could have had MSgt. Beckwith perform the jumpmaster inspections. However, doing them himself demonstrated he was a hands-on, lead-from-the-front commander who wanted to personally make sure his men's equipment had been put on right and to have a chance to exchange a few words with each jumper in the stick. The exercise helped establish the point that loyalty in Raiding Forces flowed down from the top of the chain-of-command as well as up from the lowest ranking level.

The effort was not lost on the men of B Company, 10th Ranger Battalion, on board the plane tonight. The Colonel conducting the jumpmaster inspection— impressive. Cut down on horseplay.

When the jumpmaster inspection was completed, Col. Randal had worked his way from the tail to the front of the airplane. He stepped inside the cockpit again. Everything out the windscreen was still black.

Capt. Mossberg asked, "You want the good news or the bad news, sir?"

Col. Randal said, "I could use some good news."

"If you look out my port side window, you will see the navy down below."

Col. Randal craned his neck and spotted a column of ships steaming toward, hopefully, Sicily. "What's the bad news?"

Capt. Mossberg said, "We aren't supposed to *see* the invasion fleet. That is, if we were on our correct heading. The air plan called for us to fly down the corridor between the British and American fleets sailing to their designated assault beaches."

Col. Randal said, "Sicily should be up ahead."

"There's no guarantee on that, sir."

"I'm going back to get ready for the jump. Give me the red light ten minutes out."

Capt. Mossberg said, "Turning it on now, sir."

Col. Randal airborne shuffled his way to the tail of the Dakota.

MSgt. Beckwith pointed out the open door. "Land in sight, sir."

Col. Randal looked. Sure enough, there was land. It was on the wrong side of the airplane.

King said, "You would not think the navy would be lost . . ."

"There's no telling where we are," Col. Randal said. "Sicily, Italy or even over the Balkans."

Then he turned to face the nose of the C-47 and could see the expectant faces of fifteen paratroopers who'd had enough of the long flight and were ready to exit the aircraft. "SIX MINUTES!"

Col. Randal turned back to the open door. He wedged his canvas-topped raiding boots against both sides, reached up spread-eagle, grasping the rim that ran around the interior of the door with his fingertips and arched his body outside the aircraft. The wind tore at his face, distorting it.

The idea was to check for other aircraft that could pose a hazard to his jumpers when they exited. He looked to the front, to the rear, above and below. There was not another aircraft in the sky.

Wherever his planeload of Rangers was invading, they were doing it by themselves. At this stage Col. Randal was no longer a regimental commander. He was a glorified squad leader.

Col. Randal swung back inside, turned, and gave the dual commands, "STAND UP AND HOOK UP!"

The pitching and yawing of the Dakota did not make hooking up easy. Both hands were required to click on the snap link, then put the wire safety pin in the tiny hole and bend it down, making it hard to maintain balance. Men were cursing and struggling, but they were ready to get out of the airplane.

"CHECK STATIC LINES!"

There was the screeching of metal-on-metal rasping as the Rangers shook their snap links back and forth to make sure they ran free. This was also the point in the command sequence when paratroopers' blood started to run hot. They wanted the door.

"CHECK YOUR EQUIPMENT!"

Not that it mattered. Everyone was jumping. No matter what problem might have developed since the jumpmaster inspection.

"SOUND OFF FOR EQUIPMENT CHECK"

Starting at the tail end of the stick, "OK, OK, OK. . . ."

Col. Randal arched himself out the door for one last check. He did not see anything. Their plane was all alone.

"ONE MINUTE!"

Then the green light came on. The men at the front of the stick saw the signal and surged forward. Col. Randal jammed his arm across the door, blocking it.

The C-47 was still over the water.

The green light went out and the red light came back on. Capt. Mossberg had flipped the switch prematurely. His first combat mission was about a hundred times more stressful than he had ever imagined. Not one thing was going as planned.

Capt. Mossberg had strict orders from his boss to put Col. Randal down on time on target. He was not looking forward to explaining everything that had gone wrong when he gave his after-action report to Bronc Blackwell upon returning to base.

The Dakota was thundering toward somewhere. Exactly where was anyone's guess. The beach flashed below.

Col. Randal gave the totally unnecessary command, "CLOSE ON THE DOOR!"

King and the Lovat Scouts had already been struggling to hold the Rangers back. MSgt. Beckwith was at the end of the stick to be the pusher. His efforts were not going to be needed. These paratroopers would not require any extra motivation to exit the airplane this night.

The light flashed green.

Col. Randal shouted, "GO!" And he was out the door. The stick charged after him.

Inside his head, he was screaming, "One thousand, two thousand..."

The X-type parachute cracked open before four thousand like it was supposed to. He was in a tight tuck position, and the opening shock was gentle. Suddenly, silently, everything was unfolding exactly the way all the training and his previous operational jumps had prepared him for. This one was letter perfect.

He was the right officer, in the right place with the right command to carry out his mission. Until that is, the chute fully deployed. Then the winds—thirty miles per hour gusting to forty-five miles per hour—pulled the canopy over almost parallel to the ground below and took off for parts unknown.

Col. Randal realized immediately these were the most excessive winds he had ever jumped in—gale force. He was sailing backward, unable to see the ground. The thought, *this is going to hurt* occurred to him.

No other parachutes were in sight. There was a blur out of his peripheral vision.

Then he was down.

With no conscious thought, he hit the quick release and was free from his harness before he had quit rolling from his parachute landing fall. This was one of—if not the—softest PLFs he had ever made. There was a reason. Col. Randal had come down in a vineyard, landing on the manicured ground between rows of grapes.

There was only one problem—well, actually, two. His cherished 9mm Beretta MAB 38 submachine gun was broken at the stock. And—he was all alone, with no idea where, not even sure he was in Sicily.

The next move was automatic. Col. Randal set about rolling up the stick. The technique was simple. Move in the direction the plane had been flying and start picking up jumpers.

He was armed only with his 9mm Browning P-35 and his .22 High Standard pistol with silencer—he had left his Colt 1911 .38 Supers at RFHQ because a resupply of ammunition for them would not be readily available. Ammo for the Browning was not going to be a problem. He jumped with eight hundred rounds of 9mm for his now out-of-action submachine gun.

Moving rapidly but stealthily, Col. Randal followed the direction of the C-47's flight. The moon was down now. The night was pitch-black.

Every time he came to a bush, he challenged softly, "George."

No joy.

Col. Randal was alone, lost, and possibly not even in the right country.

MAJOR DUKE SLATER, THE COMMANDER OF 1ST BATTALION, 575th Parachute Infantry Regiment was the first man out the door of the Dakota transporting his headquarters element and ten jumpers from C Company. Raiding Forces typically operated with skeletal staff personnel because every man was needed to be a trigger puller. His HQ party was limited to five people.

Maj. Slater was in trouble right from the start.

When he performed a "check canopy"—the first action a paratrooper always takes after his chute has deployed—he discovered he had an inverted main, which meant the parachute had opened inside out. In airborne-speak, this was officially "not good," although not *automatically* a fatal malfunction. Deploying the reserve is the recommended school solution.

Unfortunately, at the low 500-foot combat jump altitude, there is no time to reflect. Popping the reserve has to be a split-second reaction or you are already on the ground.

Hitting the reserve in a situation like this is no small decision because the action can result in a number of things happening—most of them bad. The reserve does not deploy automatically. The parachute has to be pulled out by hand and tossed into the breeze to open. Sometimes it can blow back in your face or fall down and wrap around your jump boots, as famously happens in the official paratrooper jump song, "Blood on the Risers." Or the silk can fly up above your head partway and get tangled in the lines, which causes no additional harm but does not help. By that point, you will have expended what little time is left to take up a good body position before making your PLF, ready or not.

Worst-case scenario, the reserve will deploy fully, but because its lines are shorter, it will steal the air from the main chute, causing it to collapse. In that event, two things can result . . . both "not good": (1) The jumper can hit the ground as the main is collapsing and before the reserve is fully deployed; (2) The main collapses and falls down on top of the reserve canopy, causing it to collapse.

Maj. Slater didn't stop to think about all the things that could go wrong. He immediately deployed his reserve.

Then he slammed into the ground. For what seemed like a long time—but was actually only a matter of seconds—Maj. Slater could not breathe. He did have enough time to ponder why he had ever volunteered to jump out of an airplane in flight in the first place.

No immediate good answer to that question came to mind.

Checking, he found nothing was broken. All his equipment had made it down in one piece. He had no idea where he was or in which direction the bridge lay.

Totally disoriented, Maj. Slater glanced at his big, olive, airborne-issue, liquid-filled wrist compass, manufactured by the Superior Magneto Corp. of Long Island, New York. He selected an azimuth. In the military, there's what are known as "WAGs," which stands for wild-assed guesses. And, there are "SWAGs," which are scientific wild-assed guesses.

Maj. Slater's choice of direction was a WAG. It did not meet criteria to be a SWAG.

PRIVATE FIRST CLASS WALLY MALINOWSKI WAS THE FOURTH man in his stick. Lieutenant Clint Hays was the jumpmaster. Their C-47 was supposed to be in the last serial carrying A/1/575th. The pilots, all flying their first combat mission, were supposed to maintain a tight formation. That was a pipe dream. Three hours of flying over open ocean, blacked out, on radio silence, in a high wind, had caused the pilots to change their priorities.

Surviving the ordeal became their only goal.

All down the aerial stream of planes behind Colonel Sam Houston Blackwell, pilots began to open up the formation, more concerned about the possibility of midair collisions than any enemy threat. Then the winds aloft caused more dispersion. Soon the Provisional Troop Carrier Group had ceased being a compact military organization moving in lockstep and was spread all across the sky.

PFC Malinowski was blithely unaware of all the problems the United States Army Air Force was experiencing tonight. As far as he was concerned, the aircrew had it easy. Their work was done when his was getting started.

The red light was on. Normally it stayed on for ten minutes. Tonight, it flashed to green almost as soon as it lit up.

Lt. Hays shouted, "GO!"

The jumpers all began rushing forward, charging the exit, almost running, shouting, "Go, Go, Go . . ."

The man in front of PFC Malinowski stumbled at the door, fell forward and went out headfirst. No problem, Malinowski dived over the man's shoulder. Neither of these were the school approved method of exiting an aircraft in flight.

So what? Got the job done.

The opening shock was gentle. However, something was not right. Then PFC Malinowski realized he was up about 3,000 feet. He had never jumped from this high.

The pilot must have felt safer at altitude than the 500-foot level he was supposed to descend to before dropping his planeload of paratroopers. PFC Malinowski had a great view, though he was feeling exposed. The purpose of making a low-level jump was to get down fast so that you did not get shot.

On the other hand, there was always the "big sky, little bullet" theory. PFC Malinowski was not necessarily a subscriber to that concept—it being a matter of perspective. It was lonely up there, and he felt like a sitting duck.

The sky was brightly lit by tracers and flares. In the glow, he could see the other parachutes in his stick as they were being swept along by the breeze. That was when he realized how fast the winds were carrying him.

When his parachute dropped below the horizon, the lights disappeared, and it became pitch-black. He lost sight of the rest of his stick. The ground was rushing up.

WHAAAAAM! He was down. Hard.

In the distance, PFC Malinowski could hear the retort of rifles and the rattle of machine guns. He knew the fighting was fairly far off because up close, those weapons did not sound like that. All around him was dead silence.

It was eerie.

CAPTAIN BILLY JACK JAXX WAS IN THE LEAD PLANE OF THE Provisional Troop Carrier Group piloted by Beverly's father, Colonel Sam Houston "Bronc" Blackwell. He was in the cockpit, kneeling between the pilot and co-pilot's seats. Out the windscreen dead ahead, a glowing gold dot appeared.

Col. Blackwell said, "There she blows. Our first checkpoint. Right on the money."

Flying on radio silence meant that the enemy could not listen in on your conversations and discern your intentions. It also meant you could not talk to your own people. Bronc Blackwell would have been really unhappy to know the other forty-nine aircraft in his formation were scattered all over the sky, straggling in ones and twos strung out behind him.

Capt. Jaxx said, "That's Linosa, sir. The Headhunter captured it last night— he's what they had in mind when they invented the word 'stud.' Looks like Butch is burning every stick of wood on the island."

"You know, Jack, I'm the president of the Texas Longhorns Football Booster Club. Talked to some of the members and what they want me to do is pin down if you're planning on coming back and playing out your eligibility after the war," Col. Blackwell said. "We're counting on you to help us win the Southwest Conference—get you one of these, son."

Bronc held up his hand with the big National Championship ring.

Capt. Jaxx said, "Looking forward to it, sir."

The C-47 droned on past Linosa.

Col. Blackwell said, "What I've been meaning to ask, Jack, is Brandy Seaborn as good-looking in real life as she is in that photo you sent?"

Capt. Jaxx said, "Brandy's so hot people rub her for luck."

Another dot appeared in the far distance. This one had a bluish tint. As the plane flew closer, it was possible to see they were pencils of light aimed skyward.

Col. Blackwell said, "Malta in sight. We will begin our turn to the left in one five. Decent job of navigation back there, Norm."

Captain Norman Nesbitt, the group navigator, said, "Thank you, sir."

As they flew closer, the lights on the one hundred twenty-five square mile island filled up the entire horizon. Malta was the most bombed place on earth. This was the first time since the war started that anything other than antiaircraft search lights had been turned on. Everyone had flipped on their houselights, then gone outside to light candles and shine flashlights.

Col. Blackwell said, "I've been thinking, Jack. That cannon back there in the troop compartment weighs two thousand pounds. A quarter of a mile from the DZ to the bridge is a long haul. What say I drop you right on your target?

"That possible, Norm—locating the bridge?"

Capt. Nesbitt, the navigator, said, "Can do, sir. Have to allow for the winds aloft, which are higher than we anticipated. At five hundred feet, we should be able to see the structure—green light on visual."

Col. Blackwell said, "Norm's the Merlin the Magician of celestial navigation. Best in the business. Want to give it a shot, Jack?"

"That's a rodge, sir — let's do it."

Neither Bronc Blackwell nor Jack Cool thought there was anything out of the ordinary to having spent virtually the entire flight en route to invading Fortress Europe talking about football and women.

They knew what they were fighting for.

Capt. Jaxx went back and conducted his jumpmaster inspection on the airborne artillerymen of E Battery, 567th Parachute Field Artillery. He had no idea if the gun was rigged correctly to be air dropped, having never jumpmastered one before. Lieutenant Christopher Issacs was well-pleased when he learned about the change of plans. A 75mm howitzer is a small gun, but it is a beast to manhandle cross-country.

The safety checks out the door were tricky. The short barrel of the 75mm gun was almost sticking out, which required working around. Capt. Jaxx was surprised but not alarmed to see no other aircraft trailing behind.

He swung back inside and went up to the cockpit.

Col. Blackwell said, "Tell your boys back there I'm dropping 'em a little lower than planned. Need to get your paratroopers down fast because of the excessive winds. We don't want you scattered all over kingdom come."

Bronc did not mention jump altitude was now 250 feet.

"Red light, Jack. Hook 'em, Horns!"

The instant the green light flashed, the 75mm howitzer went out, followed by Capt. Jaxx, Lt. Issacs and the 567th Parachute Field Artillery gunners.

"One thousand, two thousand, three thousand . . ." crack—*WHAAAAAM!*

In comic books, the characters see stars in fist fights and crashes. That is exactly what Capt. Jaxx thought he saw—with a couple of planets thrown in at the end of his PLF. Not that it could be called a parachute landing fall, exactly. The chute opened. He hit the ground flat on his back.

No checking the canopy. No slipping into the wind to slow his descent. No taking up a good prepare-to-land position. Crack, wham—pain.

The landing fall might not have been as bad except for all the equipment he was carrying. It really hurt because none of his gear was soft. He rolled over and struggled to his knees, wondering if he might be dying from internal injuries. Then Capt. Jaxx noticed the abutment of the bridge about fifteen feet away.

Jack Cool had taken his objective. Now all he had to do was hold it. At all costs.

COLONEL JOHN RANDAL HAD BEEN ATTEMPTING TO ROLL UP THE stick for two hours. Nothing. He had not encountered a single one of his men. It was like the 575th had jumped into darkness and vanished from the face of the earth.

He came to a dirt road. With the moon down, visibility was limited. Col. Randal crouched down to evaluate the situation. Walking on a road or trail behind enemy lines is a guaranteed method to find the enemy. The objective for every man in the regiment was to get to the bridge—not engage in a meaningless firefight.

From out of the darkness, the faint sound of whistling could be heard. He did not recognize the tune, but whoever was doing the whistling was approaching. If he was one of the 575th PIR, Col. Randal was first going to hug him, then he was going to court-martial the idiot.

A dim figure materialized, walking along whistling off-key as if he did not have a care in the world. Col. Randal waited until the man was right on top of him before he gave the challenge.

"George."

The counter sign tonight was "Marshall."

"*George*?" Came the response in a thick Italian accent.

Wrong answer.

WHIIIIIICH, WHIIIIIICH, WHIIIIIICH. Col. Randal shot the man three times fast with the silenced .22 High Standard.

The whistler went down hard.

"George." Came from the other side of the dirt road.

Col. Randal immediately covered the direction of the challenge and responded, "Marshall."

Private First Class Wally Malinowski whispered, "That you, Colonel?"

"Roger. Have you seen anyone else, Malinowski?"

"A guy from the 10th Rangers. Broke his leg. Had to leave him, sir, but I got his antitank mine and flares. Oh yeah, I brought the ammo for his BAR too."

Col. Randal said, "Give me the mine. I'll carry it. Let's get out of here."

MASTER SERGEANT MACK BECKWITH WAS THE LAST JUMPER OUT of Colonel John Randal's C-47. The 10th Battalion Rangers in the stick may have set the record for exiting an aircraft. When he cleared the door, there was not a single parachute in sight.

MSgt. Beckwith came in hot. He was landing backward, which was not at all unusual, but he was traveling fast. His PLF was a textbook example of how to perform a rear parachute landing fall.

The drill for the last man out was to land and stand fast while the stick leader, in this case Col. Randal, rolled up the stick moving in the direction of the jump aircraft's line of flight. Raiding Forces had rehearsed this so many times it was second nature. However, tonight the orders were to get to the bridge.

So MSgt. Beckwith waited for thirty minutes, which should have been more than an adequate amount of time. When no one had showed, he moved out. Not having any idea where he was, walking in the direction the C-47 had been going seemed like as good an idea as any.

The only thing MSgt. Beckwith knew for sure was that he had not landed on the intended DZ. He was all alone, armed with his cut down BAR modified to Colt Monitor specs by his buddy Sergeant Roy Dunlap at the 27th Ordnance outside of Cairo, and 400 rounds of .30 caliber ammunition, six frag grenades plus his 1911 .45 Colt Government Model automatic.

The first response to his challenge, "George," was a plaintive "mooooo."

His second try a few minutes later brought better results. Two privates, one from the 10th Rangers and one from the 3/504th responded with "Marshall" right on cue.

The 82nd Airborne Division trooper was really far off-target.

Crouching beside a rock wall that ran along a dirt road, MSgt. Beckwith took out his poncho, crawled under it and studied his map with a pen light. Nothing. He did not have enough information to definitively locate his position on the topographical map. After folding up his map, he held a brief conference with the two paratroopers.

Voices and the tramp of feet could be heard on the road. A detachment of soldiers was approaching. They had their weapons slung and were talking openly among themselves.

MSgt. Beckwith whispered, "Grenades—on my command."

The enemy marched closer. They had no idea any Americans were in the area. They did not seem aware there was an invasion in progress.

As the formation was passing on the other side of the wall, MSgt. Beckwith whispered, "Now!"

Three fragmentation grenades arced over the low rock wall. They went off almost simultaneously. *BLAAAAAM! BLAAAAAM! BLAAAAAM!* Sounding like 500-pound bombs in the still of the night.

Screams of pain intermixed with yells of panic came from the road. The bad guys had no idea what had happened. MSgt. Beckwith waited ten long agonizing minutes until he heard voices again. He whispered, "Now!"

Three more grenades looped over. They sounded equally as loud. Judging from the screams and moans, dead and dying enemy troops now littered the roadway.

MSgt. Beckwith did not feel like hanging around to find out. He gave the order, "Move out."

They needed to get to the bridge—wherever that was.

LIEUTENANT CLINT HAYS LED THE STICK OUT OF THE SAME PLANE Private First Class Wally Malinowski was aboard. It was a very high drop. The flight had drawn antiaircraft fire when it strayed over Gela on the way in. The pilot panicked and put his aircraft into a steep climb trying to get away from it.

It was a beautiful night. Tracers and flares lit up the sky, putting on a light show better than any Fourth of July celebration Lt. Hays had ever seen. Then he was coming in backward and crashed into a clump of tall trees. He never saw them coming.

His canopy caught in the branches. He continued falling until brought up short. Looking down, Lt. Hays could see that he was dangling two feet off the ground. Not a problem, although it would have been if he had been jumping the U.S. Army's T4. But all that was necessary now was to hit the quick release on his chest. The straps popped out, and he stepped onto the ground. Lt. Hays was really glad he had not been forced to cut his way out of his rigging with a jump knife—no way would he have been able to unbuckle the canvas straps on the T4.

The airplane he had jumped was never supposed to have been anywhere near Gela, much less flown over it. Lt. Hays did not have a clue where he was. There was not a single terrain feature to guide on in the dark.

"George."

"Marshall."

Lovat Scout Munro Ferguson stepped out of the shadows.

Lt. Hays said, "What are you doing here, Ferguson? You're supposed to be traveling with the colonel. My plane was a long way in front of his."

Scout Ferguson said, "No idea, sir. I have six men with me—10th Rangers and Five Seven Five troopers—all lost. This drop's a bloody mess."

Lt. Hays said, "We need to get to the bridge. Any idea which direction it might be?"

Scout Ferguson said, "Negative, sir. There's a farmhouse we were about to approach when we saw you landing. We were going to interrogate the farmer and commandeer any mules he may have to carry our equipment."

"Good plan."

The patrol approached the house. It was completely dark. Lt. Hays pounded on the door and the lights came on. The farmer came out. No one in the group spoke Italian. However, the Sicilian was able to point to where his farm was on the map.

They were twelve miles from the bridge.

CAPTAIN BILLY JACK JAXX WAS ALL ALONE AT THE BRIDGE. HE'D had his bell rung but did not appear to have any permanent damage.

Being there on the objective all by himself was one of the loneliest feelings he had ever experienced. He could not shake the mental image of one million bad guys coming across the bridge at him. What to do?

Capt. Jaxx was getting ready to put up a flare when he heard someone approaching.

"George."

"Marshall."

Lieutenant Christopher Issacs walked up, "One 75mm gun of E Battery reporting for duty, sir."

Capt. Jaxx had never been so happy to see anyone in his life—unless you counted the time at UT when the Alpha Delta Pi pledge scratched on his door at 0200 hours.

Jack Cool.

15

THE BRIDGE

COLONEL JOHN RANDAL AND PRIVATE FIRST CLASS WALLY Malinowski had been traveling as fast as they could in the dark. The terrain was fairly open, and the going was not difficult. The hope was they were traveling in the right direction.

They struck a dry riverbed that was running on the right east-west line and could be the intermittent stream they were looking for. The question was, which side of the bridge had they landed on? There was no guarantee the two were not traveling *away* from their objective.

Then at about 0430 hours, firing could be heard in the distance. Col. Randal decided to march toward the sound of the guns. Not sure that it was the right decision, but at least he would find a fight. Since shooting the whistling Italian soldier, they had not encountered a live person—enemy or friendly.

When the sun began to break, Col. Randal decided to press on. They were behind enemy lines. Lost. And the countryside was fairly open.

It might not have been the best decision.

The bad guys could spot them from a long way off, while they might not be able to see any Italians who were utilizing the precaution of basic cover and concealment. However, Col. Randal had no intention of spending the day in hiding, waiting for the cover of darkness to move again if he could help it.

In the distance a flare was visible. Five minutes later, another went up. Now it was apparent that the bridge was straight ahead, and a battle was in progress. The firing was not heavy, but it was steady with no letup.

This was a time for Col. Randal to exercise care. The enemy might have managed to push light infantry over the intermittent stream out of sight of the bridge in an attempt to encircle his paratroopers. If that was the case, he and PFC Malinowski might stumble into them.

A 75mm howitzer boomed from time to time. A clump of trees masked the bridge from their sight. It would also conceal any enemy forces attempting to envelop the 575th PIR.

With Col. Randal leading, they moved into the woods. The only sounds were of the small arms fire up ahead. The cracking of incoming rounds made it clear the fight was both ways.

Moving stealthily through the woods, armed with his 9mm Browning P-35, not knowing what to expect next, required patience and skill. Kill or be killed if anyone was there. Fortunately, no one was.

Col. Randal stepped out in the open on the far side of the patch of forest. He could see Lieutenant Christopher Issacs' 75mm howitzer in action. Flanking it were men from the 10th Ranger Battalion and the 1/575 PIR—only there were not very many of them.

His Rolex said 1015 hours. He had been moving since 2430 hours. Col. Randal had been dropped over twenty miles from his DZ.

The first thing he noticed was a knocked-out Sd.Kfz. 234 on the far side of the bridge. The Italians did not have Sd.Kfz. 234 armored cars. The Enemy Forces intelligence brief prior to the jump had been dead wrong.

There *were* German maneuver units on Sicily.

One dead Sd.Kfz. 234 did not mean a Panzer Division was trailing behind it, but there was no guarantee it wasn't.

Col. Randal realized the mission to hold a strategic bridge with lightly armed paratroops until relieved by friendly forces attacking overland from the sea had become even more problematic than originally conceived. If there *was* a German Panzer Division somewhere on the other side of the bridge, the 575th PIR was going to be nothing more than a speed bump—if even that.

Walking up to the concrete slab over the intermittent stream, he found Captain Billy Jack Jaxx in command. Neither Major Duke Slater nor Major Jack Dance had arrived. Only a handful of troops were in sight.

Capt. Jaxx, clearly in his element, saluted, doing it by the book, "Captain Jaxx reports, sir. Objective secured. Mines out as ordered. Seventy-three effectives—seventy-five now that you've arrived."

There were supposed to be 610.

COLONEL JOHN RANDAL TOOK IN THE SITUATION IN A SINGLE glance and reached the conclusion that there was no way to defend the bridge. The ground on their side of the intermittent stream was flat. On the far side in the distance, a gentle ridge line ran behind the Y of the road.

The mines scattered down the roadway in plain sight were an obstacle. There were not the 600 hoped-for, but seventy-three anti-tank mines were a lot. And they were covered by the 10th Rangers and 1/575th PIR's interlocking fields of grazing fire.

An obstacle not covered by fire is merely an impediment.

No one was going to clear those mines.

The problem was, if so much as a single platoon of German Mark III or Tiger tanks arrived, they could take up a hull-down position on the ridge. From complete safety, the Nazis would be able to blast the 575th's fighting positions to pieces with their main guns. And there would be nothing his men could do about it.

If the Germans brought up infantry to support their tanks, as their doctrine called for, the 575th PIR would not have enough troops—even if the entire regiment arrived—to prevent the Nazis from forcing the intermittent stream above or below the bridge, with an eye to putting in a flanking attack—or even worse, execute a double envelopment.

The position was a death trap.

Only one of the airdropped 75mm howitzers had arrived. There were eight high explosive (HE) rounds remaining for it. One of the Naval Fire Control

Teams had made it, but their radio had been destroyed in the drop, making it impossible to call for fire support from the big guns of the fleet. Captain "Dynamite" Dick Coogan was there; however, only two of his demolition men had showed up so far and the team's externally dropped explosives were missing.

Col. Randal spoke to Capt. Coogan first.

"As more of our people arrive, have them place their mines under the abutment of the bridge. If the Germans show up with armor, stand by to blow it. Don't let 'em cross."

Capt. Coogan said, "Yes, sir."

To Captain Billy Jack Jaxx, Col. Randal said, "Panzer outfits send out motorcycle reconnaissance elements, followed by armored cars, followed by mechanized infantry with tanks and other mechanized infantry interspersed in close support. Is that what happened here?"

Capt. Jaxx said, "Just a pair of motorcycle riders and what appeared to be a platoon of armored cars—four of 'em, sir. We shot the motorcyclists when they reached the bridge and Lieutenant Issacs got one of the Sd.Kfz. 234s."

Col. Randal asked, "Can you recover a German bike?"

"One crashed off the side of the bridge—it's a no go. The other's in the ditch on the far side. Been thinking about using the chopper to search for our missing door bundles."

Col. Randal said, "Bring it in."

King arrived. He was by himself. The Merc looked at Col. Randal and shook his head in disgust. "Never saw anyone on the way in, Chief—close to twenty-five miles. My guess is the regiment is scattered over thirty—maybe forty—square miles."

On the far side of the intermittent stream, the thunder of a motorcycle firing up could be heard. The motor cut off, then two Rangers started pushing it across the bridge, not taking any chances on riding over a mine. Col. Randal noted the machine was a BMW R75 with a sidecar.

King asked, "You understand what that Sd.Kfz. 234 out there means, Chief?"

Col. Randal said, "I do."

Lieutenant Nick Bellefonte, the naval fire control officer attached to the 1/575ᵗʰ, came over.

"Our radio pancaked on the jump, sir—sorry."

Col. Randal said, "We have a detachment of the 82ⁿᵈ Airborne's 307ᵗʰ Engineer Battalion. Any chance they can be of help in the event they ever make it here?"

"Negative, sir," Lt. Bellefonte said. "Army radios are not compatible with navy radios. The army and navy can't talk to each other. How stupid is that?"

The two Rangers rolled the BMW R75 to where Col. Randal was standing. He climbed on and kick-started it. The Wehrmacht grey machine was not much to look at, having seen hard service. But its motor was purring like only a BMW motorcycle could.

Col. Randal said, "Captain Jaxx, take charge. If Major Slater or Major Dance show up, turn over command to them—go back to your company. If not, you've got it no matter who arrives or what their rank is.

"Is that clear?"

"Roger that—where're you going, Colonel?"

Col. Randal said, "Gela . . . to bring back a radio Lieutenant Bellefonte can use for naval fire support."

Capt. Jaxx said, "Let me do it, sir."

"Negative, the navy may not be excited about giving away one of their radios. They'll have a hard time telling me no. I need you here doing what you do best, Jack."

"Yes, sir."

Col. Randal said, "If, in your professional opinion, you feel it's necessary—have Coogan blow the bridge."

Capt. Jaxx said, "Don't worry, sir . . ."

But Col. Randal was already gone.

The ride to Gela, approximately fifteen miles, was uneventful in that he did not encounter any Italian units actively resisting the Seventh Army. He did ride past a half-dozen abandoned French Renault R35 tanks along the road that appeared to have broken down from mechanical problems and been abandoned. The Nazis had captured the Renaults when they overran France in 1940 and given the little tanks to the Italians to bolster their meager armored forces. These bore the markings of the 131st Tank Infantry Regiment.

Down the road were more Renault R35s that had been knocked out. Dead Italian tankers were hanging out of the turrets or lying on the ground. It was creepy to roll on by the motionless R35s and dead enemy soldiers because there were no signs of battle to indicate what had caused their destruction.

Could it have been the pre-invasion aerial bombardment by the USAAF? Naval gunfire from the USS *Boise* or the *Savannah* directed by catapult-launched Curtis Seagull spotter planes? Col. Randal had no idea.

The most unusual thing of all was passing the line of massive concrete bunkers outside of Gela running along the military crest on the ridge overlooking the town. They were fully manned by the troops from Italian XVIII Coastal Defense Brigade. White flags tied to the barrels of Carcano rifles were poking out the firing slits.

These Blackshirts had already had enough.

By the time Col. Randal arrived, the fighting had died down in Gela. Lieutenant Colonel William O. Darby's X Force, consisting of the 1st Ranger Battalion, 4th Ranger Battalion, 83rd 4.2 Mortar Battalion and 1st Battalion 39th Combat Engineer Regiment, had been fighting Renault R35 tanks in the narrow streets of the town earlier. In the far distance, faint sounds of heavy fighting could be heard from where the 505th Regimental Combat Team had dropped.

Driving down the road toward the town, Col. Randal spotted a small group of officers standing together, conferring on the beach. Not having any better plan, he rode toward them. When he pulled up, he recognized Lieutenant General George S. Patton Jr., Seventh Army Commander—riding boots, swagger stick, ivory-handled .45 Single Action Army revolver, three bright silver stars on his helmet. The general was in a discussion with two other officers.

When Col. Randal pulled up, Lt. Gen. Patton shouted, "Randal, you magnificent bastard, why isn't your helmet buckled?"

Col. Randal was bareheaded, having discarded his helmet in the vineyard where he landed following the jump. He noted that the general was wearing a steel pot with no chin strap. So, his was not buckled either.

"Sir, the Five-Seven-Five seized its objective within minutes of landing," Col. Randal said. "Unfortunately, our drop was widely dispersed. Less than a hundred men were present at the bridge when I left."

Lt. Gen. Patton said, "That's not many effectives."

"My people are facing German armor, General."

Lt. Gen. Patton turned red in the face, instantly furious. "G-2 claims there's not any German panzer formations on Sicily. Sure about your information, Colonel?"

"Sir, my people knocked out an Sd.Kfz. 234 at the bridge. This motorcycle has Hermann Göring Fallschirm-Panzer Division identifiers. I need immediate assistance or we're going to be overrun."

Lt. Gen. Patton turned to one of the officers next to him, Brigadier General Theodore Roosevelt Jr., the son of President Teddy Roosevelt of San Juan Hill fame. He was the assistant division commander of the U.S. 1st Infantry Division. "Do you have anyone you can send, Ted?"

Brig. Gen. Roosevelt said, "Negative, General. We were supposed to have already relieved Colonel Randal en route to the Ponte Olivo Airfield by now. The bad weather, the hidden sandbars offshore, unusually high surf, and the Italian counterattack here in Gela have thrown off our timetable. In the confusion, some of my Big Red One troops were put ashore on 45th Division beaches down the coast.

"In addition, as you can hear, Gavin's Five-O-Five is in a pitched battle. They have priority to be relieved, being in the most immediate proximity to Gela. Be tomorrow at the earliest before the Big Red One can free up a battalion, sir."

Lt. Col. Darby, the 1st Ranger Battalion commander, said, "If those panzers break through at the bridge, they can be here in less than an hour. If the HGFPD slams into Gela on our right flank, holding the town will be impossible. We had a tough enough time this morning when those dinky little Italian Renaults attacked."

Lt. Gen. Patton said, "Anything I can do for you *besides* reinforcements, Colonel? Can't give you any air support. The navy, in its infinite wisdom, failed to detail a single aircraft carrier to support HUSKY."

"A naval fire support team jumped in with us, sir," Col. Randal said. "Unfortunately, its radio was a write-off. I need a replacement and immediate naval fire support on-call around the clock until we're relieved."

Lt. Gen. Patton turned and started yelling at another group of officers farther down the beach. The men turned to see the cause of the commotion, then immediately started jogging their direction. The senior officer, Captain Millard Thompson, USN, was the navy beachmaster on Red Beach.

He was not having a good day. The landing was chaotic. Having the Seventh Army Commander on his beach looking over his shoulder was not making things any better.

Lt. Gen. Patton immediately lit into Capt. Thompson, having already blamed him for all things nautical and/or amphibious related that had gone wrong on Red Beach in a previous one-sided conversation.

"Colonel Randal needs a ship-to-shore radio for his navy fire control team and he needs it *now*! I want you to give him absolute top priority for his fire missions. I don't care how many rounds you sailors have to fire in support of his regiment—just do it. And I want the biggest guns you've got in the fleet in direct support."

Capt. Thompson turned to a commander wearing wire-rimmed glasses, the senior fire control officer on Red Beach. "Make it so!"

Commander Charles Malcom, USN, turned to the officer standing next to him, Lieutenant Brian Sontag, USN. "Bring me an SCR 284 radio if you have to physically take it away from one of our other teams."

"Yes, sir!"

Cdr. Malcom said, "What's the name of your naval forward observer, sir?"

Col. Randal said, "Lieutenant Bellefonte."

Cdr. Malcom thumbed through a small book he had pulled out of his breast pocket. "You drew a good card on your fire support officer, sir. Nick's a pro. Let's see, his call sign is Lightning Six.

"What are we going to be shooting at, Colonel?"

Col. Randal said, "Tanks in the open."

Cdr. Malcom said, "Inform Lieutenant Bellefonte to use the code word *Antarctica* in the event a major attack develops, sir. Upon receipt of that code word, we will try to put up a spotter plane to assist in adjusting your fires. Unfortunately, we are running out of our Seagulls—been getting shot down all morning."

Lt. Sontag arrived, huffing and puffing, with two sailors helping him carry an SCR 284 radio—it was heavy. He placed it in the sidecar attached to the motorcycle.

Lt. Gen. Patton said, "Stand fast there, Colonel Randal, I'm going to send one of my aides, Captain Rockford, with you. Climb in, Frank. Hold that radio in your lap like it's one of those priceless Russian Fabergé eggs, son."

"Yes, sir!"

Lt. Gen. Patton said, "If anything goes wrong—the navy doesn't cooperate for any reason—you know who to contact at Seventh Army HQ afloat to straighten things out. Or call Admiral Hewitt direct."

Captain Frank Rockford said, "Yes, sir."

Lt. Gen. Patton asked, "What else can we do for you, Randal?"

Col. Randal produced his map and spread it out over the handlebars of the motorcycle. "Commander Malcom, I need you to arrange for an immediate fire mission along this ridgeline from here to here. We need a parallel sheath on top of the ridge and on the reverse slope. That's where the panzers will be assembling.

"Continue harassing and interdictory fires until Lieutenant Bellefonte comes up on your net to direct the shoot."

Lt. Gen. Patton said, "Turn that ridge into a moonscape."

Cdr. Malcom said, "That is one order the navy will be delighted to comply with, sir."

As Col. Randal kick-started the BMW motorcycle, Lt. Col. Darby said, "We need those panzers kept out of Gela, sir. A determined counterattack by hardcore Nazi fanatics will drive us back into the sea. Nearly got overrun this morning, and those were supposed to be second-rate Italian troops suffering from low morale."

Col. Randal said, "You'd best start working on a series of preplanned fire missions along the road I rolled in on. There's a chance the Five-Seven-Five won't be able to hold if the Germans maneuver on my people."

Lt. Col. Darby said, "You know they will, Colonel."

"Yes, I do," Col. Randal said. "Up the road a ways, there's a line of concrete bunkers with white flags waving. Might want to send a few of your Rangers to bring 'em in. You wouldn't want those people to have a change of heart."

Lt. Col. Darby said, "Wilco."

With Capt. Rockford in the sidecar clutching the SCR 284, Col. Randal peeled out, spraying gravel, heading back to the bridge.

Lt. Gen. Patton shouted, "Get a helmet on!"

The BMW raced up the road, past the Italians in the bunkers waving the white flags and past the knocked-out tanks.

Then the motor sputtered.

It cut out.

Overhead could be heard the tearing silk sound artillery makes. The big guns of the U.S. Navy were in action firing on the map references.

Col. Randal was frantically trying to kick start the motorcycle. Nothing. Out of gas.

Capt. Rockford shouted, "What are we going to do, sir?"

Col. Randal said, "We've got to haul this radio to the bridge."

Capt. Rockford said, "Colonel, it weighs over one hundred and fifty pounds!"

Somewhere, Col. Randal dimly remembered hearing that the SCR 284 could be broken down into three fifty-five-pound components, batteries, hand-cranked generator auxiliary antenna, handset and spares. Only he had no idea how to disassemble it. And no time to learn.

The radio itself came mounted on a frame with shoulder straps. So at least part of the SCR 284 was meant to be man portable. The problem—it was close to ten miles to the bridge.

Col. Randal knelt down and slipped the straps over his shoulders. Since he was already carrying thirty pounds or more of other gear, rations, grenades, ammunition, etc., standing up required a major effort. He nearly toppled over.

The normal combat infantryman carried a seventy-five-pound combat load. Men in mortar platoons, machine gunners and BAR men, more.

He was none of those and had not trained to carry heavy loads. Raiding Forces moved fast, hit hard—"high speed, low drag." Individual Raiders did not carry two hundred pounds of equipment on an operation.

Col. Randal said, "Rockford, you take off up the road until you reach the bridge. Have Captain Jaxx send help to transport this radio. Don't stop until you get there."

Capt. Rockford said, "But sir, you will be attempting to carry more than your own body weight."

Col. Randal asked, "Got any better ideas?"

Capt. Rockford said, "And I thought being a general's aide was going to be all white tablecloths and fingerbowls, sir."

"Move out, Rockford—better not let me overtake you."

Capt. Rockford had played football and run track at West Point. He took off in a sprint. His idea was to go wide open.

Col. Randal realized he was in trouble almost immediately. There were men in Raiding Forces who could throw a SCR 284 on their back and double time to the bridge with no problem. He was not one of them. His ribs had been injured two years previous on a jump during the siege of RAF Habbaniya. Then reinjured recently on the Castelrozzo jump. They were burning like fire from the first step.

Beverly had wrapped him in fresh bandages prior to his flying out to Tunisia to stage for HUSKY. The blond Texas beauty queen had opted for the "P for Plenty" formula and put the dressings on extra tight. Maybe that was saving him now.

But it did not make breathing any easier.

Col. Randal had done a lot of tough training over the years, but nothing had prepared him for this march. Besides, this was different. He was not trying to complete a selection course. Today was for all the marbles. This radio was all that stood between an elite formation of German Paratrooper Tankers and his handful of lightly armed men at the bridge. When the HGFPD realized the naval gunfire coming in now was being fired on fixed coordinates and not being adjusted by forward observers, it would simply skirt the impact area and put in their attack.

Without the SCR 284, the 575th PIR would be annihilated.

Col. Randal was marching as hard and fast as he could go . . . which meant he was staggering forward one labored step at a time. He had his head down. His whole body was a solid mass of red-hot pain.

Time froze.

He remembered something Waldo had once told him, "Dinosaurs can't stick out their tongue."

The road ahead was endless. One boot in front of the other. He started singing "Blood on the Risers" to himself—"*What* a *hell of a way to die . . .*"

Can't quit. Don't stop. Drive on, drive on, drive on . . .

He thought about his high school student teacher, Miss UCLA.

Col. Randal hurt so bad he wished a belligerent Italian Fascist would show up and shoot him.

Lady Jane had been walking beside him for some time now. "You can do it, John."

And then there was a white flash.

When Col. Randal regained consciousness, he was at the bridge, lying on the ground propped up against the stump of a tree with someone's pack as a pillow. Lt. Bellefonte was talking on the SCR 284 radio, coordinating the naval gunfire. Capt. Jaxx and King were studying the fall of the rounds through their binoculars. Lovat Scout Munro Ferguson was standing nearby, cradling his 7X57 Rigby rifle.

Master Sergeant Mack Beckwith brought a metal canteen cup of water.

Paratroopers wandered by from time to time, giving him a thumbs up.

Col. Randal wondered if he had experienced a heart attack.

In the distance, behind the ridge across the intermittent stream, were a dozen tall, black plumes of smoke rising high into the sky. Huge shells were screaming in and erupting, throwing up geysers of dirt high in the sky, making the earth shake. The 2nd Battalion, 2nd Brigade, Hermann Göring Fallschirm-Panzer Division was being decimated. Violent secondary explosions were occurring as ammunition in one burning tank or another cooked off.

A Panzer Mark III's turret shot fifty feet in the air from a blast. The men of the 575th PIR stood up and cheered, shaking their fists and waving their weapons at the bad guys. Everyone was having fun now that the situation had changed, and they were not all going to die.

Payback. Big time. Go Navy.

A reinforced battalion of the HGFPD was caught in their assembly area on the far side of the ridge by the naval gunfire, which meant the tanks and their support vehicles were concentrated, making them an easy target. The timing was fortuitous. The tankers had been organizing for an attack on the bridge.

The battalion of the HGFPD was an incredibly powerful armored force. There was no way lightly armed paratroopers in the small numbers at the bridge could stand against them. But now the Nazi tankers were being shattered.

There was no defense against the guns of the U.S. Navy.

Across the bridge, coming in on the right side of the Y, were hundreds of Italian troops waving white flags—actually towels. The 1st Battalion, 3rd Brigade, 4th Mountain Infantry Division Livomo had been assigned as infantry support for the battalion of HGFTD tanks—which is what made the panzer battalion reinforced—but the Italian Mountain Infantrymen were through with being shelled.

This fight was over.

Capt. Jaxx said, "You were face-down in the road, sir. Thought you were dead at first. Then I realized—you were still trying to crawl."

Groggy from exhaustion and dehydration, Col. Randal said, "How did Jane get here?"

Capt. Jaxx said, "Colonel, we found you about a mile away—Lady Jane's at RFHQ in Egypt, sir."

Col. Randal decided not to ask any more questions.

Capt. Rockford asked, "How are you feeling, sir?"

"I've had better days."

He reached inside the jacket of his faded green battle dress uniform and found a handful of Waldo's custom-rolled cigars. Beverly had put them there, wrapped in a handwritten note tied with a ribbon. Col. Randal stuck one between his front teeth and distributed the rest to Capt. Jaxx, Lt. Bellefonte, Capt. Rockford—who was not looking quite as spit-shined after his ten-mile run— MSgt. Beckwith, Scout Ferguson, and King.

Col. Randal unfolded the note from Beverly. It was a list of the major exports from the Congo. He had asked her to compile the list what seemed like a long time ago, hoping to establish why "Wild Bill" Donovan, Chief of the Office of Strategic Services, was so fixated on the Belgian colony.

The list read:

1. Copper
2. Palm oil
3. Lumber
4. Industrial Diamonds
5. *Uranium*

~ ~

THE MISSION CONTINUES IN

– ALWAYS SO FEW –

BOOK XIV IN THE RAIDING FORCES SERIES

~ ~

The Raiding Forces series continues…all the way to VE Day.
To be on our notification list for the next book, contact
phil@philward.com.

~ ~

ABBREVIATIONS
ORDERS & AWARDS

Bt   Baronet

CB   Companion of the Bath

CMG   Companion of the Order of St. Michael & St. George

DCM   Distinguished Conduct Medal (Awarded to non-commissioned
            officers for distinguished conduct in action in the field.)

DFC   Distinguished Flying Cross (Royal Air Force)

DSC   Distinguished Service Cross (Royal Navy)

DSM   Distinguished Service Medal (Awarded to ranks up to and
            including Chief Petty)

DSO   Distinguished Service Order

GC   George Cross

GCB   Grand Cross in the Order of the Bath

GM   George Medal

KBE   Knight Commandeer of the Most Excellent Order of the
            British Empire

KCVO   Knight Commander of the Royal Victorian Order

LG   Lady Companion of the Order of the Garter

MC   Military Cross

MM   Military Medal

MVO   Member of the Royal Victorian Order

OBE   Order of the British Empire

SS   Silver Star Medal

VC   Victoria

TIP OF THE SWORD
ACRONYMS

AO	Area of Operation
AP	Assembly Point
BAR	Browning Automatic Rifle
BDU	Battle Dress Uniform
CG	Commander General
COPP	Combined Operations Pilotage Parties
CP	Command Post
DDOD(I)	Deputy Director Operations Division (Irregular)
DZ	Drop Zone
GHQ	General Headquarters
GP	General Purpose
GSSRF	Greek Sacred Squadron, Raiding Forces
HE	High Explosive
HEAT	High Explosive Anti-Tank
HGFPD	Hermann Göering Fallschirm Panzer Division
I & I	Intoxication and Intercourse
IDB	Illicit Diamond Buying
IO	Intelligence officer
IP	Initial Point
ISLD	Inner Services Liaison Department
KIA	Killed in Action
LBSM	Life Boat Service Men
LCT	Landing Craft Tank
LRDG	Long Range Desert Group
LSF	Levant Schooner Flotilla
LSS	Levant Schooner Service
MAS	Motoscafo armato silurante Italian: "torpedo armed motorboat" (boat)
MGB	Motor Gun Boat
MEHQ	Middle East Command Headquarters
MP	Military Police
MTB	Motor Torpedo Boat
NCO	Non-Commissioned Officer
OP	Observation Post
OSS	Office of Strategic Services previously Office of Coordinator of Information
PIR	Parachute Infantry Regiment
PLF	Parachute Landing Fall
PM	Prime Minister
PPA	Popski's Private Army

PT	Patrol Torpedo (boat)
PWE	Political Warfare Executive
RAF	Royal Air Force
RCT	Regimental Combat Team
RFC	Reconstruction Finance Corporation
RFHQ	Raiding Forces Headquarters
RN	Royal Navy
R&R	Rest and Recreation
RS	Radio Station
SAS	Special Air Service
SBS	Small Boat Service
SBS	Special Boat Squadron
SI	Secret Intelligence
SIME	Security Intelligence Middle East
SOE	Special Operations Executive
SOG	Small Operations Group
TO&E	Table of Organization and Equipment
USAAF	United States Army Air Force 6
USO	United Service Organizations
WAG	Wild Ass Guess
WASP	Women's Army Service Pilot
WIA	Wounded in Action
WRNS/Wrens	Women's Royal Navy Service

LIST OF CHARACTERS
THE TIP OF THE SWORD

ACM Sir Arthur Tedder, DSO, OBE, DFC
Acting Provisional S/Lt. Skipper Warthog Finley, OBE, DSO, DSC, RNPS
Aleksy
Alexandra (Mandy) Paige, OBE, RM
Antonopoulo
Beverly Blackwell, SS
Brandy Seaborn
Brig. Dudley Clarke
Brig. Raymond J. "R.J.' Maunsell
Brig. Gen. Theodore Roosevelt III,
Brig. Gen. William "Wild Bill" Donovan
Capt. Billy Jack Jaxx
Capt. Butch "Headhunter" Hoolihan, DSO, MC, MM, RM
Capt. Delbert Ragsdale
Capt. "Dynamite" Dick Coogan
Capt. Frank Rockford
Capt. "Geronimo" Joe McKoy
Capt. Hawthorne Merryweather
Capt. Millard Thompson, USN
Capt. Norman Nesbitt
Capt. Pamala Plum-Martin, DSO, OBE, DFC, RM
Capt. Patrick "Paddy" Leigh-Fermor
Capt. Penelope "Legs" Honeycutt-Parker, OBE, GM, RM
Capt. Preston Butterfield III
Capt. "Pyro" Percy Stirling, DSO, MC
Capt. Roy Kidd, MC
Capt. Roy "Mad Dog" Reupart,
Capt. Stephanie Fawcett-Tatum, RM
Capt. Tisdale-Peterson
Capt. Wallace Mossberg
Cdr. Charles Malcom, USN
Cdr. Ian Fleming, RNVR
Chief-of-Station Cuthbert Bowlby *aka* "Curly", RN
Chief-of-Surgery Dr. Stephen Milam
Col. James M. "Slim Jim" Gavin
Col. John Randal
Col. Sam Houston "Bronc" Blackwell
Col. Zaher
Cpl. Danny Hale
Cpl. Micky Fontain

CWO Hank W. Rawlston
Ens. Theodore "The Great Teddy" Hamilton, OBE
Flanigan
Gen. Moustafa
Guido "GG" Grazinni, MC
Guns
Jamil Twins
Jeff Stillingworth,
King
Lana Turner, Zār Cult priestess
Lt. Brian Sontag, USN
Lt. Christopher Issacs
Lt. Clint Hays
Lt. Douglas Fairbanks, Jr.
Lt. Eddy Ryder
Lt. Karen Montgomery
Lt. Nelson
Lt. Nick Bellefonte
Lt. Randy "Hornblower" Seaborn, DSO, OBE, DSC, RN
Lt. Cdr. Maurice Steadman
Lt. Cdr. Nigel Willmond, DSO
Lt. Col. Marvin Woodbine
Lt. Col. Sir Terry "Zorro" Stone, KBE, DSO, MC
Lt. Col. William O. Darby
Lt. Gen. Angelico Carta
Lt. Gen. George S. Patton Jr.
Maj. A.W. "Sammy" Sansom
Maj. Baltimore 'Mongo' Farquhar, MC
Maj. Clive Adair
Maj. Duke Slater
Maj. Jack Dance
Maj. Jane Seaborn, LG, OBE, RM
Maj. Jeb Pelham-Davies, DSO, MC
Maj. Taylor Corrigan, DSO, MC,
Maj. Zargo
Maj. Gen James "Baldie" Taylor, OBE
Moe
Mr. David Smithers
MSgt. Mack Beckwith
MSgt. Mack Brown
PFC Wally Malinowski
Pvt. Danny Costello
Pvt. Dean Voight
Pvt. Fred Harwich
Pvt. Joe Malarkey

Pvt. Komansky
Pvt. Willie Sipowich
Pvt. Zeke Swearington
Red, The Clipper Girl
Rikke (Rocky) Runborg
Rita Hayworth, Zār Cult priestess
S/Lt. Trevor Montclair
Scout Lionel Fenwick
Scout Munro Ferguson
Sgt. Fred Waltmier
Stavos
VAdm. Sir Randolph "Razor" Ransom, VC, KCB, DSO, OBE, DSC
Vegas
Veronica Paige, OBE
Vitalis
Waldo Treywick
Wg. Cdr. Paddy Wilcox, DSO, OBE, MC, DFC
Wg. Cdr. Tony Dudgeon

ABOUT THE AUTHOR

Phil Ward is a decorated combat veteran commissioned at age nineteen. A former instructor at the Army Ranger School, he has had a lifelong interest in small unit tactics and special operations. He lives in Texas on a mountain overlooking Lake Austin.

~~

OTHER BOOKS IN THE RAIDING FORCES SERIES:

Those Who Dare
Dead Eagles
Blood Wings
Roman Candle
Guerrilla Command
Necessary Force
Desert Patrol
Private Army
Africa 1941
The Sharp End
Raiding Rommel
Strategic Services
The Tip of The Sword
Always So Few
The War That Never Was
Economy of Force